North Kingstown Library
100 Boone Street
North Kingstown, RI 02852
(401) 294-3306

NIGHTSHADE

*Also by John Saul
in Large Print:*

The Presence

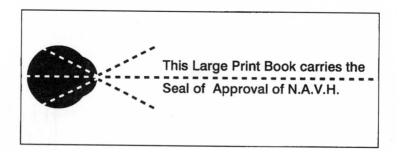

This Large Print Book carries the
Seal of Approval of N.A.V.H.

NIGHTSHADE

JOHN SAUL

G.K. Hall & Co. • Thorndike, Maine

Published in 2000 by arrangement with The Ballantine Publishing Group, a division of Random House, Inc.

G.K. Hall Large Print Core Series.

The text of this Large Print edition is unabridged.
Other aspects of the book may vary from the original edition.

Set in 16 pt. Plantin by Minnie B. Raven.

Printed in the United States on permanent paper.

Library of Congress Cataloging-in-Publication Data

Saul, John.
   Nightshade / John Saul.
     p. cm.
   ISBN 0-7838-9070-2 (lg. print : hc : alk. paper)
   1. Teenagers — Fiction. 2. Large type books. I. Title.
PS3569.A787 N5 2000b
 813'.54—dc21   00-039680

FOR COCO VERA
AND MICHAEL ALEXANDER

Welcome to our World!

Prologue

The child lay still; anyone observing it would have been certain it was sound asleep. But it was not, for long ago — so long ago that there was no memory of how it began — the child's mind had learned to defend itself from the agony that the body it inhabited was forced to bear. Someday — in a future so far away that the barely formed mind could not begin to comprehend it — it might be able to defend the body too.

But not yet.

For now, all the mind could do was retreat from the enemy, hiding deep inside the body, leaving the body to bear the pain as best it could.

Now the child's mind hovered on the fringe of consciousness, neither fully awake nor fully asleep, but lurking furtively in some shadowy nether region, ready to drop back into unconsciousness if it sensed that the enemy was near.

Beyond the eyelids — which the mind had learned very early to keep carefully closed — a growing brightness hinted that the terrors of the night would soon succumb to the onset of dawn.

But what about the terrors of the day?

The mind shifted its attention to the ears, sifting

through the sounds, sorting them, searching for signals of danger.

Nothing threatened: only a voice, laughing; a bird, singing.

The mind ventured closer to full consciousness.

It allowed the eyes to open — just the tiniest crack.

Brilliant yellow light flowed through the single small window.

The mind edged further into wakefulness.

Then a new sound — the creaking of an unoiled hinge on a sagging door — rasped in the child's ears, and the mind darted back, shying instinctively away from the noise that so often signaled approaching danger.

It closed the eyes again, lest they betray the mind's presence.

The creaking sound stopped, but the mind cowered where it was, ready to retreat into the black safety of unconsciousness at any moment.

Another sound came.

. . . *click-click-click* . . . The mind hesitated, still waiting, warily listening.

The sound came again.

. . . *click-click-click* . . .

The sound drew closer and closer, and the mind, uncertain, waited.

The *click-click-click* stopped, and a familiar scent filled the child's nostrils, a scent that instantly eased some of the fear in the child's mind.

"Doggie," the mind let the child whisper as the animal's tongue lapped at its face.

The furry mass of one of the animal's forepaws left the cracked cement floor upon which its claws had been clicking and gently prodded the child.

The child's eyes opened, and its arms wrapped around the animal's neck.

"Nice doggie," the child whispered as it peered into the dog's great brown eyes.

The dog whimpered, its tongue slurping across the child's face again.

The child giggled as its fingers stroked the animal's fur, but a second later the happy sound died on its lips and its fingers jerked away as if they'd been burned as the door at the top of the stairs was suddenly slammed open, crashing against the wall behind it.

"Out!" a voice commanded, the single word lashing down the steep flight of stairs like a snaking whip.

The child's body reflexively recoiled from the lash of the voice, and as the dog darted up the stairs, the child's mind began to retreat.

"How dare you?" the voice demanded, but even as the words rained down on the child, its mind began rejecting the signals that were funneling in through the ears and turning away from the bright sunlight the eyes perceived, retreating into the dark quiet safety of unconsciousness.

Too late. Despite the mind's effort to reject them, the furious words filtered through. "How many times have I told you not to touch that animal? Do you want me to make it go away forever? I can do that, you know! I made your father go away!" The mind felt the child trying to curl up, trying to make itself small.

Don't, the mind commanded. *Lie still. Be asleep.*

But it was far too late, for the mistake had already been made and for the child's body there was no longer any way to escape from the fury that hovered above.

"I'll teach you!" the voice rasped.

As the mind raced toward the safety of darkness, the first blow struck. Though the mind struggled once more to keep the child from reacting, a howl of pain and fear escaped its throat, and once more the voice spoke.

"Evil child! Nasty, vile, evil child! Well, I won't have it! Do you understand? I won't stand for it!"

As the raging voice ranted on, the child tried to pull its body away from the blows, but there was no escape.

The mind, reacting in an instant to the agony of the blows, retreated into the blackness, closing out what was happening. It closed off the ears and the voice began to fade away until the individual words could no longer be distinguished and the only sound that filtered through was an indistinct hum.

Next came the nerves. *It doesn't hurt,* the mind insisted. *It won't hurt. It can't hurt. Nothing can hurt. Nothing . . . nothing . . . nothing. . . .*

The sting of the slashing blows began to fade and the mind turned further away, retreating into the safety, darkness and silence of unconsciousness, sheltered from all the terrors the world held.

An eternity — or perhaps only a minute — passed.

The child's mind began to creep out of the cavern into which it had retreated. This time, though, it was even warier than before, refusing to let the child twitch even the smallest muscle until it was certain the danger had passed.

Beyond the closed eyelids there was no glow at all, which told the mind it had been gone all day, and that night — the long darkness that held its own unique terrors — must have fallen.

From the ears came no signal at all — no creak of the door, or whimpering of the dog, or voice sharp with anger. Yet the mind sensed no safety in the silence.

The lungs expanded, and the mind, suddenly stimulated by the scent captured by the child's nose, paused. The odor was strong, and very familiar.

And comforting.

It was the smell of the blanket that had given the child comfort long before its conscious memory had formed. Now, reacting to the deep emotions stirred by the scent, the mind let the child reach out to pull the comforting blanket more closely around its aching body. But the fingers touched nothing — the warm softness of the material was nowhere to be found.

Slowly, the mind became aware of the pain in the child's body. But there was more than the fading sting of the hands that had struck the child.

The mind had long since learned to deal with that. This time there was an ache as well — an ache that had settled so deep into the child's legs and arms that at first the limbs refused to obey the mind's commands. But finally — agonizingly — the child reached out into the darkness.

After moving only a few inches, the child's fingers found something hard, something immovable.

The fingers probed in another direction; the same hardness blocked them once more.

In an instant the mind knew: it wasn't the scent of the blanket at all, but the scent of the chest where all the blankets in the house were kept through the summer.

The cedar chest.

The cedar chest that sat against the wall below the cellar's single tiny window.

The lungs expanded again, and the scents of cedar and mothballs filled the child's nostrils once more. But this time, instead of reminding the child of the comfort, warmth, and softness of the blanket, the scent seemed to wrap around it like a serpent's coils, pressing tighter every second.

Panic took over and the child thrashed and cried — sobbed and choked — as it struggled to free itself from the imprisoning walls of the chest.

But the chest was strong, the child weak.

As the terror and the blackness and the scent closed around the child's body, the mind — as it had grown so used to doing — began once more to slip away, to disappear into a safer world.

This time, as the mind retreated once more into the dark haven of unconsciousness, it wondered if it would come back at all. But then, even as it dropped away into the darkness, it knew.

It would come back.

But it would be changed.

And it would strike back.

Chapter 1

It was the kind of perfect fall afternoon that erased even the memory of the blanket of heat and humidity that summer's end had laid over this part of New Hampshire. The first frost had struck a week ago: the leaves of the ancient maples and oaks that lined the streets of Granite Falls were just beginning their annual transformation, their edges barely hinting at the riot of color that would develop in another couple of weeks.

As Joan Hapgood slid her Range Rover into the slot that seemed to have been left just for her only a few steps from the Rusted Rooster — whose original name had long ago given way to the condition of the sign that hung over its door — she considered the possibility of driving up to Quebec for the weekend. She'd heard of a terrific little inn with a view of the St. Lawrence, and just that much farther north the trees would already be in full regalia, their colors so brilliant as to be almost blinding. But as she glanced at her watch — exactly one minute before two, when she and Bill had agreed to meet for a late lunch — she was already beginning to catalog the reasons why they wouldn't be able to take off for the weekend.

First, there was the opening day of hunting

season, which she knew Bill wouldn't miss. Her husband — along with nearly every one of his friends — regarded the opening day of hunting season with the same reverence most people reserved for religious holidays. But it had always been that way in Granite Falls: the hunting fervor had become so entrenched among the Granite Falls families that could trace their roots back to the seventeenth century that Joan (whose own roots went back only to her mother) suspected it was actually in their genes. But it wasn't the kind of hunting that was fashionable in other places — in the small enclaves of old, if somewhat diminished, wealth farther south, where ducks and foxes were the favored prey.

In Granite Falls, it was deer.

"We've always hunted deer," Bill Hapgood had explained. "It's just the way it's always been. We're not pretentious people up here — it's not like it is down in Connecticut and places like that. We hunt in the woods, we hunt on foot, and we eat what we shoot."

But Joan knew that it wasn't only the opening day of hunting season that stood in the way of their slipping away for the weekend.

There was Matt's football game, too. He'd finally made the starting lineup last week, and Bill was — if possible — even more excited than she at the prospect of seeing Matt score for the Granite Falls team for the first time. That was one of the things she loved best about the man she'd married a decade ago — he'd always treated Matt as if her son was his own. And neither of them would miss the biggest game of his life.

But it was the next problem that was the worst, and not just for the coming weekend, but for every weekend — indeed, for every day — in the foreseeable future.

That was the problem of Joan Hapgood's mother.

As thoughts of Emily Moore filled Joan's mind, the exhilaration which the weather had brought her began to drain away, and as she stepped through the door of the Rusted Rooster, the closeness of its low beamed ceilings and half-timbered walls only accentuated the depression that was settling over her.

"You all right?" her husband asked, half rising from his chair as Joan sank into the one the waitress held for her.

Joan smiled thinly as she automatically scanned the menu despite the already certain knowledge that she would have the Cobb salad. "I was just fantasizing about running away for the weekend," she sighed, holding up a hand as if to hold back the flow of objections she could already see forming on her husband's lips. "I did say I was fantasizing," she reminded him. "Believe me, I haven't forgotten about hunting season."

"And Matt's game," Bill added. "And, of course, your mother." It wasn't only the careful delivery of his last words that betrayed his defensiveness, but his tone as well. Joan stared at the menu, steeling herself against the same automatic defensiveness

16

that had risen like a wall around her husband. When she was certain she had herself under control, she looked up from the stiff white card whose contents hadn't changed in two generations, took a deep breath, and nodded.

No point in trying to avoid the issue.

"And my mother," she agreed. "And I know I'm going to have to do something about her. But I can't just . . ." Her voice trailed off, but Bill finished the sentence with the words they both knew she'd been unable to utter.

"Throw her in the home?" he asked, his aristocratic brow rising in a sardonic arch. When she made no reply, he reached out and laid his hand over hers. "That *is* what she's always saying, isn't it?" He screwed his face into an imitation of Emily Moore's angriest expression, which would have been comical if it had not been quite so accurate, and his normally gentle voice took on her mother's furious rasp. " 'Don't think I don't know!' " he mimicked, shaking his finger in Joan's face. " 'You're going to throw me in the home! Well, I won't let you. And when Cyn— ' "

"Stop!" Joan cried, pulling her hand away and glancing around to see who might be listening.

"I wish *she'd* stop," Bill replied, his features reverting to their usual composure, his voice to its familiar baritone. Then his lips tightened and he took a deep breath. "But we are going to have to decide what to do," he went on. "She can't go on living alone much longer."

"Try telling her that, Joan sighed. "It doesn't

17

matter what I say —"

"It doesn't matter what anyone says," Bill cut in. "She doesn't know what she's saying, Joan. She has Alzheimer's. And even before she got Alzheimer's, she wasn't the easiest person to get along with."

The trouble was that Emily Moore no longer remembered that she forgot things.

At first, when she'd just started to get sick, it hadn't been too bad: she'd known her memory was slipping, but for a while it was only a matter of a few minor annoyances. Not being able to find her keys, or forgetting exactly why she'd stopped in at Martha Thatcher's Needle Shoppe — thing like that. She'd solved the first problem easily enough by hanging her door key on a chain around her neck, and since practically everyone in Granite Falls — or at least everyone she knew — was perfectly well aware that she had "Old-Timer's Disease," (that's what her friends called it) she was pretty well-taken-care-of. Martha Thatcher would take some extra time helping Emily remember exactly why she'd come into the Needle Shoppe, and Ned Kindler would even have one of his bag boys walk her home from the market and help her put her groceries away.

After a few years, though, she'd stopped walking the few blocks into the village, letting Joan do the shopping for her. Joan only lived a little more than a mile from the edge of town, and it wasn't as if she had much else to do. She didn't work, not like

Emily had. Emily Moore had kept going to her job as a cashier at the drugstore right up until the day the Rite Aid people had taken over and let her go. She'd even looked for another job then, but by then the sickness had been starting, and she just couldn't do it. After that, she'd had to let Joan and Bill take care of her.

But she hadn't liked it — she hadn't liked it at all. Not that her daughter Joan did a very good job helping out, either. Even though she tried, Joan had never been able to clean her house quite the way Emily liked it, and as for the shopping — well! Most of the time she didn't bring Emily half the things she wanted, and there were always other things that Emily was absolutely certain she hadn't asked for. Well, at least Joan didn't try to make her pay for all those things anymore. Emily had set her straight on that right away. "Don't you look at me like I'm crazy!" she'd told Joan the first time she'd found all the wrong things in the grocery bag. "And don't think I'm going to pay for all this, either!" She'd brushed aside the list Joan had shown her, too. All it did was prove that Joan had learned how to copy her handwriting, which at least explained why there was money missing from her checking account every month. Joan had lied about it, of course, but that hadn't surprised Emily at all.

After that, she'd started hiding money in her house, where Joan wouldn't be able to find it. Then Joan had tried to trick her by offering to hire someone to "help" her. Emily had known right away what that was about — Joan just wanted to

19

get someone into her house to hunt for her money! But Emily hadn't fallen for it. It wasn't long after that that she'd seen people — people that looked sort of familiar, but to whom Emily couldn't quite put any names — walking by her house, spying on her. After one of them waved to her — just like he knew her! — Emily had started keeping the curtains closed.

Then they'd started coming to her door, talking to her like she was supposed to know who they were. She'd shut the door in their faces, and after a while, when she stopped answering the door at all, they stopped coming. But she knew they were still watching her, so she stopped going out of the house.

She liked that much better, because she no longer had to worry about anything. And she wasn't alone either, not really.

She still had her memories, and after a while it wasn't like they were memories at all. Sometimes, when she was fixing supper she'd make enough for two, and set out a place for Cynthia, too. She had a dim memory of Joan telling her that Cynthia wasn't coming home, but Emily had known that wasn't true — it was just another of the ways Joan was always trying to trick her. Besides, Joan had always been jealous of her sister, ever since she was a little girl. So Emily simply ignored what Joan said, certain that Cynthia had just gone away for a little while, and would be back any day now.

So she stayed in her house, and after a while one day seemed just like another, and one week blended into the next, and the months and the seasons and the years all ran together.

And Emily waited for Cynthia to come home.

Today, though, something was different.

Something didn't quite feel right.

But what was it?

She peered dimly at the frying pan sizzling on the front burner, in which a quarter of an inch of oil was already bubbling. She tried to remember what she'd been intending to do with the skillet and the hot oil. Make breakfast?

She wasn't sure. In fact, she wasn't really certain what time it was. But it was light out, and she was hungry, so it must be morning.

Then, from the front of the house, she thought she heard a sound.

Cynthia!

She must finally have come home!

The frying pan immediately forgotten, Emily pushed through the swinging door that led to the little dining room that was furnished only with a worn oak table so small that even if you crowded it, you couldn't get more than six people around it. Not that anyone ever sat around it anymore, and it was certainly big enough for herself and Cynthia.

Emily hurried through the dining room into the little foyer, and eagerly opened the door, certain Cynthia would be on the porch, ready to accept her mother's hug.

But the porch was empty except for the pile of newspapers that Emily never bothered to bring into the house anymore. Frowning, she looked out

21

into the street, but all she saw was a man in a blue uniform, carrying a leather bag. As he raised his hand to wave at her, Emily quickly shut the door.

Another one of Joan's spies.

Then she knew!

Cynthia had her own key! She'd come in by herself and gone up to her room!

In the kitchen, the oil in the frying pan bubbled, then began turning black as curls of smoke rose from its surface.

Emily started toward the stairs, but paused as she sensed something vaguely amiss. Something in the air? But even as her nostrils caught the first faint fumes drifting in from the kitchen, her old eyes fell on the threadbare brocade chair that stood just inside the archway leading into the parlor. Now how had that happened? Hadn't it just come back from the upholsterers, covered with the bright, colorful material Cynthia had picked out the day before she'd gone on her trip? She would have to speak to the upholsterer about the shoddy material they'd used!

But that could wait. Cynthia finally coming home was far more important than any chair!

The original reason she'd paused at the foot of the stairs having vanished from her mind as completely as if it had never been there at all, Emily hurried up the stairs and into the front bedroom. "Cynthia?" she called. "Oh, it's so good to finally have you . . ."

Emily's voice faded into silence as she realized the room was empty.

Her clouded eyes searched the room. "Cynthia?" she whispered. "Cynthia, when are you coming home?"

The oil in the frying pan burst into flames just as the breeze outside caught one of the lace curtains that hung on each side of Emily Moore's kitchen window. The breeze fanned the flames higher, the fire licking at the flimsy material as a beast might taste its prey before leaping to consume it. . . .

Emily moved into the room on the second floor, her eyes falling on the photograph of her older daughter that hung on the wall exactly where she and Cynthia had placed it when they'd picked it up from the photographer the week after Cynthia's eighteenth birthday.

The beautiful gown Cynthia wore in the portrait still hung in Cynthia's closet, along with all her other clothes.

The book she'd forgotten to take with her on her trip still lay open, facedown on her nightstand.

Everything was exactly as she had left it —

How long ago?

A week?

A month?

Surely no longer than that.

And she'd be home any day now! Of that, Emily was absolutely certain.

She moved slowly around the room, touching

the objects on Cynthia's vanity table, all the perfume and lipstick and eye shadow and mascara that Cynthia loved so much.

Every one of them was in its place, waiting for Cynthia.

She opened one of the drawers of Cynthia's bureau, her trembling fingers caressing the soft cashmere of the sweater that lay within, her eyes oblivious to the depredations of the moths and the yellowing of the fraying fabric.

She closed the drawer and let her eyes sweep over the room one last time.

All was as it should be, exactly as Cynthia had left it.

Emily left the room then and headed toward the sewing room, but as she passed the top of the stairs, an acrid odor filled her nostrils.

Smoke?

She frowned, trying to remember if she'd lit the fire that morning.

She couldn't remember.

If fact, she wasn't quite sure she'd even been downstairs that morning.

Clutching the banister, she started down the steep flight.

The odor grew stronger as she came to the foot of the stairs, but when she peered into the parlor, the fireplace was dark.

But she was certain she smelled smoke!

The kitchen?

Why would there be smoke in the kitchen? She'd just come downstairs, hadn't she?

She moved toward the kitchen, pushed open the door that separated it from the dining room. She saw it: flames boiling up from a skillet someone had left on the stove. More flames consuming the curtains around the window and charring the wood of the cupboards.

Hurrying across to the stove, Emily picked up the frying pan and started toward the sink, but the skillet slipped from her fingers and fell to the floor. The burning oil quickly spread across the linoleum, and an instant later the floor was covered with a sheet of fire.

Emily stared at the flames in frozen horror for a moment, then turned and fled from the kitchen. "Cynthia!" she called out. "The house is on fire! Hurry!"

Moving as quickly as her old legs would carry her, Emily made her way to the front door, pulled it opened, and lurched out onto the front porch.

From the other side of the fence that separated her yard from the one next door, an elderly man — whom Emily was certain she'd never seen before — looked at her worriedly.

"Emily?" asked Ralph Gunderson, who had lived next door to Emily for nearly thirty years. "What is it? What's wrong?"

"Fire," Emily managed to say, looking back at her house. "Someone set my house on fire!"

As Ralph Gunderson's gaze followed Emily's the first tongues of flame flicked out the kitchen window. Feeding voraciously on the wind, the fire began climbing the dried wooden siding of Emily's old frame house.

Matt Moore crouched at the scrimmage line, his eyes looking straight through the boy opposite him, knowing that his refusal to acknowledge his opponent's presence was already undermining Eric Holmes's confidence. It was a trick he'd been using on Eric since they'd first started playing football in fourth grade and even eight years later Eric hadn't figured out exactly what it was that made Matt's movements so hard to predict. Matt's body tensed as he listened to the quarterback call the signal to the center, and the second the ball was snapped, he sprang into action, feinting to the left then reversing to the right so quickly and smoothly that Eric, already rattled by Matt's patented blank stare, had already thrown himself off balance and was unable to bump Matt off stride. Matt streaked downfield toward the goal line, faked right and went left, then spun around as he crossed into the end zone and reached up, his hands closing on the ball, which seemed to have been placed there by some kind of magic.

Except there was no magic involved.

Rather, it was nothing more than Pete Arneson playing his role with the same precision that Matt had performed his own maneuvers. Though neither Pete nor Matt had so much as glanced at each other during the play, the quarterback had trusted Matt to be at the right position at the right moment.

A moment, both of them knew, that was absolutely predetermined by the silent counting they had perfected over the years they'd been playing together. They'd started counting together in seventh grade, practicing out loud until they found the fastest pace they could both comfortably maintain. Then they began working in silence. Whenever they were together — hiking, or going to a movie, or just hanging out — sooner or later one of them would say "Go!" and both of them would begin silently counting in their heads. After a few seconds one of them would say "Stop!" and they'd compare where they were. By the time they got to high school, the two were never more than a couple of digits off at the stop signal, and the system had given them an edge. They'd simply decide where Matt would be when they hit a certain number, and Pete would throw the ball to that spot, no matter where Matt was when he cocked his throwing arm. By last summer their coordination was so good that the coach had put Matt in the starting lineup even though his lithe frame carried at least thirty pounds less than any of his teammates.

"I don't get it," Eric Holmes groused to Matt afterward. "He wasn't even looking at you! Everyone thought he was going to pass to Brett Haynes. And you weren't paying any attention at all — you didn't even look until you turned around to grab the ball!"

"Never count us out," Matt said, cryptically repeating the only phrase he and Pete ever used when anyone asked how they managed to communicate without looking at each other. So far, no one had figured it out, not even their coach.

Eric's eyes rolled as he heard the answer for the billionth time, but he knew better than to try to worm the secret out of either one of his friends. Even though Pete told him practically everything else, he'd always ducked the question of how he knew exactly when to throw the ball. As for Matt, there'd always been things Matt wouldn't talk about — secrets Matt kept from him and Pete.

Eric eventually decided there wasn't any secret to Pete and Matt's precision at all — that they probably didn't know how they did it themselves. Besides, all that mattered was that if they kept it up, there was no way anyone was going to beat Granite Falls on the football field this year. As Matt joined his team's huddle, half a dozen boys gathered around Eric. "Well?" someone asked.

Eric shrugged. "How the hell should I know?"

"Maybe we should just always take Matt out," Mark Ryerson suggested, flexing his huge tackle's body to let Eric know he was prepared to do exactly what he'd suggested. "There's always been something weird about that guy."

Eric eyed Ryerson balefully. "You break one of his legs and there goes our shot at the championship."

"I didn't mean *really* hurt him," Mark said quickly. "I meant like — just keep him covered, you know?"

"If that's what you meant, why didn't you say it?

28

Just make sure that's all you do," Eric replied. Though he was playing opposite Matt and Pete today, Pete was still his best friend. And even if he didn't care that much about Matt, there was still no way he would let Mark Ryerson mess up their shot at the school's first winning season in more years than Eric could remember. He saw a flicker of anger in Ryerson's eyes, but before the other boy lost control of his temper, their attention was diverted by the wailing of a siren, which was quickly coming closer.

As the boys huddled around Matt Moore and Pete Arneson turned toward the blaring sound, a fire truck — immediately followed by a second one — came around the corner off Manchester Road onto Prospect Street, raced by the practice field, then braked hard and turned onto Burlington Avenue.

No more than a house or two from the corner, a curl of smoke was rising up into the afternoon sky. The sirens died away, and for a second an almost eerie silence fell over the football field. Then a girl's voice called out.

"Matt? Matt!"

The boys on the field watched as Kelly Conroe — dressed in her gym clothes for cheerleading practice — ran across the field from the gym. "It's your grandmother's house!" Kelly gasped as she came up to Matt. "We could see it from where we were practicing!"

For a moment Matt didn't seem to comprehend what Kelly was saying, but then, as the smoke from

Burlington Avenue billowed up, he came to life. Grabbing Kelly's hand, he started running, Pete Arneson and Eric Holmes right behind him.

"Let go of me!" Emily Moore demanded, struggling to pull her arm free from the fireman's grip. "It's my house! Don't you understand? It's mine!"

"I know it's yours, Mrs. Moore," Sean McCallum replied. He cast an eye around the quickly gathering crowd in search of the old woman's daughter. "But I can't let go of you unless you promise you won't try to go in!"

Emily's eyes flashed dangerously. "I can go in if I want to! It's my house!"

"No, you can't, Mrs. Moore," McCallum said doggedly. "Not until the fire's out and we know it's safe."

"I have to go in," the old woman insisted. "I have to —"

Before she could finish, Matt Moore appeared, panting and sweating from his dash from the practice field. "Gram? Gram, what happened? Are you okay?"

"Mrs. Moore is your grandmother?" Sean McCallum asked. When Matt nodded, he eased Emily toward the teenager, finally releasing his grip on her arm. "She's trying to go into the house. Make sure she doesn't."

Before Matt could reply, the fireman was gone, disappearing around the corner of the house toward the kitchen.

"What happened, Gram?" Matt asked again.

Emily's eyes were still fixed on the house, and when she took an unsteady step toward it, Matt reached out to steady her. She recoiled from his touch and turned her angry gaze on him.

"Don't touch me!" she cried. "Don't —" Her words died on her lips, and her eyes seemed to lose some of their anger. "I know you," she finally said. "You're — You're —"

"Matt," he prompted, dropping his voice so no one would hear him having to remind her who he was.

"Joan's brat!" Emily hissed the two words, and now it was Matt who recoiled.

"I'm your grandson, Gram," he said. Just as Sean McCallum had done a few moments ago, Matt scanned the crowd in search of help in dealing with the old woman. "You know me, Gram," he went on. "It's Matt! You've known me all my life!"

"It was you, wasn't it?" Emily suddenly demanded, her eyes narrowing to suspicious slits as she peered into Matt's face.

"M-Me?" Matt stammered.

Emily took a halting step forward, jabbing at his chest with her bony forefinger. "You did it! Don't lie to me! It was you!"

Matt could see Pete Arneson and Eric Holmes standing behind his grandmother. Both of them were grinning, and while Pete grotesquely rolled his eyes, Eric mockingly twirled a finger around his ear.

"If you two jerks don't want to help, why don't

31

you just go away?" Kelly Conroe said to them as she moved close to Matt and his grandmother. "You might be a little confused, too, if it was your house that was burning." As their grins faded, she turned to Emily Moore. "It's going to be all right, Mrs. Moore," she said, gently taking Emily's hand in her own. "We're going to take care of you."

The old woman peered into Kelly's soft blue eyes. "Cynthia?" she said, her voice barely a whisper.

"It's Kelly," Matt replied. "You know her, Gram — Kelly Conroe."

But Emily didn't seem to hear him. Her eyes remained fixed on Kelly, and now she was holding both of the girl's hands, her fingers digging deep into Kelly's flesh. Her lips worked for a moment, then she found the words. "She did it, didn't she?"

"D — Did what?"

Emily's rheumy eyes shifted to the burning house. "She did it," she muttered so softly that Kelly and Matt couldn't be certain she was speaking to them. "It was her. I know it was her."

Seeing his mother and stepfather coming across the lawn, Matt breathed a silent sigh of relief.

"Mother?" Joan Hapgood cried, her voice reflecting the relief she felt as she spotted Emily. "Mother, what happened? Are you all right?"

The sound of her daughter's voice brought Emily out of the reverie into which she'd fallen, and she wheeled around to face Joan. "Now look what you've done!" she said.

Dear God, Joan silently begged, knowing from

years of experience what was coming. *Please don't let her do this. Not right here. Not right now.* But even as she offered the silent prayer, she knew there was no hope of it being answered, for Emily was already shaking an accusing finger in her face.

Emily's voice rose querulously. "How many times have I told you?" she demanded. "How many times have I told you not to leave the skillet on the stove?"

Joan's heart skipped a beat as she realized what must have happened. How close had her mother come to burning herself up entirely? And what had she been doing cooking at three-thirty in the afternoon in the first place? But she knew better than to try to argue. Better just to try to calm the old woman down. She glanced at the house, where the smoke had given way to steam and the fire appeared to be under control. "It's all right, Mother," she said. "Whatever happened, it's almost over with. Everything's going to be all right."

But Emily Moore wasn't about to be appeased. "You did it on purpose!" she accused. "Don't think I don't know . . . don't think you can fool me —"

Joan looked beseechingly at her husband, and Bill moved closer, laying a placating hand on his mother-in-law's shoulder. "It's going to be fine, Emily," he assured her. "They almost have the fire out, and it doesn't look like it got past the kitchen."

Emily brushed Bill's hand away as if it were a mosquito buzzing around her. "You don't care! None of you care!" Her gaze shifted back to Joan.

"You're protecting her! That's all you're doing! Just protecting her!" Her voice was rising again, and Joan was acutely aware that the crowd of Emily's neighbors had fallen silent to listen.

"Nobody's trying to protect anybody," Joan tried to assure her. "Whatever happened, it was just an accident."

Emily adamantly shook her head. "It wasn't an accident! You did it on purpose!"

Again Joan cast her husband a pleading look. "Help me get her into the car." With Matt trailing behind, Bill and Joan led Emily Moore to Joan's Range Rover. "I'm going to take you home, Mother. You'll stay with us until we decide what to do." They were at the car now, but suddenly Emily balked.

"No! I have to stay here — I have to be here when Cynthia comes home!"

As Emily made a move to turn away from the Range Rover, Joan's hands closed gently but firmly on the old woman's thin shoulders, and when she spoke, her voice showed none of the frustration she was feeling: even when the house was burning down, her mother was still obsessed with Cynthia. "Cynthia's not coming home, Mother," she said softly. "You know she's not."

Joan's words struck Emily like a physical blow. She staggered for a moment, seemed about to topple over, and both Matt and Bill reached out to support her. But then she rallied, and her eyes glowed with anger again.

"Don't ever say that!" she commanded. "Don't

34

you dare ever say that!" But finally, exhausted as much by the confrontation with her daughter as by the fire that had preceded it, Emily allowed herself to be helped into the backseat of the Range Rover. As they drove away, though, she turned to look back at her house once more. The kitchen window was broken, the white siding blackened with smoke. "What will she do?" she asked, her voice breaking. "What will Cynthia do when she comes and I'm not there?"

Finally, Joan's own self-control gave way, and she turned around to face Emily. "Cynthia won't do anything at all, Mother," she said. "She's dead, remember? Cynthia's been dead for years!" Regretting her words almost as soon as she spoke them, Joan turned back, and for several long moments silence hung in the car. As Bill Hapgood turned through a pair of wrought-iron gates and started up the winding driveway toward the house that sat in the midst of the three hundred acres that had been his family's home for five generations, Emily seemed totally unaware of where she was. But as the house finally came into view, she suddenly spoke.

"She's not dead," she said. "Not Cynthia. Not my perfect Cynthia."

Chapter 2

Emily Moore made no move to get out of the car as Bill Hapgood pulled up in front of the sprawling house his thrice-great-grandfather had begun building as a farmhouse in the early part of the nineteenth century. Originally nothing more than a cabin built at the edge of the first small field that Luther Hapgood had carved out of the forest surrounding the hamlet of Granite Falls in the early part of the nineteenth century, the house had been remodeled and expanded, as had the farm, by the next three generations of Hapgoods. Its architecture was vaguely Federal, but with so many bastardizations that it was nearly impossible to assign it to any particular style. "Eclectic" was how either one of the agents in Bill Hapgood's real estate business would have described it, though Bill himself refused to label his home. "It's just what the family wanted" was all he said if anyone happened to ask how the house had come to be. No one in Granite Falls, of course, would ever ask; everyone in town not only knew Hapgood Farm, but knew its history as well. Emily Moore, though, was now staring suspiciously at the rambling, ungainly brick edifice as if she'd never seen it before.

"Is this a hospital?" she asked, her voice trembling with sudden fear. "I'm not sick — I don't need a hospital."

"It's not a hospital, Mother," Joan replied. Her frustration with her mother, which had boiled over a few minutes ago, was back under control, and as she opened the rear door of the Range Rover to help Emily out, she explained what was happening once again. "It's our house, Mother. You remember it — you've been here hundreds of times."

"I don't want to go to your house," Emily fretted. "Take me home."

"You can't stay at your house, Gram," Matt said, reaching in to take his grandmother's hand. "There was a fire, remember?"

Emily's eyes clouded and she pulled her hand away from Matt. "Of course I remember," she muttered. "Joan did it."

"Mom wasn't even there —" Matt began, but his mother didn't let him finish.

"It was an accident, Mother," she said, knowing better than to argue with the old woman right now. "And I'm sure the damage isn't too bad. I'll get you settled in, then Matt and I will go get whatever you need."

Her eyes filled with suspicion, Emily reluctantly let herself be guided into the house and up the wide staircase to the second floor. Joan opened the door to a spacious guest room in the southeast corner and drew her mother inside. "Isn't this lovely? You'll have sun all morning, and most of the afternoon too."

Emily peered around the room. The walls were papered with a bright floral pattern on a pale yellow background, with curtains and a bedspread to match. Besides the bed, night table, and dresser, there were a pair of wing-back chairs flanking a small fireplace, and a door leading to a bathroom that was shared with another guest room. Emily ran a finger over the small occasional table that stood next to one of the wing chairs. She scowled disapprovingly at the dust she saw on her finger.

"I'll dust it in a little while, Mother. Would you like to take a nap?"

Clearly not yet certain where she was, Emily eyed her daughter suspiciously. "Why do you want me to go to sleep?" she demanded. "What are you going to do to me?"

It's the sickness, Joan reminded herself. *It's just the sickness, and it doesn't mean anything.* She silently repeated once more what Dr. Henderson had explained to her when Emily's Alzheimer's had first been diagnosed: "There will be times when she's angry about everything, and times when she gets paranoid. But for a while at least, there will also be times when she's just like her old self, and you'll think she's actually getting better. But there's no way of reversing her condition, and in the long run she's only going to get worse. You just have to try to be patient with her, and remember that she doesn't always even understand what she's saying, let alone mean anything by it." And as the illness progressed, Joan had managed to deal with it.

She'd learned to ignore the criticism her mother heaped on her.

She'd tried to keep her patience as she explained to her mother again and again that Cynthia would not be coming home. But Cynthia's death was only one of the things she had to explain over and over again, for as the months of Emily's illness turned into years, and the fog of the disease clouded more and more of her mind, Joan found herself having to repeat almost everything over and over again.

Twice recently Emily had failed to recognize Bill when they stopped by to bring her groceries, and last week she hadn't been sure who Matt was. But perhaps that would change, now that she was going to be living in the same house with her son-in-law and her grandson. Maybe if she saw them every day, she'd remember who they were. Except that Dr. Henderson had also explained to her that as the disease progressed, it would become nearly impossible for Emily to assimilate anything new.

Joan pushed the thought away. Somehow, it would work — she would make it work! Because if her mother couldn't adjust to living here, then there was only one alternative.

She would have to do what her mother had been accusing her of wanting to do for years: she would have to find a nursing home.

Her mother would never forgive her for that.

But worse, Joan would never forgive herself for it.

No matter how bad Emily's condition got, her

mother was still her mother, and it was her duty to take care of her.

Once again in firm control of her roiling emotions, Joan put a gentle arm around her mother's stooped and rounded shoulders and tried to ease her toward the chair. "I'm not going to do anything to you," she soothed. "I'm just going to take care of you, that's all. You'll see — everything is going to be fine. You'll like it here."

Emily's mouth worked as if she were about to say something, but finally she sank into the chair. Her eyes darted around the room as if searching for a hidden enemy, and then she rubbed her arms, shivering despite the warmth of the room.

"Would you like me to light the fire?" Joan offered.

For a moment Emily seemed not to have heard her at all, but then she looked up and her eyes fixed on her daughter. Joan could see the unreasoning anger of the disease start to burn in her mother's eyes, and braced herself against whatever her mother was about to say. When Emily finally spoke, she confirmed Joan's fears: "Isn't it bad enough that you tried to burn me up in my own house?"

Joan flinched not only at the words, but at the bitterness in her mother's voice, but forced herself to turn away from the pain they caused, telling herself once again that it was the disease talking, not her mother. "I'll put on a pot of tea," she said. "You've always loved tea — it will make you feel better."

As Joan started from the room, she braced herself for whatever parting words her mother might have for her, but Emily said nothing more.

The eye of the storm, Joan thought. *I feel like I'm in the eye of the storm.*

And she knew that no matter which way she turned, the storm lay dead ahead.

Though Joan knew she was driving far more slowly than safety might demand, she made no effort at all to accelerate the Range Rover along the winding mile that separated Hapgood Farm from Granite Falls, ignoring Matt's groans as half a dozen honking cars raced past them. The last traces of the pleasure she'd taken in the perfect autumn morning had gone up in the smoke of the fire, and the forest, which only a few hours ago had beckoned to her to spend the weekend basking in its splendor, now appeared to be closing around her, suffocating her. As she rounded the last curve and the town itself came into view, she slowed even more. Her eyes fixed for a moment on the sign announcing that the town had been founded in 1684, and she remembered her third grade teacher — Miss Rutherford, who had died just last year — explaining to her class that Granite Falls had begun as a fur-trapping outpost. It grew slowly over the centuries, retaining the tidy orderliness of so many small New England towns, sufficient unto itself and far enough from any major city that it never became inundated with weekenders and summer people.

She crossed the bridge over Granite Creek, which wound along the western edge of the town before meandering south through a corner of Hapgood Farm on its way to drain into the Merrimack River, a dozen miles southeast. As Joan turned onto Prospect Street and drove by the high school — as unchanged in the last century as everything else in Granite Falls — she found herself wondering once again why her parents had come here in the first place. All she really knew was that it had happened before either she or Cynthia were born, and that after her father left — when she was still too young to remember him — her mother had stayed. Even before the disease had robbed her of her memory, Emily Moore had steadfastly refused to talk about why her husband had left. As for why she herself had stayed in a town where almost everyone else had roots that went back generations, Emily only shrugged her thin shoulders. "There was a job here," she said. "What was I supposed to do? I had two children to raise. I couldn't leave."

A trap, Joan thought now, her grip tightening on the steering wheel as she pulled around the corner onto Burlington Avenue. *The whole town is a trap. Mother sounded just as trapped back then as I feel now. And today she looks like a trapped animal.* Another thought came to mind: Had the animals for whose hides the town had been built felt the same fear when the traps closed on them? But even as the idea came to her, Joan rejected it. *It'll be all right,* she told herself. *Whatever happens with Mother, I'll get through it, just like I've always gotten through things.*

She braked the Range Rover to a stop in front of the house in which she'd grown up. The crowd, its enthusiasm for the fire quenched along with the flames themselves, had all but disappeared, though Ralph Gunderson was still chatting in his front yard with Phyllis Adams, who had come over from her house across the street. As soon as Joan saw the disapproving look on Phyllis's face, she knew what her mother's neighbors had been talking about. Phyllis confirmed it: "It's such a shame, isn't it? Of course, we've all known Emily shouldn't have been living alone, haven't we?"

Joan tried to ignore the sting of Phyllis's words. As late as yesterday afternoon her mother had refused even to discuss the possibility of leaving her little house on Burlington Avenue, let alone allow someone to come in and care for her; but Joan knew that all Phyllis and her friends would remember was that she'd left her mother alone, and the house had caught fire.

She offered Phyllis a smile that feigned more warmth than she felt. "You know my mother," she replied. "She's always been independent, and obviously she was able to get help before the fire got out of control."

Phyllis smiled thinly. "I suppose God looks out for those who have no one else." Her eyes bored into Joan's. "Will you be putting her somewhere?"

"She'll be with us," Joan replied. "At least for a while."

The other woman's expression hardened. "Well, at least you and Bill are in a position to be able to do what you want."

So there it is, Joan thought. Leave it to Phyllis to assume that enough money can solve everything. But instead of rising to the bait, she reminded herself that Phyllis had undoubtedly been drinking most of the afternoon, and was now probably feeling even more sorry for herself than she did when she was sober. Joan made herself smile again. "I'm just glad we can take her in," she replied evenly.

Before Phyllis could say anything else, Joan mounted the steps leading to her mother's front door and went into the house, with Matt right behind her.

"What's with Mrs. Adams?" her son asked. "Why's she mad at you? Or is she already drunk?"

"I think she's just mad at the world," Joan replied, answering Matt's first question but ignoring his second. "She resents anyone who she thinks is a little better off than she is." Her nostrils filled with the acrid smell of smoke as she quickly scanned the living room and dining room of the little house. Though everything looked exactly as it always had, the house somehow felt different.

The fire, she thought. It's just the smell of the fire.

But it was more than that, for as she closed the front door behind her and moved farther into the house, the strange sensation grew stronger.

Behind her, Matt echoed the feelings she hadn't

44

yet voiced: "This is weird. It's like the house knows Gram's not coming back."

As Joan's eyes took in the living room — its tables covered with the cheap china figurines her mother had been collecting since she and Cynthia had been children — Matt once again gave voice to what she was thinking.

"What are we going to do with all her stuff? Move it into our house?"

Joan heard a note of anxiety in his voice, and her mind went back ten years to the time when she and Matt had been living here in this house, before she married Bill Hapgood.

She could still remember her mother chiding Matt as his small fingers reached out to the china collie dog that lay on the floor under the end table. "Don't touch that!" she'd said. "That's very valuable, and not for children." Matt jerked his hand away as quickly as if he'd touched a hot stove, and her mother had turned on Joan herself. "Can't you control your brat? If you didn't know how to raise him, you shouldn't have had him in the first place!"

Even years later the words still stung her, and though she hoped that Matt had blocked them from his own memory, the way he was staring at the porcelain dog told her that he had not.

"I suppose we'll have to take some of it," Joan said, already dreading the task of sorting through the scores of figurines her mother had crammed into the house over the years. Nor would it matter how careful she was, or how hard she tried to

45

choose her mother's favorites. Whatever she did, it would be wrong. "But we won't take any of them right now," she decided. "We'll just get a few of her clothes, and I'll bring her over tomorrow to start going through everything."

Matt's gaze shifted from the collie to his mother. "Gram's going to live with us from now on, isn't she?" Despite the inflection at the end of the sentence, Joan knew it wasn't a question; he was asking for confirmation of what he already knew.

"I don't see what else we can do," she said gently. "I know she's difficult, and I know —" She hesitated, but knew there was no need to cushion Matt from the truth. After all, they'd both lived with his grandmother through four of the first five years of his life, after Joan had finally faced the fact that she couldn't raise him by herself in New York City. "Matt, I'm sorry. I know how she treats you, but what else can I do? She's still my mother."

"Jeez, Mom, it's not just me — look how she treats *you*. It's like you can't ever do anything right, no matter how hard you try!"

"I know." Joan sighed. "But it still doesn't change the fact that she's my mother, and I have to take care of her as long as I can. I can't just —" She cast around in her mind, searching for the right words, but could find none better than the ones her mother always used. "I just can't bring myself to 'throw her in the home.'"

Matt took a deep breath, then slowly let it out in a sigh of resignation. "I guess," he agreed, and Joan could see how much effort it took for him to give

46

her even that. But then he brightened. "Hey, who knows? Maybe she'll be better once she's out of here. Let's go up and get whatever she's going to need, and go home." He wrinkled his nose against the acrid smell of the fire that hung heavy in the house. "This place smells even worse than ever." But as they started up the stairs, Matt's step slowed, and when they came to the landing, he paused, gazing through the open door to the room that had belonged to the aunt he'd never known. "She's not gonna make us move Aunt Cynthia's stuff too, is she?"

Joan hesitated at the door to her sister's room, then stepped through it. And suddenly she heard her mother's voice again. *"Get out! That's Cynthia's room, and those are Cynthia's things, and no one is to touch them! No one! And keep your bastard brat out of there too!"*

As the echo of the words slowly faded away in her mind, Joan shook her head. "No," she told Matt. "She can't ask us to do that." She smiled at her son, and offered him a conspiratorial wink. "After all, we can't move what we can't touch, can we?" But even as she spoke the words, her mother's voice rang in her mind once more. This time she recalled a day when Matt was three, and she had suggested to her mother that he was old enough to have his own room.

"Cynthia's room? You want me to give your sister's room to your little brat? Never! As long as I'm alive, I'll keep your sister's room ready. When she comes home to me, all her things will be waiting for her! All of them!"

47

Joan, eyes glistening with tears, had said nothing, knowing it was useless to argue with her mother.

Now, she reached out and pulled the door to Cynthia's room closed, hoping that by blocking the view of her sister's room, she could also block the pain of her mother's words.

She didn't mean it, Joan told herself. *She was already starting to get sick, and she didn't know what she was saying.*

"Come on, let's pack up what she's going to need and get out of here," she said to Matt, unconsciously repeating the same words he'd spoken a few moments before.

It seemed nothing could thaw the icy chill that had settled over the Hapgoods' dining room: not the fire that Matt had laid in the hearth, nor the dozens of candles Joan had lit to cast a warm glow over the family's dinner. Though she'd cut the last of the fall flowers and set the table with the set of Limoges that had been given to Bill's grandmother as a wedding present from the Vanderbilts, and though she'd carefully prepared only things she knew her mother liked, nothing had gone as Joan planned.

She'd felt a faint flicker of hope when she first led her mother into the room. Emily stopped short when she stepped through the dining room doors, her eyes moving through the room, lingering on the gleaming silver and crystal that shimmered in the flickering candlelight. *It's going to be all right,*

Joan had told herself. But then Emily said, "How could you light all those candles? Don't you even care about what happened?"

"I was just trying to make it nice for you, Mother," Joan ventured as she helped the old woman into the chair opposite Matt.

"Why bother? You know you don't want me here." Emily peered balefully at her son-in-law and grandson. "And I don't want to be here."

Joan did her best to keep a conversation going, but no matter what she said, her mother either ignored her, disagreed with her, or changed the subject.

Emily glowered at the plate of food Joan set in front of her, and after objecting that she'd been served far too much, asked if the chicken was spoiled. "Nobody could eat this," she declared.

"It's good, Gram," Matt said.

"It's rotten," Emily said, pushing her plate away. "Take me home."

Joan silently appealed to her husband.

"You are home, Mother Moore," Bill said. Seeing Emily's eyes flash, he quickly added, "At least for a while, until we can decide what would be best for you."

It was as if Emily hadn't heard him. "Where's Cynthia?" she asked. "Why isn't she here? I want Cynthia!" She stood up, pushing her chair back from the table so abruptly that it fell over. As Joan and Bill leaped up to help her, she brushed them aside. "Leave me alone. I'm going to find Cynthia."

Emily left the dining room and Joan started after her, but Bill caught her arm. "Let her go," he said.

"But she doesn't know what she's doing," Joan protested. "She barely even knows her way around."

"Matt can keep an eye on her," Bill replied. Then, to his son: "Don't try to argue with her, Matt, and don't try to make her do anything. Just keep an eye on her and don't let her hurt herself. Okay?"

Only when Matt was gone and he'd closed the dining room door did Bill speak to his wife again. "This isn't going to work," he said gently.

"I can make it work," Joan began. "All she needs is a few days, and she'll know her way —"

Bill held up a hand to cut the flow of his wife's words. "She won't know anything. And she won't get better." His voice took on a slight edge. "You know she won't, Joan. Every doctor we've talked to for the last two years has told you she'll only get worse." He hesitated, then pressed on. "We have to find a place for her. A place where they can take care of her."

Joan shook her head. "Bill, she's my mother! And when all this started — when she first got sick — I promised that no matter what happened, I'd never put her into a nursing home. I promised I'd take care of her myself. I can't just put her away!"

"It wouldn't be putting her away — it wouldn't be anything like that. We'll find the best place in the area, and we can hire around-the-clock care if you want. And you'll be able to visit her every day."

Joan shook her head. "I can't," she repeated, her voice trembling. "I promised her! She's my —"

Again Bill cut her off, and when he spoke this time, the edge in his voice had sharpened. "I know she's your mother, but I also know how she treats you. Most of the time she has no idea who I am, and as for Matt —"

"I know," Joan said, breaking in before he could finish his indictment. "But what am I supposed to do? Could you have broken a promise you made to your father?"

As Joan's tears overflowed, Bill put his arms around her. "I know," he said. "I know how hard it is. But if she stays here, she'll tear this family apart. I know it." He looked deep into her eyes. "And you know it too." Joan didn't answer, but to Bill the conflicting emotions that struggled within her were written clearly on her face, and finally he held her close. "A week," he conceded. "We'll give it a week."

They stood together, their arms wrapped around each other, each of them reflecting upon the words Bill had just spoken.

In a week, Bill thought, *I can find the best nursing home in the Northeast, and do whatever it takes to get her admitted.*

In a week, Joan thought, *she'll be used to the house, and recognize Bill, and everything will be all right.*

Chapter 3

The week went by.

Bill Hapgood steered his Audi through the gates of Hapgood Farm, slowing the powerful car to a crawl as he made his way up the familiar curves of the long, graveled drive leading to the house. Until this week, this had been the best part of any given day of his life; the time when he left all his problems outside the gates and slipped back into the safe and familiar comfort of the only home he had ever known. It had always been that way: from the time he was a child this house had always been the final refuge from everything.

Once — just once — he had doubted the house's ability to offer him sanctuary from the world. That had been the day he was in school in Hanover and received the news that the boat his parents had chartered out of St. Lucia had been found abandoned and washed up on Macaroni Beach on the windward shore of Mustique. His parents had vanished. At first he'd simply refused to believe it — he and his parents had been sailing on Penobscot Bay every summer for as long as he could remember, and his father was an expert sailor. But he must have accepted the fact of their disappearance, for when he'd gone home that day, he hesitated before going through the gates, certain that the place would have changed, that it would feel hollow and empty with his parents forever gone.

Instead, to his surprise, it seemed to welcome him even more warmly than ever, and far from finding the house filled with memories that intensified his grief, it gave him comfort instead. It was as if the house, having already known the loss of four generations of Hapgoods, now knew how to deal with death, and the moment he'd passed through the gates of the Farm, his healing had begun.

But over the last week he'd actually dreaded coming home, and as he slid the Audi into the space in the carriage house next to Joan's Range Rover and shut off the engine, he hesitated before reaching for the door handle, as he'd once hesitated so long ago. Had the car, rather than his home, become his refuge? That was ridiculous! All that had happened was that his mother-in-law had moved in, and even that was only temporary.

Yet as he walked out of the carriage house — converted just over a century ago into a garage to hold the very first car in Granite Falls — he could feel the change. Not that there was anything tangible, anything visible. The house looked exactly as it always had. Lamps had already been turned on against the gathering dusk, but even the light that spilled through the mullioned windows seemed to have lost its warmth, and when Bill stepped through the French doors of what had once been the porte cochere, the change that had been

creeping through the house all week was more pro-
nounced than ever.

He called out to Joan and Matt. There was no
answer, and as he hung his coat in the hall closet,
he knew why: from the second floor he heard
Emily Moore's petulant voice hectoring his wife.

"Not there! It doesn't belong there! How many
times do I have to tell you?"

Taking the stairs two at a time, Bill started toward the open door to Emily's room when he
heard the old woman's voice again, and realized
the sound was coming from the room next to his
mother-in-law's. He continued down the wide
hallway to the door and pushed it open.

Except for the basics — the wallpaper, carpet,
and upholstery — the room had completely
changed. The four-poster bed, the Queen Anne
chair by the window, the Chippendale chiffonier
— all were gone, replaced by a cheap set of painted
furniture that Bill didn't quite recognize, though it
looked vaguely familiar.

Then it came to him.

Cynthia's room.

Everything that had been in his wife's sister's
room — the room that his mother-in-law had always kept in readiness for her long-dead daughter's return — was now in this room.

In this house.

In *his* house.

The pictures that had hung on the walls — three
original Currier and Ives prints — were gone, replaced with the hodgepodge of posters and snap-

54

shots that had been plastered on the walls of the little house on Burlington Avenue.

The Winslow Homer — minor, but original — that had hung over the mantel of the room's small fireplace had been replaced with the large portrait of Cynthia that in Emily's house had hung on the wall opposite her beloved daughter's bed.

And his entire family — his wife, his stepson, his mother-in-law — were all gathered in that room.

"What's going on?" he asked, keeping his voice carefully modulated so it betrayed nothing of his suddenly churning emotions.

Joan, reacting as if she'd been stung, whirled to face him. The color drained from her face, and her eyes flicked back and forth between her husband and her mother, as if she were unable to decide where her safety lay.

Matt, who was standing on a stool adjusting the portrait of his aunt, dropped to the floor. "We were just helping Gra—" he began, but Bill cut him off before he could finish.

"I thought we decided all of this would stay where it was," he said to Joan, still managing to keep his voice from betraying his feelings.

"I know, but Mother —" Again Joan's eyes darted toward her mother, who was now glowering at Bill. When his wife spoke again, her voice was trembling. "She said she wouldn't stay here without Cynthia's things. They mean so much to her, and I thought —"

"I see," Bill said.

Matt, sensing the storm that was suddenly

brewing between his mother and his stepfather, slipped out of the room, retreating to his own at the far end of the hall.

Joan tilted her head almost imperceptibly toward her mother. "Can't we talk about this later?"

Bill hesitated. Fragments of conversations flicked through his head:

His wife's voice: *Nothing I do is ever good enough.*

His own: *She's always been that way. That's one of the reasons she can't live with us — she'll destroy this family.*

His stepson's voice: *How come she's so mean to you, Mom?*

And once again, his wife's voice: *She doesn't mean it. She's just old. And she's my mother.*

Every night that week they'd waited until Emily — and Matt too — had gone to bed, and then tried to talk about it. Or, to be honest, they talked about it the first two nights.

Then they started fighting about it, and no matter how hard each of them tried, the fight had grown steadily more bitter.

This morning at breakfast the atmosphere had been so tense that none of them talked at all. Matt, pleading unfinished homework, had escaped from the house half an hour earlier than he ever left, and Joan, on the pretext of feeding her mother, had disappeared upstairs. But the simple fact was that what he feared had come true.

His home was no longer what it had been all his life, no longer offered shelter and comfort.

Not for him.

Not for his family.

Instead it had become a battle zone under the control of a woman whose disease had robbed her of any regard for anything but the preservation of her own delusions.

Hapgood Farm was no longer his home.

"Maybe we can talk about it a lot later," Bill finally said, his voice reflecting the sadness and pain in his soul as he answered his wife's question. "Maybe we can talk about it next week, or the week after. But not tonight. Not if it means going through what we've been going through every night this week."

He left the guest room and went through the master bedroom to his closet. Taking out his suitcase, he began to pack. Twice, he almost changed his mind, almost took the clothes out of the suitcase and hung them back in the closet. But what good would it do? If he stayed, he wouldn't be able to keep silent, wouldn't be able to prevent himself from trying to protect his family from the wounds Emily Moore inflicted nearly every time she spoke.

At least if he left — even for just a few days — the two people who meant the most to him would no longer be caught in the jaws of a trap with the teeth sinking in from both directions. Then, in a few days — certainly no more than a week — he and Joan could talk again.

Reluctantly, he finished packing. He paused at the closed door to Matt's room, wondering if he should try to explain why he was leaving. But even as he stood in the hall outside, he could see the hurt that would come into the boy's eyes, the hurt that would melt his resolve in an instant. Better just to go, and try to explain it all to Matt tomorrow, or perhaps the next day.

He paused at the door to the guest room too, wanting to see Joan one more time, to put his arms around her and protect her from her mother's wrath. But as he reached for the doorknob he heard Emily's strident voice once again. As he felt his fury rise again — a fury he was as helpless to control as Emily Moore was helpless to control either her illness or her tongue — he made himself turn away from the door.

Let them be, he told himself. *At least for tonight, don't put any more pressure on them.* Clutching the suitcase tightly, he hurried down the stairs and out of the house that was the only home he'd ever known. As he backed the Audi out of the carriage house a few minutes later, he glanced up to the window of the guest room that had been given over to the memory of the woman who lived only in the diseased mind of Emily Moore. He saw his wife standing in the window, looking down at him. As their gazes held, she shrugged her shoulders helplessly and mouthed three words:

She's my mother!

Then, without waiting to see what he would do, she turned away.

Matt tossed restlessly in bed, rolling first one way, then the other, pushing the blankets down, then pulling them up again. Finally he gave up trying to sleep.

Maybe he'd feel better if he went downstairs and got something to eat.

Clad only in his bathrobe — the thick velour one his stepfather had given him for Christmas last year — he slipped out into the hall and headed toward the stairs.

Everything about the house felt different tonight. Part of it was having his grandmother there. At first — the day after the fire — he'd thought it felt different because there was someone besides the three of them in the house. In a few days, he'd told himself, they'd all be used to having Gram in the house, and things would be just like they always were.

It hadn't happened. Instead, as each day crept by, he felt the tension between his parents growing. They tried to hide it from him, but even though they weren't exactly fighting, he knew they weren't getting along.

And tonight his father had left.

Matt had watched him from the window, seen him stow his suitcase in the trunk of the Audi, back the car out of the garage, then look up at the house for a few seconds, and drive away. At first he told himself that his stepfather would come back. He was just angry, and when he got over it, he'd return home. But as the minutes had turned into hours and he'd listened as the big clock at the foot of stairs tolled midnight, he knew his dad wasn't coming back.

59

Not my dad, Matt reminded himself as he paused outside the closed door to his grandmother's room. *He's only my stepfather.* But the words did nothing to make him feel better: no matter what he called him, Bill Hapgood was the only father he'd ever known. Even now, ten years later, he could still remember how frightened he felt the night after his mother had gotten married and they'd come to live here. The house had seemed so huge, with so many rooms, that at first he was afraid to sleep by himself in his own room. For as long as he could remember he'd had nightmares at night — terrifying dreams that he could never quite remember in the morning — but at least in his grandmother's house he had known his mother was right in the next bed, ready to hold him if he got too scared. But in this house his mother would be way down the hall, and he'd be all by himself in a room that was bigger than his grandmother's living room. But that first night his stepfather had come in and told him about how this used to be his room, and that there was a special knight — named the Night-Knight — who always protected him while he slept. Matt had lain in bed listening as his stepfather told him all about the Night-Knight, and finally fell asleep.

And it had worked. The Night-Knight had kept the nightmares at bay, and the next morning while they were eating breakfast, Matt looked shyly up at his stepfather

"Will you be my dad?" he'd asked doing his best not to let anyone see how scared he was. What if his stepfather said no?

But his stepfather hadn't said no, and from then on, everything had been fine. He'd never been frightened again, during the daytime or at night. And even when he'd gotten old enough to understand that the Night-Knight existed only in his imagination, the nightmares had never come back.

But tonight his dad had left, and everything about the house felt different.

He went downstairs to the kitchen, poked around among the leftovers, and finally ate a dish of ice cream. It was weird sitting by himself in the kitchen, because usually when he was worried about something and couldn't sleep and came down to get something to eat in the middle of the night, his dad would show up too, and the two of them would sit there talking until they'd worked out whatever was bothering him.

But tonight he was by himself, and there was no chance his dad would come to talk to him.

Shit!

Leaving the empty ice cream dish on the sink, he started back up the stairs. When he got to the top, he paused, listening. Behind the closed door to her room, Matt could hear his grandmother muttering to herself. Though the words were indistinct, her voice droned on and on, and he had the feeling that even though he couldn't make out exactly what she was saying, she was talking to someone.

His mother?

He moved closer.

But it wasn't from his grandmother's room that he was hearing the voice — it seemed to be coming from the room next door.

He made his way silently to the room adjoining his grandmother's.

The old woman's voice was clearer now, but he still couldn't distinguish the words.

Reaching out, he placed his hand on the door-knob and turned it.

He pushed the door open just far enough to peer into the room.

Though none of the lamps were on, the moon was glowing just brightly enough to let him see the interior of the room. His grandmother was standing in front of the fireplace, staring up at the portrait of his aunt.

Her lips were moving, and though her voice was low, Matt could distinguish some of her words: ". . . time to come home . . . need you . . . help me . . . come home, Cynthia . . ."

"Gram?" Matt asked uncertainly. "Are you okay?"

No response.

He hesitated. Should he say something else? But then, as he was trying to decide what to do, his grandmother slowly turned and her eyes, barely visible in the moonlight, fixed on him.

"Joan's bastard," she whispered. She took an unsteady step toward him, her eyes flashing venomously. "Damn you . . ."

Recoiling from his grandmother's curse, her words ringing in his head, Matt pulled the door closed and hurried back to his room.

He shut his own door too, against the sound of his grandmother's muttering, but it was still audible from the room down the hall, and he couldn't deafen himself to the last words she had spoken to him.

Joan's bastard . . . Joan's bastard . . . The words resounded in his mind, taunting him.

Dropping his robe on the chair in front of his desk, he slid naked into his bed and pulled the covers tight.

Still his grandmother's voice tortured him: *Damn you . . . damn you . . .*

Her curse echoed in his mind and he clutched the covers tighter still, willing the hateful words away.

At last, hours later, he slept.

Once, he awoke, and for a moment thought he smelled a strange scent in the air, a scent that seemed to trigger some deep memory from his childhood, from before he had come to live in this house. But even as the strange, musky aroma filled his nostrils, he dropped back into his restless sleep.

That night, for the first time since he left his grandmother's house when he was five years old, the nightmares of his childhood came back to torture him.

Nightmares from which neither his stepfather nor the Night-Knight could now defend him.

The clouds hanging over Granite Falls were nearly as dark as Matt's mood, and the morning looked every bit as cold as the house felt. Turning away from the window, he eyed his bed — still rumpled and tangled from his restless night — and felt an uncharacteristic urge to creep back into the warmth and comfort of the blankets. They had offered no solace last night, though, and even as the impulse flitted through his mind, he knew that retreating to the bed would accomplish nothing. After pulling on his clothes, he put his books in his backpack, added what little homework he'd managed to get done last night, and went down to breakfast.

Except there was no breakfast.

The kitchen was as cold and cheerless as the rest of the house.

The coffee maker — the one he'd given his dad for Christmas last year, that measured the beans, ground them, then brewed the coffee to be ready at whatever time was required — hadn't been set last night. Matt reached out to push the manual start button but stopped short of actually pressing it. As he turned on the gas burner under the old tea-kettle, he told himself that the coffee maker would take too long, and that there wasn't that much difference between fresh-ground and instant, anyway. But once again he knew the words weren't quite true.

It was his dad's coffeepot, and he should have been there to start it himself.

Fuck him! Matt thought, shutting off the burner and starting the coffee maker. *If it was so easy for him to just walk out, why should I care?*

The machine came to life, gears turning as it shifted beans into the grinder, blades clattering as the beans were pulverized. While the coffee began to brew, Matt rummaged through the refrigerator. Usually they had bacon and eggs for breakfast, but as he stared at the slab of bacon and the dozen fresh eggs, he had no appetite for any of it.

Cold cereal was a much better match for his mood this morning.

He had a cup of coffee, ate the cereal, and was just putting the bowl and spoon into the dishwasher when his mother finally appeared. Her skin was so pale — her face so drawn — that Matt knew at once she hadn't slept any better than he had.

Mother and son eyed each other, both waiting for the other to speak, neither quite sure they wanted to know what the other was thinking or feeling.

The silence built like a wall between them. It was finally Joan who breached it. "Are you all right?" she asked, her voice betraying the fragility of her nerves.

"Are you?" Matt countered, keeping his voice carefully neutral.

His mother hesitated, then shook her head. "I didn't sleep much last night."

Matt's eyes shifted from Joan to the coffee maker. "Do you think Dad'll come home this afternoon?" he ventured as he refilled his cup and poured one for his mother.

Once again the chasm of silence widened until it threatened to engulf them while Joan tried to decide what to say. Her first impulse was to try to reassure him, as she had when Bill Hapgood first came into their lives eleven years ago. But then she remembered that he was not a little boy anymore. "I don't think so," she admitted. "I'm not sure what's going to happen."

Suddenly Emily's voice could be heard drifting down from the floor above. Though her words were indistinct, both of them heard the anger in her tone. Joan flinched, and the hot coffee slopped out of the cup onto her hands. "I'd better go up and see what she wants."

His mother started toward the door. "Maybe Dad's right," Matt said, and though his voice was soft, his words stopped Joan short. "Maybe Gram shouldn't be here. Maybe you should let Dad find a place for her." He saw a flicker of something in his mother's eyes. Fear? Anger? He couldn't be certain, and it was gone as quickly as it had come.

"No," she said. "She's my mother and I have to take care of her." Then she was gone and he could hear her hurrying up the stairs as his grandmother called out again.

Matt drained his coffee, picked up his backpack, and went out into the cold morning, walking quickly down the long driveway. Kelly Conroe was waiting for him by the mailbox, just as she always did, but as he came out the gate her usually sunny smile faded.

"Matt?" she asked, unknowingly echoing the words he'd asked his mother a few minutes earlier. "Are you all right?"

He fell in beside her, taking her hand in his own. They'd been going to school together almost as long as they could remember, first waiting for the grade-school bus at the stop halfway between the Hapgood house and the Conroes', then riding their bikes, and then, when they got to high school, walking. It wasn't until last spring that they started holding hands, and though neither Matt's parents nor Kelly's had said anything, both of them were sure that their mothers, at least, were already speculating on the future possibilities, happily ignoring the fact that since Kelly was planning on going to medical school and Matt was toying with becoming a lawyer, whatever "future possibilities" there might be were at least eight or ten years away.

"My dad left last night," Matt told her.

Kelly stopped short. "What do you mean, he left?"

Matt suddenly felt annoyed with Kelly. "You know — *left?*"

"But why?" Kelly asked.

"Why do you think?" Matt demanded, his voice harsh. "Because of my grandmother moving in."

"But he's coming back, isn't he?"

Matt dropped Kelly's hand. "How should I know?" He hesitated. Then, as the rain that had been threatening began to fall, all the feelings that had been building in him through the night poured out. "It's not like he told me if he's coming back or not! He didn't say anything at all. There wasn't even a fight, or anything." The whole story of what

67

had happened the night before tumbled from his lips.

"He'll come back," Kelly decided when Matt was finished. They were in front of the school, and the first bell rang as she spoke. "I mean, your dad's not going to leave just because —"

Matt's eyes, as stormy as the sky, fixed on her. "He's not my dad, remember? He's only my step-father. So who cares if he comes back? I don't!" Turning his back on her, he hurried up the front steps and into the shelter of the school.

Kelly, oblivious to the rain, watched him go.

You care, she thought. *You care if he comes back.*

Chapter 4

"That doesn't go there! Why can't you do anything right?"

Joan's hands tightened on the dress she was holding. Pale blue, the bodice covered with seed pearls, the satin dress had been her mother's favorite. But that was years ago, and even though the dress had been kept carefully hung in the closet since the one time it was worn, the color had begun to fade and the material to rot. In fact, it should have been given away years ago, while someone could still use it. Now it was beyond repair — not that it would be worth repairing, since the seed pearls were plastic and the satin was made of rayon instead of silk. But in her mother's eyes the dress was still beautiful.

As beautiful as it had once been . . .

Joan stood at the door to her sister's room, her eyes fixed on the large gray cardboard box on Cynthia's bed. She knew what was in the box, for it was all her mother and sister had been talking about for weeks.

The dress.

The dress Cynthia would wear tomorrow night when she went to the prom with Marty Holmes.

The dress that Cynthia and their mother had

started planning weeks ago, on the day Marty asked Cynthia to the prom.

The dress that Mrs. Fillmore had made, making Cynthia come over for fittings day after day.

"I'm starting to hate that dress," Cynthia had whispered to her last week. "I can never stand still enough for Mrs. Fillmore, and she always sticks pins in me, like I'm some kind of voodoo doll or something."

"But Mom says it's going to be the most beautiful dress anyone's ever seen," Joan said. "If she finds out you don't even like it —"

Cynthia, four years older than her twelve-year-old sister, fixed her eyes on Joan. "Why would she find that out?" she asked. "I'm not going to tell her — if she wants me to wear the stupid dress, I'll wear it. What do I care?"

"Don't you even want to go to the prom?" Joan asked wistfully. Since the moment she'd heard about the prom, she thought everything about it sounded wonderful. All the boys would be dressed up in dinner jackets, and the girls would wear beautiful dresses, but none of them as beautiful as Cynthia's. The wonderfully soft and smooth satin from which Mrs. Fillmore was making the dress was the exact same blue as Cynthia's eyes, and the dressmaker was even letting Cynthia wear a string of her own pearls.

"They're not quite real," she'd admitted to her mother when she brought them over. "But they match the seed pearls on the bodice perfectly."

Joan had stared longingly at the pearls, wishing she could try them on, but knowing she shouldn't even ask.

Maybe in four years, when it was time for her own prom . . .

"I don't care if I go or not," Cynthia said, finally answering the question that had begun Joan's reverie. "And I sure don't want to go over to old Mrs. Fillmore's again." She cocked her head then, her eyes fixed on her younger sister. "Why don't you go to the fitting tomorrow?"

Joan's eyes widened. "Me?"

"Why not?" Cynthia countered, her eyes sparkling with mischief.

"But it won't fit —" Joan began.

Cynthia didn't let her finish. "It won't matter if it doesn't fit perfectly, because she's only doing the hemline tomorrow! Stand up."

Joan scrambled off Cynthia's bed.

"Stand next to me."

Joan moved next to her sister, who was standing in front of the full length mirror on her closet door.

"See? It'll be perfect!"

Joan gazed at the two images in the mirror. There was no resemblance at all. Cynthia's figure was almost perfect — Joan's own chest looked completely flat compared to her older sister's, and where Cynthia's body was all soft curves, her own was nothing but straight lines and gangly limbs.

She didn't have a waist, and she didn't have hips, and she didn't have a bust.

Even her hair — dark and straight — paled by comparison to Cynthia's wavy blond tresses.

"See?" Cynthia said. "We're exactly the same height! So you can go to the fitting tomorrow, and I —" Abruptly, she fell silent.

"You can what?" Joan had asked.

Cynthia smiled. "Never mind. What you don't know can't hurt you."

So she went to the fitting instead of Cynthia, and Mrs. Fillmore had lowered the dress over her head, and she'd turned to look into a mirror, certain the dress would somehow transform her into as beautiful a creature as her sister.

It hadn't.

Instead of seeing the fairy princess she'd let herself imagine — even hoped for — she was still the same gawky girl she'd been before.

"It's just not your color," Mrs. Fillmore had tried to reassure her, reading her thoughts as clearly as if she'd spoken them out loud. "When it's time for your prom, I'll make you a red dress. It wouldn't be right on Cynthia, but red will be perfect for you. You'll see."

Joan had made no reply, because even though she was only twelve, she was already sure no one would ever ask her to the prom. But she'd stood perfectly still, and Mrs. Fillmore hadn't stuck any pins in her, and that night when their mother asked Cynthia how the fitting had gone, her sister lied so smoothly that even Joan almost believed it had been Cynthia who went to Mrs. Fillmore's that afternoon.

And then the dress arrived, carefully folded and wrapped in tissue paper and packed into the gray cardboard box. And even though Joan knew she should wait until Cynthia got home and tried it on, she couldn't contain herself. The unfinished dress had looked so beautiful that she could hardly even imagine what it must look like now.

The box drawing her like a magnet, Joan moved toward it, her fingers untying the string and lifting the lid almost of their own volition.

And then, from behind her, she heard her mother's voice.

"What are you doing? How dare you touch that box?"

Joan spun around, her hands going behind her back as if to hide from her mother's wrath.

"Useless!" her mother said, shoving her out of Cynthia's room and closing the door so she couldn't even see the box, let alone the beautiful dress inside. "What if you'd ruined it? What if you'd spoiled the most wonderful night of your sister's life?"

But she hadn't ruined the most wonderful night of Cynthia's life.

And, despite what Mrs. Fillmore had promised, she'd never had a prom dress of her own.

"Useless!" she heard her mother mutter behind her. "You're just as useless now as you ever were. I don't know why I ever had you!"

I don't either, Joan thought. *I truly don't.* But she said nothing, reminding herself once more that her mother didn't mean what she was saying.

It will be all right, she insisted to herself as she carefully hung the dress in the exact spot her mother wanted it. *I'll get through this.*

I'll get through this, just as I've gotten through everything else.

But even as she repeated the reassurances to herself, she still heard her mother's angry words echoing in her mind.

Bill Hapgood gazed down the fourth fairway of the Granite Falls Golf Club course. The fourth hole had always been his favorite — the fairway ran 180 yards from the tee, then veered sharply to the right to proceed another 150 yards to the hole. There was a dense stand of forest to the right of the first run, and if you couldn't control your slice, there was no chance of finding the ball. On the left was a grove of pines that Bill's father had planted ("Why should the hookers get off easy?" George Hapgood, a notorious slicer, had complained, instantly earning himself a reputation as being a stalwart foe of prostitution, a profession that no one in Granite Falls was practicing anyway.) But once you got successfully through the narrow slot off the tee and made the turn to the right, you discovered that your troubles had just begun. The woods were still on the right, but now there was a pond on the left, and six deep bunkers guarding the green, which most members were absolutely certain was becoming smaller every year. There were even rumors that Bill himself sometimes snuck onto the course at night to cut away small sections of the fourth green, making the sand traps even larger than they already were.

Though the rumors weren't true, no one would have been surprised to find out that they were: indeed, there wasn't a soul in Granite Falls who could even remember a time when a Hapgood wasn't tinkering with the course; Bill's grandfather carved the first nine holes out of his farm sixty years earlier, and he and his friends had built the original clubhouse themselves. Bill's father had figured out how to add enough new tee boxes to at least half convince the membership that eighteen holes wasn't just a matter of going twice around the original nine, and Bill himself hadn't missed a workday since he'd inherited his father's membership when he was still in college. Indeed, the old hickory clubs his father had sawn off to teach Bill the game when he was four — and that Bill had used to teach Matt when he was five — were still stored in the club's locker shed, waiting for the day when he could use them to teach Matt's son.

Matt's son.

His grandson.

Not his grandson, he reminded himself. His *step-*grandson. Not for the first time, he wondered if he'd made a mistake not adopting Matt when he and Joan first got married. But it had been impossible then, for his grandfather was still alive, and Bill would never forget the scene he'd had in the den the night before his wedding when he broached the subject to the old man, who had only reluctantly left his retirement home in Scottsdale to come to the wedding.

"Never!" William Hughes Hapgood had roared. "It's bad enough that you're marrying that Moore girl at all. But to even think of adopting her bastard —"

"Come on, Grandpa! Nobody uses that word anymore. It's archaic!"

75

"Morality is not archaic," W.H. had growled, his brow furrowing dangerously. "And don't begin prattling about modern times."

"I won't prattle about them if you won't try to pretend they don't exist," Bill replied.

W.H.'s features had grown as hard as the New Hampshire granite from which he'd sprung. "I'm not forbidding you to marry this Joan person, am I? But I draw the line at adopting her —" He cut himself short, reading the danger signals in his grandson's eyes. "— her son," he finally went on. "We have no idea who the child's father was, and I can only assume that since she's never told anyone, she's not terribly proud of whoever he was. And while you may find it old-fashioned, I still believe that in the long run, breeding will win out. Know the lineage, and you know the man. But if you don't know the lineage —"

"You can't trust the man." Bill finished the phrase that had been drilled into him since childhood like a catechism, and in the end he'd given in to his grandfather's wishes.

Just as Joan had given in to her mother's wishes.

But it wasn't the same thing, Bill told himself as he teed up his ball and took a couple of practice swings. Matthew Moore had never disrupted his life; if anything, Matt had been the son he'd always hoped for, and in the end even old W.H. had grudgingly conceded that Matt wasn't "as bad as I was expecting."

Emily Moore, on the other hand, was even worse than Bill had been expecting, and now, as he lined up his drive, his eyes rested for a moment on the chimneys of his house, just visible above the grove of trees that stood at the far end of the fairway, beyond the dogleg.

Maybe he should have gone back this morning, just to make certain things were all right. After all, if Emily could set fire to her own house, there was no reason she couldn't do the same to his.

But no — if he'd gone back so soon after leaving, Joan would take it as a sign that he might move back in, and until Emily was gone, that wasn't going to happen. Not given the condition Matt had been in when he'd first moved from his grandmother's house into Hapgood Farm. Even now, ten years later, Bill remembered how afraid Matt had been to go to sleep those first few nights. Though the boy had never been able to tell him exactly what his nightmares were about, Bill was certain he knew the cause: Emily. Though he suspected the woman had never exchanged more than a word or two with his grandfather in her life, she seemed to share W.H. Hapgood's archaic ideas about lineage and breeding, even though she had none herself.

None, at least, that anyone knew of.

Joan's bastard.

That's how she'd always referred to her grandson. And with her feeling that way, how could Matt not have nightmares? So Bill had come up with the Night-Knight, and stayed up with Matt, reading to him and reassuring him that there was nothing to be afraid of anymore, and afterward

77

the nightmares that had plagued Matt in Emily Moore's house had vanished.

But with Emily in the house, how long would it be before they came back?

Now, his hands clenched tightly on his driver, Bill began his downswing, and immediately knew that the shot would go wrong. As the ball curved off into the woods, cracked against two trees, then dropped into a thicket of mountain laurel, he heard Gerry Conroe chuckle.

"Thought you said you were just fine," the publisher of the *Granite Falls Ledger* said sardonically.

"I am just fine," Bill growled, sounding more like his grandfather than he would have liked.

"That's the third drive you've blown," said Marty Holmes, who, along with Paul Arneson, made up the rest of their regular foursome. "A couple more drives like that and I might be able to retire early."

His jaw clenching, Bill teed up a second ball, told himself to relax, and swung again.

As the second ball disappeared into the woods, he decided that Gerry Conroe was right.

He was upset. He was very upset, and he was going to do something about it.

The only question was what. But even as the question came into his mind, so did a possible answer.

Maybe it was time to do what he'd been thinking about doing for two years.

Fishing his cellular phone out of his golf bag, he dialed his lawyer's number.

"That better not be business," Marty Holmes said as Bill began talking. "You know the club rule about discussing business on the course."

"And you know how often it's enforced," Bill replied as he waited for the attorney to come onto the line. "But it doesn't matter. This is just about as personal as it gets."

As the other three started down the fairway, Bill hung back.

No sense letting the whole town know what he was thinking of doing.

"Jeez, Moore! What's wrong with you today?"

The anger in Pete Arneson's voice grated on Matt, and his right hand clenched into a fist. What was Pete so pissed about? All he'd done was miss a catch!

Except that it wasn't just one catch. So far, he'd missed every pass Pete had thrown him, and on two of the plays he hadn't even been able to remember which pattern he was supposed to run. On the last play, Eric Holmes had somehow managed to knock him off stride as he began to run, and that had never happened before. But long before he was ready to receive Pete's pass, the ball sailed over his head, dropping to the ground near the goal post.

Fifteen lousy yards, and he hadn't even come close to hitting his mark!

"Screw you," he snarled.

Pete's eyes widened. " 'Screw you'?" he repeated. "That's all you've got to say? Then fine, Moore — screw you too." He turned to Kent

Stackworth. "After that last play, they'll expect me to try to run this time. So I'm passing to you."

"Me?" Stackworth repeated. What was going on? Pete always passed to Matt — they were like a team within a team.

"Yes, you," Arneson shot back. "You can't do any worse than Moore, can you? As for you, Moore, you're blocking on this play."

A few seconds later Matt, seething, was back on the line, facing Eric Holmes.

Concentrate, he told himself. *Just forget about everything else and focus.* But as he crouched down, Pete Arneson's words kept running through his mind, and when he heard the last number of the count, something happened.

Instead of launching himself into Eric Holmes and blocking him, Matt spun out to the right, letting Eric lunge past him. A second later he heard Pete Arneson's outraged howl as Eric took him down, but it didn't matter.

Matt was already off the field.

"Moore!" he heard the coach shouting as he started toward the locker room.

Matt kept walking.

"Moore! Hold it right there!"

Matt hesitated, but then turned to face the coach, who was walking quickly toward him.

"You want to tell me what's going on?" Ted Stevens asked. "Since when do you just walk off the field in the middle of a play?"

Matt's jaw tightened and his right hand clenched into a fist.

The coach's tone changed when he saw the uncharacteristic anger in Matt's face. "What is it, Matt?" he asked. "What's going on?" For a moment Matt's expression didn't change, but then, as if he'd made a decision, Matt unclenched his fist and his shoulders slumped.

"I just don't feel very good today."

"You sick?"

Matt shrugged. "I didn't sleep very well last night." He hesitated, then: "And my dad left."

Suddenly, Ted Stevens understood. No wonder the boy's game had been off. "You want to talk about it?" he offered. "It can be pretty rough when your folks split up."

"He's not my father," Matt said, a little too quickly. "He's just my stepfather."

Stevens knew better than to challenge the defensiveness in Matt's words, but instead slung a friendly arm around the boy's shoulders. "Tell you what," he said. "Why don't you call it a day and hit the showers? And if you want to talk, I'll be in my office. Okay?"

Matt shrugged the coach's arm off. "Hey, it's no big deal," he said. "Everybody's folks split up, right?"

Again the coach knew better than to try to argue. "I'll be in my office," he repeated. "The door's always open."

Right, Matt thought as he went to his locker, stripped out of his jersey and padding, then headed for the showers. *Everybody wants to talk about it.*

81

He turned the hot water up until the needle spray was nearly scalding and stepped under it, letting it sluice the sweat off his body. But even the stream of hot water could do nothing to ease the tension that had been building in him all through last night and then the long day at school. He finally shut off the shower, toweled himself dry, and pulled on his clothes.

As he headed for the door he didn't even glance in the direction of the coach's office.

Nor did he head out Manchester Road toward Hapgood Farm.

Instead he found himself walking toward Burlington Avenue.

Five minutes later he was standing in front of his grandmother's house. From where he stood, there was no sign of the fire at all, but even though it had been only a week since his grandmother had moved in with his own family, the house had already taken on a look of abandonment.

"It's weird, isn't it?"

Matt turned to see Becky Adams smiling at him. Before Matt's mother had married his stepfather and they'd moved away from Burlington Avenue, Becky had been his best friend. Now, ten years later, he wasn't sure if they were friends at all; it wasn't just his family and address that had changed, but the crowd he hung out with as well. And there was Becky's mother too. His eyes automatically flicked across the street toward the Adams house as he wondered if Becky's mother was drunk, but a second later he pulled his gaze self-consciously away. Then he relaxed: even if Becky had noticed his glance, she couldn't know what he was thinking.

"What's weird?" Matt countered. "It's just a house." But even as he spoke the words, he knew it wasn't "just a house" at all. It was the house of the nightmares and nameless terrors of his early childhood, along with the frightening woman who was his grandmother. Now, as he gazed at it, a thought crept into his head.

Why couldn't it have burned to the ground? And why couldn't she have been in it?

"All the little kids on the block think it's haunted," Becky said.

"I bet they think my grandmother's a witch too."

Though Becky shook her head, her blush told him the truth.

"Well, she's not," he went on. "She's just —" He fell silent as fragments of the last few days flitted through his memory. *Crazy,* he wanted to say. *She's just crazy.* But when he spoke, his words were carefully tempered: "She's just sick, that's all."

"How come your mom didn't put her in a nursing home?"

"Why would she?" Matt countered.

Becky Adams's flush deepened. "Well, I mean —" she stammered. "Like — everyone knows how she treats your mom. And my mom said —"

"I don't want to talk about it, okay?" Matt said, his voice harsh enough to make Becky flinch. "Look, Becky, I'm sorry," he quickly went on when he saw her reaction. "It's just — oh, Jeez, I don't know . . ."

His voice trailed off and he turned away, suddenly wanting to be by himself.

"Matt?" Becky called.

He turned back.

"If there's anything I can do . . . I mean to help . . ."

"There's not," Matt said. "There's nothing anyone can do."

Chapter 5

Bill Hapgood slowed his car to a stop as he came to the black wrought-iron gates of the home he'd left almost three weeks earlier. This would be the first time he'd set foot on the property since the night he packed his suitcase and moved into the Granite Falls Inn. He was still there, camping out in the two-room suite on the second floor whose main attraction, for him, was that it faced away from his own house. Even tonight he was reluctant to go back; indeed, he'd almost called Joan an hour ago to tell her he wouldn't be there after all. In the end, though, he succumbed to his mother's social dictum that the only valid excuse not to attend a dinner party is death. "People like us do not ruin someone's evening merely because we don't feel well, or are out of sorts," she'd instructed him when he was a child. "We attend the dinners we've accepted, and eat whatever is put before us. And we expect no less of others."

Aside from his mother's rule, tonight's dinner party was a special event that had been on the calendar for months. In truth, the dinner had been on the calendar for years, for every Hapgood boy was given a formal dinner on the eve of his sixteenth birthday, and it had never occurred to Bill not to continue the tradition for Matt simply because his name was Moore instead of Hapgood. "I raised him," he said when Gerry Conroe suggested that perhaps the dinner was inappropriate for a stepson. "I've brought him up to be a Hapgood, and I'm proud to be able to say that I've succeeded." So tonight the table would be set for six: Gerry and Nancy Conroe would bring Kelly to join Matt and his parents.

Tomorrow, the rest of the Hapgood sixteenth birthday tradition would be carried out:

At dawn, he and Matt would go hunting, along with Marty and Eric Holmes, and Paul and Pete Arneson.

In the afternoon, he and Matt would play a round of golf.

And tomorrow night would be the big party at the house for Matt and all his friends.

Tonight and tomorrow, at least, they could all pretend that nothing was wrong. And the next day . . .

The next day will take care of itself, Bill told himself as he put the car back in gear and drove through the gates. Pulling up in front of the big brick house a few moments later, he switched off the ignition, but didn't immediately leave the car. Instead he sat there, looking at the house, trying to get a sense of what might be happening inside. And he wondered if he really wanted to go back in, with Emily Moore still there. *She's just an old woman,* he reminded himself. *None of this is her fault.* Getting out of the car he strode up to the front door, then hesitated before knocking.

Should he just go in? It was his house, wasn't it?

He opened the door and stepped inside.

And instantly noticed the change.

The warmth — the sense of welcome and comfort — was gone.

Though everything in the house looked exactly the same, everything had also somehow changed.

Something doesn't want me here!

The thought seemed to come out of nowhere, but even as Bill tried to banish it, it took root in his mind. It was as if some kind of hostile force had crept into the house, and as he moved from room to room on the first floor, the feeling that this was no longer his home grew stronger. But that was ridiculous! The furniture was exactly as it had been for decades; the paintings were in their proper places on the walls. In the dining room, the table was set, laid with the best china and his great-grandmother's sterling flatware, along with the Venetian crystal his grandparents had shipped back from their honeymoon tour long before World War II.

He started out of the dining room, then abruptly turned back.

There were seven places set at the table instead of six.

So Emily Moore would be joining them for dinner.

Again Bill felt an urge to leave, and again he put

it aside. *She's Matt's grandmother,* he reminded himself. *She has a right to be here.*

"Hello?" he called out as he started up the wide stairs toward the second floor. "Anybody home?"

Joan suddenly appeared at the top of the stairs, but before she could speak, he heard his mother-in-law calling out from what had been a guest room: "Make him go away. I don't want to see him! Not after what he did to me!"

"What *I* did to her?" Bill said, hurrying up the stairs. Then, as Joan stepped back and the light from the chandelier in the corridor shone full on her face, he stopped short. His wife's face was ashen, and she seemed to have aged ten years in the short time since he'd last seen her. "Joan? Are you all right? You look —"

Joan's chin trembled, and for a moment Bill thought she would start to cry, but she regained control of herself. "I'm just a little tired, that's all," she said. "I'll be all right." She managed a slight smile. "And it's not you she's angry at. Right now, it's my father."

"Your father? But your father's —"

Joan held up a hand to silence him. "She has Alzheimer's, remember? She's been pretty good the last couple of days, but today —" Her voice broke and she shrugged helplessly. "She's been muttering about my father all day. She seems to think he's coming home, and when she heard your voice, well . . ." Her words trailed off into silence, and Bill pulled her into his arms.

88

"This can't go on," he told her, gently stroking her face as if to caress the strain away. "Look what she's doing to you. And from what I'm hearing about Matt —"

Joan abruptly pulled away from him. "I thought you were coming to his dinner party," she said, her voice taking on a bitter edge. "But if you're going to start about Mother, maybe you shouldn't stay. She's just having a bad day, but by tomorrow she'll be fine." In a near desperate tone she added: "She will be. I know she will be!"

Before Bill could say anything, Emily Moore's voice erupted from the guest room again. "Cynthia? Where are you?"

"I'm coming, Mother!" Joan called. As Bill opened his mouth to say something, she shook her head. "Don't," she pleaded. "Sometimes it's easier if I just pretend to be my sister. At least she's always nice to Cynthia." She moved toward the door to her mother's room, then turned back. "Are you staying for dinner?" she asked. "But before you answer, remember — I don't want to talk about Mother tonight. For Matt's sake, let's just try not to fight about her, all right?"

Bill nodded, managing a smile. "For Matt's sake," he agreed quietly.

While Joan went to tend to her mother, he went to his closet and began laying out his tuxedo.

The Hapgood tradition, he decided, could survive Emily Moore.

Whether his marriage could remained to be seen.

Matt lay sprawled on his bed, staring up at the ceiling.

Why the hell did they have to have a dinner party, anyway?

But he knew why — because tomorrow he'd turn sixteen, and whenever a Hapgood boy turned sixteen, they had a dinner party the night before.

And then they went hunting.

And then they played a round at the Granite Falls Golf Club.

And then they had a big party for all the birthday boy's friends.

It was the way his dad's family always did it.

Except Bill Hapgood wasn't his dad. Not anymore. He was just his stepfather, and three weeks ago he'd walked out, leaving him with his mother and his grandmother.

And everything had turned to crap.

From that night, when he'd watched his dad leave without even looking up at him, let alone saying good-bye, nothing had been right. At first he told himself the nightmares would go away — that they'd just begun again because of what had happened with his parents. After a week, he thought, he'd get used to the way things were and the nightmares would stop. But when they were still plaguing him in the middle of the second week, he began dreading going to bed, knowing what would come. For a while the house would be silent, but it wasn't the kind of quiet he was used to, when you could hear owls hooting softly as they hunted, and listen to the gentle rustling of the wind in the trees outside the window. Instead it was a foreboding silence that enveloped the house.

But soon it would be broken by his grand-mother's voice. At first Matt had gone out into the hall to listen, in case she needed help, but every night it was the same. His grandmother was always in the room that was filled with his aunt's stuff, al-ways talking to his mother's sister as if she were ac-tually there. So he would go back to his room and try to go to sleep.

And every night the dreams would come. Dreams he could never quite remember in the morning, but that left him so tired he could barely stay awake at school and couldn't concentrate on the lessons even if he managed to keep his eyes open.

This week he'd actually failed a history test.

It should have been an easy test — history was his favorite subject, and he'd been studying the textbook the night before the quiz. Except that even as he pored over the book, trying to memorize the major points of the Monroe Doctrine, the first tentacles of the terror of the nightmares were al-ready creeping up from the dark depths of his sub-conscious, distracting him from his work, setting his nerves on edge, making his skin crawl as if some unseen creature were slithering over him.

So he failed the test in the morning, and then after lunch Mrs. Clemens wanted to know why his math assignments — always perfect until three weeks ago — were no longer being turned in at all.

91

And today Ted Stevens had dropped him from the first string of the football team.

Shit!

The last thing he felt like doing was putting on his tux and sitting in the dining-room pretending like there was something to celebrate!

Screw it — maybe he'd just stay in his room. If they wanted to pretend to have a party, let them do it by themselves.

There was a rap at his door then, and he heard his mother's voice. "Matt? The Conroes will be here in fifteen minutes!"

He hesitated. Should he tell her he was sick? But he wasn't — not really. Just tired, and pissed off, and —

— and it would just make things worse if he didn't show up downstairs. "Okay," he sighed as he rolled off the bed.

He put the studs in his shirt, put it on, then pulled on his trousers and fastened the braces. He was still struggling with the bow-tie when he heard the muffled sound of the doorbell ringing. Jerking the half-done knot loose, he replaced the tie with a pre-tied one on a ribbon that fastened under his collar, pulled on his socks and shoes, and arrived in the living room just as his father was pouring drinks for Kelly's parents.

His grandmother, her tiny body all but lost in one of the wingback chairs flanking the fireplace, seemed unaware that there was anyone else in the room at all, not even looking up when he came in.

"How come you didn't wait for me after

school?" Kelly asked as he found a Coke in the refrigerator under the bar.

Matt shot a quick glance at his parents. He hadn't even spoken to his dad yet, nor had he told his mother about what happened at school that afternoon. "I just didn't feel like it," he said, trying to signal Kelly to drop the subject.

" 'Didn't *feel* like it?' " Gerry Conroe echoed, his brow arching as his lips curved into a tight smile. "I'm not sure I like your attitude, young man! That's my daughter you're talking about!"

Though Conroe tried to make it sound like he was joking, Matt still felt the sting of the words. His face flushed, but Kelly leaped to his defense before he could say anything. "He didn't do anything wrong, Daddy! It's just that Mr. Stevens kicked him off —"

"I quit the team," Matt cut in quickly, but it was already too late.

"You quit?" Joan Hapgood asked. "But you love playing football! Why would you quit?"

Matt felt his face burning. "It — I —" His eyes darted from his mother's face to his stepfather's, then back to his mother's. "It was just taking up too much of my time, that's all."

"From what I've been hearing, maybe you're right," Bill Hapgood said. "It seems your grades haven't been what they might be lately."

Matt felt his face burn hotter, and his temper began to smolder. "How would you know about my grades?" he demanded. "It's not like you've been around here to find out what's going on!"

"Matt! Don't speak to your father like —"

Matt's angry eyes shifted to his mother. "My father? I don't even know who my father is, remember?"

"Now see here, young man," Gerry Conroe began, his own face darkening with anger. "Boys don't speak to their mothers in that tone of —"

Bill Hapgood raised his hands as if in supplication, saying, "Can we all just hold on a minute? This is a party, remember? A sixteenth birthday party, and in my family —" He hesitated, and his eyes fixed on Matt. "— and this is my family — sixteenth birthdays are important. So let's just not worry about anything tonight except having a good time. All right?"

An uncomfortable silence fell over the room, and it seemed as though everyone was waiting for someone else to break it. Nancy Conroe was the one who finally spoke. "I agree with Bill," she declared, struggling to infuse her voice with a gaiety that no one was feeling. She raised her glass. "Happy birthday, Matt. And may we all celebrate many more of them together."

Though everyone lifted their glasses, Nancy Conroe's words couldn't quite dispel the pall that had been cast over the party by the angry exchange between Matt and his parents. Only Emily Moore, who spoke not a word during dinner and barely ate a bite of her food, seemed unaffected by what had happened. Even after the Conroes left — almost as soon as dinner was over — there was still an air of tension in the house.

94

"We have to talk," Bill said quietly to Joan as he closed the front door behind his departing guests. When his wife's eyes flicked toward Matt, who was standing at the foot of the stairs, he shook his head almost imperceptibly. "Just us."

Without a word, Matt turned away from them and disappeared up the stairs.

Shut out! Just plain shut out, as if he didn't even exist!

Well, then, fine! To hell with them too.

Matt's simmering anger was about to boil over. What had Kelly been thinking about, blabbing to his folks that he'd been dropped from the football team? Couldn't she keep her mouth shut, just for one night? Coming to the top of the stairs, he started down the hall toward his room. At least there he'd be by himself, away from everyone, at least for a little while. But as he came to the room next to his grandmother's, he hesitated.

His grandmother was still downstairs, and he could barely hear his folks, who must have shut the door to the library, which meant that they didn't want him to hear what they were talking about.

Which meant that he was alone upstairs.

He eyed the closed door to the room next to his grandmother's, her warning echoing in his mind. "This is Cynthia's room," she'd said as he and his mother finished unpacking the boxes filled with his aunt's things. "Nobody goes in it except me." Her eyes, sunk so deep in her wrinkled face as to be almost invisible, had flicked from Matt to his mother, then come back to rest on him. "Nobody!" she'd repeated. He'd wondered why she thought he'd even want to go in there — there was nothing in the room but a bunch of old pictures stuck on the walls, a closet full of clothes that no one would want even if they weren't so old they were starting to fall apart, and some ratty old furniture that Gram had insisted on using instead of the stuff he'd had to drag up to the attic. Why would anybody want to go in there?

But every day — and every night too — his grandmother spent hours in the room, talking as if someone were in there with her. But of course there wasn't — Gram's Alzheimer's had just made her forget that his aunt was dead.

But what was it that made her go in there? Why didn't she just sit in her own room and talk to Aunt Cynthia, if that's what she wanted to do?

Matt went quickly back to the top of the staircase and peered down into the empty foyer. He still could barely hear his parents' voices, muffled and indistinct, through the closed library door. And there was no sign at all of his grandmother.

His movements unconsciously furtive, he went back to the closed door and tested its knob.

Unlocked.

Slowly, praying that no squeaking hinge would give him away, he pushed the door open and slipped into the room.

He stood still, waiting for his eyes to adjust to the dark, and took a deep breath to try to calm his now-pounding heart.

As his lungs filled with air, his nose was flooded with a scent that instantly transported him back to the house on Burlington Avenue.

But that was crazy! This room was much bigger than the one in the other house, and nothing like it at all except for all his aunt's stuff.

Yet even as he told himself that it made no sense, the aroma washed over him and the walls seemed to close around him, just as the walls of his grandmother's house had. In the gloom of the night, the terrors that used to come to him in his dreams surrounded him again, even though he was wide-awake.

Feeling as if he couldn't breathe, he strode across the room to pull a window open and suck the cool evening air deep into his lungs.

A little better.

He took another breath, and the strange suffocating panic began to release its grip on him.

And then he felt something else.

Eyes.

Eyes watching him in the darkness.

Caught!

Someone had come upstairs and —

He spun around, his eyes searching.

Nothing! The door was still closed, the room still empty.

He started toward the door, and again was seized by the irrational feeling that unseen eyes were following his every move.

Once again he turned, and this time he saw it.

A pair of eyes pierced the darkness, seeming to hang suspended in the blackness, fixing on him with an intensity that made his skin crawl. As his heart raced, he fumbled for the light switch by the door, found it, and flipped the toggle. He blinked as light flooded from the chandelier in the center of the ceiling, and then he saw it.

The picture!

It was the picture of his aunt that hung over the fireplace. Now, in the bright light of the chandelier, the eyes lost the terrible intensity they had possessed in the darkness, and he found himself looking at nothing more than a carefully posed photograph of a beautiful girl who appeared to be no more than a year or two older than he was.

Nothing that bore any threat at all. Then why had her eyes frightened him so much? Why had they seemed to glow in the dark almost as if they were lit from within?

His fingers trembling, he reached for the light switch, to plunging the room back into darkness. As he waited for his eyes to readjust to the gloom, the strange suffocating claustrophobia closed around him again, but this time he fought it, his fingers clutching at the doorknob, tightening on it harder with every second that passed. Then, very slowly, Cynthia Moore's eyes emerged out of the darkness, fixing on him.

No, he told himself. It's not possible — it's just some kind of trick of the light! But even as he tried to reassure himself, the eyes seemed to reach out to him, reach into him, peer into the depths of—

"No!"

The word exploded from him in a choked gasp

of panic, cut off even before it was fully formed. Reflexively, his hand twisted the doorknob and he pulled the door open, spun out into the corridor, then jerked it closed behind him. He stayed there a moment, his heart pounding, his breath coming in panting gasps. As the panic slowly ebbed, as the terror drained away, he began to understand what must have happened.

Of course he'd been reminded of the house on Burlington Avenue: the odor in the room his grandmother had filled with all his aunt's stuff smelled just like it. Until tonight he'd always thought the strange musky scent in his grandmother's house was just the way that particular house smelled.

Now he knew it wasn't that at all. It had been his aunt's perfume, filling his grandmother's house the way it now filled the room he'd just left.

And as for the eyes — the eyes that seemed to loom in the darkness as if lit from within — that was easy. It must have been a beam of moonlight straying in through the window, hitting the portrait at just the right angle. Putting the last of his fear aside, Matt went to his room, stripped off his tuxedo, and, even though it was barely ten o'clock, climbed into bed.

When he finally turned out the light an hour later, he fell asleep before noticing that the moon had not yet risen.

So it never occurred to him that it must have been something else that lit his aunt Cynthia's eyes. . . .

The darkness around him was redolent with the same musky scent that had filled his aunt's room, and Matt knew he was no longer alone.

Gentle fingers touched his naked skin, caressing him.

He moved, trying to pull away from the touch, but the fingers followed him, moving down his back, across his hip to his thigh. . . .

"No," he whispered, but his throat constricted so tightly that no sound at all emerged from his lips.

"It's all right," a voice whispered. "I love you. You know I love you. . . ."

Again Matt tried to pull away from the touch and the voice, but there was no escape. No escape, at least, for his body.

But as the gentle hand caressed, and the soft voice whispered, his mind pulled away, sinking into a darkness where, no matter what might happen to his body, it, at least, would be safe. . . .

Chapter 6

Though the morning was clear and crisp and the whole world seemed suffused with the golden light that filtered through the fall foliage, Matt's mood was as dark as when he had awakened an hour ago to the shrill buzzing of the alarm. He'd snaked one hand out from under the quilt — wrapped so tightly around him that it felt like a shroud — silenced the clock, and wondered why he couldn't just stay in bed.

It was his birthday, wasn't it? Why couldn't he just do whatever he wanted to do? Besides, it didn't feel like he'd slept at all. Then he rolled over, turning his back on the morning light streaming through the window; closing his eyes against it.

It had not worked.

His skin still crawled with the memory of the touch during the night — the touch that had to have been no more than a dream, but that even now he could still feel in his loins. Better to face the day than risk slipping back into the nightmares of sleep.

But he was starting to think he was wrong, that maybe he should have just stayed in bed.

When he'd come downstairs to find his stepfather waiting for him, he knew right away that nothing from last night had yet been forgotten. His dad hadn't said anything, but Matt could tell he was still pissed off. As they checked over the guns on the big refectory table in the den, Matt waited for the storm to break, but as the minutes had ticked by and the silence held, he finally figured out his dad's game. *He's gonna wait for me to apologize. Well, why should I? What did I do? It's not my fault. None of it's my fault!* He thought things would get better when Eric and Pete got there, but as soon as they came in with their fathers, he could tell that Pete was still pissed at him too.

And now, an hour later, the six of them were deep in the woods to the west of the house, and hadn't had so much as a glimpse of a deer, and it seemed that nobody was speaking to anybody.

"Why don't we just give it up?" Matt asked, stopping abruptly.

"What's the matter, Moore?" Pete Arneson said, his voice edged with sarcasm. "You want to quit on this the same way you quit on me?"

Matt glowered at him. "What's that supposed to mean?"

Pete and Eric Holmes exchanged a glance, silently sharing the moment on the practice field when Matt had purposely let Eric charge through, then Pete's eyes settled on Matt again. "You know what it means."

The two boys stood glaring at each other, and their fathers remained silent as well. Then Bill Hapgood said, "What's he talking about, Matt?"

"I don't —" Matt began, but Pete didn't let him finish.

"You're screwing up! You're screwing up every-thing. What the hell's wrong with you lately?"

"Nothing!" Matt flared. "Why don't you all just leave me alone, okay?" The words were out of his mouth before he even realized he was going to say them, and now it was too late to snatch them back. He could see the anger burning in Pete's eyes, and feel Eric glaring at him too. "Who needs any of you?" he shouted. He turned away, pushed past Eric and Pete, Marty Holmes and Paul Arneson, and started down the trail.

"Matt!" his stepfather barked, breaking the tense silence in the aftermath of Matt's outburst. From force of habit, Matt stopped and turned back. "You don't talk to your guests that way."

Matt's face burned with humiliation at the tone of Bill's voice but he wasn't about to back down. "They're not my guests," he shot back. "This whole thing was your idea. I didn't even want to come."

Bill Hapgood's jaw tightened. "Be careful, Matt. You're walking a very thin line. Just because it's your birthday doesn't give you the right to talk to your friends or your father —"

"You're not my father!" Matt exploded. "I don't have a father, remember? You're just the man my mother married!"

"Now just hold on, Matt," Marty Holmes cut in. "If I were you —"

"You're not me," Matt flared. "None of you are!

So why don't you all just —"

Pete Arneson grabbed Matt's arm. "Look!" he whispered excitedly, pointing upward. They were standing on the bank of Granite Creek, a quarter of a mile above the falls for which the town was named. Across the stream a craggy face of stone rose in a steep bluff for nearly forty feet. A seven-point buck gazed down at them from the top of the bluff. "Jeez!" Pete whispered. "Did you ever see one that big before?"

They gazed up at the buck, and the enormous animal, feeling their eyes on him, looked back at them for a moment. But as Eric Holmes lifted his rifle to his shoulder, the deer shied away and disappeared.

"It's not going to be that easy," Bill Hapgood said as Eric lowered his rifle. "Any buck that's been around long enough to get that big isn't going to just stand there and let us shoot him." The storm between Matt and his friends dying away almost as quickly as it had come up, Bill began issuing orders. "If we're going to get him, we'll have to split up. Matt and I will cross the stream and climb the bluff here, and you guys spread out. Marty, you and Eric head downstream toward the falls, while Paul and Pete go the other way." He glanced at his watch. "We'll meet back here at ten — that gives us a little less than two hours. If none of us have him by then, we're not going to get him." His voice dropped. "And just make sure that if you shoot at something, it's that buck, not one of us."

"If he's still up there at all," Marty Holmes muttered, warily eyeing the steep face of the bluff and wondering how sure the footing might be.

"He'll be up there somewhere," Bill replied. "He wants to come down to the river to drink, so he'll stay close. See you back here at ten."

The group split up, and as his stepfather picked his way across the shallow stream and began working his way up the bluff, Matt hesitated.

Maybe he should just go home right now.

But that would only make things worse than they already were. And maybe if they were by themselves for a while, he and his dad could straighten things out. Taking a deep breath, Matt made his way across the stream, then slung his rifle over his shoulder and followed his stepfather to the top of the bluff.

Ten minutes later, as they were working their way along the edge of the bluff searching for the deer's tracks, a flicker of movement caught Matt's eye.

The buck was standing in a thicket about fifty yards away, its ears flicking rapidly as it searched for sounds that might indicate danger. But as Matt raised his rifle, the deer vanished into the woods.

"He smells us," Bill said softly. His eyes still fixed on the spot where the deer had been, he tilted his head to the left. "Circle around that way. We're upwind of him, so if I stay here, he'll still have my scent. And you can bet that he's in there somewhere, watching us. But if you circle around so he can't smell you, you might get close enough to get a good shot." When Matt made no move to start closing on the prey, Bill's voice hardened slightly, leaving no room for argument. "Just because it's your birthday doesn't mean you're entitled to do any damn thing you want. "It's time for you to grow up. And it's time for you to bag your first trophy. Understand?"

Matt's face burned. All he'd wanted to do was talk to his dad, to try to straighten things out. But —

But the hell with it!

Without a word he disappeared into the woods.

A quarter of an hour later Matt was on the other side of the thicket. For the last two minutes he thought he could hear the deer moving restlessly in the underbrush, and now, as he moved slowly toward the sound, the big buck came into view.

It was standing about forty yards away, its head up, its ears pricking as it tried to pick up sounds that might indicate danger.

Matt eased his rifle — a brand-new Browning BAR 30-06 with a Bushnell sight — off his shoulder and flicked the clip and chamber open. Putting one shell in the chamber and four more in the clip, he snapped the clip closed and released the safety. His fingers tightening on the satiny maple of the Browning's stock, he braced its rubber butt firmly against his shoulder. His right forefinger curled around the trigger as his left hand steadied the semiautomatic rifle.

He squinted, peering through the sight.

The deer's head appeared in the cross hairs.

Matt hesitated.

It was such a magnificent creature — why should he shoot it?

Then, as he gazed at the buck's uplifted head, he became aware of a strange scent on the morning air: a scent that jerked him out of the brilliant morning light and plunged him back into the depths of last night, when he had wakened in darkness.

The scent grew stronger, and now he heard the voice whispering to him.

"You know what you have to do, Matthew."

Darkness began to close around him, until all he could see was the head of the deer.

The deer, and something beyond . . .

"Do it, Matthew," the voice whispered. *"Do it for me. . . ."*

The darkness deepened.

"No," Matt whispered.

The shroud of darkness tightened, and now he felt the touch, the same touch he'd felt last night, stroking his arms.

Moving over his hands.

Curling around his fingers.

"Do it," the voice whispered once more. *"Do it . . ."*

A shot sounded.

Then another.

And another.

Matt, lost in the darkness, was utterly unaware that the shots echoing through the morning had come from the weapon in his hands. . . .

"Matt? Hey, Matt!"

Matt jumped at the sound of Eric Holmes's voice.

"What's going on?" Eric asked, approaching and cocking his head as he looked at Matt. "You okay? You look —"

"I'm fine," Matt said, the words coming quickly. But he wasn't fine. He felt strange, almost as if he'd been half asleep and Eric's voice had jerked him out of a dream. But that didn't make any sense — he was still standing in the same spot as when he caught sight of the deer a few minutes ago, the Browning still in his hands. And you couldn't sleep standing up.

Could you?

Of course not! So Eric's voice must have just caught him by surprise. Except nothing looked quite the way that it had a minute ago. The light filtering through the trees appeared different, and —

And the sun was higher than it had been.

A lot higher!

"You sure you're okay?" Eric pressed. "I've been looking for you for an hour!"

An hour? What was he talking about? It hadn't been much more than half an hour since he and his dad had crossed the stream and started up the bluff while Eric and his father headed toward the falls and the Arnesons went farther upstream. So it couldn't be much later than eight-thirty, maybe quarter to nine. Except when he looked down at his watch he saw that Eric was right — it was almost nine-thirty.

But that was nuts! It couldn't be that late — it was just a minute or so ago that he'd spotted the deer, and raised his rifle and —

— *and what?*

There was something playing around the edges of his memory, something he couldn't quite bring into focus, and now, as he struggled to remember it, it vanished the way the ephemera of the night dissolve in the morning light, erased from the memory as cleanly as if they'd never existed at all.

But it wasn't night, and he hadn't been dreaming.

Then what had happened?

Where had the missing time gone?

His thoughts were disrupted by Eric shouting to his father. "I found him, Dad! He's over here!" Again his eyes fixed on Matt. "How come you didn't answer me?" he demanded. "We've been calling you for half an hour."

"I — I guess I didn't hear you," Matt stammered. But that didn't make any sense either! What was going on? He tried to force his mind into focus, and went over it all again.

He and his dad had spotted the deer, and he'd circled around. Then he'd heard the deer, and moved toward it so silently that it hadn't heard him at all. He'd loaded the clip, raised the 30-06 rifle to his shoulder, and drawn a bead on the buck.

And then . . .

There it was again! Something touching the very

edge of his memory, just beyond his grasp! He'd been aiming at the deer — had it in his sight!

But something had happened.

Had he heard something?

Felt something?

Smelled something! That was it! There'd been a strange aroma in the air — the same aroma he'd smelled last night after he'd gone to bed, when —

Suddenly, his skin crawled and he felt a sheen of cold sweat spread over him. He felt sort of dizzy, and —

"Jeez, Matt!" he heard Eric say. "What's going on with you? How come you didn't even go look at the buck?"

"G-Go look at him?" Matt stammered. "I thought — I mean, he got away, didn't he? I had him in my sights for a second, but then —"

Eric stared at him. "You mean you didn't shoot him?"

Shoot him? What was Eric talking about? He shook his head.

"Then who did?"

"Maybe my dad —" Another image flicked through Matt's mind. While he had the gun trained on the deer, he'd seen something else, beyond the deer. Something like . . .

A face?

No! It couldn't have been! Besides, what did it matter? He hadn't even pulled the trigger!

"We can't find your dad either," Eric told him. "Come on — I'll show you the buck."

Eric led him toward the thicket in which the deer

had been standing, and as they threaded their way through the trees, Matt kept trying to make sense out of it all. But no matter how hard he tried to figure it out, he was still missing almost an hour from the morning.

An hour during which he'd apparently stood absolutely still, holding the Browning in his hands.

Half an hour during which Eric Holmes had been calling him, and he'd heard absolutely nothing.

Half an hour in which . . .

What?

As he followed Eric through the trees a terrible feeling came over him. It was the same feeling he had when he woke up in the morning from the nightmares that left nothing in their wake except fear, and a feeling of terrible exhaustion, as if he hadn't been sleeping at all. Suddenly he wasn't sure he wanted to remember the missing hour. And then, a few yards ahead, he saw it.

The big buck lay on its side at the exact spot where he'd seen it standing earlier. Marty Holmes was crouched over it, and as Eric and Matt approached, he stood up and grinned at Matt. "Good shooting. One clean shot right through the head."

Matt said nothing. The buck's eyes were wide open, and as he gazed down at it, Matt had the eerie sensation that the buck was staring back at him.

Accusing him.

"But I —" he began, but quickly fell silent, his eyes still fixed on the deer.

111

"Matt says he didn't shoot it," Eric said.

"What do you mean, you didn't shoot it?" An uncertain look came into Marty Holmes's eyes. "Where's Bill?"

Matt pointed in the direction of the bluff. "He was right over there," he said. As he gazed at the spot, the memory of the flicker of movement he'd seen in the gun sight popped back into his mind. Could it have been his dad? Of course not! If it was, surely he wouldn't have pulled the trigger! He grasped at the idea like a straw in the wind. "That's why I didn't shoot," he said. "I didn't want to risk hitting my dad —"

Marty Holmes's expression darkened as he turned and started toward the bluff, pushing his way through the branches that blocked his path, Eric following right behind him. As a terrible fear began to gnaw at his gut, Matt looked once more at the deer he'd last seen in the sight of his rifle, then hurried to catch up with Eric and his father. A few moments later they were on the trail that ran along the top of the bluff. Almost against his own will, Matt made himself look down.

For a moment he saw nothing, but then, almost hidden by the bushes it had fallen through, he saw it.

A body.

And even though it lay face-down, he knew exactly who it was.

His stepfather.

"No," he breathed. "I didn't shoot. I know I didn't shoot!"

But when he opened the Browning's clip, he knew he was wrong. Of the five cartridges he'd loaded, only two remained.

Three bullets — bullets he clearly remembered loading himself — were missing.

Joan Hapgood eyed the stacks of frozen pizza as if they were so many cobras waiting to strike. Which, in truth, they might as well have been, since she knew it wouldn't matter which one she finally reached for — when she got home it would turn out to be the wrong one, and her mother's words would certainly be sharper than a serpent's tongue. *Make up your mind,* she told herself. *Just make up your mind, put them in the cart, and go home. If it's wrong, you can bring it back tomorrow.*

But it wasn't just that. If she chose the wrong pizza — and she knew there was no possibility of choosing the right one — her mother would harp on it all day long. On the other hand, her mother would find something to harp on anyway, so what did it matter if it was the pizza or something else? Pulling the freezer open, she tried to remember whether it was pepperoni or sausage her mother had declared inedible, then gave up and tossed two of each into the grocery cart. No worse to be hanged for being spendthrift than for bringing the wrong thing.

She finished the shopping, went through the checkout stand, and loaded the groceries into the Range Rover, then glanced at her watch: almost ten. Where had the time gone? The shopping had taken far longer than she'd planned. She would have to hurry if she was going to get home, put everything away, tend to her mother, and still get to the caterers by eleven to go over the last details for Matt's party tonight.

After the dinner last night, she almost wished she could simply cancel the party.

But that wouldn't happen — it would just be four times worse than last night — or, more accurately, ten times worse, since they'd had only three guests last night, and there would be thirty tonight. She was not looking forward to it, hadn't been looking forward to it since the night Bill left. She'd been sure he was bluffing then, assumed he'd stay away that night and be back the next morning. Except Bill hadn't come back.

He hadn't even called.

The days had crept slowly by, and she just as slowly came to understand that he might not be back, at least not right away. Over and over again she'd replayed the arguments they'd had about her mother, and eventually she had to admit to herself that Bill was more than half right — he'd tried to talk about the problems her mother was causing them — and all she'd done was put him off. When she came to that conclusion, she'd picked up the telephone book and begun looking for someplace to put her mother. But even as she stared at the listings in the yellow pages — beautifully scripted advertisements for Continuing Care Facilities and Leisure Living Centers and Retirement Environments — she knew she would never be able to do it. She would never be able to send her mother to a nursing home — no matter what they called it, or how nice it looked. The only reason she'd even considered finding a place for her mother was to repair her marriage, not to give her mother the best life she could.

But as the time Bill was gone lengthened, she'd started feeling as if she were literally being torn apart, her mother pulling at her from one side, her husband from the other. And she was caught in the middle, with no escape.

The problem was that deep in her heart, she knew that Bill was right, that for his sake and for Matt's sake — even for her own sake — she should find a place for her mother. Matt was already suffering, though she hadn't realized just how much until last night. And she'd seen the unhappiness in Bill's eyes too.

She'd tried to ignore what she herself was going through, but as she steered the Rover back toward Hapgood Farm, she found herself going slowly, putting off as long as she could the moment when she would have to start dealing with her mother again.

Her mother, and Cynthia.

Cynthia had become almost as strong a presence in the house as her mother. Not an hour went by that her mother didn't speak of her long-dead sister.

If it goes on much longer, I'm going to start to hate her, Joan thought as she turned through the gates. And she'd never hated Cynthia. Even now she could remember how she'd adored her older sister when they were growing up. Cynthia had been everything she had not — blond, and beautiful, and graceful. She'd loved nothing more than sitting on Cynthia's bed, her arms wrapped around her knees as she watched her sister get ready for a date.

And Cynthia had many dates — practically every boy her age wanted to go out with her. Cynthia went out with them all, and every night when she got home Joan would sneak into her room and the two of them would whisper in the darkness for hours as Cynthia told her everything that had happened.

Now, though, it was her mother who whispered in the darkness for hours. But it wasn't always whispering, and it wasn't always in the darkness. But it was always about Cynthia, and what would happen when Cynthia got home. Every day, her mother spent hours in what Joan had already come to think of as Cynthia's room, going through everything over and over again, making certain that everything was in its place, that nothing had been touched.

And screaming at her if she so much as set a foot through the door.

Would the screaming of her guilt be any worse, if she put her mother into one of the facilities she'd found in the yellow pages? Joan wondered. She had actually driven by one of them a few days ago. It was a lovely three-story brick Colonial surrounded by beautiful gardens, and if you didn't notice the people in wheelchairs sitting under the trees — wrapped in heavy scarves against the nip in the fall air — it would be easy to mistake it for someone's private home. But even as she enjoyed the beauty of the place, Joan remembered the things she'd read about how the elderly were sometimes treated.

Tied into a chair and left in the hall for hours.

Strapped into bed at night and kept so drugged they didn't even have the will to complain.

She could never do that to her mother. Never.

And so, tonight, she would stand next to Bill in the receiving line at Matt's party and try to pretend that nothing was wrong, that they were just going through what some of her friends called "a bad patch" in their marriage, though she suspected that what her friends usually meant by "a bad patch" was that their husbands were having an affair. Bill would be fine, of course; a talent for always being gracious and never letting his true emotions show had been bred into him for generations.

I'll get through it, she told herself. *I'll get through it somehow.*

She came around the last curve in the driveway and was pulling the car into the carriage house when she noticed that a fourth car had joined the group parked in the area behind the house.

The brand-new black-and-white Ford Taurus that the town had bought for Dan Pullman in recognition of his tenth year as the Granite Falls police chief.

Mother! she thought. *Oh God, what's happened? What's she done?*

Leaving the groceries in the car, she hurried to the house, letting herself in through the back door. Dan Pullman was standing in the kitchen, and there was something about the look in his eyes as he turned to face her that told Joan the problem wasn't her mother.

"What is it?" she breathed. "What's happened?"

Pullman hesitated, but knew there was no way to break the news gently. "There's been an accident, Joan," he said, running a hand through his shock of steel gray hair as he uncomfortably shifted the weight of his six-foot-two-inch frame from one foot to the other.

"Not Matt!" she gasped, her heart racing.

Pullman shook his head. "It's Bill," he said softly, the emotion in his voice telling her just how bad it was.

"Oh God," she whimpered, sinking onto a chair. "No. Please . . . no . . ."

Chapter 7

This isn't happening, Joan told herself. *It can't be happening.*

The whole scene seemed somehow surreal — she was sitting next to Dan Pullman in the front seat of his Taurus, and everything beyond the windshield looked perfectly normal. It was a perfect late fall morning; the ancient maples, birches, and oaks that had been protected by generations of her husband's family were clothed in brilliant foliage that was almost blinding against the clear turquoise of the sky.

But it was all wrong!

The sky should have been a heavy leaden gray.

There should have been a cold drizzle falling through sodden leaves.

A chill wind should have been blowing, which would at least have accounted for the terrible cold that had fallen over her, making her shiver even in the warmth of the car.

They were half a mile from the house, moving along one of the narrow unpaved tracks that twisted through the woods. The road eventually wound around to the base of the waterfall and the swimming hole that was a favorite picnic area not only of the Hapgoods, but of everyone else in town. She and Bill were always careful to leave it undisturbed until late in the season, when the trees were bare and the road would be covered with shimmering leaves. Then, on a morning as perfect as this one, they'd go out and walk the road, hand in hand, listening to the rustle and crunch of the leaves underfoot, sometimes even abandoning their adulthood to roll around in them like children, their noses filling with dust until they were sneezing helplessly. But this morning the leaves that had already fallen were crushed, the ruts in the road laid bare by the wheels of . . . How many cars? Had they called an ambulance? For some reason — maybe to keep from thinking about what had happened — Joan found herself trying to remember if she'd heard the wailing of a siren while she'd been moving through the aisles of the market, doing the shopping as if nothing was wrong.

And nothing should have been wrong — she should have gotten back to the house just as Bill and Matt returned from their morning hunt. The scene began to play itself out in her mind: the two of them bursting into the kitchen through the back porch and the mud room, their faces flushed with the chill of the autumn air, regaling her with details of the hunt, each giving the other the credit for whatever they'd bagged.

Matt, grinning at Bill, saying, "I wouldn't have even seen the deer if it hadn't been for Dad."

Bill, sloughing off the compliment: "Matt's got the eye — and he's a better shot now than I ever was! Another couple of years and he'll be good enough for competition!"

But as the car rounded a sharp bend in the road and braked to a stop, the happy scene in her mind was shattered by what she saw.

Two police cars, their lights flashing incongruously in the morning light, were parked haphazardly beneath the canopy of immense maples. And a boxy ambulance, bearing the orange and white paint of the aid unit of the fire department. Its lights, though, were not flashing, and her heart sank as she realized why: for the ambulance, at least, no emergency existed.

Then Joan saw it.

Bill lay facedown on the other side of the stream. If she had stumbled upon him while walking in the woods, she might have assumed he'd merely fallen asleep.

She might even have left him undisturbed, and enjoyed watching him sleep. But the activity around his motionless figure betrayed the truth of what had happened as clearly as the lack of flashing lights on the ambulance.

Yet even in the face of what she had heard from Dan Pullman and what she saw before her, a glimmer of hope still flickered inside her. Before the police car came to a complete stop, Joan scrambled out, waded across the stream, and hurried toward her husband, crouching down beside him.

Reaching out to him.

Touching him.

His skin was cold, his flesh unresponsive.

His hair was matted with blood.

The flicker of hope in her heart guttered and went out.

As the terrible finality of what had happened settled over her, she could no longer bring herself to look at her husband's body, and raised her eyes. Seeing the bluff rising a few feet away, she suddenly understood.

An accident — just a stupid accident! He and Matt had been on the trail at the top of the bluff, and Bill had lost his footing! "How could it have happened?" she blurted, barely even conscious she was speaking aloud. "He knows that trail so well! He —"

Then Dan Pullman was beside her. "It wasn't the fall," he said softly.

Joan gazed blankly at him, as if the words he'd just spoken had been uttered in some foreign language. Not the fall? What was he talking about? Then, slowly, she became aware of the figures around her.

Figures — not people.

The paramedics, in their white uniforms, made sense to her.

So did the police officers.

But Marty Holmes and Paul Arneson were standing with their sons a few yards away.

Looking at her.

Looking at her, but not talking to her.

And Matt! Where was Matt?

Then she saw him. He was sitting in one of the

police cars, his face ashen, his eyes staring straight at her.

Staring at her, but not seeing her.

"What is it?" she whispered, turning back to Dan Pullman. "What killed him?"

When Pullman still said nothing, she reached out again, took Bill by the shoulder, and turned him over.

His body rolled onto its back, and now she could see it.

A hole exactly in the center of his forehead.

Perfectly formed.

But not bloody.

Shouldn't there have been blood?

She reached out, her fingers hovering over the strange hole, but in the end she couldn't bring herself to touch it. Then her gaze shifted back to Dan. "How?" she breathed. "Oh, God, Dan, how . . . ?"

"We think Matt shot him," he said softly.

"An accident," she breathed. "It had to be . . ."

Dan's jaw tightened, and she saw the pain in his eyes, and finally he shook his head. "We don't know, Joan. It might have been an accident, but — well —" He bit his lip, then forced himself to go on. "Apparently there was some kind of argument."

He continued speaking, but Joan didn't hear his words; as the full reality of what had happened broke over her, a wailing scream of grief rose in her throat. "Nooo," she howled, shattering the eerie quiet that had fallen over the scene. "Noooooo . . ."

123

It was the ringing telephone that first told Gerry Conroe that something had happened. After twenty years of running the little paper that managed to serve most of Granite Falls' needs with its one edition a week, he had grown accustomed to a certain pattern: Tuesdays, Wednesdays, and Thursdays were the big news days, if you could really call the stories in the paper news at all. In truth, he thought of most of what he published as features, not news. Perhaps the scores of the high school athletic teams might be considered news; even the latest slate of officers for the Lions Club, Rotary, or the Gardening Ladies might fall into that category. But for hard news the people of Granite Falls turned to the *Manchester Guardian* rather than the *Granite Falls Ledger.* Thus, it fell to Gerry to keep them abreast of local doings, and everyone knew that if you wanted something in the paper on Monday morning, you'd absolutely better let Gerry know before lunch on Friday, and even then you'd better be able to convince him that there was a good reason to make changes that close to press time. So in Gerry's life, Saturday mornings were generally quiet, spent helping his two-person staff finalize the layout of the paper so it could be sent down to Manchester to be printed on Sunday, coming back to Granite Falls just in time to be delivered Monday morning. So when all three of the office lines suddenly lit up at ten o'clock on Saturday morning, he knew immediately that something in town had gone wrong.

And when Kelly, who had started working Saturday mornings a year ago, appeared at his office door — her face ashen and her eyes glistening with tears — he knew it was serious, and very close to home.

Not Nancy. Please, not Nancy.

But when Kelly spoke, the blow her words dealt him was almost as powerful as if she'd told him something had happened to her mother. "It's Uncle Bill," she whispered, her voice trembling. "He — They say he's dead!"

For a moment Gerry Conroe's mind simply refused to accept it. Dead? Bill Hapgood couldn't possibly be dead! They'd just had dinner at Bill and Joan's last night, and this morning Bill was taking Matt —

In a flash, it came to him.

A hunting accident! Another damned hunting accident!

Suddenly, his shock at what had happened was tempered with fury. Every year it was the same — every year he printed the same editorial, questioning the whole idea of men going out hunting deer in this day and age. And every year he heard all the arguments from all his friends: if they didn't argue that hunting was "in their genes," they tried to raise it to a constitutional issue.

"What's the point of having the right to own guns if we don't own them?" Bill Hapgood himself had argued just a few weeks ago. "And we have to own them — some day we just may need to defend ourselves against our own government. So if we own them, it follows that we should know how to

125

use them." When Gerry had suggested that Bill had just named the exact purpose of shooting ranges, his friend only laughed. "Don't give me that nonsense about target shooting — that's all well and good for a novice, but once a man's learned to shoot, he wants a challenge!"

And now Bill Hapgood was dead.

Mindlessly, stupidly, dead.

Then, through his anger, he heard Kelly speak again.

"They think Matt might have done it," she whispered.

Once again his mind reacted without thought. "That's the stupidest thing I've ever heard —" he began, but the words died on his lips as he remembered the scene at the Hapgoods' last night.

Until he'd heard Matt argue with his father, he hadn't thought him capable of such anger and bitterness.

Except Bill wasn't Matt's father.

Bill was Matt's stepfather.

Not that it had ever made any difference to Bill. How many times had he heard Bill say that Matt was exactly the son he'd always wanted? Recalling the angry dinner, Gerry did his best to banish the idea that came with that memory. What was he thinking of? Was he seriously thinking that Matt might have shot Bill on purpose?

Ridiculous!

It was an accident.

It *had* to be an accident.

"I'd better get out there," he said as he pulled on

126

his jacket. "Where did it happen?"

"Not very far from the falls," Kelly said. She followed him as he walked out of his little office and through the single large room where the two-person staff worked. "I want to go with you, Daddy."

Her words jolting him to a stop, Gerry Conroe turned to look at his daughter. Go with him? But she was just a little girl!

"I'm almost sixteen," she said, seeing his thoughts etched on his face. "I'm not a baby anymore."

"For God's sake, Kelly — why would you want to go out there?" As she hesitated, he knew exactly what she was going to say, and didn't need to hear her explanation before he made up his mind. He was already shaking his head when she spoke.

"I want to see Matt. If they really think he —"

Gerry held up a hand to silence her. "No," he said. "You're only fifteen years old. You don't need to see —" His throat tightened and he couldn't bring himself to finish what he'd been about to say. It was going to be hard enough for him to see Bill Hapgood's lifeless body himself, and he knew it was an image he would never forget. There was no reason for Kelly to have to bear the memory of that image. "No," he said again, his voice much softer now. He cast about for some words that would neither offend Kelly nor upset her more than she already was. "Look," he finally went on, reaching out and pulling her into his arms, "it's going to be crazy out there. There'll be police, and medics,

127

and God only knows how many other people. I wouldn't even go myself, except Bill's my best friend, and I have to be there."

"But Matt's my boyfriend —" Kelly began.

Gerry stiffened, then let his arms drop to his sides. "No," he said one last time. His voice took on a tone that warned Kelly against pressing him further. "And I really don't want to talk about it." But even as he spoke, the hurt in her eyes made him relent slightly. "Let's just wait until we know what happened, okay?"

As he drove away from the office, though, Gerry found himself wishing that Kelly had not been dating Matt at all, and in the back of his mind he could hear his own father explaining how to judge his friends. "The apple never falls far from the tree, Gerald," Jerome Conroe had taught him when he was no more than six or seven. "Know the father, and you will know the son. That's why you must always know who your friend's families are."

But no one except Joan Hapgood knew who Matthew Moore's father really was. So maybe Bill had been wrong.

Maybe Matthew Moore hadn't been the son he'd always wanted.

Maybe none of them — not even Bill Hapgood — really knew Matthew Moore at all.

"Matt?"

His name sounded muffled, as if it were coming from somewhere far off in the distance — or perhaps even from underwater — and it wasn't until he heard it a second time that he slowly looked up to see his mother standing close to him, her eyes anxious, her face pale. She reached out to touch his cheek, but her fingers were like ice and he reflexively pulled away from the chill of her touch.

Joan winced at the rejection of what she'd intended as a gentle caress, but told herself it meant nothing — that he was still in shock from what had happened. "It's going to be all right," she told him softly. "Everything's going to be all right. I'll take care of you."

Again Matt barely heard the words. From the moment when he'd looked down from the top of the bluff and seen his stepfather's body lying in the thicket of brush next to the stream, something had changed. It was as if in that instant a barrier of some kind had fallen between him and the rest of the world.

Everything was different.

He'd seen it first in Eric Holmes's eyes. They'd all stared down at the broken body in the brush, a terrible silence falling over them. Then, after what seemed an eternity, Eric had spoken. "Jeez, Matt," he'd breathed. "What happened? What'd you do?"

Matt's gaze had slowly shifted from his stepfather to Eric, and that's when he'd seen it. There was something in Eric's eyes that told him in an instant that everything had changed. Seemingly out of nowhere, a memory rose in his mind. He and Eric were in biology class, dissecting a frog. As he had cut through the skin of the frog's belly, laying it back in neat flaps, he'd glanced up at Eric. The expression on Eric's face — and the look in his eyes — as Eric watched him lay open the frog's abdomen were exactly the same as the look he'd given Matt as he asked what Matt had done.

Revulsion, only slightly tempered with curiosity.

On the bluff above the river, he'd seen Eric turning away from him, just as he turned away from the frog in the lab that day.

From that moment, Matt sensed everyone watching him, and there was no friendliness in their eyes.

Now they were watching him as if he were some kind of specimen, some individual of another species, no longer part of what had been his world only a few hours ago. He'd been squeezed out of it in an instant.

But why?

He hadn't done anything!

Or had he?

He hadn't answered Eric's question when they were standing on the bluff, and even now he had no answer. Rather, there were just more questions, questions and images, tumbling through his mind in a jumble of confusion.

The deer.

He'd been aiming at the deer! And his stepfather hadn't been there —

Had he?

Of course not! He'd have seen him!

But even as he tried to reassure himself, he kept seeing another image, just the faintest flash of a memory, of something else in the gun sight, something he'd barely been aware of as the strange aroma filled his nostrils, spreading like a mist over his mind, sending him —

Where?

Even now, long after Eric's voice had brought him out of the strange reverie he'd fallen into, he had no real idea of what had happened. It wasn't as if he'd been sick, even though he hadn't slept well last night. So what had happened? Had he just passed out? Had it been some kind of fumes he'd smelled, that knocked him out for a while? But if he'd passed out, how come he hadn't fallen?

So he couldn't have passed out.

The questions kept churning in his mind.

He had no memory even of following Eric and his father down the bluff, though he knew he must have. And he'd been only vaguely aware of everything that had happened since, of Dan Pullman arriving, and the ambulance, and then more deputies. He vaguely recalled one of the deputies asking him what had happened, and putting him in the backseat of one of the cars, but he'd been no more able to tell the deputy anything than he'd been able to tell Eric.

"I don't know" was all he'd said. And now, as he looked up at his mother, he could only repeat the same question the deputy had asked him.

"What happened, Mom?" he said softly. "What happened to Dad?"

Before his mother could answer, Dan Pullman appeared next to her, and as Matt's gaze shifted to the police chief, he saw the same look in Pullman's eyes that he'd seen in Eric's.

"I think you know what happened to your dad," Pullman said softly. "Do you want to tell us about it?"

"I —" Matt began, then fell back into silence.

Immediately understanding the implication of Pullman's words — and seeing the pain they brought to her son's face — Joan's anguished eyes fixed on the police chief. "How can you even think that?" she breathed, her voice trembling as she struggled with her roiling emotions. "Matt loved his father! He'd never do anything to hurt —"

Pullman raised both his hands as if to fend off her outburst. "I never said that, Joan. Whatever happened, I'm sure it was an accident. And Matt was there. Who else can tell us —"

Joan shook her head as if to throw off the words as a dog sheds water from its coat. "Not now," she said. She reached out and took Matt's hand in her own, and this time, at least, he didn't try to pull away from her. "How can you expect him to say anything now?" she asked. "How can you expect either of us to —"

"It's all right, Joan," Dan cut in. "Nobody has to say anything right now." He glanced around, then signaled to Tony Petrocelli, in whose squad car Matt was sitting. "Can you drive them home, Tony?"

Knowing from long experience that his boss wasn't asking a question, Petrocelli nodded. "Right away."

As his deputy moved around to the driver's door

132

and Joan Hapgood joined her son in the backseat, Dan Pullman spoke. "It's going to be all right, Joan," he said, trying to reassure the woman whose husband's body was at that moment being loaded into the ambulance to be transported to the coroner. "I'm sure it was an accident." He shook his head, sighing. "I'll come by later, okay?" When Joan didn't respond, he reached through the open window and laid his hand on her shoulder.

Just as her son had pulled away from her own touch a few moments ago, Joan now recoiled from the police chief's gesture. "I know what you think," she said, looking directly into Pullman's eyes. "You think Matt shot Bill. But I'll never believe that. He couldn't have. He just couldn't have."

Dan watched the car until it disappeared from view, then went back to his examination of the scene of the accident, taking careful notes as both Marty Holmes and Paul Arneson recounted the argument between Matt and his stepfather that morning.

Then, when Gerry Conroe arrived, he heard about the scene that had transpired at the Hapgoods' last night.

"Go up on the bluff and start searching," he finally told his deputies. "I want the casings of every bullet Matt fired. And I want the bullets too. But first find the casings. Then at least we'll know how many bullets we're looking for."

"What about the buck?" one of the deputies asked. "Seems like we shouldn't just let it rot."

Pullman hesitated. He couldn't imagine why either Joan or Matt would ever want to see the buck again, but on the other hand, Matt had shot the deer on their property, and the last thing he needed was anyone accusing him of disposing of it without permission. "There's a shed behind the Hapgoods' carriage house — that's where Bill always hung his game. Guess you might as well put it there. Someone call Petrocelli and have him tell Mrs. Hapgood where it'll be. If they want to get rid of it, they can do it themselves."

As the deputies set to work, Dan Pullman turned to Gerry Conroe. Like almost everyone in Granite Falls, they had both been born there, had known each other all their lives. "Well?" Pullman asked. "What do you think? Was it an accident?"

Conroe hesitated only a second before shaking his head. "I'd like to say it was," he replied. "But I can't. I just can't."

Chapter 8

Numbness fell over Joan as Tony Petrocelli drove her and Matt back to the house. When the deputy pulled the squad car to a halt in the circular drive at the foot of the wide steps leading up to the front door, she neither said anything nor made any move to open the door. Instead she gazed through the car window at the sprawling brick house she'd lived in for the last ten years.

It looked completely different now.

But what had changed?

Not the facade, for the columns supporting the porch roof were just as they'd always been. Nor was it the windows, with their dark green shutters hooked open, or the porch or the eaves. Every detail of the house looked the same, and as her eyes wandered over it, she almost convinced herself that she'd been wrong, that nothing had changed at all.

"Mrs. Hapgood?" Petrocelli glanced worriedly in the rearview mirror. Joan Hapgood appeared puzzled, as if she wasn't quite sure where she was. "Is everything —" He stopped himself. He'd been about to say "okay," but how could anything be okay for her right now? Petrocelli licked his lower lip nervously, and began again: "Is there anything I can do for you, Mrs. Hapgood?" For a moment it seemed she hadn't heard him, but then she slowly came back to life.

"No," she said, "I — Well, thank you for bringing us home." The words were little more than a breath of air, and the wan smile she managed appeared to cost her most of what little composure she had been able to muster.

As Matt got out of the backseat and moved around the car to his mother, Petrocelli wondered what he should do. Go in with them? Just wait there until they were in the house? Or head right back to the scene? He tried to figure out what Dan Pullman would do in this situation, but then decided that if it were his own wife who had died, he wouldn't want anyone around except maybe a couple of really close friends. "If you need anything . . ." he began, then his voice trailed off. "I guess I better be going, unless you want something else."

Neither Joan nor Matt replied, and finally Petrocelli drove on around the circle of the driveway heading back the way he'd come. It was at times like this that he wished he'd gone into partnership with his brother on the pizza parlor. When he glanced back and saw that neither of them had moved, he wondered if he should go back. But what would he say? Feeling utterly inadequate, Tony Petrocelli kept driving.

And Joan Hapgood kept gazing at the house.

Though nothing about it had changed, nothing was the same either, and as she looked at it, she

136

began to understand. *It's not mine anymore.* But why? She'd lived in it for ten years, and never had any feeling about it except that it was where she and Bill and Matt lived.

Home.

In fact, she realized, it had felt more like home than any other place she'd ever been. Certainly the house on Burlington Avenue should have felt like home, but for as long as she could remember, that house had always been associated with her mother's constant belittlement of everything she did. Nor had any of the places in New York felt like home either, even before she'd found herself unable to support herself and Matt, and been forced to bring him back to her mother's house. Then, nearly five years later, she'd married Bill and moved here and finally felt as if she truly was at home.

She and Bill and Matt.

But now Bill was dead, and now it didn't seem like her house anymore.

Now her mother was waiting for her, not Bill.

As if in response to her thoughts, the door opened and Emily Moore came out onto the porch. She stood at the top of the steps, her eyes fixing on her daughter. "Where have you been?" the old woman demanded. "I'm hungry! I want my breakfast!"

The words — so totally unexpected — stunned Joan for a moment, and her eyes clouded with tears. How could her mother be so callous? Then she remembered — in her rush to get to Bill, she'd

137

completely forgotten her mother. She didn't know what had happened.

"Maybe I should have asked Cynthia for my breakfast," Emily said. "She would have fixed it for me!"

"Cynthia?" Joan echoed. "Mother, you know —"

"She was here," Emily cut in. "She was here this morning! But now I can't find her either!" Turning away, she started back toward the front door.

"Gram?" Matt called. The old lady turned to peer down at her grandson. "It's Dad," Matt said, his voice quivering as he struggled to say the words. "He — He's dead, Gram. There was an accident, and he — he got shot!"

Emily Moore pursed her lips and appeared to struggle to process what her grandson had just told her. Finally, though, she shook her head. "Accidents don't happen," she declared. "There's always a reason." She turned away and disappeared back into the house, closing the door behind her.

Joan slipped her hand into her son's. "She didn't mean that, Matt," she said softly. "Most of the time she doesn't even know what she's saying."

Matt's fingers tightened on her hand, but before he could say anything, they both turned at the sound of a car coming up the drive.

Seconds later Nancy Conroe pulled her Saab to a stop, then jumped out and put her arms around both Joan and Matt.

"I just heard," she said. "I don't know what to say — it's just so — so awful!" With her best friend's arm around her, the fragile fragments of

Joan's composure collapsed, and she began sobbing helplessly. "It's all right," Nancy Conroe crooned, gently smoothing Joan's hair as if she were a child. Then, hearing her own words, she pulled Joan close. "Oh, God, what am I saying? It's not going to be all right, is it? But we'll get through it. Somehow, we'll all get through it. Now let's get you both into the house."

With one arm still around Joan, she put the other around Matt, steering them both up the steps and into the house. "Let's get some coffee on, and then I'll —" Nancy abruptly fell silent, unsure about what she should do. But when Joan said nothing, and Nancy could bear the silence no longer, she said, "I'll do whatever you need me to do."

Again there was a silence, then Joan began speaking, and Nancy could hear in her voice that the full reality of what had happened was closing in on her. "We need to call people," Joan said. "All the people that were coming to Matt's party tonight . . ."

"Of course. Where's the list? Oh, never mind — I know who's coming as well as you do, don't I?" She set up the coffee maker, then picked up the phone that sat on the breakfast bar behind the big six-burner cook top.

"And our lawyer," Joan added, almost as an afterthought. "You'd better call Trip Wainwright too."

The afternoon passed in a haze. Every now and then a familiar face emerged and Joan would listen to the same words spoken again and again:

"It's just so terrible — unbelievable!"

"I can't believe Bill's gone! How will any of us get along without him?"

"Such a tragedy — how could something like this happen?"

"God works in mysterious ways, but we must trust in Him."

"If there's anything I can do, Joan, anything at all . . ."

But there was nothing anyone could do, and they seemed to know it. Almost as quickly as they uttered the expected platitudes, they left, and by five o'clock the trickle had dwindled away to Arthur Pettis, who wrung his Uriah Heepish hands for the last time and took his leave with promises that she needn't worry about anything — "insurancewise, your husband was absolutely scrupulous about making sure his loved ones were covered." She somehow knew that for today at least, there would be no more visitors.

After Nancy Conroe steered the insurance agent to the front door, however, Joan wondered which would be harder to bear: spending the evening alone in the house, or trying to make conversation with all of Bill's friends.

Bill's friends?

Where had that come from? Of the somewhat more than half-dozen people who had stopped by that afternoon, bringing some kind of casserole, or cold salad or pie or cake, most had been *their* friends, people she'd known her entire life.

Except that as they passed through the house, squeezing her hand and offering condolences, she'd begun to sense something. At first she thought it was nothing more than the fact that no one knew quite what to say. But then she started picking up on other things.

Little things.

The glances that some of them had shot toward Matt.

Not that anyone said anything — they'd taken Matt's hand every bit as warmly as they'd taken her own, and murmured the same words they were speaking to her. But after they'd spoken to her and to Matt, they began talking among themselves, their eyes darting toward Matt, then quickly shifting away again, as if they feared being caught doing something not quite polite.

As the afternoon wore on and the first numbness of shock wore off, she tried to tell herself she was wrong — that she was imagining things. But she knew she wasn't imagining things.

They were talking about Matt.

And about Bill.

They thought Matt had killed him.

Slowly, without quite realizing what was happening, fear for her son began to thaw the terrible cold of Joan's grief for her husband, and through the tears that still glazed her eyes, she began to see her friends in a different light.

Her friends?

Were they really her friends? Had they ever been her friends?

She kept trying to tell herself that she was wrong, that they were as much her friends as Bill's. But even as she tried to convince herself, she knew it wasn't quite true. These were the people who had grown up with Bill, and though she'd always known them too, it wasn't until she'd married Bill that she became a part of their group.

They'd never been inside the house on Burlington Avenue where she'd grown up.

None of the men had ever taken her to a dance when they were in high school.

She hadn't been a song-leader at the football games, or part of the homecoming court, or anything else. For most of these people, she hadn't really existed at all until the first night Bill Hapgood had taken her to dinner with his friends. And that night had been one of the most frightening of her life. . . .

"They're staring at me," she whispered. "Bill, why are they staring at me? Am I dressed wrong?"

"They're staring at you because you're the most beautiful woman they've ever seen," Bill told her. Then he winked. "It's when they stop staring at you that you have to start worrying."

She didn't believe him, of course, because she'd never been beautiful. Cynthia was the beautiful one, and even tonight, sitting with Bill on a perfect August evening, she'd been sure that if Cynthia were still alive, she herself wouldn't be sitting here at all. It would have been Cynthia who Bill had come to the house on Burlington Avenue to pick up.

Her mother would have welcomed him, and taken him into the parlor, and made conversation with him while Cynthia put the finishing touches on her makeup.

And Cynthia wouldn't have been praying that she wouldn't break out in a sweat and stain the armpits of her best dress.

But it hadn't been Cynthia — it had been her, trembling in front of Cynthia's closet as she searched for a dress that might be suitable for an evening out with Bill Hapgood.

And instead of chatting with Bill, her mother had come upstairs and lectured her on making certain she behaved herself. "I already have one grandchild," her mother had reminded her. "Don't make me another one tonight."

Her face burning, she had gone down to greet Bill, and found him playing with Matt. By the time he'd brought her home, he'd actually succeeded in making her feel like the most beautiful woman at the restaurant, and she knew she'd begun falling in love with him.

And now, ten years later, with the pain of Bill's death still so sharp it felt like a knife twisting in her belly, she had the sickening feeling that a need to offer her their condolences wasn't what had brought all these people to her home.

The real reason they'd come was to find out exactly what had happened in the woods that day.

But now, except for Nancy Conroe, the last of them were gone, and suddenly the only thing Joan wanted was to be alone.

Alone with Matt.

Alone with their grief.

Half an hour later she closed the door behind Nancy too and at last was able to turn her full attention to her son. He was sitting on one of the wingbacks flanking the fireplace, and she knelt in front of his chair, taking his hands in hers. "We're going to be all right, Matt," she said softly.

Matt, his sixteenth birthday drawing to a close neither of them could have imagined the day before, looked bleakly into his mother's eyes.

"I know what they were thinking, Mom," he said. "I know what they were all thinking. That I killed Dad."

Should she try to argue with him? Tell him he was wrong? But how could she, when she knew he'd spoken the truth.

"It doesn't matter," she said, needing to comfort her son even more than she herself needed to be comforted. "What they think doesn't matter. What matters is that we both know you didn't do anything."

Matt said nothing.

Emily Moore watched suspiciously as the last of the cars wound down the graveled driveway and disappeared into the trees. Several cars had come and gone today, but if anyone had asked her exactly how many, or how long any of them had stayed, she wouldn't have been able to say. All she knew was that ever since Cynthia had come, everything was somehow different than before. Though the memory of seeing her beloved daughter was blurry, she'd been clinging to it, turning it over and over in her mind, trying to absorb every detail. But there was so little to hang on to. All she remembered was that she'd been in the bathroom, and suddenly knew that Cynthia had come home.

Just *knew* it!

She'd reached out to open the door that led to Cynthia's room, but paused before turning the knob. What if she wasn't there? But she was! Emily could feel her. So she turned the knob and slowly pushed open the door. And there she was — sitting at her vanity table, carefully finishing her makeup, just like she was getting ready to go to school. As Emily watched, Cynthia set aside her eyelash curler, examined herself carefully in the mirror, then reached for her perfume. As she opened the bottle, the musky scent of Nightshade filled the room. Her heart fluttering with excitement, and her knees weakening as the fumes surrounded her, Emily steadied herself against the doorjamb. When she tried to speak, even her voice was so faint it was barely a whisper: "Cynthia? My Cynthia?"

At first she didn't think Cynthia heard her, but then Cynthia turned and smiled at her. "I'm home, Mama," she said. "I'm finally home!"

One hand clutching at her breast to calm her hammering heart, the other stretched out toward Cynthia, Emily moved toward her perfect child. But she'd gone no more than a step or two when Cynthia, silent as a wraith, had risen from the little chair in front of the vanity and vanished through

145

the heavy mahogany door leading to the hall. Emily tottered after her, but by the time she managed to pull the door open, Cynthia had disappeared.

Disappeared as completely as if she'd never been there at all. Emily had gone after her, making her way from room to room, searching every corner of the house, calling out to her, but it was no use.

Cynthia was gone.

When Joan finally came home, Emily told her about Cynthia, and then the cars started coming. She'd known why they were there right away. Joan didn't want Cynthia here, so she'd made all these people come to look for her and take her away. Emily watched from the safety of her room, holding the curtain back just enough to peek out, terrified that at any moment they might find her perfect daughter. But now all the people and all the cars were gone, and finally, exhausted from her vigil by the window, Emily unsteadily made her way over to her chair and gingerly lowered herself into it.

Her eyes closed. . . .

Minutes passed.

Perhaps hours.

Emily drifted up from the unconsciousness into which she'd fallen. Her body felt stiff and there was a sour taste in her mouth. The room was dark, but she wasn't aware of it. Slowly, her old bones protesting, she lifted herself from the chair and shuffled into the bathroom. Fumbling in the medicine cabinet, she found a can of powder and shook

146

some into the palm of her left hand. Her fingers found her toothbrush; she scrubbed it in the powder, then put it in her mouth. It didn't taste quite right, and felt dry, but she kept brushing anyway, trying to rid herself of the sour taste.

Then, in the mirror, she glimpsed something. A movement, all but lost in the shadowy darkness.

Dropping the toothbrush, Emily turned and peered into the darkness.

The door to Cynthia's room stood open.

And she could *feel* Cynthia's presence. Her senses came alive. Her ears, weakened by the passing years, were filled with unfamiliar sounds: the ticking of a clock, the low hooting of an owl beyond the window, the rustling of a prowling animal.

Her eye, its focus softened with age, now caught every beam and flicker of light, and her daughter's room was filled with a silvery glow.

Cynthia sat once more at the vanity table, her blond hair flowing in gentle waves over her shoulders, her diaphanous nightgown shimmering around her like a cloud.

Barely trusting the vision not to vanish before her like a mirage, Emily took an unsteady step forward.

Then another, and another.

Finally she stood behind Cynthia, gazing into the angelic face reflected in the mirror. Her hands trembling, she held them above her daughter's shoulders, afraid to touch her child's flesh lest it dissolve away to nothingness.

"I'm so glad, Cynthia," she whispered, her voice as palsied as her hands. "I'm so glad you've come home."

In the mirror, Cynthia's eyes met hers, and a smile curled her lips. "Do you love me, Mama?" she asked softly.

"More than anything," Emily whispered. "More than anything in the world."

Cynthia rose from the chair and turned so Emily could gaze up into her perfect face.

Her eyes glowed in the silvery light.

Her smile widened.

Both her hands came up and rested on Emily's thin shoulders.

A warmth she hadn't felt in years suffused Emily's body, washing away the cold that constantly gripped her. She reached up to touch her daughter's cheek.

And in an instant, everything changed once more. Cynthia's fingers suddenly felt like talons sinking painfully into Emily's withered skin and flesh.

The silvery light that had magically filled the room faded away, and the gentle sounds of the night that a moment ago had filled the old woman's ears died out.

The talons on Emily's shoulders tightened, and she felt a stabbing pain in her chest. Then, as if impelled by some terrible force, she staggered backward.

Her balance failed her.

She struggled, fought to stay on her feet, reached

out to grasp something — anything — to break her fall.

"Cynthia!" she cried out. "Help me, Cynthia!"

But it was too late. Her body crumpled to the floor, a flash of blinding pain shot through her, and in an instant she sank back into the unconsciousness from which she had emerged only minutes ago.

Emily awoke sometime before dawn, her body aching, her mind muddled. Struggling to her feet, she groped in the darkness until she found the bed, then dropped onto it. The pain in her body easing slightly, she drifted back into a fitful sleep. When next she awoke, the gray light of dawn filled the room, and she heard a voice speaking to her.

"Mother? Mother, are you all right? What are you doing in here?"

Her body aching, Emily pulled herself up to rest her back against the pillows. For a moment nothing around her looked familiar, but then, slowly, some of the fog began to lift from her mind.

"Cynthia?" she asked. "Is that you?"

"No, Mother," she heard. "It's not Cynthia. It's Joan. Let me help you back to bed."

Too tired and too sore to protest, Emily let Joan take her back to her room, half carrying her. Barely aware of what was happening, searching in the mists of her memory for some fragment of the beautiful vision that had come to her last night, she let herself be put in her own bed. Then, struggling to hold on to the memory of Cynthia, she fell once more into a restless sleep.

Matt felt as if he hadn't slept at all; though the clock by his bed insisted it was eight-thirty, both his mind and his body were as exhausted as if he'd been up all night. A grunt of frustration boiling out of his throat, he turned over, punched at his pillow, and jerked the covers tight over his head, as if by shutting out the morning he could shut out not only the nightmares of the early hours before dawn, but the even worse nightmare that had been his birthday.

But it wouldn't go away, because what had happened yesterday wasn't a nightmare at all — it was real.

His stepfather — the only father he'd ever known — was dead, and there was no way that pulling the covers over his head could shut out the image he would carry in his mind for the rest of his life: the image of his stepfather's expressionless face when Pete's dad had turned the body just enough so they could see it.

The empty eyes that had stared straight at Matt.

The hole in the forehead.

The neat, oddly bloodless hole, that looked as if it had been made with a drill rather than a bullet.

Matt's hand went to his own forehead, and a whimper of pain escaped his lips as he imagined what it must have been like. But it couldn't have felt like anything, could it? His dad wouldn't have even heard the shot, let alone felt the bullet entering his brain.

Alive one second.

Dead the same second.

The image of his stepfather's face — and the hole puncturing his forehead — had stayed with Matt all day long, and he'd barely been aware of the steady stream of people who passed through the house all afternoon. But he had been acutely aware of some of the people who *hadn't* been there.

Eric Holmes.

Pete Arneson.

Even Kelly Conroe.

He was pretty sure he knew why Eric and Pete hadn't come — they were probably still telling the police what had happened. Or at least what they thought had happened. And they thought he'd killed his dad.

But why had Kelly Conroe stayed away? He kept looking for her, kept waiting for her to come in the front door. She wouldn't even have had to say anything — it would have been enough if she'd just sat with him, and let him hold her hand. But she hadn't come, and most of the time he'd sat by himself while people came through the house, telling his mother how sorry they were about what had happened.

Some of them had spoken to him, but he could tell by the sound of their voices — and the way they looked at him when they thought he didn't see them — what they were thinking: *You killed him.*

151

You killed our friend.

You killed your dad.

But mostly they didn't speak to him at all — mostly they just whispered to each other, and looked at him.

Looked at him like he was some kind of strange insect.

But if he didn't even know what had happened, how could any of them?

The whispering and staring went on and on, and the terrible image of his stepfather's face hung before his eyes, and a numbing coldness began to fall over him.

By the time he'd finally gone to bed, he knew his life was forever changed.

He felt cold.

He felt alone.

He lay in the darkness, trying to shut it all out, trying to drive the image of his stepfather's face from his memory, trying to protect himself from the cold by wrapping the blankets tightly around his body. But there was no escape from the image etched in his mind, or the chill that had imbued his soul. Yet finally he slept.

And in his sleep, his aunt had come. A whimper emerged from his throat as the memory of his dream — for it had to have been a dream — rose into his consciousness:

The blackness around him receded until everything was suffused with a silvery light. He was still in his bed, still in his room, and it was still night. Dimly, he could hear a clock chiming, but when he tried to count the hours, he lost track, and the chiming went on and on. Then, at the door to the room, a figure appeared. A woman, her long blond hair flowing over her shoulders, a beautiful gown billowing around her body. As the silvery light fell on her face, he recognized it at once.

His aunt.

His aunt Cynthia.

But how could she be here? She was dead, wasn't she?

She came across the room, her arms stretched out to him.

He lay perfectly still, watching.

She stood by the bed and smiled down at him.

"I'll take care of you," she whispered. "I'll always take care of you."

The nightgown fell from her body, and a musky perfume filled the air. As Matt breathed deeply of the scent, his aunt reached down and gently pulled back the blankets and the sheet.

Her fingers brushed against the skin of his chest.

The scent grew stronger, and a faint moan drifted from Matt's lips.

Then his aunt was on the bed, her body pressing close to his, and he could feel the heat of her flesh finally driving the cold from his soul. He drew in his breath, sucking the musky aroma deep into his lungs, and his body began to respond to her touch.

He wrapped his arms around her and pulled her to him.

Her hands moved across his back, caressing him, then moved lower.

And lower still.

He felt her fingers between his legs now, felt the warmth in his body ignite into flames.

"Let me," his aunt whispered. "Let me love you."

His heart throbbing, his breath coming in desperate gasps, the strange aroma transporting him, Matt surrendered to the warmth, the comfort — the ecstasy — of the vision that had appeared out of the darkness.

A dream.

It had only been a dream.

But even now, with the morning sun streaming through the window, his body felt spent.

And his skin felt sticky, even though he had showered last night before he went to bed.

Throwing back the covers at last, Matt went into his bathroom and turned on the shower, letting the near-scalding water wash over him. But even though he scrubbed his skin again and again, he couldn't rid himself of the unclean feeling.

Nor could the steaming water rid him of the chill that had entered his soul.

Chapter 9

I can't face this. I can't face any of it.

The thought was already in Joan Hapgood's mind as she woke from a restless sleep to begin the day that would culminate with her husband's burial. The dread of it — a dread that had been building for the last two days — held her in bed for a few more minutes, and she found herself checking her body for symptoms — a fever, perhaps, or nausea — anything that would give her a legitimate excuse to avoid facing the day entirely. Like a ten-year-old, she chided herself. Like a little girl who doesn't want to go to school. A memory came back to her — a memory of being in the fourth grade.

"Just be sick," Cynthia had told her. It was a Friday morning, and even though Joan had studied the words for the spelling test, she knew that when she was faced with the blank sheet of paper, and Mrs. Van Sant began reading the words to the class, it would be as if she'd never heard them before. "I do it all the time," Cynthia blithely told her. "It's easy — all you have to do is act like you're trying to be brave and really want to go to school, but if you let out a little moan, sort of clutch at your stomach, Mom will send you back to bed. I'll show you!"

155

So they went into the kitchen and sat down at the table, and while their mother was facing the stove, Cynthia winked conspiratorially at her. Then, as their mother placed a plate of scrambled eggs and bacon in front of each of them, Cynthia flinched and her hand went to her stomach. "Cynthia?" their mother said, frowning anxiously. "Are you all right?" Joan watched as Cynthia forced a wan smile.

"It's okay, Mama," she said, somehow managing to make her voice sound both weak and brave. "I'll be fine."

But their mother was already at Cynthia's side, her wrist pressed gently to Cynthia's forehead. "I think you're a little feverish — you go right back to bed, and I'll bring you a tray."

As Cynthia trooped out of the kitchen, winking at Joan once more behind their mother's back, Joan took a deep breath and tried to make her voice as much like Cynthia's as she could. "I don't feel very good either, Mother," she ventured.

Her mother glared at her. "Don't think you're going to get away with that with me, young lady! You just want to stay home with your sister."

That had been the end of it. She'd gone off to school, while Cynthia settled down on the sofa in the living room with a blanket wrapped around her to watch television all day while their mother brought her apple juice and hot tea and whatever else she wanted. But in school that day, when the teacher read the words for the spelling test, Joan managed to get them all right, and until this morning she'd never even thought of playing sick again. In fact, she hadn't even realized she remembered that long ago day.

So I'll face it, she decided. I'll face all of it, and get through it, and I'll be all right. And Matt will be all right too. But even as she silently reassured herself, Joan knew the reassurance itself reflected her growing worry about Matt. Instead of starting to recover from the terrible trauma of three days ago, it seemed that each day the experience was weighing more heavily on him. Each morning he seemed a bit paler, a bit more nervous, a bit more withdrawn than the day before.

Time, she told herself. We both just need time. After the funeral — after Bill is buried — he'll start to recover. We both will.

Pulling on her bathrobe, she began her new daily ritual. First she went downstairs to put on a pot of coffee. She never got it quite right, never got it quite the way Bill had always been able to do it, but at least the measuring and the grinding, and the wait while the coffee brewed, gave her a little time to herself before she had to face her mother each morning.

A little time to pray that this would be one of her mother's good mornings.

On the good mornings, Emily knew where she was and why she was here. She would ask when she could go home again, and want to know what was being done to repair the damage to her house.

And criticize anything and everything Joan might do.

On the bad mornings, she barely recognized Joan at all, seeming lost in some world of the past. On those days, Joan could barely get through to her at all, and though Emily at least didn't rant at her, it could sometimes take an hour just to get her out of bed and into her clothes. After her mother was dressed, Joan would have to spend most of the day just looking out for her, making certain she didn't try to start cooking, or wander off for a walk, or simply get lost in the house. The worst so far had been the morning after Bill died, when she'd found her mother on the floor in the guest room, insisting that Cynthia had been there during the night.

Still, given the cruelty of the words Emily was capable of speaking on the "good" days, versus the rambling near-incoherence of the "bad" days, Joan often wondered if the two appellations shouldn't be reversed. Finally, when the coffee was done and she'd drunk a cup, she knew she could put it off no longer, and made herself go back upstairs.

She tapped softly at her mother's door, then opened it. "Mother? Are you awake?"

"Did you bring me a cup of coffee?" Emily countered.

No "Good morning," Joan thought. No. "How are you?" And why was she asking for coffee? The last time she had brought her mother a cup of coffee, Emily had refused to touch it.

"I'm not an invalid," she'd grumbled. "I'll drink my coffee in the kitchen, like I always do."

"I'm sorry," Joan now said. "I'll bring a cup up

right away." She paused, then: "This is the day of the funeral, Mother." Her voice trembled as she spoke the words, praying that at least her mother would remember what she was talking about. "We have to decide what you're going to wear."

"I'm not going to any funeral," Emily announced. "I don't want to go anywhere."

Not going? What was she talking about? "Don't you feel well?" Joan asked. "Would you like me to call Dr. Henderson?"

"I'm fine. But I'm not going to sit at that funeral and be stared at."

"Stared at?" Joan echoed. "What are you talking about? Why would people stare at you?" Even as she asked the question, she she knew the answer but despite being forearmed her mother's next words lashed at her with the sting of a whip.

"Your son murdered him," Emily said, her eyes fixing balefully on Joan. "Everyone will be staring. They'll be staring at him, and they'll be staring at you. But they won't stare at me, because I won't be there. I'll stay here, with Cynthia!"

Joan recoiled, pain and anger churning within her. "That's not true, Mother. It was just an accident! A stupid hunting accident that wasn't anybody's fault! And it certainly wasn't Matt's fault!"

"Wasn't it?" Emily shot back. Her eyes narrowed accusingly. "It was his finger on the trigger, Joan."

Joan stared at her mother. What was she talking about? Why was she talking as if she'd seen what had happened? "Who told you that?" she asked. "How could anyone have told you that?"

159

"It's true," Emily insisted. "Cynthia told me!"

Joan's eyes widened in shock, and before she could even think about them, angry words began pouring from her lips: "Cynthia didn't tell you anything, Mother! She's dead! She's been dead for years!"

"She's not!" Emily cried, pulling herself off the bed and onto her feet. She took an unsteady step toward Joan. "She's here!" she insisted. "She's in this house, and she talks to me!"

In the face of her mother's wrath, Joan backed toward the door. "That's not true, Mother. You're just confused . . . you're just . . ."

"Get out!" Emily spat the words at her daughter. "Just get out and leave me alone."

Too hurt — too upset — to argue, Joan escaped into the hall, pulling the door closed behind her. Her chest heaving, her pulse racing, she leaned against the door for a moment, willing herself to calm down. She doesn't know what she's saying, she insisted to herself. She doesn't know.

Slowly, she regained control of her emotions, but her mother's words still echoed in her mind. At least Matt didn't hear her, she told herself. At least —

But then she opened her eyes, and there, standing in the corridor only ten feet away, was her son. And she knew by the look on his face that she was wrong.

He'd heard what his grandmother had said.

He'd heard it all.

The stone facade of the new Congregational Church on Hartford Street looked almost as dour as the face of its founding minister, Seth Frobisher, whose portrait — darkened with age — hung in the parish hall that adjoined the church. As the car bearing Joan and Matt to Bill Hapgood's funeral pulled up and stopped in the space reserved for it directly in front of the great double doors — carved from a single tree that had been felled to make way for the building its wood now adorned — Joan almost wished she'd chosen another site for her husband's memorial service. Yet where else could the funeral have been held? Bill's family had worshiped in the Congregational Church for more years than the edifice itself had stood. It was Bill's great-grandfather who had commissioned the doors when the "new" church was constructed seventy years ago to replace the original wooden structure built by Seth Frobisher. Except for a handful of Catholics, nearly everyone in town prayed at the New Congregational Church, was married in it, and was buried in the cemetery that took up the rest of the block upon which it stood. So when it came to Bill's memorial ceremony, there really hadn't been a choice at all.

Stepping out of the car, Joan tucked her right hand under Matt's left arm. "Are you going to be all right?" she asked softly as they started up the walk toward the doors.

Matt, his face strained and looking thinner than it had just three days earlier, shook his head. "I'm

161

never going to be all right again."

Joan squeezed his arm, certain he was remembering the cruel words his grandmother had uttered earlier. "You're not responsible, Matt. You have to believe that whatever happened, it was an accident."

Before Matt could reply, the double doors were pulled open by two of the pallbearers, and a terrible sensation of déjà vu suddenly gripped Joan. Except it wasn't déjà vu at all, for ten years earlier she had stood at the doors to this same church, with Matt at her side, nervously waiting to start down the aisle to the altar where Bill Hapgood was waiting for her.

Waiting for her to marry him.

She could still remember how terrified she'd been, wondering what all the people gathered inside the church — Bill's friends, every one of them — really thought of her. Were they snickering behind their smiles? Were they laughing at the dress she'd chosen? That day, it had been Matt who squeezed her hand and looked up into her face. "You look beautiful, Mommy," he'd told her, and his words had been enough. Taking a deep breath, she'd strode down the aisle, her son beside her, to marry the one man she'd ever loved.

Now all of Bill's friends were gathered in the church once more, and once more Bill was waiting for her in front of the altar.

Waiting for her to bury him.

The casket stood open, but as she paused at the top of the aisle, Joan refused to let herself look at it, knowing her tenuous hold on her emotions might easily give way the moment she saw her husband's face. Taking a deep breath — just as she had a decade ago — she started down the aisle toward the front pew, Matt on her right, Gerry Conroe, who was serving as chief pallbearer, on her left.

Ten years ago Gerry had been standing beside Bill, serving as his best man.

Now, murmuring the same sympathetic words Joan had heard so many times over the last few days that they no longer seemed to have any meaning at all, he saw them into their pew, then retreated to his own, one pew back and on the other side of the aisle.

The pew directly across from Joan and Matt was as empty as their own.

As soon as they were settled in, Myra Conklin began muting the organ and Reverend Charles Frobisher, whose ancestor had founded the church, slipped through the side door and entered the pulpit. His eyes scanned the quiet mourners, then came to rest on the front pew, and as he began to speak, his gaze fixed on Matthew Moore. "We are gathered together to mark the tragically premature passing of our dear brother William Apperson Hapgood into the company of angels," he began.

Matt, his mother's fingers squeezing his left hand, did his best to concentrate on the minister's words. All the way down the aisle he'd kept his eyes riveted on the face of his stepfather, terrified that if he let his gaze waver at all, he'd see the accusing looks on the faces of everyone he'd ever known.

They don't care, a voice had whispered inside his head. *They don't care what really happened. They've already made up their minds. Your fault. All this is your fault.*

Somehow he had survived the walk and slipped into the pew and kept his mind on what the minister was saying. But his eyes kept going back to his stepfather.

He's not dead, he kept thinking. *He's just asleep, and in a minute he'll wake up and sit up, and everything will be all right again.* But as quickly as the words ran through his mind, he knew they weren't true, for even though his stepfather's face looked as peaceful as if he were merely sleeping, it was still framed in the coffin like a mask of death.

The minutes crept by.

As the congregation rose to sing or knelt to pray, Matt numbly reacted to every cue. But through every second of it his eyes remained fixed on the figure in the coffin. Then, as the prayers and the eulogy and the singing began to draw toward an end, something amazing happened.

Something that Matt knew was impossible.

He saw his father sitting up and turning to look at him in exact imitation of the fantasy that had entered Matt's mind when he first slid into the pew.

His stepfather was smiling at him, and reaching out a hand toward him.

Matt rose from his place in the front pew and stepped out into the aisle, reaching out as if to touch his stepfather's hand.

But as he stared at the impossible apparition, it

abruptly changed: his father's head transformed into the head of the buck he'd been stalking that morning.

The finger of Matt's right hand slowly curled as if he were gently squeezing a trigger.

In his mind, he heard the report of the rifle once more.

As the terrible sound echoed in his brain, the apparition shifted again, and once more he was gazing at his stepfather's face.

Now his stepfather's eyes were open and in the center of his head was a neat, round hole.

A bullet hole.

A bullet hole from which fresh blood was oozing, running down his stepfather's face, into his eyes and down his cheeks, to drip onto the perfectly pressed blue suit and starched white shirt in which he would be buried.

"I'm sorry," Matt whispered. He lurched forward, half tripping on the step that led to the altar, his arm still stretched out as if in some kind of supplication. "I'm sorry."

He was at the coffin then, gazing down into his stepfather's face, and still he could see the bullet hole, see the open eyes accusing him.

"I didn't —" he began, and his voice faltered. What if it was true? What if everything his grandmother had said that morning — everything his friends and everyone he knew was thinking — had actually happened?

"I'm sorry," he moaned again, his voice choking on the terrible constriction in his throat. "I didn't want anything to happen. I just wanted you to come home. Just come home. . . ." His voice trailed off as his mother slipped her arm around him and gently led him back to the front pew. As the final prayer began, he repeated the words: "All I wanted was for him to come home. . . ."

Silence fell over the cemetery next to the church as the pallbearers slowly lowered the coffin into the grave. Even the birds that had been chirping in the trees paused in their song, as if sensing the solemnity of the ritual being carried out below. As the coffin came to rest on the floor of the grave, the church bell began to toll, but as Matt gazed down at the lid of the coffin, he barely heard the striking of the hours, for a terrible fear was slowly growing inside him.

Suddenly it was no longer his stepfather in the coffin being lowered into the grave.

It was himself. But it was a mistake, a terrible mistake — he wasn't dead at all, even though everyone thought he was.

As Reverend Frobisher whispered the final benediction and dropped a clod of earth onto the casket, Matt flinched, imagining the hollow sound it must make inside the coffin.

What if that sound woke him up? Would he even know where he was? No, of course not — how could he know? He would be surrounded by a darkness so intense he could feel it even as he imagined it. There would be no flicker of light —

not even the faintest glow would penetrate the seal of the coffin.

In his mind he heard the hollow *clunk* as the next clod fell into the grave. Would he know then?

Now he imagined himself reaching out to explore the darkness, but feeling only the satiny softness of the casket's interior, a softness whose deception would be exposed as he felt the unyielding walls behind the padded fabric.

He was pushing against the lid now, trying to raise it, but already there was too much earth on top, and even as he struggled, more and more was piling onto the top of the coffin, until he could almost feel its weight. He tried to scream, but there was no way his voice could penetrate the coffin and the earth above. How long could he survive? How long before he suffocated?

Would it hurt?

Would he tear his fingernails off scratching at the walls as he tried to free himself?

Or could he force the panic back, make himself lie still and await the death that now would surely come?

But even in his imagination the darkness bore down on him, and the walls of the coffin closed around him, and an ineffable terror rose within him. The scream that no one would hear rose in his throat, but as he opened his mouth to give it vent, he felt something.

A hand, squeezing his elbow.

"Matt? Matt!" Though his mother's voice was low, there was an urgency to it that jerked him out of the daydream. "It will be all right," he heard her say. "Just do what I do."

Numbly, he stepped forward to the edge of the grave and stood beside his mother as she stooped, picked up a clod of earth with her gloved hand, then dropped it onto his stepfather's coffin.

Matt crouched, reached down, touched the pile of crumbling loam beside the grave.

And the terrible image of being trapped inside the box, knowing what was happening even as you were being buried alive, leaped again to the forefront of his mind.

He couldn't do it!

Standing up, he turned away. His eyes glazing with tears, he threaded his way through the crowd around the grave, barely aware of the murmur that was passing through the throng of mourners, the eyes that watched his every move. Finally he was away from the crowd, and a moment later his mother was beside him.

"Matt? Darling, what happened?"

Matt shook his head. How could he explain the terrible, irrational fear that had suddenly taken hold of him? "Nothing," he blurted. "I just . . ." His voice trailed off and his eyes moved back to the grave, where one by one the mourners were stooping to pick up a clod to add to the earth that was on the coffin. "I — I just couldn't do it, that's all," he finally finished, his voice trembling.

His mother put her arms around him. "Just a little while longer," she said. "Just a little while, then we can go home."

But the little while seemed to stretch into a terrible eternity as he stood beside his mother just inside the door to the parish hall. As the mourners filed by, he heard them whisper words of sympathy to his mother, the women leaning forward to kiss her cheek, the men holding her hand in theirs.

But as they came to him, they fell silent.

Their eyes refused to meet his, instead darting first one way, then another, as if seeking some means of escape.

They think I did it on purpose. The first time the dark thought rose in his mind, he tried to ignore it, tried to tell himself that they just didn't know what to say to him. But the thought kept coming back, jabbing at him over and over again. *They think I did it on purpose. They all think I meant to kill my own dad!*

Finally, though, the last of the throng who had come to bid their final respects to his stepfather had spoken to his mother, and one or two even nodded to him. His friends had gathered in the far corner of the room, whispering among themselves just out of earshot of their parents.

Both Eric Holmes and Pete Arneson were in the group, and so was Kelly Conroe. By force of habit, Matt made his way over to them, but instead of widening their circle to include him as they always had before, today they moved closer together, falling silent as he approached. A memory flashed into his mind. He was four years old, and he'd just come out the front door of his grandmother's house, only a block away from where he was right now. A group of other children were playing in Eric Holmes's yard across the street. He wanted to play with them, but when he started to cross the street, Eric and his friends had abruptly stopped talking. And he knew, without any of them saying anything, that they didn't want to let him play with them. Doing his best not to cry, he'd turned around and gone back into his grandmother's house.

Today, though, in the parish house next to the church, they didn't stay silent. When Matthew was still a few feet away, Eric Holmes spoke. He kept his voice low enough so it wouldn't fill the room, but loud enough so Matt would hear his words clearly.

"How did it feel?" he asked. "How did it feel to shoot your dad?"

Matt stopped short, the words slashing through him like a razor. For a moment he couldn't speak — couldn't even think. Then his mind slowly began to function again, yet still he didn't speak, for he knew there was nothing he could say.

They had made up their minds: he was guilty.

His eyes moved from face to face. For ten years they had been his friends, the people he'd gone to school with! They'd known him! They'd liked him!

Or had they? Was it possible they'd never been his friends? That they'd only pretended to be because of who his stepfather was? Suddenly Matt felt as if he were four years old again.

Then, as his eyes fell on Kelly Conroe, he felt a flicker of hope. There was something in her expression that told him she wasn't as certain about what had happened as the rest of them. He took a step toward her, but as if reading his thoughts, she shook her head in a quick movement and she edged toward Eric Holmes.

Another stab of pain shot through Matt, and as he felt his eyes sting with tears, he turned quickly away.

At least he didn't have to let them see the pain he was feeling.

Out!

He had to get out!

His head down so no one could see his glistening eyes, Matt hurried toward the door, brushing past his mother and pushing his way out onto the loggia that connected the parish hall to the church. Breathing deeply, he tried to swallow the lump that had blocked his throat, and to conquer the tears that streamed from his eyes.

How can they know? he silently demanded. *If I don't even know what happened, how can they?*

But it didn't matter — nothing mattered now.

Everything was gone.

His stepfather.

His friends.

Even Kelly.

When he heard the door open behind him, he held very still, refusing even to turn around.

"I'm really sorry about your dad, Matt."

When he failed to face her, Becky Adams moved around in front of Matt and looked directly into his face. Her mousy brown hair was cut in bangs that made her face look even rounder than it was, and she seemed almost lost in the bulky brown sweater she was wearing. Her brow was furrowed with worry, and her eyes looked enormous behind the thick lenses she'd been wearing since they were little. "I don't care what anyone else thinks," she said. "I don't believe it. I don't believe any of it."

Matt's first impulse was to turn away, knowing what his friends would say if they caught him actually talking to Becky Adams. But then he remembered that it didn't matter anymore what his friends might say.

He no longer had any friends.

"Thanks," he said. "And thanks for at least talking to me."

Thirty minutes later, as the limousine pulled away from the front of the church, Matt looked back to see Becky Adams still standing on the loggia. She raised a hand to wave to him, and he waved back, though he wasn't sure she could see him through the car's dark windows.

Chapter 10

Trip Wainwright — whose full name was Wallace Fisher Wainwright III — had been involved in the affairs of Bill Hapgood since the day he graduated from law school twenty-six years ago. Five months later, when he'd passed the bar and received his license to practice, his father added his name to the shingle that hung outside the old stone building at the corner of Main and Chestnut, which had originally been a post house. It had been Bill Hapgood's suggestion that at such time as Trip's own son, currently in his second year at his father's alma mater, took over Senior Wainwright's desk in the old post house, the name of the firm should be modernized to WW, an appellation that Trip suspected might very well prove prophetic if and when he broached the idea to his father. "Don't worry about that," Bill had assured him. "I can handle your dad. He's always liked me better than you anyway."

Though Bill had said it half jokingly, it was more than half true, and as Trip sat through the funeral that morning, he'd realized just how much he was going to miss the man who had been not only his first client, but one of his best friends as well. Now, as he went through his briefcase one last time to make certain he had all the files that might be relevant to whatever questions Joan Hapgood might have, he reflected that he was far from the only person in Granite Falls who had thought of Bill Hapgood as their best friend. Besides himself and Gerry Conroe, Trip suspected that Paul Arneson and Marty Holmes would have placed Bill at the top of their list of friends, and even beyond those three, nearly everyone in town had liked and respected Bill.

Granite Falls wasn't going to be the same without him.

Sighing, Trip snapped the latches of his briefcase closed, started out of his office, then turned back to pick up the telephone and call Dan Pullman, whose office was just down the block in the town hall. "I'm on my way out to talk to Joan," he said. "Is there anything I can tell her?" He listened, grunted noncommittally, then hung up. Finally leaving his office, he got into the little Miata that his father never failed to remind him was too flashy for a lawyer — which was the primary reason he'd bought it — and headed out to the Hapgood house. But he found himself driving slowly, turning the two-minute drive into a ten-minute run for no other reason than to put off the inevitable. That was another thing his father never failed to needle him about: "Never put things off, Trip. You never know when a client might drop dead, and you don't want to have papers still waiting to be signed." Sometimes, when he wasn't feeling particularly charitable, Trip wondered if that was all the clients were to his father: nothing more than sheaves of paper, neatly filed away in manila folders, to be shuffled about and eventually disposed of.

But Bill Hapgood had been his friend, and he was not looking forward to the next couple of hours. Yet as he turned through the gates and started up the long driveway to the house, he knew his father was right — the sooner he got it over with, the better.

Joan answered the door as he was about to press the bell a second time. She was still wearing the same black dress she'd worn to the funeral, and the single strand of pearls still hung around her neck. She'd taken off the pearl earrings, though, and removed her makeup.

As had happened every time Trip Wainwright had seen Joan since she'd first come back to Granite Falls fifteen years ago, his heart had skipped a beat and he felt a hollowness in his stomach. It wasn't that Joan had turned beautiful while she was away, for her features hadn't so much changed as simply matured. It was that she didn't seem to have any idea how beautiful she was. Of course, Trip — already married and with a son of his own — had been careful never to reveal the crush he'd developed on Joan Moore, and even when she married Bill Hapgood, he carefully betrayed none of the sense of loss he felt. Then, after Adrienne died three years ago, he'd been even more vigilant in guarding the secret of his feelings toward Joan Hapgood. Now, even without her makeup, and with her eyes still red from the tears she'd shed at the funeral, he still thought she was the most beautiful woman he'd ever seen.

And she still seemed utterly unaware of it.

"Come in, Trip," she said, pulling the door wide. She managed a weak smile. "I'd intended to change and be all ready for you, but —" Her voice cracked, but then, with a visible effort, she pulled herself back together. "It hasn't been the easiest day for any of us, has it?"

"If you'd like to do this another day —" Trip began, but Joan shook her head.

"I don't think there's any point in putting it off, is there?" she sighed. "Matt and my mother are in the library." Suddenly, she looked uncertain. "Should they be part of this?"

"Actually, I'd like Matt to be there," Wainwright replied. "As for your mother," he went on, shrugging, "that's really up to you." He hesitated, then: "How is she today?"

Joan's hands spread helplessly. "Right now she seems almost like herself. But this morning —" She shook her head, shuddering. "You don't want to know. I keep thinking that Bill was right, that I should have found someplace for her."

The lawyer shook his head. "She's your mother. If it had been Eloise Hapgood, Bill never would have heard of her being put anywhere. He would have hired whatever staff she needed, and she would have stayed right here, where she belonged."

"That's what I keep trying to tell myself," Joan

said as they moved into the den. Emily Moore, a shawl wrapped around her knees, was almost lost in a corner of the sofa in front of the fireplace. Matt, his face pale and his eyes anxious, stood next to the big globe that was suspended in a mahogany stand. He seemed unaware that he was nervously spinning it.

"Are you here to see Cynthia?" Emily Moore asked, peering up at Wainwright. "Call your sister, Joan."

Before Joan could speak, Wainwright took Emily Moore's hand. "I'm here to see you," he said. "And Joan and Matt too."

The words seemed to mollify the old woman, and she relaxed back onto the sofa. For the next fifteen minutes the lawyer went over the terms of the will. "Basically, it's a trust," he explained to Joan. "In the short term, you're in charge. You're the sole trustee, with very broad powers. You can liquidate anything you want, including the business, but in the end, Matt inherits."

Matt's eyes widened. "Me?"

Trip Wainwright had been deliberately watching Matt as he uttered the last two words, and he was sure the surprise in the boy's face — and his voice — was genuine.

"Why would Dad have done that?" he asked. "Why didn't he leave everything to Mom?"

"He said he wanted to make certain you knew he didn't think of you as a stepchild," Wainwright replied. "When he had me draw up the papers, he told me it was his way of letting you know he truly thought of you as his son." Matt's eyes glistened, and Wainwright could see him struggling to control his emotions.

When Matt finally spoke, his voice was barely audible. "Everybody thinks —" he began, then fell silent, unable to finish.

"What everybody thinks doesn't matter," Wainwright said. His eyes shifted to Joan, and his voice dropped. "I've been talking to Dan Pullman," he said. "They think they've found the casings of the bullets Matt fired. There are four of them, and they're the right caliber. It'll take a lab to match them to Matt's rifle, but I suspect that will happen."

Joan's eyes widened, and the color drained from Matt's face. "Are they going to arrest —" Joan began, but Wainwright quickly shook his head.

"Of course not. They haven't found the bullet that killed Bill, and I suspect that if they haven't found it yet, they're not going to. But even if they find it, it doesn't mean anything. Matt was shooting at the deer, not at Bill. There was no way Matt even could have seen him — not through that thicket."

"But everyone thinks I did it on purpose," Matt whispered.

Wainwright's voice hardened. "It doesn't matter a whit what people think, Matt. The only thing that matters is what they can prove. And at this point, there's no way they can prove you even shot him, let alone shot him on purpose. Dan Pullman says that even if he finds the bullet and can prove it came from your gun, he doesn't think anyone would charge you. Not unless they want to go back and charge everyone who's accidentally shot someone during hunting season."

Suddenly, Emily Moore spoke again. "It wasn't an accident," she said, her voice crackling as she peered at Trip Wainwright.

The lawyer frowned, his eyes fixing on the old woman. "I beg your pardon, Mrs. Moore?"

"I said it wasn't an accident," Emily piped. Her flinty eyes darted toward her grandson. "He did it on purpose."

"Mother, how can you say that?" Joan protested.

"Because it's true," the old woman insisted. "Cynthia told me. She told me exactly what happened."

Trip Wainwright felt the tension drain out of his body as quickly as the old woman's accusation had brought it, and his gaze shifted sympathetically to Joan. "If there's anything I can do . . ." he said, and deliberately let his voice trail off.

Reading his meaning perfectly, Joan shook her head. But as she walked him to the front door a few moments later, she sighed. "I wish I knew what to do," she admitted. "I'm not sure how much longer I can keep her here."

"If you need help . . ." Wainwright offered again, and this time Joan smiled at him.

"If I need help, I'll call you," she promised him.

As she started to close the door behind the lawyer, they both heard Emily's voice rising. "He never loved you," the old woman raved. "The only person he ever loved was your aunt! Don't you understand? It was Cynthia he loved! Not you, and certainly not your mother!"

Taking a deep breath, Joan quickly closed the door behind Trip Wainwright and hurried back to the library.

Her mother still sat in the corner of the sofa.

Matt was gone.

"Mama? Mama?"

The voice was barely a whisper, no more than a breeze that might be drifting through the open window, but still Emily Moore stirred restlessly in her bed and her clawlike fingers tugged at the sheet as if to shield herself from a draft.

"Can you hear me?"

The voice was louder now, as if the breeze had strengthened.

"It's me, Mama. Can't you hear me?"

Emily's lips worked, and an unintelligible sound escaped her lips. Once again she stirred, turning from her side onto her back. Her right arm rose up, as if to fend off a mosquito.

"Mama!"

This time the voice cracked like a whip, jerking Emily from her restless slumber into instant wakefulness. Her whole body convulsed, and a cry of pain burst from her throat as the arthritis in her joints protested against the sudden movement.

But even though she was wide-awake, her mind was still fogged with age and her disease, and for a few moments she couldn't quite remember where she was. Then, slowly, it started coming back to her.

Joan's house.

She was in Joan's house, in her room, in bed. But what had awakened her? She strained her ears, but heard nothing; the silence of the night was almost complete. Yet even in the silence, there was the faintest echo of a memory.

A memory of a voice.

A voice calling out to her.

Cynthia?

Her heart fluttered, and once more she strained her ears.

Still hearing nothing, she left her bed, slipped her feet into her slippers, and shuffled slowly toward the window, steadying herself first on the bed, then on a chair, and finally on the table that stood in front of the window. She gazed out into the night, but age and the darkness beyond the glass hid anything that might be outside.

"Mama . . ."

Emily's breath caught as she heard the word. There was no mistaking it this time — she would know her beloved daughter's voice anywhere. She turned away from the window and started toward the bathroom, moving so quickly that she nearly lost her balance. Recovering herself, she tottered through the bathroom and put her shaking hand on the knob to the door connecting it to the bedroom next to hers. Then, with Cynthia's voice still ringing in her ears, she pushed the door open.

The room was illuminated by a dozen candles

burning on Cynthia's vanity table.

The air was filled with the musky aroma of Cynthia's favorite perfume, a heavy scent called Nightshade that never failed to bring images of her beloved daughter into Emily's fogged mind.

"Cynthia?" she called out, her voice choking with eagerness. "Cynthia, darling, where are you?"

Something flickered in the mirror of the vanity. A moment later she saw it again — a movement near the door!

A small cry catching in her throat, she turned, and there she was.

In the glow of the candlelight she could just see Cynthia, standing at the door to the corridor. Her daughter was facing her, her lovely figure draped in a diaphanous negligee that Emily herself had given her years ago. Her hair, framing her perfect features and flowing down over her shoulders nearly to her waist, seemed to radiate with a light of its own.

As Emily gazed at the perfect vision, Cynthia raised her arm as if to beckon to her mother.

Then she turned and disappeared through the door.

"No," Emily croaked, her heart pounding. "No, Cynthia — don't leave me! Not again." She lurched toward the door, moving as quickly as she could, once again steadying herself against the furniture. "Please," she breathed as she came to the door. "Please — wait for me!"

She stepped out into the hall. The darkness was almost complete, save for a faint bluish glow coming from a night-light at the top of the stairs. But as her eyes adjusted to the dim light, she could once more make out Cynthia starting down the stairs toward the floor below. "Wait!" she cried out once again. "I'm coming, Cynthia! Don't leave me! Please?"

Bracing herself against the wall, she hurried toward the top of the stairs as quickly as her thin legs would carry her. Coming to the landing, she braced herself against the banister and peered down into the entry hall below.

Cynthia was there, beckoning to her, waiting for her!

She was halfway down the stairs when she thought she heard another voice, a voice calling out from somewhere above her, but she shut it out of her mind, every part of her focusing only on the apparition below.

"I'm coming!" she cried out. "Just don't leave me. Not again, Cynthia. Please, not again."

Coming to the bottom of the stairs, she paused in the darkness.

Where was she?

Where had she gone?

A flicker of movement, toward the front of the house.

A faint glimpse of flowing blond hair.

The musky scent, heavy on the night air.

Emily's heart pounding with excitement, her breath coming in ragged gasps, she pushed herself onward, struggling to keep up with Cynthia, determined to follow her wherever she might lead.

This time, she wouldn't lose Cynthia.

This time, wherever Cynthia went, she would go too.

Her heart racing, a spurt of adrenaline giving her a strength she hadn't felt in years, Emily Moore followed her adored daughter into the darkness. . . .

Chapter 11

The house on Burlington Avenue was silent, and she could feel its emptiness.

But that wasn't right — her mother and sister should both have been there. Why weren't they? Where had they gone? She got out of bed and crept to the closed door of her room. Pressing her ear against the wood, she strained to listen.

Silence.

Then something changed.

The room behind her seemed different.

The hairs on the back of her neck stood on end and she felt a rippling chill as goose bumps covered her skin. Unconsciously holding her breath, she struggled against the panic that threatened to overwhelm her, then forced herself to look back over her shoulder.

Empty!

The room was empty — her bed was gone, and so was the pretty white dresser the woman next door had given her last month for her tenth birthday. The pictures on the walls — the stuffed bear that had kept her company as long as she could remember — all of it was gone! A terrified squeal bursting from her lips, Joan jerked the door open and ran downstairs to the living room.

It was as empty as her room, stripped of its furniture,

even the curtains gone from the windows.

In the kitchen, the familiar chipped enamel table had vanished, the cupboards were empty, and a gaping empty place was all that remained of the refrigerator.

Her heart thudding with the terror of abandonment, her cheeks wet with tears, she went back upstairs.

Her mother's room was as empty as the rest of the house, but in her sister's room one single piece of furniture remained.

Cynthia's vanity table.

All her cosmetics were still there — all the wonderful things Cynthia liked to put on her face. Why had Cynthia left them?

Mesmerized by the sight of the bottles and boxes and pots and tubes, she took a step into the room, then another.

Could Cynthia have left them for her?

The terror of a moment ago now giving way to excitement, she went to the vanity and sat down. Opening a container of powder, she began patting it onto her face. Then, in the mirror, she saw her sister — Cynthia was standing right behind her, glowering at her.

"How dare you?" Cynthia demanded. Her arm lashed out, knocking the open powder container to the floor, its contents exploding into the air. Joan's nostrils filled with talc and she began coughing and choking.

She heard another voice then — her mother's voice. "What's going on in here? What are you doing?"

"It's Joan's fault, Mama," she heard Cynthia saying. "Look what she did! It's all Joan's fault!"

Now she was looking up into her mother's angry face, and she knew what was about to happen. "No,"

186

she whispered. Her mother's arm rose, and she cowered away. "No," she cried. "No!"

The sound of her own voice jerked Joan out of the nightmare, and she instinctively reached out to Bill, needing to feel his strength — his warmth — against her flesh.

But he wasn't there, and as the vestiges of the bad dream faded away and she saw the gray light of dawn beginning to drive the night away, the terrible empty feeling of the house she'd dreamed about was replaced by the even worse emptiness that now imbued her.

Bill was truly gone, and would never lie next to her again.

He'd abandoned her, just as her mother and sister had abandoned her in the dream.

No! she reminded herself, unconsciously echoing the final protest she'd uttered before she woke up. *No! He didn't abandon me. It was an accident, and he would have come home! He would have come back!*

She turned over, wanting to escape back into sleep, but even as the urge to retreat into unconsciousness came over her, she knew it would do no good. The dream would only reach out to her again.

And even if she managed a few more minutes of escape, the day — and reality — would still await her. Pulling on her robe, she went out into the corridor toward the head of the stairs. But as she passed the guest room and noticed that the door was ajar, she paused.

187

Why was the door open? Even now she could hear the echo of her mother's voice. "Stay out of that room! That's Cynthia's room, and I won't have you ruining her things!"

Cynthia's room. Not the guest room at all anymore.

Suddenly the dream came back to her, and she moved into the doorway. The vanity table was exactly as she'd seen it in her dream. All her sister's makeup laid out as if Cynthia had only stepped out for a minute or two and would soon be back. Joan's eyes darted over the rest of the room — the pictures of Cynthia — her magazines, still open, as if she were in the midst of reading them — her favorite negligee still thrown over the end of the bed, as it had been for years, first in the house on Burlington Avenue, now here.

Here, in Cynthia's room.

Cynthia's room!

Joan's eyes fixed on one of the images of her sister that covered the walls and stood in frames on every piece of furniture. "Leave us alone," she whispered. "Why can't you just leave us alone?"

She started to turn away, but the silence that followed her words was broken by a sound.

An impossible sound.

The sound of her sister laughing.

Laughing at her.

Mocking her.

Joan whirled back to face the room, almost expecting to see Cynthia sitting at the vanity, her eyes sparkling with mischief as she gazed at the shock on Joan's face. But there was nothing.

Nothing except the laughter that had echoed out of the past.

Turning away from the room — and everything in it — Joan started once more toward the stairs, but again paused, this time outside her mother's room. She listened, knowing that if she heard the deep sound of her mother's snoring, she would have a few minutes to herself before her mother awoke. But if her mother was already awake, she would begin calling for her the moment Emily heard her going down the stairs.

She listened, but heard nothing.

Joan's breath caught as she realized what the silence might mean, and for a moment she was almost afraid to open the door.

If her mother had died —

Steeling herself, she turned the knob and opened the door.

Empty!

Her mother's bed was empty.

Joan hurried across the room to the door leading to the small bathroom between her mother's room and Cynthia's.

Empty!

Downstairs.

Her mother must have gotten up early and gone down to the kitchen! Hurrying down the stairs, she searched the lower floor, calling out her mother's name.

The rooms were silent and empty.

Her mother was no longer in the house.

189

We'll find her, she told herself as she rushed back up the stairs. *Matt and I will find her! She can't be far away!* At the top of the stairs Joan started toward Matt's room, but as she passed the open door to Cynthia's room, her eye was caught by the portrait of her sister that hung over the fireplace.

She stopped short.

The portrait, like the laughter she'd heard earlier, seemed to be mocking her. Then she remembered the nights when she heard her mother inside that room, talking to Cynthia.

Talking to her as if she were still alive.

"What have you done with her?" Joan whispered, her eyes locking on her sister's. "What have you done with Mother?"

This time she heard no laughter.

This time she heard nothing at all.

"Matt? Matt, wake up!"

Wide-awake in an instant, Matt knew by the look on his mother's face that something had happened, and even before she said anything, he was certain he knew what it was.

"Mother's gone," Joan said, confirming the thought that had gripped him.

"You mean she isn't in the house at all?"

"Just get dressed and come help me."

Five minutes later he joined his mother in the kitchen, and together they searched the entire house, even going up into the dusty attic beneath the steeply pitched roof. After they'd searched the

190

basement as well, they came back to the kitchen.

"What are we going to do?" Matt asked.

"Look outside. If we only knew how long she's been gone —" Her anxious eyes fixed on Matt. "Did you hear anything last night? Anything at all?"

Matt hesitated. He'd dreamed about his aunt Cynthia again, dreamed that she came to him in the night and crept into his bed and — He shuddered at the memory, trying to force it out of his mind. But there was something else as well . . .

Then it came back to him! He'd had another dream. A dream about his grandmother. He'd heard her talking, and gone to look out into the hall. And he'd seen something . . .

For a second he wasn't sure what it was — just a sort of hazy figure, almost invisible in the darkness. But then he'd known — it was a ghost.

The ghost of his aunt, her long blond hair flowing down her back, wearing the same white nightgown she always wore when he dreamed about her. Frozen by terror, his heart pounding, he'd watched as the ghostly figure disappeared down the stairs. Then his grandmother appeared in the hall and started after his aunt. He tried to call out to her but had barely been able to utter a word, and when he was finally able to make himself go to the top of the stairs and look down, he had seen . . .

Nothing!

Nothing but the empty entrance hall.

Nor had he heard anything, for a silence had

fallen over the house that seemed somehow unnatural. Finally he retreated to his room and back to his bed. He'd lain in the darkness for a long time, listening, but he heard nothing else. Certain that what had happened must have been a dream, he tried to put it out of his mind.

But then the other dream came, and once again his aunt was in his room, in his bed, touching him, caressing him.

"No," he said, finally replying to his mother's question. "I didn't hear anything. I just had a dream, that's all."

Though he wasn't looking quite at her, he felt his mother's eyes on him.

She thinks I'm lying!

But he wasn't lying — it had only been a dream! He was sure it had! There was no such thing as ghosts.

Were there?

No!

Suddenly the walls of the kitchen — the whole house — seemed to be closing in on him.

He had to get outside!

"I'm going to look in the garage and the shed," he said. "If she went outside, maybe she just got confused in the dark or something." Without waiting for his mother to reply, he went out the back door. Pausing on the steps, he took a deep breath, then another.

What was happening to him?

Where were the dreams coming from?

What did they mean?

Nothing, he told himself. *They don't mean anything.*

But what about his grandmother? If what he'd seen last night was only a dream, why hadn't Gram been in her room this morning?

It was a coincidence. Just a coincidence. Wasn't that one of the reasons his mother had moved her into the house? Because people with Alzheimer's disease sometimes just wandered away from their homes, and got confused, and couldn't find their way back? Of course! Gram was out here somewhere, in the carriage house, or the old stable. She had to be somewhere.

Except she wasn't. Matt searched the buildings, then went through them again, calling out to his grandmother, opening every door, even climbing into the hayloft in the barn.

Nothing.

Finally he went back to the house, re-entering through the same door he'd come out of fifteen minutes earlier. As he stepped into the mud room, he heard his mother talking in the kitchen.

"Trip? I need you to come out — Mother's gone."

Mr. Wainwright? Why had she called him?

"I think she must have wandered off sometime in the middle of the night. If you'll just come out and —" Her voice broke off abruptly, then: "No, don't call the police, Trip — at least not yet. The chances are she's somewhere on the property and —"

Once more his mother fell silent, and when she

spoke again, her voice had dropped so he had to strain to hear her. "I really don't think you should call Dan Pullman. Not after — well, not after what happened, and what they're already thinking about Matt. Besides, we don't really know that anything's happened to Mother, do we?" Her voice took on a pleading note. "Please? Just come out, and then we can decide what to do."

For an instant Matt felt an impulse to go back out the door, to get away from the house, to escape to —

To where?

Nowhere.

There was nowhere at all to go.

What was happening? Was he going crazy? How could his mother even think —

But then, before he could finish the thought, his mother was standing in the door of the mud room, looking worriedly at him. "Matt? What is it? You look —"

"You think I did something to her, don't you?" he whispered. Finally he managed to look at her. "You think I did something to Gram."

The abject misery in her son's face wrenching at her heart, Joan pulled Matt close, wrapping him in her arms.

"No," she whispered. "Oh, no, Matt. Of course not! How could you even think such a thing?" But even as she spoke the words, Joan remembered the look on Matt's face when she'd asked him if he'd heard anything last night.

She remembered the hesitation in his voice as he

194

told her that he hadn't heard anything at all.

Trip Wainwright didn't need to look at his watch to know that it was getting close to ten: if the angle of the sun hadn't told him it was mid-morning, the gnawing in his belly would have; ever since he'd given up breakfast in the latest of his ongoing battles against an irreversibly expanding waistline, his stomach had begun demanding food — preferably an apple Danish — at exactly nine-thirty. By ten o'clock, when his teeth literally began to hurt and he was unconsciously snapping at his secretary, the need for a Danish usually became so overwhelming that he left his office and went next door to the bakery, promising himself that tomorrow morning he would find the strength to resist his stomach's demands. So far his broken promises had resulted in five more pounds and an extra half inch on his waistline, and he was still only a month into the no-breakfast diet.

But it was more than his stomach that was gnawing at him right now, for during the nearly three hours he had spent helping Joan and Matt search for Emily Moore, they found no trace. They had started in the house, searching every room again, opening every closet. Then the lawyer retraced Matt's route through the outbuildings, even climbing the ladder to the hayloft himself, though he knew by the third step that there was no way Emily Moore could have made it even as far as that.

Certain that the old woman wasn't in any of the

buildings, they searched the grounds. For an hour they had slowly moved back and forth in an ever-widening semicircle through the forest that half surrounded the house. But finally, half an hour ago, Wainwright had insisted that they give it up. They were in the midst of a thicket of underbrush which had twice nearly succeeded in immobilizing the attorney, whose hiking — for the last twenty years, anyway — had been confined to the neatly trimmed fairways of the Granite Falls Golf Club, which, if not exactly kept up to the standards of some of the wealthier country clubs down around Boston, were at least mown once a week.

"There aren't even any trails, Joan. There isn't any way your mother could have gotten in here — not even in the daylight, let alone in the middle of the night."

For a moment he thought Joan would refuse to give up, would insist that they keep on pushing through the heavy undergrowth, but then her shoulders sagged and the hope had gone out of her eyes. "I know," she sighed. "I know you're right, but . . ." Her voice trailed off, and the defeated look in her eyes made him want to reach out and comfort her.

"We'll find her, Mom," Matt had said. "I know we will."

Barely responding, Joan followed along as Matt started guiding them back toward the house.

They were at the edge of the forest now; the house was visible through the trees, and the low stone wall that edged the lawn was only a few yards ahead. Joan suddenly stopped short.

"What is it?" Wainwright asked, scanning the area but seeing nothing except a trail that would lead them to a gap in the wall, and the broad expanse of closely mown grass that surrounded the house.

"The river path," Joan said, her voice hollow, her gaze fixed on the narrow path. "We never looked there." She looked at Wainwright. "The trail leads to the falls. Mother always liked the falls." Her eyes glistening with hope again, she started down the path. "That's where she would have gone! I know it!"

Wainwright's first instinct was to try to stop her, but the sudden buoyancy in her step made him abandon the impulse. Determinedly ignoring his growing hunger, he followed Joan down the trail, Matt behind him.

They were no more than two hundred yards from the falls, and starting to feel the chill of its mists in the air, when Joan stopped so abruptly that Trip Wainwright almost bumped into her.

"Look!" The word was more of a yelp than anything else, and when Wainwright followed her gaze, he at first saw nothing. But then he spotted it.

Half buried in the soft dirt of the path was a slipper.

A worn shearling slipper, the same kind that Wainwright himself liked to wear when he was home alone at night. "It's a man's slipper," he said, starting forward.

Joan's hand closed on his arm, stopping him.

"Mother has a pair just like that," she said, her voice trembling. Wainwright wasn't sure whether the quaver in her voice was from fear or excitement, but her next words made it clear. "She came down here! I know she did!" Snatching up the slipper before the lawyer could stop her, Joan hurried down the trail, her step now quick and eager. "Mother?" she called out. "Mother, where are you?"

With Matt still following him, Wainwright started after Joan, but they'd gone no more than fifty yards when his own eye was caught by something.

A scrap of thin, white material was caught on the jagged end of a limb that someone had broken off to prevent it from blocking the trail. "Joan?" the lawyer called out. "Joan, look at this." But before Joan could get back to the scrap of cloth, Matt had told him what he needed to know.

"Gram's nightgown," he said.

Now Joan was next to Wainwright, and he stopped her as she instinctively reached out to touch the scrap of cloth. "Let's just leave it exactly where it is," he said. Joan's eyes met his, and for a moment he wasn't sure she understood what he was saying. But then her eyes cleared.

"It's going to be all right," she said. "We're going to find her — I know we are!" Turning away, she hurried on down the path.

They came to the last bend in the narrow trail, and a few yards farther stepped out onto the bare expanse of granite that surrounded the pool at the base of the falls. Forty yards away the cataract tumbled from an uneven crag that split it into three separate streams. The base of the falls was all but lost in the plume of mist that hung over the pool, and though the water was crystal clear, the roiling surface concealed anything that might lie on the pool's floor.

It was at the very edge of the pool that they found Emily Moore's other slipper. Joan's breath caught as she spied it, and a strangled cry rose in her throat as she realized what it might mean. But even as she stared at the slipper, she refused to give up hope. "Mother?" she called out, her voice breaking. She tried to call once more, but this time her emotions overflowed, stifling her words.

Now Trip Wainwright put his arms around her, clumsily trying to soothe her. "We'd better call Dan Pullman," he said. "I just don't think we can wait any longer."

For a moment he thought Joan might still object, and then she nodded. "But she's all right," she said. "I know she is." She looked into his face, as if seeking confirmation of her own feelings. "If she was dead, I'd know, wouldn't I? Wouldn't I feel it?"

Though Trip Wainwright made no answer, he had a feeling of his own.

A feeling that was the exact opposite of Joan Hapgood's.

Chapter 12

Dan Pullman listened in silence as Trip Wainwright explained why he was once more needed at the Hapgood house. Dan, like nearly everyone else in Granite Falls, had attended Bill Hapgood's funeral yesterday and — also like nearly everyone else — had found himself paying more attention to Matthew Moore than to the service itself. Hardly an hour had gone by since Bill Hapgood's death that someone hadn't called him to ask why the boy hadn't been charged in his stepfather's killing. Though most of his callers had at least made an attempt to feign nothing more than the interest of a responsible citizen, more than one had spoken what the rest thought but wouldn't admit: "Everybody knows he did it."

Dan, who had long ago learned that anything he might say would instantly be ground into unrecognizable dust by the Granite Falls rumor mill, had ventured nothing more than that the case was "still under investigation," and that any charges to be brought would be filed "at such time as is deemed appropriate by the county prosecutor." He'd steadfastly resisted the urge to tell the callers that what everybody knows often proves to be completely wrong, since he'd also learned very early in his tenure as the town's police chief that when "everybody" knows something, the last thing they want to hear is even a hint of a contradiction.

Still, he'd kept a careful eye on Matt Moore at the funeral, trying to fathom what might be going on in the boy's mind. Matt had looked pale and tired, but that was only to be expected. The question Dan had been trying to answer was whether his pallor and exhaustion were a product of grief or of guilt.

Either one could keep a person from sleeping; either one could drive someone to the ragged edge of emotional collapse. But as he'd watched Matt Moore, Pullman hadn't been able to make up his mind which problem was preying on the boy. Certainly his display of emotion at the coffin seemed genuine, but even that could be interpreted in more than one way:

Matt could have been apologizing for being at the root of a terrible accident.

Or he could have been apologizing for a murder.

Indeed, Pullman had been pondering it when the call from Trip Wainwright came in, and even as the lawyer explained what had happened that morning, Pullman found himself wondering what part Matt might have played in Emily Moore's disappearance.

None, he told himself as he drove the two miles from his office behind the fire station to the gates of Hapgood Farm. Emily Moore had Alzheimer's, and most likely she just wandered off. *Don't turn into the kind of cop who sees crimes everywhere he looks.*

But as he followed the same path that Trip Wainwright, Joan, and Matt had trod only half an hour earlier, he found himself wondering.

"The first slipper was right here," Wainwright told him. "Joan picked it up before I could stop her."

"I didn't know I was doing anything wrong," Joan said, her eyes begging him to understand. "When I saw it, I just —"

"It's all right," Pullman assured her. "There's no harm done. She probably didn't even notice it was gone." But in his own mind, Pullman wasn't so sure — even if you were lost, you'd still feel your slipper go, feel the mud oozing between your toes. Though he'd said nothing, his eyes had quickly scanned the path for signs of a bare foot, but all he saw were the faint prints left by several pairs of shoes.

Nothing that looked like either a bare foot or one that might have been clad in a slipper. Of course, it was possible that whatever tracks Emily Moore might have left had simply been covered over by the three other people who had walked the path this morning.

They continued on, pausing at the spot where the scrap of cloth still clung to the broken branch. Again Dan Pullman found no signs of tracks that might have been left by a bare foot, but on the other hand, the path here was hard enough that he could barely make out the signs of any footprints at all.

Finally they came to the shelf of rock bordering the pool at the base of the falls, where Emily's other slipper still lay. Now, as he listened to Joan Hapgood recount every detail of what had happened that morning, his eyes were drawn to Matt, just as they had been yesterday at the funeral.

The boy looked even paler than before, and more exhausted.

But there was something else in his face too.

Not guilt, exactly, but something close to it — a furtiveness, as if there was something he didn't want to be asked about. When Joan finally fell silent, Pullman decided to take a shot in the dark.

"What happened last night, Matt?" he asked. The boy flinched, and Pullman knew he'd struck a nerve. When Matt said nothing, he pressed harder. "Something did happen, didn't it, Matt?"

Matt's eyes finally met Pullman's, and the police chief could see the misery in them.

The boy's eyes flicked away again.

Looking for a means of escape?

Then, hesitantly, Matt said, "I'm not sure," choosing his words carefully. "I thought it was a dream, but now . . ." His voice trailed off, and he gazed off into the distance, as if he were looking at something far away.

"What, Matt?" Pullman asked, feeling faintly uneasy as he sensed that Matt might be on the verge of confessing something. Until now, most of the confessions Pullman had heard from frightened teenagers involved nothing more serious than minor vandalism or "borrowing" someone's car for a joyride, and it had always been his hope that he would be able to retire without having to hear anything worse. Right now, though, it looked as if that might not happen. "What did you see?"

Slowly, Matt recounted hearing his grandmother's voice and going out into the corridor to see if she was all right. Again the strange look came into his eyes, as if he were looking far into the distance. "I didn't see Gram right away," he said, his voice so low that Pullman had to strain to hear it. "I — I saw someone else."

Pullman glanced at Joan, then at the lawyer. It was obvious that neither of them had heard this before.

"Someone else?" Pullman urged. "Someone you knew?"

Matt's eyes darted as if he were once again seeking escape, but at last he nodded. "It was my aunt," he said. "My aunt Cynthia."

Pullman's eyes narrowed. "Your aunt Cynthia," he repeated, his brow furrowing. "Now come on, Matt, you know —"

"I *know* she's dead," Matt broke in, his words suddenly coming in a rush. "That's why I thought it was a dream! And after I saw Aunt Cynthia, Gram came out of her room, and she was calling Aunt Cynthia. Then Gram followed her downstairs!" Quickly, he recounted the rest of it: being so shocked by what he'd seen that he couldn't move, then finally going to the head of the stairs and looking down.

Looking down, and seeing nothing.

"And that's it?" Pullman asked when Matt was finished. "You didn't see anything, so you just went back to bed? You didn't even go downstairs to check on your grandmother?"

A look of panic came into Matt's eyes. "I didn't know what to do — I thought — oh, God, I don't know what I thought." His eyes shifted from Pullman to his mother. "I thought it was a dream, Mom."

Joan slipped a protective arm around her son. "It's all right," she said. "We're going to find Gram. We're going to find her, and she's going to be all right." But even as she said it, Joan could see in the chief's eyes that Pullman didn't believe it would happen that way.

Chapter 13

The air sparkled with the shimmering of a million flecks of gold, making the woods glow with a light Matt had never seen before. *Dust,* he told himself. *It's just dust.* But it didn't seem like dust; it seemed like magic, suffusing everything it touched with a luminescence that made his spirit soar.

He wasn't certain where he was, or exactly how long he'd been wandering through the trees, sometimes following a trail or path, but mostly following his urges wherever they led him. He paused, partly to try to get his bearings, but even more for the sheer enjoyment of the perfect morning. He sucked in his breath, filling his lungs with the cool forest air. As he was letting it out again he saw a flicker of movement out of the corner of his left eye. His hand tightening on the rifle that was slung over his shoulder with a leather strap, he searched the forest. At first he saw nothing, but a moment later caught the movement again, and this time knew what it was right away.

A deer — a large buck — standing still, but flicking its ears in search of any lurking danger.

It was no more than fifty yards away, perhaps less.

Feeling a twinge of excitement at the sight, Matt

froze too. A rush of adrenaline heated his blood as his senses peaked in synchronization with the stag's. A faint breeze on his face told him he was downwind of the animal, and as he took a step forward, his tread was so light that there was no crackling underfoot.

He took a second step, then a third.

The buck was staring straight at him, its head high, its ears still flicking. It waited until Matt was within twenty yards, then slowly — almost languidly — turned away and moved silently through the trees. When it had once more placed itself some fifty yards from Matt, it stopped again, and turned back to look.

Almost as if it were expecting him to follow.

As if it *wanted* him to follow.

Matt moved forward again, and again the deer waited until he was only fifteen or twenty yards away before retreating. The cat and mouse game continued, the buck leading him deeper and deeper into the woods. But after a while the forest took on a more familiar cast. The deer was in a thicket now, visible, but indistinct. Again it turned to face him, its ears still flicking as it tracked his progress, and Matt edged closer until his view was clear.

He raised his rifle, pressing its butt firmly against his right shoulder, laying his cheek on the smooth walnut of the stock as his right eye lined up with the telescopic sight.

The deer's head appeared in the cross hairs.

Matt's finger curled around the trigger, and he felt an almost physical surge of strength flow into him, as if the power of the gun had become a part of him.

Then, as he concentrated on the image in the scope, the deer's head began to change. Its antlers faded away and its muzzle contracted.

Its wide-set eyes drew closer together, and as the muzzle turned into a nose, the lips also began to transform.

Now, through the scope, Matt was looking at a human face.

His stepfather's face.

The heat in his blood drained away, and a terrible cold fell over him. He began to shiver, and tried to pull his finger away from the trigger for fear the palsied trembling that had overcome him might inadvertently fire the weapon. But his finger seemed frozen to the metal now, and when he tried to lower the gun, his arm refused to obey the demands of his mind.

The gun held steady on the face of his father.

Then he heard the voice.

"You know what you have to do, Matthew."

A faint memory stirred deep within Matt's consciousness. "No," he whispered. "No . . ."

"Do it, Matthew," the voice whispered. *"Do it for me. . . ."*

"No," he whispered again. But even as he uttered the plea, he felt his finger tightening around the trigger.

"Do it," the voice whispered once more. *"Do it."*

Matt felt the gun recoil against his shoulder, but heard nothing at all.

In the sight, his father staggered.

He felt the gun recoil again.

His father spun away.

The gun recoiled a third time.

His father fell.

The light changed, the golden glow fading. As Matt walked toward the spot where his father had fallen, the cold in his body seemed to seep out into the world around him. He shivered as if fall had suddenly given way to winter. At last he came to the spot where his father had fallen.

Only the corpse of the deer lay on the ground. Blood oozed from the three wounds Matt's bullets had caused: two in its chest, the third in the center of its head, directly between its eyes.

He gazed in horror at the body of the animal that had led him so trustingly through the forest.

Why? Why had he shot it?

Then the voice spoke again, this time from somewhere beyond the deer. "You killed him because you wanted to, Matt."

He looked up. Standing a few feet away was the white-clad figure of a woman.

Blond hair flowed over her shoulders.

His aunt Cynthia gazed steadily at him. "You killed him because you wanted to," she said again. Her eyes shifted from Matt to the corpse that lay at his feet, and a moment later, as if under some kind of spell, Matt too looked down.

He was staring at the body of his father.

He gasped, tore his eyes away, and once more looked at his aunt.

She spoke again, her voice soft, seductive. "You always do what you want to do, Matt. Always." Once again her gaze shifted.

Once again, Matt looked down.

Now he was staring into the open eyes of his grandmother.

Open, and lifeless.

"No," Matt whispered. Then he screamed it, bellowing out his denial of what his eyes — and his aunt — had told him. "NOOOOooo . . ."

It was that final jerk that tore him from the nightmare. His body convulsed as he howled out the word, and a split-second later he was wide-awake. But the images of the dream hung against the black canvas of the night, as clear as if they were illuminated from within. He lay in bed, trembling from the memory, his mind still crying out the denial he'd bellowed a moment before.

It couldn't be true. It *couldn't!*

Could it?

But as he lay awake in the darkness the rest of the night, the images — and his aunt's voice — stayed with him.

Taunting him . . .

Torturing him . . .

The moment Matt came into the kitchen that morning, Joan knew he'd slept no better than she. His face looked almost as gray as the clouds that hung in the sky, dropping a steady drizzle whose chill seemed to have come right through the walls of the house. But Joan could see that it was something more than lack of sleep that had brought the pallor to Matt's face and the dark circles to his eyes.

Something inside him had changed.

Though he still looked like the son she'd raised, there was something in his eyes that she'd never seen before. Or, more exactly, something that she'd always seen before was suddenly gone. Where always before Matt's eyes had been clear and bright and full of eagerness, now the life seemed to have gone out of them, and even when he faced her, his gaze didn't quite meet her own. He's tired, she told herself. And why wouldn't he be? All through the long hours of the previous day, he continued to search for his grandmother, moving in ever-widening circles around the area where they'd found her slippers and the scrap of cloth from her nightgown. Only when it was too dark had he finally given up and come back to the house with her.

The house — empty now, but for the two of them. Except it hadn't felt empty, and in the hours before they finally went to bed to try to sleep, both Joan and Matt found themselves moving restlessly from one room to another.

Though neither admitted it aloud, they were both feeling the same thing.

Cynthia.

She's dead, Joan kept reminding herself. But all night, as she lay in bed trying to sleep, the feeling persisted that though neither Bill nor her mother were there anymore, she and Matt were not alone.

As the hours crept by and sleep refused to offer her its solace, she had felt something — some presence — lurking just beyond her door. Three times she had left her bed and stepped out into the corridor.

Cynthia's room.

It was coming from Cynthia's room.

It was as if somehow her mother had brought her sister's spirit into the house. But though her mother had seemingly simply vanished — the searing pain of the loss of her husband was still far too great to let Joan even imagine that her mother might also be dead — Cynthia had not.

Joan could still feel her.

And so, she was certain, could Matt, for even after a night in which he should have been able to rest, he still looked —

A word popped into her mind.

Haunted.

He looked haunted.

"You didn't see her, darling," she said quietly. Though they hadn't spoken of the strange experience Matt had recounted to Dan Pullman yesterday, he knew immediately what she was talking about. "You couldn't have seen her — it's simply not possible." But even as she spoke, Joan wondered if the words sounded as hollow to Matt as they did to her.

Matt only nodded, sank into his chair, and looked disinterestedly at the plate of food Joan placed before him. "I — I'm not really hungry," he finally said. "Maybe I'll just go back to bed."

He started to get up, and for a moment Joan was tempted to say nothing, to let him retreat back to his room. But then she heard Bill's voice in her head, as clearly as if he'd spoken aloud: *Don't let him. He has to deal with what's happened. He has to deal with it head on.*

"No!" she said so sharply that Matt jumped. Joan took a deep breath and began again. "I don't think you should go back to bed. I think you need to go to school today."

Matt's eyes changed again. Joan saw fear in them now, and knew the words she'd spoken so sharply to him were the right ones. If he didn't go back to school today, it would only be harder tomorrow, or the day after, or the day after that.

"I think you've been away from school long enough." She went to him and put her hands on his shoulders. "The funeral was two days ago, Matt. You should have gone back to school yesterday."

"But Gram —" Matt began.

Joan laid a finger over his lips to stop him. "We don't know what's happened to your grandmother. But you looked for her all day yesterday and didn't find her. You can't do it again today." She put her arms around him, hugging him close. "I know you want to look for her, darling. But sometimes we can't do what we want to do. So today I want you to go back to school." She felt Matt stiffen in her arms.

"Everyone thinks —" he began, but once again she didn't let him finish.

"What everyone thinks doesn't matter," she told him. "And the only way people are going to stop talking about you is if you face them and show them you're not afraid of anything they might say, because you didn't do anything. So this morning you're going back to school, and face all your friends, and start living again." She stepped back so she could look into his eyes, but her hands still gripped his shoulders. "You can't hide here forever. Neither of us can. So I want you to go to school today. I'll take care of everything else."

The nightmare from last night flashed back into Matt's mind, and he saw his father's bleeding wounds and his grandmother's dead eyes.

He recalled his aunt whispering to him. "*Do it . . . do what you want to do. . . .*"

But even as he remembered, he knew what would happen if he went back upstairs to try to sleep.

The nightmare would come again.

And again.

Surely whatever might happen at school could be no worse than the terrors that plagued him whenever he slept.

Matt turned the corner onto Prospect Street. The school was only half a block away, and he found himself slowing, finally coming to a dead stop just as he should have been stepping off the curb to cross the street. How many mornings had he been here before? Hundreds. And on every one of those mornings, he'd looked forward to the day

— looked forward to his classes, to eating lunch in the cafeteria with his friends, to going out for football practice as soon as his last class was over. But this morning it had all changed.

Was it really possible that less than a week had passed since he'd been here? How could the facade of the main building look so different? But it did — the brick walls had taken on a foreboding cast that the white-painted shutters and trim did nothing to soften.

His eyes shifted from the building itself to a group of his friends who were clustered on the lawn — Eric Holmes was there, talking to Pete Arneson and Brett Haynes. When Eric glanced his way, Matt raised his arm to wave.

Eric turned away as if Matt had suddenly become invisible.

He won't even wave to me. If Eric won't even wave to me, what's everyone else going to do?

The nervousness and apprehension that had been gnawing at Matt as he walked to school congealed into a nearly irresistible urge to turn away from the school, as Eric had turned away from him. If everyone treated him like Eric had —

The echo of his mother's words broke through his thoughts: "Face them . . . show them you're not afraid of anything they might say, because you didn't do anything."

Dropping the hand he'd raised to greet Eric Holmes, Matt stepped off the curb and crossed the street.

But it wasn't just the facade of the building that

215

had changed since Friday afternoon. Everything about the school now felt foreign, as if he'd wandered into a place he'd never seen been.

And a place where he wasn't wanted.

It was worse than his stepfather's funeral, for at the funeral he hadn't felt as totally alone.

His mother had been beside him, and people — at least some people — had spoken to him.

This morning, though, as he made his way through the crowded halls to his locker, no one slapped him on the back, no one stopped him, no one asked him how he was. He told himself that they just didn't know what to say, but he knew it was more than that. Wherever he went, the other kids fell silent, and though they were careful never to meet his eyes or even look directly at him, he could feel their eyes on his back, sense the whispered conversations he didn't quite hear.

When he entered a classroom, the hum of conversation instantly quieted, and when he took his seat, no one acknowledged his presence.

Even the teachers seemed no longer to see him. When he raised his hand three times in his advanced algebra class — twice to offer a solution to the equation scrawled on the old slate blackboard, once to ask a question — Mrs. Tokheim's gaze passed right over him as if he didn't exist.

At lunch he went through the cafeteria line and automatically headed toward the table he'd always shared with Eric Holmes, Pete Arneson, and — the last few months, anyway — Kelly Conroe. But today his usual seat between Eric and Kelly was already occupied by Mark Ryerson.

Nor had any of the other seats at the table been left empty.

He knew it wasn't a coincidence — as long as he'd been in high school, one of the chairs at that table had always been his. So they'd done it deliberately. They'd shut him out. A wave of anger rose in him, and his jaw tightened. Maybe he should just go over and dump his tray on the whole bunch of them!

No — that was the last thing he should do. If they knew they'd gotten to him, it would just get worse. Struggling to keep his emotions from showing, he searched the cafeteria for someplace else to sit. Half a dozen tables had empty seats, but the people at every one of them looked away as soon as he turned in their direction. His appetite deserting him as the hard knot of fury expanded inside him, Matt finally dropped his tray — and everything on it — into one of the trash bins, and walked out of the cafeteria.

The rage building inside him kept him from noticing Becky Adams gesturing for him to come and sit at the table where she, on most days, sat feeling as alone as Matt felt today.

By quarter past two, when he was making his way toward the computer room for his last class, he knew what to expect, so he was almost able to ignore it when the low hum in the room died away as he entered.

He glanced around at the tables. They were all there. Eric Holmes and Pete Arneson were huddled with two other football players. And Mark Ryerson and Brett Haynes were pretending they were engrossed in a game on the screen in front of them.

But Matt had seen all of them look at him when he came in.

Well, the hell with all of them. He wouldn't sit with them now even if they invited him!

He looked for an empty niche where he could be by himself and ignore all the people who were so carefully ignoring him. Spotting a vacant seat in front of one of the computer carrels, with empty chairs on either side, he sat down, tucked his book bag under the table, and logged onto the computer.

He'd start by searching for a site that might offer him the answer to the algebra question Mrs. Tokheim hadn't let him ask. But a fraction of a second after the log-on screen disappeared and the navigation program booted, a message popped up on the screen:

Hey, Matt — What does it feel like to kill someone? (;-)

The words slashed at Matt, and without thinking he began to type in a furious denial. But before he'd finished the first word, another message flashed onto the screen:

Did you shoot the deer first, or your dad?

He could feel eyes watching him as he read the second message, and he spun around in time to catch Mark Ryerson and Brett Haynes signaling to someone else, whom he couldn't see. Then another message jumped up on the screen in front of him:

> What about your grandmother, Matt?
> Did you kill her too?

Something inside Matt snapped, and he leaped to his feet, his chair crashing to the floor behind him. "I didn't do it!" he shouted, the pent-up fury that had been building inside him all day suddenly erupting. "I didn't do anything!" Grabbing his book bag, he stormed out of the classroom, racing down the corridor toward the front door. Bursting outside, he paused at the top of the steps and sucked air deep into his lungs, struggling to hold back the tears that seared his eyes. Then, behind him, he heard a voice.

"Matt? What's going on? What happened?" Matt spun around to see Jack Carruthers, the computer teacher, looking worriedly at him. As the teacher moved closer, Matt backed away. "Tell me what's wrong, Matt," Carruthers went on. "Tell me what I can do to help."

"What's wrong?" Matt echoed, his voice rising sharply. "What's wrong? My dad's dead, and my grandmother's missing, and everyone thinks I did it! That's what's wrong!"

Spinning away from the teacher, he charged down the steps and away from the school, but even as he sprinted down Prospect Street, the words he'd seen on the computer screen taunted him.

What does it feel like to kill someone?
Did you shoot the deer first, or your dad?
What does it feel like to kill someone?
What does it feel like?

He kept running until he could go no farther, but there was no escape from the terrible words, and deep in his heart he knew there never would be.

But even worse than that was the fear that kept growing inside him.

The fear that maybe — just maybe — everyone was right.

No more, Joan prayed silently. *Please, God, no more.*

But as she watched Matt coming up the driveway, she knew that her silent prayer was not going to be answered, for on any other day Matt wouldn't have been home from school before five.

Today it wasn't even quarter past three, though from the way she felt, it should have been later. Much, much later.

All day long she'd moved back and forth between the house and the pool at the foot of the falls. She'd barely even felt the chill of the steady drizzle as she waited while a diver searched the depths of the pool, then began working his way downstream until the river widened out a mile below the falls and became so shallow that there was no possibility of the water hiding —

Joan had shuddered at the image that had risen in her mind of her mother's lifeless body caught in a crevice under a boulder, her hands reaching toward the surface as if seeking help.

She had only been able to escape the vision by returning home, but a few minutes later she was drawn back to the bank of the stream again. One of Dan Pullman's deputies had brought his dog — a gentle German shepherd named Sheba — but the dog had been unable to pick up a trail. "Not surprising, with this rain and all," Pullman told her. Sometime in the middle of the morning they'd brought the dog to the house, but the animal was no more successful picking up a scent there than on the paths by the stream.

As the hours passed, Joan felt the hope of finding her mother slipping away, and knew that soon — if not today, then tomorrow or the day after — the men Dan Pullman had sent into the forest would have to stop looking, just as the shallows had stopped the diver. But not yet. She wouldn't give up yet.

Nancy Conroe had come over around noon, but Joan was unable to eat more than a bite of the salad Nancy brought, and in less than an hour Joan had sent her away, saying, "You have better things to do than sit and watch me worry."

"But you shouldn't be alone," Nancy replied. "With everything that's happened, just the idea of you being in this house all by yourself makes me shudder. Maybe you and Matt ought to go somewhere else, even if it's just for a little while."

Joan shook her head. "I can't. Not until we find Mother." She turned to gaze out the rain-streaked window. "If she's out there somewhere . . . if she somehow finds her way back . . ." Her voice trailed off, and neither woman was willing to voice what they both knew: if the temperature should suddenly drop — if the rain should suddenly turn to sleet or snow — Emily Moore couldn't possibly survive more than a few hours in nothing more substantial than a thin nightgown.

"I'll call you," Joan promised as she walked Nancy out to her car, wrapping herself against the rain in one of Bill's parkas. "And thanks for coming out. I really do appreciate it. But right now, I think I just need to be by myself."

Three times she'd gone back to the stream, each time allowing herself to hope that some trace of her mother would have turned up.

Three times she'd come home, her hopes momentarily dashed.

It was as she was leaving the house for the fourth time that she saw Matt walking up the driveway. Even if he hadn't been getting home far too early, everything about him — his posture, the shuffle in his step, the way his hands were shoved deep in his pockets told her that something — had gone terribly wrong at school.

Ten minutes later, after she dragged the truth out of him about what had happened, he at last looked directly into her eyes. "What if it's true?" he whispered. "What if what they're saying is true?" Joan reached for his hands, but he pulled away from her. "I had a dream last night, Mom," he said.

Slowly, his tone conveying the pain and fear it had caused him, he told her about the terrible vision that had come to him in the night. "And Aunt Cynthia was there," he finished, at last lifting his eyes to meet hers. "She kept telling me to do it. To do what I wanted to do." Even as he spoke the words, Joan could see the terror coming into his eyes once again. "I was pissed off at Dad on my birthday," he went on. "And I was mad at Gram night before last. What if it's true? What if I —"

Joan clamped her hand over his mouth, refusing to let him even utter the terrible words. "You didn't," she said. "You didn't do anything." Recalling the accusations that Matt had told her he'd seen on the computer monitor, her sympathy for her son hardened into anger toward his tormentors. "Go up and change your clothes," she told him. "I'll fix you something to eat. You hardly touched your breakfast, and without lunch you must be starving."

"But I'm not hungry," Matt protested.

"Maybe you will be by the time you get back downstairs," Joan replied.

As soon as Matt was gone, she picked up the phone and called the school.

"I wish I knew how kids can be so cruel," Burt Wing sighed after hearing Joan out. "Jack

Carruthers told me about Matt leaving early, but Matt didn't tell him what had happened." He was silent for a moment, then: "Joan, I wish I could tell you it won't happen again, but —"

"Then what is Matt supposed to do?" Joan asked. "By the time he got home, he was starting to wonder if maybe what they were saying was —" She cut herself short, and when she spoke again, managed to keep most of the anger out of her voice. "You're Matt's counselor. I'm just asking you to talk to him, Burt. And maybe to the rest of the kids in that class too. Matt should be able to go to school without having to hear that kind of garbage, shouldn't he?"

"Of course he should," Burt Wing agreed. "Nothing like that should happen to any child. But these days — well, you know how kids can be."

"I do," Joan sighed. "I just don't want them making Matt's life any more difficult than it already is. And Burt? Don't tell Matt I called, all right?"

For the first time since he'd picked up the phone, Burt Wing chuckled. "Don't worry. The last thing any kid needs to know is that his mother called his counselor. Believe me, he won't ever hear it from me. And I'll talk to him first thing in the morning."

As she hung up the phone, it occurred to Joan that morning was a long time away.

The voice whispered her name so softly that at first Joan wasn't certain she'd heard it at all.

When it came again, slithering out of the silence and creeping around the fringes of her consciousness as if it didn't want to be heard at all, she told herself it was just the wind. Though the rain had stopped and a breeze had come up, water still dripped from the leaves that clung to the branches of the huge maple just outside her bedroom window. Surely all she heard was the soughing of that breeze.

But then she heard the sound again, her name breathed in a long, drawn-out sigh:

"*Jo-oan . . .*"

She tried to shut it out, tried to tell herself once again that it was only the wind, or something in her imagination. But even as she tried to close her mind to it, the voice called out again.

"*Jo-oan . . . Joanie . . . Joanie-baby . . .*"

Cynthia!

Only Cynthia had ever called her Joanie-baby.

It came again, and now the voice of her sister was unmistakable. "*Come on, Joanie-baby . . . come and play with me.*"

"No!" Joan whispered, unaware she had spoken aloud. It wasn't real. It couldn't be real.

Now she heard a tinkle of laughter, and then, once again, her sister's voice. "*Come, Joanie-baby . . . come and see.*"

Joan tried to resist the voice, but even as she told herself again that whatever she was hearing could be nothing more than an illusion, she found herself getting out of bed, slipping her arms into the sleeves of Bill's worn woolen robe, and moving to the closed door of the bedroom.

She paused, listening.

Nothing.

But now, though the house was once again silent, she could feel something. Something in the hall, just outside her door.

Her heart quickened, and her fingers went to the key in the lock just below the doorknob. "Matt?" she whispered, so softly that even she could barely hear her words. "Matt, is that you?"

Nothing.

She wanted to lock the door to her bedroom, wanted to go back to her bed and wrap herself in the comfort of the down quilt. But as if held in thrall by some force she could neither see nor feel, she turned the doorknob and pulled the door open.

The corridor was dimly lit by a night-light; both its ends lost in shadows. Clutching the lapels of the robe tight around her throat, Joan slipped out into the hallway.

Though she knew it could be no more than an illusion, the corridor seemed to stretch away forever in both directions.

Every door was closed.

Yet she still felt the presence of someone — or something — lurking close by.

Very close by.

"M-Mother?" she stammered, her voice trembling. "Mother, is that you?" But even as she uttered the words she knew her mother was nowhere in the house, and when once more the tinkle of laughter pierced the silence, it stung her like a thousand needles jabbing at her skin.

Cynthia!

It was Cynthia's laugh!

The same laugh Joan had heard hundreds of times — thousands of times — when she was a child.

Steeling herself, she moved down the corridor until she stood in front of the door to Cynthia's room.

No! Not Cynthia's room!

Her room! In *her* house! It was nothing more than a guest room in which her mother had stored her sister's things!

She reached out and gripped the knob, but still she hesitated.

Why? What was she afraid of?

She was just tired — exhausted from everything she'd been through in the last few days. And her mind felt as exhausted as her body — her grief, her lack of sleep, all of it had taken its toll. Why wouldn't she be imagining things? Hearing voices? Feeling things that weren't there?

The laughter came again, and Joan shuddered as a chill rolled over her.

Go back, she told herself. Go back to bed, and go to sleep.

But even as her mind spoke the order, her hand turned the doorknob and pushed open the door to Cynthia's room.

She felt for the light switch; turned it on.

And saw her sister staring at her.

A scream rose in Joan's throat, but as quickly as it came, she stifled it. It wasn't Cynthia she was seeing at all, only the portrait that hung on the wall. Furious at her own reaction to the picture, she moved deeper into the room, her eyes locking on the image of her sister.

Cynthia's eyes seemed to come alive, holding Joan's gaze; her smile twisted into a mocking smirk.

"What do you want?" Joan demanded. Though she heard nothing, Cynthia's eyes continued to grip her.

Grip her as they had when she was a child, and Cynthia was about to tell their mother a lie, warning Joan with nothing more than a look to say nothing.

An image leaped from the depths of Joan's subconscious. . . .

She was five years old, sprawled out on the floor in the living room, poring over one of her books. Cynthia was stretched out on the sofa, leafing through a movie magazine. The phone rang, and as Joan scrambled to her feet, Cynthia reached behind her without looking and picked up the receiver. As she pulled it to her ear, the cord caught on their mother's favorite vase and it crashed to the floor. When their mother rushed into the room a few seconds later, Joan was still staring at the scattered shards. Then she heard Cynthia telling their mother what had happened.

"She didn't mean to do it, Mama. She was just

trying to answer the phone, and she knocked it off the table."

As the words — and the certain knowledge of what would happen next — sank into Joan's mind, she tore her eyes away from the shattered remains of the vase. Her mother was glowering down at her, her hand already raised to punish her clumsiness.

Behind her stood Cynthia.

Her eyes warning Joan to keep silent, Cynthia's lips twisted into a smile so cold that it froze the younger girl.

In silence, she had borne the punishment that should have gone to Cynthia, and that night, when they were both in their beds, Cynthia asked her how she could have been so clumsy.

"But I didn't do it," Joan protested. "You broke Mommy's vase!"

"Me?" Cynthia said. "But Joanie-baby, you were the one that tried to answer the phone. Don't you remember? As soon as it rang, you jumped up to answer it and knocked over the vase!"

"No, I didn't," Joan objected. "It was you!"

But Cynthia had gone over it again and again, and finally Joan decided her sister must be right — she herself must have been so afraid of what her mother might do that she'd wanted it to be Cynthia's fault. "But it wasn't my fault, Joanie-baby," Cynthia explained. "It was your fault. It was all your fault."

As the long-buried memory blazed in her mind another memory stirred in her. The memory of the strange story Matt had told about what had happened the night before last, when his grandmother disappeared from her room.

And she remembered the terrible nightmare Matt had told her about just this afternoon.

"What are you doing?" she whispered in the darkness. "Are you trying to blame Matt this time? Are you trying to blame him for what you've done?" Her eyes still fixed on the image of Cynthia, she backed out of the room. "Well, I won't let you! Do you hear? I won't let you!" Snapping off the light, Joan pulled the door closed behind her, then twisted the key in the lock, jerked it out of the door, and dropped it in the pocket of her robe. Only then — with the door securely locked behind her — did she rest against the wall for a moment while her racing heart slowed.

And once again, she heard her sister's laugh.

Chapter 14

Joan had to get out of the house.

It was mid-morning. Matt had left for school three hours ago, and for the last two of those hours Joan had been trying to concentrate on the task she could put off no longer: sorting through the contents of Bill's desk, deciding which of the stacks of papers needed to be returned to his office, which turned over to Trip Wainwright, and which to either keep or dispose of. But every time she went to the desk in the den, she turned away, unable to bring herself to begin the job. She knew what was holding her back.

It was the finality of it.

Even as she'd stood at her husband's graveside, looking down at his coffin, some small part of her still rejected the reality of it, the cold truth that she would never see her husband again, never be able to talk to him. Never feel his touch.

That same small part of her still clung to the idea that as long as Bill's things were just as he'd left them — the clothes, the papers in his desk, even the books and magazines that he hadn't finished reading — as long as none of those things were touched, he might still come back.

Like her mother with Cynthia, she told herself

that morning when her eyes had fallen on the row of Bill's suits that still hung in the closet in her bedroom. But even knowing that keeping Bill's things was as futile for her as keeping Cynthia's was for her mother, Joan still hadn't been able to bring herself to take his suits and shirts out of the closet. But she promised herself she'd start with the desk.

Yet even that proved to be too much, for every time she approached it — every time she sat down at the desk and started to open one of its drawers — she felt as if she were being watched, as if unseen eyes were peering over her shoulder, following her every move.

The first time, she simply tried to shake it off, but no sooner had she pulled the top left-hand drawer open than she felt it again, and instinctively slammed the drawer shut and whirled around to see who was watching her.

The den, of course, was empty.

The whole house was empty, except for her.

But it didn't feel empty.

It felt as if someone were there, lurking close by, stealthily following her as she moved from one room to another.

Stalking her.

Finally she left the house, telling herself that she wanted to talk to Dan Pullman, find out if any trace of her mother had been found. But she knew that was only part of it — that just as strong was her need simply to escape from the house.

The house and everything in it — both seen and unseen.

There was only one car parked at the head of the trail to the pool below the falls that morning — Dan Pullman's black-and-white Taurus — and when Joan emerged onto the shelf of rock edging the pool, she found him removing the bright yellow ribbons that had warned the curious away from the areas where traces of Emily Moore had been found.

"You're giving up, aren't you?" she asked, biting her lip to hold back the tears that threatened to engulf her. How could they do it? How could they just walk away from the search?

Pullman couldn't quite bring himself to meet her eyes. "I just can't keep my men on it any longer," he replied as if he'd read her thoughts. "It seems like if we were going to find her, we would have by now." His eyes moved toward the heavy clouds that seemed to hang just above the treetops. "With this weather . . ." His voice trailed off, but his meaning was unmistakable. "Well," he went on a few seconds later, shoving the last of the yellow tape into a plastic trash bag, "I guess I'd better be getting back to town." He hesitated again, then: "Will you be all right, Joan?"

She took a deep breath and forced a nod. "I don't have much choice, do I?" When Dan seemed uncertain about whether to leave her, she spoke again. "You go on, Dan. I'll be all right. I promise."

As Pullman started back up the path, Joan gazed out over the pool. Its clear green water — water she'd swum in hundreds of times over the years — had turned gray under the overcast sky, and when she looked up, the naked branches of a huge oak — stripped bare by last night's wind — seemed to reach toward her, as if to snatch her up and hurl her into the leaden water. As she flinched reflexively away from the tree, she thought she heard a faint sound.

She was about to call out when she heard something else.

A voice.

Cynthia's voice.

"Remember Timmy?"

Joan's heart skipped a beat, but even before the words had sunk in, her eyes flicked back to the tree she had flinched away from a moment ago. Only now it had changed.

A rope hung from one of the tree's branches, and a boy clung to the end of the rope.

Timmy Phelps.

Barely six — two years younger than Joan — Timmy laughed happily as he swung back and forth. As he swung toward her, Joan gave him a gentle push so his motion wouldn't die down.

But as she pushed, she heard Cynthia — treading water in the middle of the pool — call out to her. "Push him harder, Joan. Push him harder!"

As Cynthia urged her on and Timmy shrieked with excitement, she pushed harder and harder, until each swing took Timmy out over the very center of the pool. Then Cynthia's urging suddenly changed.

"Let go, Timmy!" she shouted. "Let the rope go! I'll catch you!"

A split-second later Timmy dropped into the water and the rope suddenly went slack, dangling loosely from the branch.

Cynthia, still treading water, was laughing.

And Timmy Phelps was gone.

Joan stared at the water — where was he?

What had happened? Why hadn't Cynthia caught him? Everyone knew Timmy couldn't swim!

Without thinking, Joan plunged into the pool. Beneath the water, she kicked hard, forcing herself down deeper and deeper.

Keeping her eyes open, she twisted around, trying to find Timmy. Then her lungs started to burn, and she knew she could hold her breath only another few seconds.

Where was he?

Her chest felt like it was on fire, and in a few seconds she would have to give up. Then, she saw him.

He was reaching out to her, just a few feet away. She kicked, then kicked again, and just as she knew she could hold out no longer, her fingers closed on his hand. She hurled herself to the surface, expelling air from her lungs all the way.

Her head finally burst out of the water the instant she could resist inhaling no longer.

Somehow, she managed to pull Timmy out of the pool and start pumping the water out of his lungs. Then her mother was there, and Cynthia was telling her what had happened.

"Joan was pushing him on the rope, Mama. I tried to make her stop, but she wouldn't. She just kept pushing him higher and higher. But she didn't mean for

him to fall, Mama. She was just having fun. It wasn't really her fault."

Joan stared at the spot where she'd saved Timmy Phelps's life, Cynthia's words burning once more in her memory.

"Is that what you did?" she finally whispered, her eyes moving once more to the dark waters of the pool. "Did you do the same thing to Mother that you did to Timmy?"

Again she heard her sister's voice. *"Mama wanted to be with me, Joanie-baby. She always wanted to be with me. But you know that, don't you? You've always known that."*

As Joan stood alone by the pool, Cynthia's laugh rang out again, harsh and cruel, and though Joan knew it was impossible, she was certain that Cynthia's laugh had not come from inside her own head.

Matt's mood was even darker than the sky that afternoon, and as he crossed the street he turned to look back at the school. What would happen if the angry clouds overhead suddenly flashed with lightning, hurling a blazing blue bolt right at the school?

Would it burst into flames? Would the windows blow out? And what would happen to all the people inside?

I hope they fry, he said to himself. *I hope they fry right where they're standing.*

Today had been even worse than yesterday. The

236

only person who spoke to him when he'd arrived at school this morning was Becky Adams; but his friends —

Friends? He didn't have friends anymore. People had hardly looked at him, at least not when he was looking at them. It was as if he'd become invisible. He told himself it didn't matter, that he didn't care, and went to his locker just like he always did.

Mr. Wing had been waiting for him.

He had known right off what that was about: his counselor was going to give him hell about what had happened in the computer class yesterday. But what about all the rest of the kids? The ones who sent him the messages? When they got to Mr. Wing's office — a little green cubicle that looked out on the Dumpsters next to the cafeteria — it turned out to be even worse. Instead of chewing him out, Mr. Wing told him that he'd talked to all the teachers, and the teachers were going to talk to their classes about what had happened yesterday.

"We're not going to tolerate anyone accusing you of anything, Matt," his counselor had said, trying to reassure him. Right then Matt knew what had happened — his mother had called the school. Nobody else would have told Mr. Wing about the messages. By the time he was out the door, they would have been gone from his screen, and no one in the room would admit to having any idea what had happened, any more than he and Eric Holmes and Pete Arneson had ever admitted to knowing how the butter patties had gotten stuck to the ceiling over their table in the cafeteria last spring, melting just in time to drip onto Mr. Wing's own head at the senior class breakfast.

So Matt knew that when the teachers started talking about him in their classes, everyone would know that he'd told someone what had happened in the computer class.

The reaction was exactly what he expected:

It was as if he'd ceased to exist.

No one spoke to him.

No one looked at him.

People even started looking the other way when they saw him coming.

He felt a flicker of hope in P.E., when the coach made Eric and Pete the captains of the football teams. For as long as Matt could remember, he had always been one of the first ones chosen.

But today neither Eric nor Pete had chosen him at all, and when the choosing of sides was done, he found himself standing alone.

Even Nate Harkins, who had never caught a football in his life, was standing in the group around Eric Holmes. "Play on Arneson's team," the coach told him.

Pete hadn't even spoken to him, let alone included him in any of the plays.

At lunch he didn't bother going to the cafeteria. Instead he found a deserted corner on the second floor of the main building and tried to concentrate on solving the same equation he'd been working on yesterday.

Somehow he had survived the endless hours of

the afternoon, but by the end of the day, all he wanted to do was escape.

Escape from the school. Escape from the people who had once been his friends. Escape from everyone and everything.

He started home, moving slowly, his head down. But even with his head down, even with his eyes focused tightly only on the sidewalk, he could feel them.

Feel them watching him from the cars that passed, watching him from the houses he passed himself.

Watching him, judging him.

He could almost feel their thoughts. *We know . . . we know what you did . . . we know . . . we know . . .*

The heavy cloak of loneliness that had fallen over him at school wrapped him tighter and tighter in its folds until it felt like he was suffocating.

He hurried his step until he was almost running, but even when he passed through the gates of Hapgood Farm he felt no relief, and when he saw the house itself, he remembered the terrible dreams that had begun to disturb his sleep each night.

Dreams that didn't feel like dreams at all.

As the rain began to fall, he headed around toward the back door and the mud room, but as he was about to go in, something caught his eye. He turned and looked directly at the shed behind the carriage house.

The shed in which one of the deputies had hung the dressed carcass of the deer he shot the day his father died. He had forgotten it was there until yesterday, when he pulled the door open to see if his grandmother had wandered in. For a moment he hadn't realized what it was. Its belly had been slit open, its guts removed. It was dangling by its hind legs from a hook. It wasn't until he saw the head — the head his dad had planned to have mounted as his first trophy — dangling a few inches above the floor, that he recognized it. Then, quickly, he shut the shed door, and tried to shut the image of the dead animal out of his mind.

But this afternoon another animal hung on the shed, on the outside wall.

It was a rabbit. A white rabbit.

It hung upside down from a single nail driven through its hind legs. Just like the deer.

Its belly was slit. Just like the deer.

But unlike the deer, bloody entrails hung from the gaping wound, and blood oozed down the shed wall.

As his eyes locked on the grisly object, Matt's subconscious opened and a terrible vision rose up from its depths.

He was five years old. He woke in the night and instantly knew he was not alone. He lay absolutely still, certain that if he moved, whoever — or whatever — had entered his bedroom would surely come and kill him. Then, in dim moonlight that seeped through his window, he saw a figure approaching, emerging from the shadows as if springing from the darkness itself.

He recognized the figure the moment the moonlight

fell on its face: his aunt Cynthia. And even though his mother had explained to him long ago that his aunt was dead, Matt knew his grandmother always talked to her just as if she were still alive. As he watched the specter in his room come closer, a strange aroma filled his nostrils — a musky odor that seemed strangely familiar. His aunt knelt beside the bed and began whispering. Though he couldn't quite make out the words, they sent a chill through his body, and when her fingers touched his skin, he felt his flesh respond. She eased the blankets back and slipped into his bed, her hands never leaving his body, caressing him, her fingers exploring every part of him. Matt wanted to scream, to call his mother to come and help him, but his voice caught in his throat and a strange paralysis held him in its grip. Though he could neither speak nor move, part of his body began to respond to his aunt's touch. "Love me, Matt," she whispered then. "Always love me." She wrapped her arms around him and pulled him close, then rolled him over and pressed her mouth to his.

He tried to shut it out, told himself it wasn't happening. And as the caresses and the kisses went on and on, as his aunt guided his hands over her body, Matt turned his mind away.

Don't think about it, he told himself. Think about something else.

His rabbit!

The white rabbit the man who was going to be his stepfather had given him.

The white rabbit that even now was in its cage in the corner of the room. He focused his mind on the rabbit, clinging to its image, shutting out the terrible reality of what was happening to him.

And it worked. He turned his mind away from what was happening to his body, letting it sink into a darkness that nothing could penetrate.

When he awoke the next morning, everything that happened during the night had vanished from his mind as completely as if it had never happened at all. But when he went to feed his pet, he found the rabbit dead in its cage.

Its belly slit open.

Hanging upside down from the top of its cage, its hind legs bound together. Sickened — and terrified — Matt stared at it for a long time, trying to imagine what might have happened.

Matt's eyes remained fixed on the rabbit as the last fragments of the terrible memory fell into place. He could still hear his aunt's voice whispering to him; could almost feel her fingers caressing his body; could still smell her musky scent.

It couldn't have been real — it couldn't have been!

It must have been a dream, like the dreams he'd been having the last few nights. He backed away from the shed, but couldn't escape the sound of his aunt's voice.

"*You know what you have to do,*" Cynthia's voice whispered. "*You want to do it. You know you do.*" Obeying the voice in his head, Matt turned away from the grisly object on the wall of the shed and started toward the house.

Slowly — almost imperceptibly — the gray fog of disease that lay over Emily Moore's mind began to lift. In a way, it was like awakening from a deep sleep, except that even now, with darkness still surrounding her, she wasn't certain whether she was conscious or not. Reality, dreams, and memories swirled around in her mind, mixing together until their strands were so tangled that she had no idea from whence any of them came, let alone where they might lead.

She had no idea where she was, nor how long she'd been there.

The blackness surrounding her was utterly impenetrable.

Death . . .

The word drifted out of nowhere, and a corner of her mind reacted to it —

Had she died?

How would she know?

No, not dead — something else.

Cynthia!

Yes! Now she could see Cynthia, smiling to her, beckoning to her.

Her lips worked, and she tried to form a word: "Cynthia."

But all that emerged from her throat was a formless sound, low, guttural, almost inaudible.

She kept her eyes fixed on Cynthia's smiling face, her sparkling blue eyes, her flowing blond hair.

Like an angel.

Her daughter was like an angel.

Death . . .

The word floated into her mind again, and more of the fog drifted away. She wondered if perhaps, after all, she was dead.

Wouldn't that be what death was like? Falling into sleep — a sleep so deep no dreams could penetrate it, no terrors reach through it, no pain disturb it.

A sleep that would finally give way to a first glimpse of eternity.

The radiant smile on Cynthia's face began to change, her lips twisting cruelly; her sparkling eyes turning to angrily glittering orbs.

Instinctively, Emily tried to lift her arm to fend off the suddenly frightening visage, and a flash of pain so intense it burned her whole body coursed through her. Then another sound emerged from her lips: a strangled howl.

Overwhelmed by agony, Emily felt herself drop back into the black chasm of unconsciousness. But even as part of her longed to drift into the welcome arms of sleep, another part of her fought against it.

She was alive! The pain told her she was alive! And if she was alive, she had to figure out where she was — what had happened.

What was going to happen.

She willed herself back to consciousness, forced herself to lie still. Slowly the pain ebbed away.

A dim memory began to take form.

A house! She'd been in a big house, a house so big she couldn't find her way around. *But Cynthia was there!* She'd seen her; talked to her.

Followed her.

Yes, that was it — she'd followed Cynthia. Through the darkness and down a flight of stairs, a flight so long it seemed endless. She tried to catch up to Cynthia, wanted Cynthia to hold her hand, to lead her through the darkness, to steady her tottering gait.

But Cynthia had always been ahead, smiling back at her, beckoning to her, urging her on.

Then, at last, she almost caught up with Cynthia, was almost able to touch her, to stroke her golden hair, feel the smoothness of her skin, the firmness of her young flesh.

Then —

What?

The fog began closing in again, but she struggled against it. She had to remember — remember everything that had happened.

She'd fallen!

Yes! She'd been only inches from Cynthia — only another step before she would be able to take her beloved daughter in her arms. And then there was nothing. Nothing under her feet.

Nothing to hold her.

She felt herself falling, felt a terrible stab of pain, and then —

Nothing.

Nothing but the terrible unfathomable blackness that now surrounded her.

Emily tried to move again, but very slowly, testing each muscle, each joint. When she at-

245

tempted to move her right arm, the same burning pain that had stopped her before stopped her again.

She couldn't move her left leg at all, and when she finally managed to twist her body enough so she could touch her thigh with her left hand, she felt nothing. Though she could touch the loose skin covering her wasted muscles with her fingers, it was as if she were touching someone else's limb, not her own.

Broken.

Her left leg and her right arm were broken.

As the thought implanted itself in her mind, the pain of her broken limbs began to creep out of whatever cage had penned it, as if released by her own realization that she was injured. The arm throbbed, and when she gingerly prodded at her elbow, it felt as if a knife had been plunged into her flesh.

Then, as the pain receded, she heard something.

A footstep.

Muffled, indistinct, as if it came from somewhere beyond the darkness.

But where? Where was she?

She tried to cry out, but though she could form the words in her mind, her throat and lips refused to obey her commands, and all that emerged was a mewling whimper.

"Please," she begged softly. "Please help me . . ."

There was another footstep, closer this time, and now she could sense that she was no longer alone. But who was there?

The fog began to gather around her again, and once more she tried to hold it back, tried to keep it from muddling her mind.

Cynthia! Cynthia must be nearby, come to help her!

But if she was hidden in the darkness — and the quickly gathering fog — how would Cynthia find her?

Again she tried to cry out, mustering her strength to utter her daughter's name. But it was too late.

The fog closed around her, the pain in her arm and leg eased, and the peace of unconsciousness once more claimed her. . . .

Chapter 15

Joan came awake abruptly, sitting up on the sofa in the library and automatically glancing at the clock — almost four! How had it gotten so late? When she stretched out on the sofa at a little after two, she'd only intended to relax for a few minutes, not waste the afternoon sleeping. But now the afternoon was almost gone, and the pile of half-finished work on Bill's desk — files she barely understood, let alone had any idea what to do with — was every bit as daunting as it had been that morning, when she found herself unable to deal with it at all. Sighing — and feeling as tired as if she hadn't slept at all — she pulled herself off the sofa and moved toward the ornately carved mahogany desk. Maybe she should just put it off until tomorrow.

"Lazy!" It was her mother's voice she heard echoing in her memory. How many times had her mother lectured her about putting things off? "Why can't you be more like your sister? You don't see Cynthia lazing around doing nothing! She always keeps her room spotless, and her things in perfect order! But you!"

In her mind's eye Joan could see her mother shaking her head in despair. "All right," she said, speaking out loud almost unconsciously. "I won't put it off. I'll heat up a cup of coffee, clear my head, and start!" She was on her way to the kitchen when she saw Matt's book bag on the table at the foot of the stairs. As she gazed at the worn canvas, she tried to tell herself that it didn't mean anything, that he could have skipped football practice for any number of reasons — maybe it had even been cancelled. But her attempt at reassurance sounded exactly like what she knew it was: wishful thinking.

All thoughts of coffee — and the files on Bill's desk — forgotten, she started up the stairs. "Matt?" she called out as she came to the landing. "Matt, are —" Her words died in her throat as she saw the door to Cynthia's room standing ajar. It had been closed this morning. She clearly remembered closing it herself — locking it! — after that terrible moment last night when she'd imagined she heard Cynthia laughing at her. She moved closer to the door, but warily, as if some unseen danger lurked inside.

"Matt?"

No response.

She reached out with a trembling hand and pushed the door wider. "Matt? Are you in here?" When there was still no answer, she reluctantly stepped inside. The room was empty.

Yet he must have been here! Who else could have unlocked the door?

But how had he found the key?

Leaving the room and pulling the door firmly shut again, she walked quickly down the hall to

Matt's room. She rapped softly on the closed door, and was about to rap again when she heard Matt's voice. "It's not locked."

Joan turned the knob and stepped into her son's room. Matt was sprawled out on the bed, flat on his back, staring up at the ceiling. He sat up as she came in, and one look at his face told her that today had, if anything, been even worse than yesterday. The pallor in his face had worsened, and the haunted look in his eyes had deepened. Now he had the eyes of a frightened animal, eyes that darted as if searching for a predator he sensed but had not yet seen. As his eyes finally fixed on her, she could see a flame of anger burning in them.

"You called the school," he said. "You talked to Mr. Wing, didn't you?"

Joan bit her lip. "I thought —"

"It doesn't matter what you thought, Mom!" Matt burst out, his voice bitter. "You want to know what happened today? You want to hear it?" Before Joan could respond, the story came out. Bitter, angry words spewed from Matt. "Someone even nailed a dead rabbit to the shed," he finished, his voice shaking, his face streaked with the tears he was unable to control.

"A rabbit?" Joan echoed. "What are you talking about?"

Matt pointed to the window. "Go look!" he said. "If you don't believe me, look for yourself!"

Joan crossed to the window and peered out into the darkening afternoon. Forty yards away, behind the carriage house, she saw the shed Matt was talking about. But there was nothing on it. "You saw it on the shed?" she asked, her voice conveying her doubt as much as her words. "The one behind the carriage house?"

"Is there another one?" Matt demanded, getting off the bed and coming over to stand beside her. "It's right —" His words died abruptly as he stared at the shed wall. There was nothing there at all. The dead rabbit was gone, and as he stared at the empty expanse of white-painted siding, he wondered if it had been there at all. Could his eyes have been playing a trick on him? "But I saw it," he murmured, more to himself than his mother.

Joan remembered, then, a morning more than ten years ago, when she found the pet Bill had given Matt, dead in its cage.

Hanging upside down, eviscerated.

It had been a rabbit — white rabbit — and Matt was unable to explain what had happened to it.

He'd clung to her then, crying inconsolably, brokenly insisting over and over again that he hadn't done anything to it, that he'd loved it, that someone must have come into the room in the night and done it. For a moment Joan had wondered if it could have been her mother. But in the end, rather than even talk to her mother about it, she put the dead rabbit in a plastic bag and deposited it in the garbage barrel in the alley. Neither of them had ever spoken of it again. Now, as her son stood trembling next to her, his eyes fixed on the woodshed, she slipped her arm around him.

"It's all right, Matt," she said. "You probably just dreamed it."

He turned to face her, the anger gone from his eyes; instead, the terrible, frightened, hunted look had returned. "Remember the rabbit Dad gave me before you got married and we still lived at Gram's?" Joan felt a chill go through her, and knew she didn't want to hear what Matt was about to say. "What if I killed it? What if I killed the rabbit myself and didn't remember?" Though he said no more, Joan knew what he was thinking. If he could have killed the rabbit and not remembered, then what about his stepfather?

And his grandmother?

Joan put both her hands on her son's shoulders. "You didn't do anything, Matt. I know you didn't." But even as she spoke the words, she knew they weren't quite true.

For the first time, a seed of doubt had been planted in her mind.

It wasn't until she was about to leave Matt's room a few minutes later that she remembered why she'd knocked on his door in the first place. "Matt," she said, turning back to face him, "did you go into Cynthia's room?" She thought she saw something flicker in Matt's eyes, but it was gone so quickly that she wasn't sure she'd seen it at all.

Matt shook his head. "Why would I do that?"

Joan hesitated, but decided to say nothing more. Leaving Matt, she went down the hall to her own room. Bill's old robe — the one she'd been wearing this morning — still hung from the hook in her dressing room, where she'd left it. But as she reached for the pocket, she paused. What if the key was gone? What would she do? What if Matt had lied about going into Cynthia's room?

She could think about that later — right now, she simply had to know. One way or the other, she had to know.

She slipped her hand into the pocket of the robe.

The key was still there.

Surely, even if Matt had found the key and used it, he would have relocked the door before he put it back. So Matt hadn't lied.

But she still had no idea why the door had been open. Then, heading downstairs to find something for their dinner, she heard Cynthia's voice again. *"Maybe I did it,"* her sister whispered. *"Maybe I opened the door myself."*

Joan jerked to a stop and spun around, as if expecting to see her sister standing on the landing, her mocking eyes sparkling with cruel mischief. "Leave me alone!" she cried. "Just leave me alone!"

It wasn't until she'd shouted the words that she realized Cynthia wasn't there at all.

Couldn't be there.

After all, Cynthia was dead.

Wasn't she?

"Am I?" Cynthia whispered. *"Come and see, Joanie-baby. Come to my room and see. . . ."*

Matt stayed by the window even after his mother left his room, staring down at the blank white wall of the shed. Its emptiness seemed to taunt him. But the rabbit had been there! He'd seen its slit belly, seen its entrails hanging down the wall, seen the bloodstains on the wall itself. Yet now, from his room on the second floor, the wall appeared as pristine as if it had been painted only yesterday. A wave of angry frustration crashing over him, Matt wheeled away from the window and bolted from his room.

A minute later he was standing in front of the shed, staring at the spot where the rabbit had hung. He moved closer, reaching out to touch the siding; there was no sign of any stain whatsoever.

His eyes moved to the storm clouds scudding across the sky. Could the rain have washed away the stains? But it didn't seem possible: the rain had almost stopped; the ground was hardly even wet. So whoever had hung the rabbit there — then come and taken it away — must have cleaned up the mess themselves.

A thought rose unbidden in his mind: *Maybe the rabbit was never there at all.*

But if it hadn't been, that meant —

He cut the thought short. He wasn't crazy! He *had* seen the rabbit. And he would find out what happened to it!

He went around behind the shed to the trash barrels and jerked their covers off one by one. Nothing!

Inside the shed?

He reached for the handle of the door, then stopped as he remembered what was inside. *It's only a deer,* he told himself. *And it can't hurt you.* Grasping the handle, he pulled the door open, and for only the second time since the day he shot it, looked at the animal he had killed. It was exactly as he remembered it: hanging from its hind legs, its belly slit, its head suspended just a few inches above the floor.

Just like the rabbit.

But it didn't mean anything — it couldn't mean anything! Yet as he stood transfixed at the doorway, the memory of what had happened the morning of his birthday came back to him.

Again he was staring down the length of his rifle barrel, holding the sight steady on the buck's raised head.

Again he could smell the musky aroma that had filled his nostrils.

And again there was the voice, whispering to him: *"Do it, Matt. Do it . . . do it . . . do it . . ."*

But do what? What was he supposed to do? His eyes remained fixed on the deer. Why was it here? Why had they left it hanging in the shed?

Because he'd shot it.

They all knew he'd shot it, shot it just the way his dad had wanted him to.

"It's time for you to bag your first trophy," his father had told him when they finally sighted the deer. And he had. He'd circled around the deer, crept up on him, and taken him.

"I did what you wanted," Matt whispered. "I did exactly what you wanted." But even as he said it, he knew he hadn't — not yet. His stepfather had intended that the buck — *this buck* — be his first trophy.

That its head be cut off and taken to Mr. Rudman, who would stuff it and mount it on a mahogany plaque with a brass plate commemorating his sixteenth birthday.

The day he'd shot the deer. The day everyone thought he'd shot his father.

"No," he whispered. "No . . ."

But how could he prove it? There wasn't any way.

Then an idea came into his mind. What if he had Mr. Rudman do exactly what his dad had wanted? That would prove it, wouldn't it? If he'd done what everyone thought — if he'd really shot his stepfather — he'd never want the deer's head around to remind him of it, would he?

His eyes darted to the bench that ran along the length of the wall. Hanging in its usual place was the skinning knife that generations of Hapgoods had used to dress their game, its razor-sharp blade protected by a leather sheath.

Matt moved closer to the bench, reaching out toward the knife, but hesitating just before his fingers closed on it. Why was he really doing it? What would it really prove?

Then the voice he'd heard before — the voice that seemed to come out of nowhere and out of everywhere — whispered again. *"Do it . . . do it . . . do it . . ."* Grasping the sheath with one hand, he pulled the knife out with the other. Its perfectly honed blade glinted even in the gray light of the afternoon, and as Matt's eyes fixed on it, the voice whispered once again. *"That's right, Matt . . . do it, Matt . . . do what you have to do. . . ."*

All the anger, all the rage, all the terrible frustrations that had been building inside him for days burst loose inside Matt, and with a single heave he lifted the buck's carcass from the hook and let it fall to the floor. Dropping to his knees, straddling the animal's body, he grabbed the animal's head with one hand and lifted it, and with the other hand went to work with the knife, plunging it through the deer's thick hide, then jerking it upward through skin and muscle and tendons. The knife stuck, jammed between two vertebrae. Matt yanked it loose, then attacked again. Nearly congealed blood oozed from the arteries and veins the blade slashed through, but he ignored the gory mess that covered his hands, hacking harder and harder with the knife, struggling to force it through the creature's spine.

Again he felt the blade strike bone, but this time he twisted it, jerking it one way and then another until he found the cartilaginous disk between the vertebrae. A moment later he lost his grip, and as the stag's head dropped to the floor of the shed, the knife stuck fast. Grunting, his rage and frustration unabated, Matt attacked the carcass again, the knife flashing as he yanked it free and raised it once more.

Raised it high over the body.

"I didn't do it," he cried out. "I didn't!"

The knife slashed downward, plunging deep into the stag's chest.

"I didn't," he sobbed again, jerking the knife loose and raising it yet again.

Over and over the knife rose and fell, slashing at the animal's chest and legs and neck. Matt was sobbing now, his breath coming in great heaving gasps. Now, as he sucked air deep into his lungs, he could smell the aroma too — the musky aroma that had filled his nights.

His nights, and his nightmares.

And through it all the soft, seductive voice kept whispering to him. *"That's right. That's a good boy. Do what you want to do. "Do what you need to do. . . ."*

At first Emily Moore barely noticed the strange light that glowed in the sky above her. She had been drifting among her memories, but in her mind they weren't memories at all, for something deep in her brain had finally given up trying to distinguish between the conscious and the subconscious, between what was real and what was not. The darkness surrounding her and the terrible pain in her failing body had at last become too much to bear, and her mind retreated into itself. Memories had become reality, and though her body — stiff and sore — still lay in the darkness, Emily herself was living in the warmth of a summer afternoon. . . .

They were all in the backyard of the little house on Burlington Avenue. Frank — his shirt stripped off — was mowing the lawn. Joan was perched on his shoul-

258

ders, her little hands clutching his hair as her tiny heels kicked at his chest.

Cynthia, her blond curls bouncing, was chasing after Frank, begging him to pick her up. But Frank ignored her.

Ignored Cynthia the same way he had begun ignoring her.

She knew when it started: the day Joan was born, two years earlier. She had been holding her new baby, and Frank lifted the corner of the blanket to look at his new daughter's face for the first time. "She's beautiful," he breathed. "She's the most beautiful thing I've ever seen." He was wrong, of course: Joan's face, framed by more straight black hair than any baby should have been born with, had looked to her like that of a tiny monkey, with a pushed-in nose and eyes that were too big. Not like Cynthia at all. Cynthia looked like a perfect china-doll from the day she was born, and it seemed to her that Cynthia had gotten even more beautiful every day since. But Frank, lifting Joan out of her arms and cuddling her against his chest, had murmured, "Are you my perfect princess?" From that moment, Frank and Joan became inseparable.

When Joan cried in the night, Frank got up to comfort her.

When she fussed about eating, Frank fed her.

Day after day she watched as her baby daughter stole her husband's heart away.

Day after day, Cynthia watched as her baby sister stole her daddy's heart away.

As Joan and Frank grew closer, so also did she and Cynthia.

259

Now, as she watched Joan cling to her father while he worked, pressing herself close to his bare flesh, resentment seethed inside her. It's not natural, she told herself. She shouldn't cling to him like that, and he shouldn't let her.

But he did let the child touch him, did let the child put her hands on his flesh.

And he liked it — she could see that. He liked it in a way he shouldn't.

In a dirty way.

When Frank was finished mowing the lawn, he went in the house, carrying Joan with him. She and Cynthia stayed outside, sprawled in the sunshine, but as the minutes ticked by, she began to wonder what Frank was doing in the house.

What Frank was doing with Joan.

Getting up, she went in the back door. For a second she heard nothing, but then heard Joan giggling.

She didn't hear Frank at all.

Moving silently through the kitchen to the hall, she followed her baby daughter's laughter to the bedroom.

The bedroom she shared with Frank.

Joan, naked, lay on her back, her little legs spread, her little arms waving.

Frank stood over her, his hands caressing her skin.

The way they had once caressed her skin.

He was smiling down at Joan.

The way he had once smiled at her.

The seething resentment that had been building in her as she watched her daughter ride her husband — ride him like an animal, rubbing her crotch on the back of his neck while she cried out with pleasure — sud-

denly erupted. "Get out!" she screamed, shoving Frank away from the bed and snatching Joan up so quickly the tiny child screamed with fright.

Frank pretended to be shocked by her sudden outburst, but she knew better. Before he could come up with some excuse — claim he had been doing nothing more than changing her diapers — she turned her wrath on him. "Do you think I don't know what you've been doing? Do you think I haven't watched the two of you? Well, it's over. Get out, Frank. Get out, and don't ever come back." He tried to argue with her, but when she told him she'd call the police, he changed his mind. Finally, he packed a suitcase and left.

Then she'd turned her attention to Joan.

It was as much Joan's fault as it was Frank's — she was as sure of that as she was sure that Frank had been getting his pleasure with his baby daughter. Frank was weak, and it had been easy for the little girl to seduce him.

She glowered at the child she knew had stolen her husband away, stolen Cynthia's father away.

"Evil," she whispered. "You're an evil child, and you must be punished."

She'd slapped Joan then, slapped her hard enough to make her cry. "Be quiet!" she told her. "That might have worked on your father, but it won't work on me!" But Joan kept crying, kept crying until she could no longer stand it. She picked Joan up then, and taken her down to the cellar and put her in the cedar chest that stood beneath the dark chamber's single tiny window. "You want to cry?" she asked. "Then cry in there!"

She closed the lid, plunging Joan into darkness. Joan had screamed, and pounded on the sides of the chest, but she refused to hear it. After a while, though, Joan stopped crying.

And she went back out into the sunshine, to be with Cynthia. . . .

Now the strange light in the summer sky was disturbing Emily's memory, and bits and pieces of reality slowly began to intrude upon her consciousness.

It wasn't a summer afternoon at all. It was a night so dark and endless that she couldn't remember how long it had gone on. But now the darkness was receding.

Light!

She could actually see light!

She tried to turn her face toward it, but pain shot through her arm and her leg, pain so sharp that a scream of agony rose in her throat.

But all she heard was a strangled gasp as the scream died before leaving her lips.

Her mouth!

She couldn't open her mouth!

The pain in her shoulders grew worse, and she realized she could no longer move her arms. And her hands felt cold and numb.

Then, in the shadows beside her, she saw a flicker of movement. Someone was there!

Cynthia! It was Cynthia, come at last to help her, to take her away.

She tried to speak her daughter's name, but

again nothing escaped her lips and the words died in her mouth.

She grunted as she was suddenly jerked up from where she lay. Why was this happening? Why wasn't Cynthia helping her?

What was —

Her thought was cut off by a sound.

Thunk!

It was a familiar sound — one she was certain she'd heard a hundred times before. But it was a sound she couldn't quite place.

Then she realized that though her arms still hurt, her hands no longer felt cold or numb.

They didn't hurt at all.

And on the floor beneath her legs she could feel something warm, and wet.

What was happening? Why couldn't she feel her hands?

Then, in a flash, it came back to her, and she knew where she had heard that familiar *thunk* before.

She had indeed heard it at least a hundred times.

It was a sound she'd made herself, working in her kitchen.

Preparing the meals to feed her family.

It was the sound a cleaver made as it sank into a butcher block. . . .

As the shock of the blow slowly wore off and the pain from her severed wrists began to penetrate her mind, Emily sank once more into the darkness of unconsciousness.

Chapter 16

Kelly Conroe wondered why she'd even shown up for song-leading practice that afternoon — she didn't feel like singing, she missed half the steps, and now the rest of the girls on the squad were mad at her. She should have followed her instincts and gone home. But when the final bell rang, and she opened her locker to get her book bag, she'd heard her father's voice almost as clearly as if he'd been standing right behind her. "You made a commitment, Kelly. Perhaps other people don't take commitments seriously, but the Conroes do. We always have, and we always will." So she dropped the bag back onto the floor of the locker and went to the girls' locker room to change into her gym clothes. But no matter how hard she tried, she couldn't focus her mind on the drill, and when it was over, she changed back into her regular clothes as quickly as possible, escaping from the locker room before anyone else was dressed. The last thing she needed was to listen to everyone talking about Matt Moore and what he'd done.

In fact, it seemed like no one had talked about anything else since Matt's birthday.

Even at home, it seemed as if it was all she heard about.

"I don't understand why Dan Pullman hasn't arrested him," her father had said that morning.

"I'm sure when he has proof of what happened, he'll do whatever needs to be done," Kelly's mother replied. But it wasn't enough for her father.

"What needs to be done is to lock that boy up before anything else happens."

Nancy Conroe had carefully folded her napkin before speaking again, which Kelly recognized as a sign that her mother was angry. "If Dan Pullman isn't certain what happened, I don't think the rest of us are in any position to judge Matt."

Gerry Conroe's face darkened with anger. "We know what happened — Matt and Bill had a fight, and Matt shot Bill! Shot him in cold blood, Nancy." He shook his head sadly. "I knew it was a mistake to take that boy in. I always say, if you don't know the father —"

"You don't know the son." Nancy finished the familiar litany. "But as far as Bill was concerned, he *was* Matt's father. He raised him as if he were his own son."

"That's not the point. Breeding is the point. Breeding will always out. Look at the condition this country is in! And it's the worst elements who are having all the children — the worst! If we knew who Matt Moore's father was, we'd know a lot more about him." His attention shifted to Kelly. "Which is why I never approved of you going out with him. Bill was my best friend, but Matt . . ." His voice trailed off, and he shook his head.

It had been the same at school. In the space of the weekend, every one of their friends — everyone she and Matt had grown up with, everyone they knew — had turned against him. By the time Matt came back to school, Kelly knew what would happen to her if she didn't join in the ostracism that had suddenly shut Matt out of everything. All her friends would turn their backs on her as coldly as they had turned them on Matt. But still she tried to stay neutral. She hadn't been willing to risk actually talking to him, let alone sitting with him at lunch. But at least she'd tried to warn him away from the table where he usually sat before anyone had a chance to humiliate him. And though she hadn't defended him — at least not out loud — she'd done her best not to listen to what everyone else was saying about him. No matter how bad the fight with his stepfather had been, she didn't believe Matt would have killed him.

So it must have been an accident.

But deep inside Kelly knew that by not defending Matt, by not speaking to him, by not sitting with him at lunch, she'd been as cruel as everybody else.

Today had been the worst — everyone treated him as if he didn't exist. Today, people hadn't even bothered to turn away as he approached, or avert their eyes, or even stop whispering to each other. Today they looked right through Matt as if he wasn't there at all and went on talking about him as if he were deaf. She saw the hurt and anger in his eyes, but it wasn't until the last period that she made up her mind to talk to him after school and let him know that she, at least, didn't believe he was guilty.

But when the time had come, when she saw Matt walking quickly away from the school, she lost her nerve. She told herself that she wouldn't be able to catch up with him, that he wouldn't want to talk to her, that she really should go to song-leading practice.

But she knew the truth: she'd lost her nerve.

Later, when she left the gym, Kelly brushed aside Sarah Balfour's invitation to go somewhere for a Coke and went to her locker to retrieve her book bag. Leaving the school, she headed toward the newspaper office three blocks away, then changed her mind. Even though it was getting late, she'd rather walk home than ride with her dad. At least if she walked she wouldn't have to listen to him go on and on about Matt while he drove.

As the afternoon light began to fade, she started out on Manchester Road along the same route she knew Matt had taken earlier — the same route they had walked together hundreds of times before. Twenty minutes later Kelly saw the gates at the foot of the Hapgood driveway. Her pace slowed, and as she came to the gates she looked up the long curving drive, hoping to catch a glimpse of Matt. If she could just talk to him — even for a minute or two . . .

But he wasn't there. And even if she'd seen him, he probably wouldn't have wanted to talk to her anyway, not after the way she'd treated him the last few days. But she didn't turn away. If she wanted to talk to him, why shouldn't she just go in? It wasn't like anyone — her friends, or even her father — were going to know. But what if someone saw her? What if someone drove by while she was walking up the driveway? She shivered as she thought about how everyone would treat her tomorrow if they saw her. She started to walk on.

And again hesitated.

Matt was her friend, and she was supposed to be his! So what could it hurt, just to talk to him for a minute or two, and tell him she didn't believe what everyone was saying about him?

She glanced up and down the street, and seeing no cars, made up her mind. Darting through the gate, she ran a few yards up the driveway, then ducked into the cover of the woods. A few moments later, when she knew she was far enough from the gate that no one could see her, she emerged from the trees and continued up the drive. When she came to the house, she ignored the front door, going around to use the back door the way she always had. She passed the carriage house and the shed behind it and was at the steps to the door leading to the mud room when she sensed something.

Something behind her.

Suddenly she wondered if maybe she shouldn't have just stayed on the road and gone on home. But that was stupid — it was just Matt, or Mrs. Hapgood, or —

An arm slipped around her neck and tightened

on it so quickly that her scream did not escape her throat. She tried to jerk away but lost her footing and fell to her knees.

In an instant, the arm around her throat was replaced by hands with a grip even stronger than the arm.

Desperately, she reached up, her own hands closing on the fingers squeezing her neck.

They felt cold to her touch, as if they were the fingers of a corpse. But their pressure was relentless, and no matter how hard she tried, she couldn't pry them loose.

Struggling to breathe, to fill her lungs with the air the hands around her neck had cut off, Kelly thrashed first one way, then the other.

Her heart was pounding now, and as her vision began to blur and she felt herself grow dizzy, the truth rose up in her mind:

She was going to die.

She was going to die right here, right now, and nobody — not her parents, not her friends — nobody in the world could help her.

Nobody even knew where she was.

Daddy! she tried to cry out, but no sound emerged from her strangled throat. Darkness was closing around her now, and she felt the strength in her body ebb. Still she tried to pull at the cold, nerveless hands that gripped her, but her fingers were growing numb, and in another few seconds they fell away.

Kelly's body went limp and the blackness closed around her.

They were right, she thought as she gave in to the darkness. *They were right. . . .*

Fred Rudman was about to close up shop for the evening, a process that wouldn't take him more than five minutes, given that it involved little more than wiping down the work surfaces, turning off the lights, and closing the door that separated the shop from the rest of the house. There had been a time, back when he'd learned the art of taxidermy from his father, when the shop was a busy place. During hunting season his father would hire two assistants, and even working twelve hour days, they wouldn't be able to keep up with the work. Nor had it just been deer, bear, and the occasional mountain lion that came through the door back in those days, for when Fred was a boy, the men of Granite Falls — at least the men of any kind of means — had hunted throughout the world, shipping their trophies home for Hans Rudman to mount. Lions, tigers, elephants, and giraffes. Polar bears, rhinos . . . even a hippopotamus head had once arrived. But as the big game dwindled away over the years — and as more people saw hunting as nothing more than the slaughter of animals for no other reason than to assuage the self-doubt of the hunters — the Rudman family business also began to dwindle away.

Fred saw the trend coming years ago, and so he prepared for the future by investing what little money he earned in a dying industry in stocks that looked to him as if they were in their infancy.

Thanks to the success of Microsoft and a few other companies, what had been the Rudman family's source of income for four generations was now little more than a hobby for its last surviving member. And this season had been the slowest ever — since the death of Bill Hapgood, no one at all had come to the shop with a trophy to be mounted. Thus, Fred Rudman was surprised to hear the bell jingle just as he was about to go out front and lock the door.

When he stepped through the door from the workroom and saw Matt Moore, the boy's shirt and pants stained with blood, Rudman's surprise gave way to concern. "Good Lord, young fellow, what have you been up to? Are you all right?" His eyes shifted to the object Matt had put on the counter — a large garbage bag from which a pair of antlers protruded — and his concern shifted to uncertainty. "That's not what I think it is, is it?"

"It's the buck I shot," Matt said. "How much will it cost to have it mounted?"

Instead of answering the question, Rudman gingerly picked up the bag and stepped back through the door to the workshop, jerking his head to indicate that Matt should follow him. "Let's just have a look at this." He set the bag down on the big stainless steel table, untied the drawstrings, and peeled it away from the buck's head. The first thing he saw was the neat hole through the skull — exactly between the animal's eyes — where Matt's first shot had struck. There was a larger wound on the back of the head where the bullet had exited, tearing away a piece of the deer's skull and a ragged patch of skin. Both were the kind of wounds he'd repaired hundreds of times before, and by the time the head was mounted, neither would show at all.

Then his attention shifted to the stag's neck, where Matt had cut it free from the body. The skin was ragged and torn, almost shredded in places. "What did you do, try to cut it off with a pocket knife?" When Matt didn't reply, the taxidermist lifted his eyes from the deer to the boy who stood on the other side of the worktable. Though Matt's eyes were fixed on the buck, it seemed to the old man that he wasn't seeing it. "You sure you want me to mount this, Matt?" he asked. For a moment he wasn't certain Matt had heard him, and when the boy finally spoke, his eyes remained fixed on the grisly object that lay on the table.

"My dad wanted me to," he said. There was a flatness in Matt's voice that caught the taxidermist's attention, and the frown lines in his brow deepened. Now he had no doubt that though Matt was looking at the deer's head, he was seeing something else. The boy's next words confirmed it: "My dad said it was going to be my first trophy."

Finally he looked up, and as their gazes met, Rudman felt a chill. Matt's eyes held an expression the old man had never seen before. There was a flatness to them — an emptiness — that made him take an instinctive step backward.

"Everyone thinks I killed my dad," Matt said, his voice dropping so low that Rudman wondered if

272

he even knew he was uttering the words out loud. "And maybe I did," he went on. "Maybe that's why I want to mount it — to remind myself of what I did."

The slamming of the back door made Joan Hapgood's body jerk reflexively in one of those convulsions that usually occur only at the moment when both the body and the mind are on the very edge of sleep. Except Joan hadn't been asleep at all — she was in the kitchen, thinking about what she and Matt might have for supper. Then, as she smelled the aroma of meat loaf wafting from the oven and saw how dark it had gotten beyond the windows, she felt oddly disoriented. How had it gotten so late so quickly? And when —

Her thought died as Matt stepped through the door from the mud room and she saw the bloodstains on his shirt. For a moment she could do nothing at all — neither speak nor move — as questions tumbled through her mind.

Where had he been?

How long had he been gone?

And what on earth had he been doing?

But a moment later the paralysis that had seized her passed. She took a hesitant step toward him, instinctively reaching out as if to help him. "Matt? What happened? What . . . ?" Her question faded to silence as Matt's eyes narrowed and sparked with a glint of anger.

"I'm fine," he told her, but the tension in his voice belied the words. "I took the buck's head over to Mr. Rudman's, that's all."

Joan felt dizzy. The buck? Then she remembered — the deputy who brought them home a few days ago had said something about putting it in the shed. But surely Matt couldn't be talking about *that* deer.

"Dad said it was going to be my first trophy," he said. The anger in his eyes was matched by the truculence in his voice.

Joan listened numbly, barely able to grasp what he was saying, as Matt told her how his clothes had gotten stained. Surely he couldn't really want to have the deer's head mounted? Just the idea of it hanging in the house made her queasy. To have it reminding them every single day of what had happened last week . . .

She shuddered.

And the sight of his clothes — the dark smears of blood —

"Take off your clothes," she said, her voice trembling. "Don't even take them upstairs. Just take them off and leave them on the washing machine."

For a moment it seemed Matt might challenge her, but then, as if he'd come to a decision, some of the anger drained from his expression. He disappeared through the door to the laundry room, and a minute later she heard him going up the back stairs. Only when his footsteps had faded did she go to the laundry room herself.

He had left the bloodied shirt and jeans on the washing machine, just as she'd asked. But eyeing the crumpled mass, she wondered if she shouldn't just burn them instead.

Just take them outside to the old incinerator, put them in it, and burn them.

But even as the thought came into her mind, she rejected it. What had she been thinking? The clothes weren't ruined — they just had a few stains on them. She would just put them in the washer, turn the machine on, and forget about it.

She reached for the clothes, but before her fingers could close on them, she hesitated again.

Did she doubt him? she wondered. Did she think he was lying? A chill passed through her as she remembered the doubt she felt when she found Matt in his room and he told her about the rabbit hanging on the shed wall.

The rabbit that hadn't been there.

Stop it! He's a good boy, and he wouldn't hurt anyone or anything, and he wouldn't lie. He'd never lie!

But even as she tried to reassure herself, the doubts kept flicking back at her. Flicking like so many tiny darts, picking at her, piercing tiny holes in the shield of confidence she was trying to build.

What had happened to the rabbit Bill had given Matt so many years ago?

What *could* have happened to it?

"No!" She spoke the word out loud, as if the sound of her voice could drive the demon thoughts from her mind. Snatching up the shirt and jeans, she opened the top of the washer and shoved the clothes inside, then added detergent and bleach.

She closed the lid and pressed the buttons to set the machine.

Finally, refusing to listen to the questions still spinning through her mind, she pulled the knob to start the machine.

Chapter 17

Gerry Conroe slowed his car as he approached the gates to Bill Hapgood's house.

Not Bill's, he silently corrected himself. *Not anymore. Now it's Joan's. Joan's and Matt's.*

But no matter how many times he reminded himself, it still didn't seem possible. Bill Hapgood had been his best friend for as long as he could remember — they'd done everything together, from the time they were little boys right up until the night before Bill had died. They'd been as close as brothers — closer, in fact, since the only thing they'd ever disagreed on had been Bill's decision to marry Joan Moore. His knuckles turned white as his fingers tightened on the steering wheel. Wrong! The whole thing was wrong! He'd told Bill he shouldn't marry Joan. "It's not really Joan," he'd said when Bill told him of his plans. "It's that boy of hers — we don't know who he is — who his father was. What kind of stock he comes from."

Bill's expression had hardened. "We're talking about a little boy, not a colt," he said.

"But he'll never be your son," Gerry insisted. "If you ask me —"

"I didn't ask you," Bill cut in, his voice taking on an edge that warned Gerry not to push the issue

277

any further. "I asked you if you'd be my best man. And that's *all* I asked you. So will you do it, or do I have to find someone else?"

That was the end of the argument, and for the last ten years Gerry had kept his misgivings to himself.

Now, ten years later, Bill Hapgood was dead.

Worse, it was starting to look like the boy would get away with it too. Dan Pullman showed no signs of even arresting the boy, and the way things were going, the whole thing might be chalked up to a hunting accident.

Accident!

As far as Gerry was concerned, a direct shot to the center of Bill Hapgood's forehead couldn't have been an accident. And everyone knew how good a shot Matt was — Bill had taught the boy himself.

For just a second Gerry was tempted to turn in at the gates, drive up to Bill's house, and confront Matt right now. Confront him, and get the truth out of him. But then he imagined what his wife would say: "It's not up to you, Gerry. What you think doesn't matter — it's what Dan and the prosecutors think that counts, and they say they don't have a case against Matt." He could feel Nancy's eyes boring into him as clearly as if she were sitting beside him. "Why are you so sure Matt killed him on purpose? What if you're wrong?"

I'm not wrong, Gerry told himself. *What happened to Bill was no accident.* But still he didn't turn in at the gates. He continued to drive on to his own house, where he left the car in the driveway in front of the garage and went into the house through the back door. Nancy was in the kitchen, standing in front of the open oven door and poking gently at a roast whose aroma made Gerry's mouth water. "I think another half-hour, and it'll be done," she said, glancing at the clock. "Dinner at seven okay?"

"Perfect. You want me to tell Kelly when I go upstairs?"

Nancy's brow furrowed. "She's not here. I assumed she stopped at the paper and hitched a ride with you."

Gerry shook his head. "I thought she must have decided to come right home after whatever it is she does every afternoon."

Nancy's frown deepened and she looked at the clock again. It was still six-fifteen, just as it had been a few seconds ago. "Maybe she went over to someone's house," she suggested, though she didn't believe it. Ever since she was a little girl, Kelly had been utterly reliable. If she was going to be late coming home, she always called.

Even if she was only going to be ten minutes late, she always called.

Always.

She could see that Gerry's thoughts were the same as hers, and when she spoke again, she didn't know if she was trying to reassure her husband or herself. "I'm sure everything's fine. She probably just stopped off somewhere for a minute and just lost track of time."

"Kelly doesn't lose track of time," Gerry said. "You know that. She's never lost track of time in her whole life." His jaw had tightened, his complexion gone pale. "I'm going to call Dan Pullman."

"I'm going to call some of her friends first," Nancy insisted. "Let's not start worrying until we know there's something to worry about." As if to preclude Gerry from calling the police chief, she picked up the portable phone and began dialing.

As Nancy began talking, Gerry poured himself a scotch, eyed the glass critically, then poured again. Adding some water, he gulped half the drink down in a single swallow, and waited for the heat of the alcohol to thaw the cold knot of anxiety that had formed in his belly.

It didn't work.

Matt Moore, Gerry thought after he drained the rest of his drink and poured a second. *Matt's done something to her. I know it. I can feel it.*

As he sipped the second drink, he listened with half an ear as Nancy made call after call. By the fifth one her face was as pale as his, and the worry he'd heard in her voice when she insisted that nothing was wrong had congealed into fear.

"What is it?" he asked when she hung up the phone and looked up at him. "What's going on?"

"Sarah Balfour said Kelly was 'weird' at song-leading practice this afternoon." Nancy told him, her voice low. "That was her word — 'weird.' She said it didn't seem like Kelly was thinking about what she was doing. Couldn't do the steps or

280

follow the routines. And when Sarah asked her if she wanted to get a Coke afterward, Kelly didn't say anything."

"Maybe Kelly didn't hear her," Gerry suggested, but his wife shook her head.

"Sarah said she heard her, but just turned around and walked away." Nancy paused, taking a deep breath, then went on. "It seems the kids have been making things pretty rough for Matt Moore at school."

"Which doesn't have a damned thing to do with Kelly," Gerry said.

Nancy's eyes flashed impatiently. "Oh, for heaven's sake, Gerry. Until last weekend he was her boyfriend. I know you didn't like it, but your not liking it doesn't mean it wasn't so. And even before they started dating, they were friends." She shrugged helplessly. "You know how loyal Kelly is, and apparently today the kids were all acting as if Matt didn't exist."

"Why wouldn't they, after what he did?" Gerry's voice grated angrily, which Nancy chose to ignore.

"Sarah thinks Kelly might have gone to see Matt —"

"I'm calling Dan Pullman," Gerry snapped, snatching up the phone. But as he started dialing, Nancy's fingers closed over his and she took the phone away from him.

"Not yet. We don't even know if that's where Kelly went. And even if she did, we don't know if anything's wrong." She could see that her words were having no effect on her husband, so she changed her tack. "Gerry, I know what you think, but I also know that Joan has been a good friend for ten years. And Matt's been a good friend to Kelly. So I'm not going to call Dan Pullman, and neither are you. First I'm going to call Joan and Matt and see what I can find out."

Gerry's eyes narrowed. "You won't find out anything," he predicted. "But if that kid's done something to my daughter . . ."

His words faded away, the sentence hanging in the air, his hands clenched into fists.

Even though the electronic buzz of the telephone had none of the harshness of the jangling bell Joan remembered from her childhood, its sound startled her, and she almost dropped the plates she was about to put on the table. The sound had made Matt jump too. When the phone buzzed a second time, Joan realized that it had come as a surprise because no one had called recently. Until a few days ago, the phone had rung constantly. It had sometimes seemed that everyone in town called someone in the house at least once a day, what with Bill's steady stream of clients calling about one deal or another, her own friends calling just to check in, and Matt's myriad friends calling to talk about whatever it was that kids talked about these days. But since the day after the funeral, it had fallen nearly silent. Today, in fact, it had been silent.

Joan knew why: if no one knew what to say to you, they didn't call. Now, instead of talking to the

Hapgoods, everyone was talking about them. In the space of a few short days, the cradling comfort of living in a town where you know everyone and everyone knows you had devolved into the misery of knowing that wherever you went, people were watching you.

Watching you, and whispering about you.

Worse, whispering about your son.

As the phone buzzed a fourth time, a voice spoke inside Joan's head. A voice so clear that for a moment it paralyzed her.

It was her sister's voice.

Cynthia's voice.

"Answer the phone, Joanie-baby. You know what it's about, don't you? It's about Matt, Joanie-baby. It's about Matt. . . ."

When the phone buzzed a fifth time, Joan was determined to ignore it, to let it ring until the answering machine on Bill's desk picked it up. But in her head Cynthia's voice was still speaking to her, whispering to her. *"Answer it, Joanie-baby. You have to answer it. You know you have to. . . ."*

Setting the plates down, Joan finally picked up the phone, and when she spoke, she could hear the nervousness in her own voice. Then, hearing Nancy Conroe, she felt a flash of hope — Nancy, at least, hadn't abandoned her. But then, listening to Nancy, the flicker of hope she'd felt quickly died, and her gaze moved to her son.

"I'm sure it's nothing," Nancy Conroe was saying, her tense voice belying her words. "But Kelly hasn't come home, and she hasn't called, and I was just wondering if maybe she'd stopped over there."

An image of the blood on Matt's clothes — the clothes that were in the washer now — leaped up in Joan's mind. *Deer blood!* she told herself. *It was only deer blood!* But when she replied to Nancy Conroe, she betrayed nothing of her terrible thought. "She's not here, Nancy," she said. "I haven't seen her at all."

There was a second or two of silence, then: "What about Matt? Is he there? Could I talk to him, Joan?"

Joan hesitated, but even that felt like a betrayal. What was she thinking? Matt hadn't done any-thing! He couldn't have done anything! "Of course," she finally said. Covering the receiver with her palm, she handed the phone to Matt. "It's Nancy Conroe. She wants to talk to you."

Matt listened in silence as Kelly's mother re-peated what she'd just said to his mother, and when he replied, his voice was tight. "She isn't here." He hesitated and then, recalling that Kelly had barely spoken to him the last two days — hardly even looked at him — his voice broke. "I haven't seen her," he said. "And why would she have come over here anyway?" He struggled not to let his voice reveal the pain his words were causing him. "She's not even speaking to me anymore."

"Not speaking to you?" Nancy echoed. "But you and Kelly are friends. You've always been friends —"

Suddenly Matt's control over his emotions

broke. "I don't have any friends anymore," he blurted. "Didn't she tell you? No one's speaking to me. No one's even looking at me anymore! It's like —" His voice broke, and the last words he spoke before he cut off the connection were strangled by a sob. "You don't care what it's like. Kelly doesn't care. No one cares."

Matt set the phone on the table, then looked up at his mother to see something in her eyes that he'd never seen before.

Doubt.

Silence fell over the kitchen, a silence that seemed to stretch into eternity. Slowly, Matt began to understand.

She thought he was lying.

She thought he had lied to Kelly's mother.

He rose from the table. "You don't believe me either," he said. "Nobody believes me!" His voice rose. "Why doesn't anyone believe me?" He started for the back door.

Joan took a step toward him, instinctively reaching out. "Matt, where are you going?"

He spun around to look at her, his face pale, his eyes anguished. "To find her! Don't you understand? If I don't find her — if something's happened to her —" His voice broke. "Oh, God, if you don't even believe me, who's going to?" A moment later he was gone, stumbling out into the darkness.

Then Joan too was out the back door. "Matt?" she called. "Matt, come back!" She listened for a moment, but heard nothing. "Oh, God!" she cried, her own voice breaking now. "Please come back."

But it was as if the night had swallowed him up.

*She thinks I did something! My own mother thinks I
did something to Kelly!*

His chest heaving as he paused to catch his
breath, Matt leaned against the wall of the carriage
house. He could see his mother framed in the light
of the open back door, and hear her voice as she
called out to him. But even though he could hear
her and see her, and stood hidden in the darkness
no more than fifty yards away, he felt as if transported into a parallel universe where everything he
had always known had suddenly changed.

It *looked* exactly the same; everything smelled
and sounded the same. Everything was familiar.

But everything was different, for the world he
had always known, and loved, had been filled with
people. His family, his friends, his teachers. All of
them had been part of his life.

And he'd thought they'd always be part of his
life.

Now they were gone. Now he was alone in the
world. What had happened?

Had the world changed?

Or was it he, himself, who was different?

I'm not! he cried silently to himself. *I'm who I always was!*

But as his mother called out to him once more
— her voice echoing through the darkness as if
through a long tunnel — he wondered.

Fragmented memories flitted through his mind.

Mr. Rudman, looking at him as if he didn't quite

know who he was. But Mr. Rudman had known him all his life!

The way his mother had looked at him when she'd handed the phone to him a little while ago.

Another memory rose in his mind.

The words that had been whispered to him as he crouched over the carcass of the deer: *"That's right, Matt . . . do what you want to do . . . do what you have to do. . . ."*

The musky aroma that had filled his nostrils . . .

And the blood on his clothes — had it really all come from the deer? Or —

No! It wasn't possible! He couldn't have done anything to Kelly!

What if he was going crazy?

A strangled, half-muted cry rose from his throat, and he started running again, sprinting through the darkness as if he were being chased by an unseen enemy. But even as he ran, he knew that the enemy lay not in the darkness of the night, but somewhere deep within the darkest reaches of his own mind.

He paused when he came to the gates. Where could he go?

But there was nowhere to go, no one to turn to. He couldn't go find Eric Holmes or Pete Arneson, couldn't just go into town and see who might be hanging out.

Not anymore.

Maybe not ever again.

But he hadn't done anything!

Without thinking about it — without even understanding quite why he was doing it — he turned away from the town and began walking in the other direction. In the direction of the Conroes' house. He walked quickly, with no thought at all, his head down, his feet carrying him along the familiar route. He paused only once as the glow of headlights appeared around a bend far ahead. As the glow brightened and he heard the rumble of a diesel engine, a new thought leaped into his mind.

What if he stepped out in front of the truck?

It would be over. There would be no more terrible dreams that stole his rest at night, nor the even worse nightmares that had become the reality of his days.

The headlights grew brighter, and as the truck came around the bend, the twin beams of light swept across him, blinding him. But instead of turning away, or even shielding his eyes from the glare, he stood perfectly still, staring into the light as if gazing at a beacon in the night.

A beacon signaling refuge, beckoning him toward safety.

As it approached, Matt almost unconsciously took a step off the shoulder onto the pavement.

The roar of the engine grew; the headlights held him in rapture. A hundred yards, then fifty. The twin halogen beams held him transfixed.

He stepped farther into the road, so he was standing directly in front of the truck as it hurtled toward him.

Only a few more seconds and it would all be over.

Thirty yards. Twenty. Ten —

The blare of the horn rent the night, shattering the trance into which Matt had slipped, and he leaped away, hurling himself into the ditch that ran alongside the road. He felt the slipstream as the truck raced past, and in another moment it was over; the roar of the diesel faded away, the glow of the headlights dimmed.

He was still alive, still living in the strange new world in which he was cut off from everyone he had ever known.

He recalled then the last words he'd spoken to his mother. "I have to find her. If I don't find her — if something's happened to her —" He hadn't finished the sentence, hadn't been able even to finish the thought. But now, alone in the darkness, he did.

If he didn't find Kelly Conroe — if something had happened to her — it would never end. The nightmare his life had become would go on, unchanged, until the day he died.

He might as well have thrown himself under the truck.

Picking himself up from the ditch, ignoring the scratches and bruises on his hands and face, Matt headed back the way he'd come.

Chapter 18

Joan stood at the back door, staring into the darkness that had swallowed up her son. Her first impulse was to go after him, but as she reached for the car keys that hung on a hook by the back door, she knew it would do no good. The second Matt saw the headlights — or even heard the engine — he would vanish into the woods as quickly as a wild animal, slipping silently along the paths that wound through the trees, leaving her to drive aimlessly through the night with no hope of finding him unless he wanted to be found.

Slowly, reluctantly, she closed the door.

Should she call Nancy back? Call Trip Wainwright?

Wait, she told herself. *Don't do anything — not yet. He'll come back. When he calms down, he'll come back.* She picked up the plates from the table and scraped the untouched food into the garbage disposal. *Clean up the kitchen,* she told herself. *Just do what you have to do, and he'll come back.* But as she tried to concentrate on her chore, she found herself looking out into the darkness beyond the kitchen window, the darkness that seemed to have devoured her son.

And as she watched it, the darkness of the night

began to creep into the house.

Creep in, and wrap itself around her.

Suddenly she felt exhausted, and the darkness around her seemed a comforting blanket. If only she could give in to it . . .

If only she could let herself sink into oblivion . . . If only she could forget . . .

. . . forget, and rest.

Yes . . . if only she could rest . . .

But there would be no rest, for now she could hear laughter.

Cynthia's laughter.

The skin on her arms began to crawl, and the tiny hairs on the back of her neck stood on end.

The house was not empty.

But of course it was empty! Matt had just left, and Bill was dead, and her mother was gone.

Yet the house was not empty.

Her fingers, still on the doorknob, tightened until the skin on her knuckles turned white, but she didn't turn the knob, didn't give in to the urge to jerk the door open and flee from the unseen presence in the house into the darkness of the night outside.

Instead, she made herself turn her back to the door.

There's nothing here, she told herself as she gazed through the door leading from the mud room to the kitchen. But a moment later, as she forced herself to walk into the kitchen, her heart began to pound.

Though the kitchen looked exactly as it had a

291

moment ago, it no longer felt the same; it was if someone had come into the room — someone she could neither see nor hear, but could feel.

Cynthia.

As her sister's name rose in her mind, Joan tried to reject it, to tell herself it was impossible. Yet even as she tried to reassure herself, the feeling grew stronger. Then she heard Cynthia's voice.

"I'm here, Joanie-baby. You know I'm here. And you know exactly where to find me, don't you?"

Joan froze. Her sister's voice was as clear as if Cynthia were standing next to her. *But she's not standing next to me,* Joan told herself. *She's dead! I saw her die!*

The mocking laughter that answered her thoughts cut into Joan like a knife, and as the pain of it sliced through her, something inside of her snapped. Her fear forgotten, replaced in an instant with a burning anger that quickly built into rage, she left the kitchen, moving through the dining room to the base of the stairs.

"I'm not dead, Joanie-baby," Cynthia's voice taunted again. *"You know where I am. Come on, Joanie-baby. Don't you want to play with me?"*

Joan charged up the stairs and burst through the open door to her sister's room. As the door slammed against the wall, she stepped into the room, her eyes searching it as if she expected to find her sister sitting at her desk, or sprawled out on her bed.

But except for her sister's things, the room was as empty as it had always been. Joan ventured

292

deeper inside, until she was standing in front of her sister's vanity table.

She heard her sister's voice again, but now it had changed. The mocking tone was gone. Now the voice was soft, almost seductive. *"That's right, Joanie-baby,"* Cynthia whispered. *"You do want to play, don't you? You always wanted to play. You always wanted to play Let's Pretend, didn't you? Let's play it again . . . let's play it now . . . let's pretend you're beautiful . . . let's pretend you're me. . . ."*

As the words swirled around her, the rage that had driven Joan up the stairs drained away, and as if guided by some unseen force, she eased the stool out from Cynthia's vanity and lowered herself onto it. Then, as her sister's voice whispered to her, she reached for a jar of Cynthia's makeup. But when she opened it, it was a memory that emerged.

She was four.

She was sitting in front of the mirror.

Cynthia was next to her, working the magic that would make Joan beautiful.

"You'll look just like me," Cynthia promised her. "Maybe not your hair, but everything else."

While Joan sat perfectly still, Cynthia carefully applied a layer of her own pale foundation, lightening Joan's complexion, making her eyes appear even darker than they were. Then Cynthia began applying rouge to her cheeks, and shadow to her eyelids, lipstick.

A new face began to emerge — a face that wasn't Joan's, but wasn't quite Cynthia's either.

"But I don't look like you," she said when Cynthia

293

was done and the two of them were peering into the mirror.

"It's your clothes," Cynthia decided. "Don't move. I'll be right back."

She sat perfectly still, staring at the image in the mirror. She knew that whatever Cynthia was planning, it wouldn't work. No matter what they did — no matter how hard she tried — she would never be beautiful.

Never look like her wonderful sister.

Then Cynthia was back, and when Joan saw what she was holding, her eyes widened. It was her mother's white fox stole. As long as she could remember, it had hung in her mother's closet, carefully wrapped in a plastic bag.

Joan had never touched it.

Never even seen her mother wear it.

"Don't," she whispered as Cynthia laid it over her shoulders. "If Mommy catches us —"

"She won't," Cynthia whispered to her. "Just feel it — feel how soft it is. Look how beautiful it makes you."

Almost against her own will, Joan's little fingers touched the fur. It was almost like touching a cloud, and when she tilted her head a moment later to feel the softness caressing her cheek, warmth flowed through her. And in the mirror, she almost did look beautiful. "I love it," she whispered. "I wish . . ."

The words died on her lips as the mirror reflected a flicker of movement behind her. Her heart pounding, she turned to look up at her mother. Still wearing the winter coat and leather gloves she'd put on before leaving the house an hour ago, she now stood in the

294

doorway, her eyes blazing with fury. "What are you doing?" she demanded. "What are you doing with my stole?"

"Cynthia —" Joan began, but before she could utter another word her mother snatched the stole from around her shoulders with her one hand while raising the other, clenched into a fist.

The gloved fist seemed to hang in the air like a hawk preparing to drop on its prey, and then, as Joan's eyes widened in terror and the leather-clad hand descended, a strange blackness began closing in on Joan.

By the time her mother's fist crashed into her cheek, knocking her to the floor, Joan's mind had already turned inward upon itself, escaping from the terrible pain of her mother's fury.

Her fury, and her blows . . .

The blackness around Kelly Conroe was almost physical, wrapped around her like a thick quilt. But it gave none of the comfort of the quilt she slept under at home, didn't make her feel safe and protected.

This quilt was heavy. Suffocating.

Inescapable.

And then there was the pain. Pain that suffused her body like some kind of poison. It was in her legs and her arms. Her neck. Her back. Everywhere. For a split-second she thought it might all be a dream, some terrible nightmare from which she would awaken to find herself in bed at home. But as she tried to move her aching limbs, she knew it wasn't a dream — that what had happened was real.

Slowly, it came back to her. Just scraps at first. She'd been on her way home, and she stopped to see Matt. She was about to knock on the Hapgoods' back door.

Suddenly those hands closed around her throat. Hands covered with some kind of strange gloves, whose leather was unlike anything she'd felt before. Yet there had also been something familiar about them, as if even though she didn't know what they were made of, she should have known. Her body jerked reflexively as she tried to escape that terrible touch, those awful fingers closing around her throat, and a cry of agony erupted from her lungs as every bone and muscle in her body screamed out against the sudden movement.

But her cry was choked back by the tape that sealed her lips, and instead of exploding out through her mouth, it seemed to grow inside her head until it felt like her head itself might explode.

Suddenly she couldn't breathe! The unuttered cry held her in its grip, her mouth filled with air, her lungs still trying to empty themselves, the pressure building as her panic grew. Then some instinct inside her took over, and she released the air through her nose. But then, with her lungs finally empty, she couldn't catch her breath. Her heart began to pound, and panic rose inside her again, a panic even more frightening than the darkness that surrounded her.

Automatically, her body started to fight for breath, but this time she overcame her instincts. *Think!* she commanded herself. Steeling her mind against the panic, she forced herself to stop trying to breathe through her mouth, stop trying to suck great gulps of air into her lungs. Instead she drew air in through her nostrils, expanding her chest slowly, forcing herself to be patient.

As her lungs slowly filled, the panic receded.

And Kelly began to think. *Where am I?* There was no way of telling; the darkness around her was as impenetrable as great slabs of iron.

Once again she tried to move, but this time slowly, methodically, knowing that if she lashed out, began thrashing in the blackness, the pain would overwhelm her.

Her mouth was covered with some kind of tape. By curling her lips back over her teeth and forcing her tongue through, she could just feel — even taste — the adhesive.

Her hands were tied behind her back, her wrists bound together so tightly her fingers felt numb.

Her ankles were bound too.

And the darkness — the terrible darkness — a darkness so complete that it almost felt as if she'd been buried.

Buried alive!

As the thought rose in her mind, a terrible feeling of claustrophobia began to close around her. Another scream rose inside her, and her body fought once more against the cords that bound her. She thrashed, rolling first one way and then another, and it was finally the agony in her joints that cut through the panic and claustrophobia.

When the wave of abject, unreasoning terror finally broke and ebbed away, Kelly lay still again, her chest heaving as she tried to draw enough air through her nostrils to satisfy her body's demands, knowing that if she gave into the panic again, she might black out.

Black out.

Part of her mind reached out, grasping at the thought, wanted to escape into the peace of sleep. But even as that temptation crept over her, seducing her, she began fighting against it as a moment ago she had fought the bindings on her wrists and ankles.

If she went to sleep, she would only wake up again; wake up to the terrors of the darkness, the pain in her body, the terror of not knowing where she was or why she was there. So she wouldn't go to sleep, wouldn't try to escape from the darkness around her to an even deeper one that might hold nightmares worse than the one she was living. Again she rose above the terror, refused to give in to the panic that had threatened to overwhelm her.

She was alive. That was all that counted. She was still alive, still able to breathe.

Still able to think.

She concentrated on her breathing, carefully taking one even breath after another until her lungs fell into a gentle rhythm.

She moved her legs in one direction, then another. When her feet touched nothing, the last of the claustrophobia drained away.

She wasn't buried alive, wasn't trapped in a grave.

She drew in another breath, and now her mind was clear enough to notice the odors filling the air.

Urine.

Her first thought was that she had wet herself, but a moment later she knew that wasn't true.

But it wasn't just urine she smelled — there was a musty odor as well, as if the air in the dark chamber was old and stale.

Then she heard a moan, so faint that for a second she wasn't certain she'd heard it at all. Then it came again, and Kelly had to fight the urge to cry out herself, knowing that with the tape over her mouth the attempt would only bring on another attack of panic. So instead of crying out, she forced a long, low sound — almost a hum — from her nostrils.

Then she listened.

And heard nothing.

She hummed again, but again there was no response. Yet even in the silence that filled the darkness, she knew she hadn't imagined it. She'd heard something — some sound — in the darkness.

But why was it silent now?

The silence itself became frightening as she imagined what might be lurking there in the darkness, creeping closer to her.

She closed her eyes, telling herself that by not seeing the darkness, it didn't exist.

Light!

She would imagine light!

She focused her mind, thinking of the chandelier that hung over the dining room table at home, its crystals refracting the light into a brilliant rainbow of color that splashed into every corner of the room.

Slowly, deep in her mind, a pinpoint of light appeared, then began to expand until it seemed she was no longer in the dark chamber, but in the center of a great pool of light.

But then, as something scuttled over her legs, the light vanished and she was plunged back into darkness. And with the disappearance of light, her hope also began to fade away.

No one — not even herself — knew where she was.

No one — not even herself — knew what had happened to her.

Slowly, the truth dawned on her.

She was going to die.

Die alone.

Die in the darkness.

Exhausted, Kelly Conroe finally gave in to the terror and sobbed.

But no one heard her. No one, at least, who cared.

The news of Kelly Conroe's disappearance spread through Granite Falls like a virus, leaping from one house to another, transmitted partly over the telephone wires, but also by people — adults and teenagers alike — who darted out of their houses to dash next door, or down the block, or even a street or two away to tell their friends what had happened. As with all stories that spread through small towns, the facts, what few there were, were soon tainted with speculation, rumor, and gossip. The simple truth — that Kelly Conroe was late coming home and that her parents had so far been unable to locate her — was far too prosaic to be passed along unadorned. So with each telling of the tale, each iteration of the facts as the teller had heard them, a detail was expanded upon, a speculation added, an interpretation mixed in.

"She just vanished, right after school!" Sarah Balfour's mother hadn't intentionally misinterpreted her daughter's report that Kelly had ignored her invitation to go for a Coke after song-leading practice. It was simply that Sarah was involved with so many things that Elaine Balfour had long ago come to think of "after school" as beginning at four-thirty or five, rather than ten past three.

"She didn't speak to anyone all day!" Marge Carson, who heard the story from Elaine Balfour, had no idea that it was only at song-leading practice that Kelly's friends had noticed she'd appeared distracted. She had no idea that Kelly had gone to song-leading practice at all.

"Everyone says Matt Moore had something to do with it!" That had started with Heather Pullman, who overheard her father's side of the conversation when Gerry Conroe finally made good on his threat to call the police chief. "Mr.

Conroe thinks Matt must have done something to her," she'd whispered to Tiffany Vail, a chill running through her as she imagined what "something" might be. She hung up when she felt her father's eyes on her, but it was too late.

"You know you're never to repeat anything you hear me talking about," he told her as he unplugged her telephone.

Though it was well-intended, Dan Pullman's suspension of his daughter's telephone privileges accomplished nothing, for the speculation on Matt Moore's role in Kelly's disappearance had begun even before Tiffany Vail passed it on to Sarah Balfour and all the rest of the song-leaders.

Gossip and the grapevine acted as prosecutor and jury, and as the story spread, the assumption that Matt Moore was involved pervaded everything.

"Everyone knows she broke up with him."

"Everyone knows he was trying to get her back."

"Everyone knows he killed his stepfather."

Everyone knows . . . everyone knows . . . everyone knows . . .

An hour after Nancy Conroe began looking for Kelly, the disease had infected nearly everyone in Granite Falls, and nearly everyone agreed on what had happened.

Kelly Conroe had tried to break up with Matt Moore, and Matt refused to accept it. So after school he followed her, and when she refused even to speak to him, he'd "done something" to her.

No one would say he "killed" her, rather than

"done something" to Kelly, but it didn't matter. Everybody knew exactly what everybody else meant.

"Well, I don't believe it," Becky Adams announced. She'd been surprised when Eric Holmes came to the back door ten minutes earlier. Even though the Holmes family had lived next door for most of her life, and she and Eric grew up together, they'd never been friends.

Not like Matt and Kelly were friends, anyway.

Becky's mother constantly speculated on how wonderful it would be if she eventually married the boy next door, but Becky knew it was never going to happen; Eric had always been part of a group that barely acknowledged her existence. So when he knocked at the back door, she'd been immediately suspicious, and as she listened to his version of Kelly's disappearance, her suspicion coagulated into anger. "I don't care what anybody says. Matt wouldn't hurt Kelly. He wouldn't hurt anybody!"

Eric rolled his eyes scornfully. "I was there the day he killed his dad, Becky!"

"Nobody even knows if he killed Mr. Hapgood," Becky flared. "They don't even know if it was Matt's gun."

"I'm telling you, I know what happened!" Eric shot back. "And what about his grandma?"

Becky's expression hardened. "Nobody knows what happened to Mrs. Moore, so why are you and your friends saying Matt had something to do with it?"

"If he didn't have anything to do with anything, how come he's acting so weird?"

Becky's fury grew. "How would you be acting if all your friends were treating you the way you're treating Matt? I thought you were supposed to be his best friend! I thought —" Before she could finish, Pete Arenson pushed through the hedge that separated the Adams backyard from Eric's. "What do *you* want?" she demanded. "If you're going to start talking about Matt, I don't want to hear it."

Pete barely even glanced at her. "You ready?" he asked Eric.

"Ready for what?" Becky asked.

"Pete and I are going to look for Kelly," Eric told her.

Becky stared at the two boys she had known all her life and wondered why she'd ever wanted to be part of their crowd. But she knew why: because Matt was part of it. But not anymore. All the people Matt thought were his friends had turned their backs on him.

Suddenly Becky no longer wanted to be part of that group. "Jerks," she said, not aware that she was speaking out loud.

"What?" Eric said. "What did you say?"

Becky flushed with embarrassment, but it quickly vanished. "I said you're both jerks," she repeated. "I thought you were Matt's friends, but you're not. If you were really his friends, you'd know he couldn't have done any of the things you think he did. He couldn't have hurt his dad or his grandmother, and there's no way he could have done anything to Kelly!"

Eric Holmes stared balefully at Becky. "We may be jerks," he said, "but at least we're not stupid." A moment later he and Pete Arneson were gone, disappearing into the night.

Chapter 19

"So where do you think he took her?" Eric Holmes asked as Pete Arneson revved the engine of his BMW. Though the car had been new the year before Pete was born, he loved it as much as if it had come off the assembly line last week, and for a moment, listening to the purr of the motor, he ignored Eric's question.

"Do you hear a valve clattering?" he asked, cocking his head as he concentrated on the car's rumble.

"How would I know what a valve sounds like? I'm gonna be a lawyer, not a mechanic. And if we're going to go look for Kelly, let's do it, okay?" As Pete pulled away from the curb, Eric repeated the question he'd asked a moment ago. This time Pete grinned at him, the pale glow of the halogen street lamps making the twisting of his lips look almost cruel.

"Same place he took his grandmother."

"They haven't even found his grandmother," Eric reminded his friend, but Pete shrugged the question off.

"They found her slippers, didn't they? Just because they didn't find her body doesn't mean anything — all they did was look in the stream and under the falls. Matt could have buried her out there, and the grave would be so covered with leaves nobody'd ever notice it."

Eric wasn't so sure. "I heard they took dogs out there. If the dogs didn't find anything, how come you're so sure —"

"Look, do you want to do this, or not? Because if you don't, I can take you back to your house and go by myself."

And then tell everyone I chickened out, Eric thought. "I didn't say I wouldn't go," he protested. "All I said was no one really knows what happened to Mrs. Moore."

Pete shot him a look. "Well, we sure know what happened to Mr. Hapgood, don't we?" As they passed the last of the streetlights, the night seemed to close around the car, and Eric unconsciously shrank back into the seat, a movement Pete caught out of the corner of his eye. "Going to chicken out?" he mocked.

"Just drive, okay? We'll see who chickens out when we get there."

Pete pressed hard on the accelerator. The car shot forward, but seconds later he had to brake sharply as they came to the mouth of the narrow dirt road that led to a small parking area the Hapgoods had carved out of the woods two generations earlier. Slowing the car to a crawl, Pete negotiated the ruts and potholes in the worn surface until he came to the deserted parking area at the trailhead of the path that led to the waterfall.

Pete shut the engine and headlights off, but as

the comforting hum of the engine died away and the silence and darkness of the night closed around them, neither boy spoke nor made a move to leave the car. Eric finally broke the silence. "So what's your plan?" he asked. "Are we just going to sit here all night?"

Spurred as much by the mocking tone as by the words, Pete Arneson jerked on the handle and pushed his door open. "Maybe you are, but I'm going to take a look around."

Eric hesitated, then he got out of the car too.

For a moment neither boy could see anything, but as their eyes adjusted to the darkness, the moonlight filtering through the branches provided just enough illumination for them to make out the trail and the trees on either side of it. "You coming?" Pete asked as he started down the trail.

As Pete moved quickly toward the path, Eric just as quickly considered his choices. He could stay by himself in the parking lot, but if he did, he knew that by tomorrow afternoon Pete would tell everyone they knew that he lost his nerve and he'd never live it down. Besides, what if Kelly was out here? What if something actually had happened to her?

What if someone had killed her? And what if that someone was still out here?

The idea of being alone in the silence and the darkness was suddenly more frightening than going with Pete, and Eric hurried after his friend before the other boy vanished completely into the darkness.

They moved quickly along the path, Pete leading the way. They had walked it hundreds of times before, but tonight it seemed longer, and they found themselves pausing every few yards.

Pausing to peer into the darkness around them.

Pausing to listen to the sounds of the night.

But they could see nothing, and all they could hear was the steadily growing roar of the waterfall that lay a quarter of a mile ahead.

A roar that would grow louder and louder, masking every other sound.

Though neither of them spoke, the same thoughts came to both of them:

What if there's someone else out here?

What if it's not Kelly? What if it's someone else, and he's right beside us?

Following us.

Watching us.

Pete began moving faster, and Eric matched his pace. The path seemed to grow narrower, the forest denser.

A faint sound stopped Pete dead in his tracks, and Eric almost bumped into him. "What is it?" he whispered, his words sounding louder than they were. "Why are we stopping?"

"Will you shut up?" Pete whispered back. "I thought I heard something!"

A chill passed through Eric, and he scanned the darkness, straining to pierce the night.

But he could see nothing.

They stood still, their bodies as tense as those of animals sensing danger, but all they could hear was the roar of the waterfall, and they slowly relaxed. Pete continued along the path, Eric following, but as the trail opened onto the broad shelf of rock that edged the pool, he stopped again, reaching back to stop Eric as well.

Pete pressed his forefinger to his lips, and as Eric moved closer, Pete pointed toward the waterfall.

At first Eric saw nothing, but then, almost invisible in the darkness, he barely was able to make out a shadowy figure.

Someone was standing on the ledge about forty yards away.

Standing on the ledge, and peering into the pool.

Every instinct in Eric Holmes told him to turn around and slip back into the protective darkness, then run back to the safety of the car. But as he started to back away, Pete Arneson moved through the grove of trees that edged the rocky shelf.

Against his own will, Eric found himself following.

They moved closer, until they were only twenty feet from the figure that was now silhouetted against the cascading waterfall. And then, over the roar of the falls, they heard a voice.

"Kelly? Kelllly . . ."

It was a voice they both recognized.

Matt Moore.

Pete and Eric looked at each other. Again Eric's instincts told him to go back to the car, to go back to town, to tell someone what they'd seen — their parents, or even the police. But before he could say anything, Pete spoke up.

"What did you do with her, Matt?" Matt spun around, and Pete glared balefully at him in the darkness. "What did you do with Kelly?"

Matt remained frozen where he was, staring at the two figures that had suddenly materialized out of the darkness. But as Pete took a step toward him, he finally recovered. "I didn't do anything to her," he said. "I'm looking for her."

"You're lying," Pete Arneson said. Keeping his eyes on Matt, he gestured to Eric. "Come on. Let's make him tell us what he did with her."

Sensing what was about to happen, Matt darted toward the trail that would lead him home. Pete, anticipating him, countered by moving quickly in the same direction and tackling him. Matt grunted as he went sprawling facedown on the rocky shelf, the cheek around his left eye slamming painfully against the granite. In an instant Pete was on top of him, rolling him over, pinning his arms down.

"Where is she?" he screamed, his face contorted with rage as he glowered down at the boy who had been his best friend only a few days ago. "What did you do to her? I swear to God, you tell me what you did with Kelly, or I'll kill you!"

The look in Pete's eyes — the cold fury that told him Pete meant what he'd said — galvanized Matt. As adrenaline shot through his system, he jerked his arm free of Pete's grip, balled his fists and slammed it into the other boy's face.

Pete bellowed in surprise, then howled in pain as blood spurted from his smashed nose. Instinctively

311

clutching at his face with both hands, he lost his balance, and Matt, both arms free now, pushed him aside and scrambled to his feet. "I didn't do anything to her," he shouted down at Pete, who was cowering on his knees as he tried to stanch the flow of blood streaming down his face and chest. "I was just looking for her!"

Leaving Eric Holmes to take care of Pete Arneson, Matt turned and fled into the woods.

Though the window was tightly closed, the chill of the night outside had crept into the room, binding itself around Joan like an icy sheet. But it wasn't just the cold that gripped her now. She was aching from the remembered pain of that terrible day more than two decades ago when she had sat before this same mirror as her sister wrapped their mother's fur around her shoulders then stood by and watched as her mother beat her. The memory of the beating, buried for so long, was as fresh now as if it happened yesterday.

Joan gazed into the mirror, her finger tracing the curve of her cheekbone where a tiny scar was still barely visible. A scar whose source had until to-night been buried so deep that she hadn't wondered about it for years.

"You fell," Cynthia told her when she was in high school and self-conscious about the scar, though no one else appeared to notice it. "Don't you remember? You were riding your tricycle, and fell off."

But that wasn't true, and now, staring into the

mirror, she saw the face of the little girl she'd once been. But it wasn't the face Cynthia had created, covering her skin with pale makeup and bright rouge.

Now she saw the face her mother had created, saw not only the scar, but the terrible purple bruise that had formed around the cut.

Saw the battered, swollen tissue that had kept her hidden in the house for days, days that, until this moment, she had forgotten about.

What had happened during those days when the swelling and the bruises kept her from leaving the house?

What had caused the pain that now — years later — was throbbing in her arms and legs, making her feel as if she'd been tied up for hours?

Hours, or even days?

Was it possible? Could her mother have done such a thing? No! No, of course not! She'd been just a little girl!

Another question rose in her mind: What did she tell her friends when her mother finally let her outside again? Did she tell them she was sick? Or had the story of the tricycle already been invented?

As Joan gazed into the mirror — gazed with the strange, shocked detachment of a bystander at the scene of a terrible accident — tears began to stream down the face of the child she had once been.

Tears she could not remember having shed.

Then, through the blur of the tears, she saw her sister and her mother standing behind her, close together. Cynthia's arm was curled protectively around Emily's waist. They were looking at each other, smiling at each other, and even in the mirror Joan could see that they shared some kind of secret, one that she was not a part of.

As she watched, first her sister and then her mother turned to look at her and laugh.

The laughter tore at her, and Joan whirled around to face them.

There was no one there; the room was as empty as when she'd come into it. For a few seconds she felt disoriented, but then her mind slowly cleared. Of course they weren't there: Cynthia was dead, and her mother had vanished.

It had all been an illusion. But an illusion so real that she could still feel the pain she must have felt as a child, still recoil from the cruel laughter she had heard in the empty room. "Why?" she whispered, though there was no one there to hear her. Rising from the vanity, she gazed at the portrait of Cynthia. "Why didn't you tell her the truth?" she asked, her voice strangling on the pain of the memory that had only tonight emerged from the depths of her subconscious, escaping from the grave where she had kept it buried for so many years. "Why did you let her do that to me?"

Her sister stared coldly back at her.

"I'm glad you're dead," Joan whispered. "I'm glad you're dead, and I hope you're burning in hell."

The sound of the back door slamming jerked Joan out of her reverie, and she turned her back on

314

the image of her sister. But as she left Cynthia's room, she heard the whispered sound of her sister's voice.

"What if I'm not dead, Joan? What if I'm alive? What if I'm as alive as you are?"

"Matt?" Joan called as she hurried down the stairs. "Matt, is that you? Where have you —" The words died abruptly on her lips when she saw her son standing in the door to the kitchen. For a moment she felt what seemed like a wave of déjà vu break over her, but then she realized that it wasn't déjà vu at all — although Matt's clothes were once again smeared with blood, this time his left eye was badly swollen and starting to turn an ugly purplish color. "Dear God," she breathed, steering him into the kitchen. "What happened? Who did this to you?"

"It's not that bad," Matt replied. "It's no big deal — just a little blood. I've been hurt a lot worse at football practice."

Joan had wet a dishcloth — the closest thing available — and begun to gently wipe the blood from his face. "For heaven's sake," she said, "don't try to tell me you were at practice."

"I was looking for Kelly."

"Kelly?" Joan echoed.

"I thought I knew where she might be," Matt went on, wincing as his mother touched his bruised eye. "I figured she might have gone down by the falls — that's where we always go when we just want to talk about something. So I thought if

315

something was wrong, maybe that's where she went."

"But surely Kelly didn't —"

"I didn't find her. But Pete and Eric found me."

"Pete Arneson and Eric Holmes?"

Matt jerked his head away as the dishcloth touched a small cut below his eye. "They said they were looking for Kelly too."

When the phone buzzed, Joan almost dropped the dishcloth, and when it sounded again, she handed the dishcloth to Matt. "Rinse it out, wrap it around some ice, and —"

"— hold it against my eye," Matt finished for her as she picked up the phone. "It's not like I've never had a black eye before."

"Yes, he's here," he heard his mother say. She was silent for a moment, then: "I really don't understand why —" Another pause, and then, "Of course he'll be here. We both will." She hung up as Matt was opening the freezer to get some ice cubes. "That was Dan Pullman," she said, and there was something in her voice that made Matt turn to look at her. The color had drained from her face, and her eyes seemed to bore into him. "He wants to talk to you."

A pair of headlights swept across the kitchen window. A moment later Joan opened the back door and the chief of police stepped into the mud room. "Matt's still here?" he asked without preamble.

"Of course he is," Joan replied, her voice cold.

"Aside from the fact that you called only two minutes ago, where would he go?"

The color rose in Pullman's cheeks, but when he spoke, there was no hint of anger in his voice. "Cell phone. I was only a quarter of a mile away when I called." His eyes shifted to Matt, who was still standing at the sink, the dishcloth and ice pressed to his left eye. "You get in a fight tonight?" he asked.

For a moment Matt said nothing, but then he lowered the dishcloth to reveal the cut and the bruise. "I didn't exactly get it in the fight," he said. "Pete tackled me, and my face hit the ground hard when I went down. And I'll bet he's hurting a lot more than I am. Did I break his nose?"

Joan's eyes widened in shock. "Matt!" she gasped. "You didn't tell me —"

Matt wheeled on his mother. "What was I supposed to do?" he demanded. "Just lie there and let him beat the shit out of me?"

Joan recoiled from her son's anger, her eyes flicking toward Dan Pullman, who seemed to be studying Matt carefully. "Matt! Don't talk like —"

Pullman didn't let her finish. "Why don't you just try to tell me what happened?" he said. As Matt hesitated, glancing at his mother as if seeking her permission to speak, he sighed heavily. It seemed as if everything in Granite Falls had changed. Up until a few days ago, he thought he had the perfect job — for the most part, all he'd ever been called upon to do was supervise a couple of deputies whose main duty was to keep tourists

317

from speeding through town. Now he had one man dead, two people missing, and no idea of what might be going on, except that he'd known everyone involved almost all his life. As Matt recounted what had happened, Pullman wondered if he shouldn't try to get some help up from Manchester tomorrow. At least a stranger would be able to look at everything objectively.

"Pete's a lot bigger than I am," Matt finished. "I got lucky, or he would have really pounded me." His jaw tightened and his eyes narrowed. "He said he was going to kill me." He spoke the last words so softly they were almost inaudible, but they weren't lost on Pullman.

"Why would he want to kill you, Matt?" the chief asked, his voice reflecting doubt that Pete Arneson would say such a thing. Pullman's eyes held Matt's gaze, and he hoped that when the boy answered — if he answered — his expression might reveal the truth of his words.

A curtain seemed to drop behind Matt's eyes, and when he spoke, his voice was flat. "He said if I didn't tell him what I did with Kelly Conroe, he was going to kill me."

Pullman's gaze didn't waver. "That's not what the Arneson boy says," he countered, his frustration evident. "He says you jumped him. And he says he's going to press charges."

Matt's eyes widened. "Why would Pete say that? I was just looking for Kelly!"

"Why would you be looking for her out there at this time of night?" Pullman asked.

"Because that's where we always went," Matt began, but his mother didn't let him finish.

"Don't say anything else, Matt." Her eyes flashing with anger, she turned on Dan Pullman. "How can you think Pete's telling the truth? He's six inches taller than Matt, and must weigh fifty pounds more than he does. And Eric Holmes was with him, wasn't he?" When Dan didn't answer immediately, she repeated her question, her voice lashed like a whip. "Wasn't he?"

"Yes, but —"

"Two of them! There were two of them, and they're both bigger than Matt. And they claim he jumped them? Do you think Matt's an idiot? The way his friends — or rather, the people who were supposed to be his friends — have been treating him, the only thing that makes any sense is what Matt already told you." She reached for the phone. "I'm calling Trip Wainwright. If you have any more questions you want Matt to answer, I want Trip to be here."

"Now, just hold on, Joan," Pullman said. "If Matt's telling the truth —"

"The truth? Nobody in this whole town cares about the truth anymore! All they care about is ruining my son's life. Well, that's not going to happen, Dan! I'm not going to let it happen!" Furiously, Joan punched the buttons on the phone, and as Dan listened to her talking to the lawyer, he closed the tattered book in which he'd been taking notes.

The truth, he knew, would come out sooner or

later, and he wasn't about to have whatever case might develop ruined by making Matt answer questions without his lawyer present.

A heavy silence fell over the house as the three of them waited for Trip Wainwright's arrival.

Chapter 20

Though Joan Hapgood hadn't told Trip Wainwright what had brought Dan Pullman to her house that evening, the strain in her voice when she called him on the phone told him how worried she was, and the moment she opened the back door to let him into the kitchen, he could sense the tension. But it wasn't until he saw the blood on Matt's clothes that his lawyer's instincts went onto full alert.

"Did you call Alan Henderson?" he asked Joan, deliberately not asking what had happened, lest Matt say something he'd rather Dan Pullman not hear.

"It's no big deal," Matt protested before his mother could reply. "It's not my blood anyway. It's Pete Arneson's."

Wainwright sat down at the kitchen table and listened in silence as first Joan and then Pullman recounted what they knew. When both of them were finished, the lawyer turned to Matt, who, among the four of them, had remained standing. "Anything you want to add?" he asked.

Matt shook his head. "It's like I said — I was looking for Kelly, and Pete and Eric jumped me."

The lawyer shifted his attention back to

Pullman. "From what I've heard so far, it sounds to me like you should be taking a complaint from Matt, not questioning him."

The police chief's eyes narrowed. "The Arneson kid says —"

"I don't really care what Pete Arneson said," Wainwright cut in, certain that if Pullman had any intention of arresting Matt, he already would have done it. "Nor do I care if Eric Holmes swears to it. Given what's been going on in this town the last few days, I've been half expecting someone to accuse Matt of kidnapping the Lindbergh baby, for Christ's sake! And you know as well as I do that both Eric and Pete are a lot bigger than Matt. So what's this really all about?"

The frustration that had been brewing inside Pullman suddenly boiled. "It's about me trying to do my job, Trip. Just like you're trying to do yours. Maybe you ought to look at this whole mess from my point of view for a change. Matt's stepfather is dead, his grandmother is missing, and now his girlfriend is missing too. What the hell am I supposed to think? What's *anyone* supposed to think?"

Matt was about to protest, but the attorney held up a hand to stop him. "So far there's nothing more than gossip to indicate that Bill's death was anything other than an accident, unless you've got something you haven't told me or anybody else about yet."

He paused just long enough for Pullman to shake his head.

"Can we agree that it's not fair to accuse anyone

of doing anything to Emily Moore until you've found her?"

He paused again, extracting another nod from Pullman. "And now Kelly Conroe is missing?"

Once more Dan Pullman nodded.

When Wainwright resumed speaking, his voice had turned hostile. "How long has she been missing, Dan?"

Pullman could see what was coming. His jaw tightened. "A couple of hours," he said, keeping his voice flat.

"A couple of hours," Wainwright repeated. "She's two hours late coming home from school, and you're out searching for her? Would you say that's standard operating procedure for your office?"

Pullman's face reddened. "Of course it is," he retorted. "I take it very seriously when one of our kids is missing."

"Especially if she happens to be the daughter of the publisher of the newspaper." He waited for Pullman to rise to the bait, which the police chief quickly did.

"That has nothing to do with it!"

"Then why did you tell Connie and Jim Delaney that you couldn't do a thing for at least twenty-four hours when Valerie took off last spring?"

"That was different," Pullman began. "Valerie wasn't —"

"Valerie Delaney was exactly the same age as Kelly Conroe, Dan," Wainwright cut in coldly. "When she took off, she gave Connie and Jim the worst night of their lives. And you didn't get involved. In fact, unless I'm completely mistaken, you told them the next day that if it ever happened again, they shouldn't waste your time until she'd been gone at least twenty-four hours. Isn't that right?"

A vein throbbed in Pullman's forehead, and for a second he was tempted to deny it. But he couldn't bring himself to do it. "Maybe I shouldn't have said that," he admitted.

"Or maybe you should have said exactly the same thing to Gerry Conroe when he called you tonight." When Pullman made no reply, Wainwright pressed his advantage. "Then I think we're done here, aren't we? Unless Matt wants to file a complaint against Pete Arneson?" Matt shook his head, and Wainwright stood up. "Then perhaps I can see you out."

Signaling Joan and Matt to stay where they were, Wainwright walked out to Pullman's car with the police chief. "You want to tell me what's going on, Dan?" he asked as Pullman opened the driver's door and got in.

"What's going on is that we've got one person dead, and two other people missing, Trip. And given where we found Emily Moore's slippers, I'd sure like to know the real reason Matt was 'looking' for Kelly down by the waterfall." He gave just enough emphasis to the word "looking" to let Wainwright know that he wasn't accepting Matt's story at face value.

Wainwright's expression remained bland. "Did

324

you ask the Arneson and Holmes boys why they went down there?"

"They said they were looking for Kelly too."

"So Matt having gone there is sinister, but the fact that two other boys — two big, strong boys who could easily have raped, killed, and disposed of a girl Kelly's size — isn't even questioned? I find that a little peculiar, Dan, especially given that they weren't happy about Matt showing up."

"They said Matt started the fight," Pullman insisted again, but the lawyer only snorted dismissively.

"Matt's story makes a lot more sense than what you've told me Eric and Pete said, and you know it, Dan. Unless you know something you're not telling me, I'd say you came over here on a fishing expedition. So consider yourself instructed that neither you nor anyone else in your department is to talk to Matt without me being present."

Pullman's lips compressed into an angry line, but he nodded. "But if Kelly Conroe doesn't show up within twenty-four hours, you can plan on hearing from me." His eyes moved from the lawyer to the kitchen window, where both of them could see Matt standing by the counter, where they'd left him. "I'm going to want every minute of that kid's time accounted for. Every single minute."

Wainwright waited until Pullman's car disappeared down the driveway, then went back into the kitchen.

"Is he gone?" Joan asked, the tension draining out of her. But when he answered her, she felt her nerves start to tingle again.

"He's gone for now," Trip Wainwright said, wishing he could spare them from what he had to say. "But he'll be back. If Kelly Conroe isn't found, believe me, he's going to be back, and he'll have a lot more questions." The lawyer turned his attention on Matt. "He'll want to know everything you did this afternoon, minute by minute. And if by some chance something actually *has* happened to Kelly, and she's found anywhere near that waterfall, you'll need a lot better explanation of why you were there tonight than 'it's where we always went.' In fact, that particular explanation might very well work against you, rather than for you."

Matt sat down at the table, his mother standing behind him now, her hands on his shoulders. She squeezed them reassuringly, and he heard her telling Wainwright that he couldn't possibly have done anything to Kelly.

But as she spoke, he remembered the strange odor that filled his nostrils in the shed behind the garage.

Remembered the voice of his aunt, whispering to him.

Remembered the hour that had somehow vanished out of the afternoon when he'd severed the buck's head.

What had happened during that hour? What had he done?

As if in answer to his unspoken question, he again recalled his aunt's voice: *"Do what you want to do. . . . Do what you need to do. . . ."*

Matthew Moore shivered with a chill that shook his soul.

Dan Pullman was still fuming as he drove down the driveway toward the gates at the end of the Hapgood driveway. Who the hell did Trip Wainwright think he was, talking to him like he didn't know how to do his own job? But as he slowed to a stop at the gates before turning back toward town, his sense of fairness broke through the wall of anger he'd built up to defend himself from the lawyer's tongue-lashing. Alone in the privacy of his car, without Trip glaring at him, he knew that Trip was right. A few months ago, when Valerie Delaney had disappeared overnight and there was no indication of foul play, he had indeed refused to take any serious action until the following morning, by which time Valerie had indeed come back.

Taking a deep breath, Dan turned in the opposite direction from the town and drove the additional half mile that took him to the Conroes' large brick Tudor house. As he pulled into the driveway he almost changed his mind — he could just as easily give Gerry a call from home as speak to him directly. But when the front door opened and he saw Nancy Conroe framed in the bright light of the entry hall, he knew it was too late to change his mind. He got out of the car, slammed the door, and started toward the house. He could see the look of disappointment that clouded Nancy's expression as she saw that he hadn't brought her daughter home. Then, as he stepped up onto the porch, a flame of panic ignited in her eyes and she reflexively shrank from him, as if to shield herself from the horrible thought that had occurred to her.

"We haven't found her," Dan said quickly.

Gerry Conroe appeared behind his wife, laying his hands on her shoulders as if to steady her. "What about Matt Moore?" he asked. "Have you talked to him?"

"I talked to a lot of people," Pullman countered. "And I'll probably be talking to a lot more, Gerry. But not before tomorrow."

Gerry Conroe's eyes smoldered. "What the hell are you saying, Pullman?" he demanded, his use of the chief's last name betraying his anger as clearly as the tightness of his voice.

Pullman braced himself. "I'm telling you that I've looked around, and I've talked to a few people, and I'll have Tony keep an eye out while he's on patrol tonight. But for now, that's all I can do."

"I don't want to hear that, Dan," Gerry Conroe replied, his voice low. "I want to hear you say you're going to find my daughter!"

"Look, Gerry," Pullman said, doing his best to keep his fraying temper in check, "I know how you feel, but —"

"But nothing," Conroe interrupted again. "A teenage girl is missing, and you're not doing anything about it?"

"Gerry, let him finish," Nancy Conroe said, sensing that her husband's temper was about to get the best of him.

Choosing his words carefully, Pullman repeated much of what he'd just heard from Trip Wainwright. "I know this isn't what you want to hear, Gerry," he finished, "but I can't accuse Matt Moore — or anyone else, for that matter — of having done anything to Kelly. Not yet."

Conroe's eyes, cold with fury, bored into the policeman.

Pullman, with a tight grip on his own anger, went on: "Unless you've got something a lot stronger than your own suspicions about Matt Moore to go on, you and Nancy are just going to have to wait until morning. You know as well as I do that in ninety percent of cases like this —"

"My daughter isn't ninety percent of anything, Pullman," Conroe snapped. "You're acting like she's the same kind of trash as Valerie Delaney. Everybody knew she was out getting laid, but my daughter isn't a slut. She'd never do anything like that. The only mistake she ever made was getting involved with Matthew Moore."

"Gerry, please calm down," Nancy pleaded once more, but Gerry shook her words off as easily as he brushed her hand away from his arm.

"I'm telling you, Pullman," Conroe insisted, "there's something wrong with that boy! There's something way wrong with him, and I intend to find out what it is. No one knows who his father is, no one knows where he came from. And I always say —"

Pullman had finally had enough. "Everyone in town knows what you always say, Conroe — God knows you say it often enough. But I'm not going after Matt Moore or anyone else just because I don't know who his father was." Conroe started to interrupt, but Pullman raised a hand as if to fend off his words before he could utter them. "I'm just trying to do my job."

"You won't have your job long enough to give anyone special treatment by the time I get through with you," Conroe warned.

Dan Pullman's voice dropped dangerously low. "Don't threaten me, Gerry," he warned. "Right now, I don't give a damn what you think you can do to me. You find anything that implicates Matt Moore in whatever might have happened to your daughter — assuming she didn't just get as sick of your snobbery as I am and just take off — and I'll do something about it. But until then, don't tell me how to do my job, and don't threaten me with what you think you can do with your two-bit gossip sheet." Without waiting for a reply, Pullman wheeled around, strode to his car, and drove away into the night.

"You want to know about Matt Moore?" Gerry Conroe whispered as he watched the departing car. "I'll find out everything there is to know about him!" Even as the car vanished, carrying the object of his wrath with it, Conroe's fury continued to grow. "You'll see . . ."

Joan hadn't realized she'd been asleep until she heard the eleventh stroke of the clock in the library. Certainly she hadn't been sleeping deeply — both

330

her body and her mind felt as exhausted as when she turned off the lights downstairs before going up to bed an hour ago. Her eyes had fallen on the TV then, and more to put off going upstairs and facing what she knew would be a sleepless night than because she was interested, she flipped on the television and dropped onto the sofa. She'd tried to concentrate on the local news, but instead of hearing the anchorman, she kept thinking about what Trip Wainwright had said: "He's going to want to know everything you did this afternoon, minute by minute." She'd seen the look on Matt's face as the lawyer spoke, the flash of panic that had come into his eyes, and she knew then that there was something Matt hadn't told her.

Hadn't told her, or couldn't remember?

Now, with the news still droning in the background, she tried to convince herself that she'd imagined it, that there was no reason for Matt to hide anything from her. As the soft note of the clock's chime faded away, she told herself that it would be all right — if Kelly weren't home already, certainly she would turn up tomorrow. She reached for the phone, to call Nancy Conroe, but changed her mind before lifting the receiver. If Kelly had come home, she would have heard. Maybe not from Nancy or Gerry, but surely they would have called Dan Pullman and he would have called her. And the last thing she needed tonight was to hear Gerry accusing her son. Turning off the television and the lights, she went through the downstairs once more, checking the windows and doors.

331

Checking them against what?

In all the years she'd lived in this house, even though it stood alone, surrounded by the forest, she had never felt frightened. Yet tonight, as she moved from room to room, she felt uneasy.

Exposed.

As if there were someone — or something — lurking in the darkness outside.

Looking in at her.

Watching her.

There's nothing, she told herself. *There's never been anything out there to worry about, and there still isn't!* Yet as she turned off the last light, plunging the downstairs into a darkness that no eye could penetrate from outside the house, the uneasiness refused to leave her, and as she started up the stairs, it grew worse.

She paused at the top of the stairs, listening.

All around her the old house creaked and groaned.

Like it always does, she reminded herself. *Nothing's different tonight.*

Nothing!

She started toward her own room, but paused at the door to Cynthia's room. Though it was closed, she could almost feel a presence behind it.

Her sister's presence? Of course not — her sister was dead!

But she'd heard her sister's voice, heard her laughter.

Seen her.

Memories, she reminded herself. The voices and

laughter she'd heard were nothing but memories! *And it's not Cynthia's room! It's a guest room.* My *guest room!* But still, her hand closed on the door-knob, twisted it, and pushed the door open.

The room was empty.

Joan stood just outside the doorway, staring into the darkness at her dimly perceived sister's things. But they weren't her sister's, not anymore. Her sister was dead, and the dead couldn't own any-thing. But as her eyes fell on the shadowed portrait of Cynthia, she heard her sister's voice, as she had before.

"They're still mine, Joan. Everything you have is mine."

"No," Joan whispered, unaware that she'd spoken aloud.

"It is, Joan. You know it is. I'm taking it back, Joan. I'm taking it all back!"

"It's not true," Joan whispered, snapping on the light and scanning the clutter in the room.

The pictures on the walls.

The makeup on the vanity.

The small bottle of Nightshade, its powerful scent hanging in the air, even though its stopper was in place.

Junk, Joan told herself. It's nothing but junk, and tomorrow — first thing — she would rid herself of it all, empty the room of everything that reminded her of Cynthia, get it all out of the house.

Get it out, and burn it.

That was it — she'd take all her sister's things, along with all the terrible memories they were kindling, and burn them in the old incinerator behind the carriage house.

Her hand still gripping the doorknob, she scanned all her sister's belongings once more, but now she saw them in flames, the dresses burning on the hangers, smoke curling from the robe that lay across the chair next to the bed, the makeup on the vanity charring into gray ash. Just the vision of it in her imagination added to her resolve, and she pulled the door closed, turning her back on the room.

Ten minutes later she was in her bed, the lights off, the door closed, the window open to let in the cold autumn air and the sounds of the night. For a few minutes she lay awake, her eyes open in the darkness. The house creaked around her; she could hear the breeze soughing through the trees beyond the window. For a moment she felt the comfort she'd always felt in this bed, in this room, in this house.

She was almost able to convince herself that in a moment the door would open and Bill would come into the room, and a moment or two after that slip into the bed beside her and take her in his arms. Then reality crept in.

Nothing in her life would ever be as it had been only a week ago. Everything had changed — everything been shattered. And there was nothing she could do — nothing anyone could do — to put it back together again. Her eyes stung with tears, but she refused to give in to them.

Matt, she thought. *I still have Matt.* Forcing herself to turn away from her grief, her worries, and her fears, she conjured an image of her son — her perfect son who, no matter what anyone else thought or said, could never have done any of the things of which he was being accused. Not Matt.

Not her perfect Matt.

Clinging to the thoughts — and to the image — Joan finally drifted into sleep.

When she awoke again, the blackness of the night still surrounded her, but its sounds — the faint murmuring of birds and insects, the soft whisper of the wind, even the familiar creaking of the house — had fallen silent.

Then, as the silence seemed to close around her, she felt it.

She was no longer alone in the room.

But that wasn't possible — of course she was alone. Who would have come in? The doors and windows downstairs were all locked — she'd checked them herself.

But as she tried to reassure herself, her heart began to race. She could hear it throbbing in the silence, feel it pounding in her chest.

And whatever had crept into her room drew nearer.

Matt! It had to be Matt!

"Matt?" she whispered, her voice preternaturally loud in the silence. "Is that you?"

It was as the echo of her words died away that she heard it.

Laughter.

Cynthia's laughter, barely audible, but coming from everywhere.

Everywhere and nowhere.

She tried to reach for the light, but it was as if her limbs had frozen, and she lay helplessly where she was, unable to move.

The presence was close to her now. She could feel it all around her, reaching out to her, groping for her in the darkness.

Her skin tingled with anticipation, and her body grew moist with a sheen of sweat. Then she felt it.

The first caress was feather light, almost as if she hadn't been touched at all. But then she felt it again, this time like the touch of a lover's fingers, stroking her limbs, tracing strange patterns on her skin.

Hands were moving over her, exploring her.

"No," she whimpered. "Don't . . . please don't . . ."

She squirmed, writhing her body in an effort to escape the strange sensations, but no matter how she moved, the touch followed her. Followed her, and found her, reaching deeper and deeper within her.

"No," she whispered again. "No . . . oh, please, no . . ." But it was too late. Whatever had come for her, whatever had her in its embrace, held her firmly in its grip, and she knew there was no escape. Now a new blackness began closing around her, a blackness far deeper than that of the night.

The blackness of unconsciousness.

She reached out to it, embracing it. As she let

herself fall into its welcoming arms, she heard Cynthia whisper, *"Go to sleep. Just go to sleep. . . ."*

Her sister's voice echoing in her mind, Joan let herself fall away into the blackness.

Chapter 21

Not dead.

At first, the words seemed to have no meaning at all.

It was as if they'd been spoken in some foreign language and were emanating from some unseen place.

But then she heard them again, and this time they were more than mere sounds.

This time they had meaning:

Not dead!

The words resounded around her, but very slowly — so slowly that it took Kelly a moment to realize they weren't coming from some unseen place, were not echoing out of the darkness around her. Instead, they were coming from within her own mind, and as the last tendrils of sleep released her from their grip, their meaning sank in.

She had survived.

Her body was cold with a chill that seemed to penetrate to the marrow of her bones. Her muscles ached with a pain that had moved beyond the level of the unbearable into another realm; it was as if her mind had come to accept that the pain could be neither alleviated nor controlled, and so must therefore be ignored. Otherwise the agony in her joints, the numbness in her hands and feet, the spasms in her muscles, would render her completely helpless.

For a moment she lay perfectly still. The impenetrable darkness still cloaked her like a shroud, but while she'd slept — or fallen into the sanctuary of unconsciousness — it, like the pain, seemed to have lost some of its power. It no longer ignited panic within her, and when she opened her eyes she had no expectation — not even any hope — that she would find so much as a glimmer of light to reveal her surroundings.

But she was not dead.

How long had she been here?

She had no idea — it could have been hours; perhaps days.

Her stomach ached with hunger; her throat was parched with thirst. How long had she given herself up to the escape of sleep?

She'd had no dreams — none, anyway, that she could remember.

Nor had she rested, for her body felt exhausted, as if its battle against the pain had drained it of all its resources.

Yet she was still alive.

Her lungs were still functioning.

Her heart was still beating.

She could hear it in the silence of the darkness, thudding almost below the threshold of her hearing.

Feel it, throbbing inside her, driving blood through her tortured limbs, refusing to give in to the pain that all but paralyzed the rest of her body.

Then, through the throbbing, she heard something else.

Her mind suddenly went on full alert, ignoring the pain in her body, filtering out the sound of her heartbeat.

She held her breath to concentrate on the sound that had come from the darkness around her.

There!

There it was again! The same sound she'd thought she heard when she first found herself in the prison of darkness, but that had faded away as quickly as it had come, as if it hadn't been there at all. But this time, with her mind focused perfectly, she knew it was real.

And she knew it had come from somewhere behind her.

She was still lying on her side; her hands still bound behind her back.

Her knees were bent.

But she had to roll over.

She stretched her legs out, then twisted her body, ignoring the agony that shot through her muscles. For a moment she lay facedown, her neck twisted sharply to keep her face from pressing into the dirt beneath her. Then she twisted again and was lying on her other side. Her lungs heaved as her body struggled to replace the oxygen she'd expended in her efforts. As her breathing returned to normal, she heard it again. But this time the sounds formed a word, then another word.

"Help . . . help me . . ."

The words were uttered in a voice so soft — so weak — that it seemed as if the darkness itself had whispered them. But then Kelly heard them again: ". . . help me . . . please . . ."

A sound reflexively formed in Kelly's throat, but as before was abruptly blocked by the tape over her mouth. This time, though, she didn't fall victim to the panic that had overcome her the last time her scream had been strangled.

Calming herself, she eased the pressure through her nostrils.

She wasn't alone! Somewhere in the darkness — somewhere close by — there was someone else.

Someone who was alive, and awake, and able to talk.

Forcing herself to stay calm despite the excitement raging inside her, Kelly made the same humming sound as the last time she thought she heard something in the darkness. Even to her own ears, it sounded pitifully faint, pathetically weak.

She resisted the urge to repeat the sound, and instead listened for a response. At first there was nothing, but then she heard the voice again.

"Cynthia? Help me . . ."

As the sound was swallowed up by the darkness, Kelly had a feeling she'd heard that voice before. Her pulse quickening, she made her muffled humming moan again, and this time the answering words came almost immediately.

"Help me . . . help me, Cynthia. . . . Please help me. . . ."

Then Kelly knew: it was Matt's grandmother! It

341

was Emily Moore. So she wasn't dead! She hadn't wandered off somewhere and gotten lost! Matt's grandmother was here, only a few feet away, trapped in the same darkness as she. Kelly felt an overwhelming need to communicate with Mrs. Moore, to speak to her, to let her know that she was there. She knew she had to find a way to talk, to rid herself of the tape covering her mouth so she could call out.

Kelly twisted her body until she was again lying facedown, ignoring the pain that shot through her. But this time she didn't turn her face away from the hard-packed earth on which she lay. Instead she pressed the right side of her face into it, scraping the tape hard against the floor, trying to get a single corner of the tape to catch on something, to snag on some unevenness in the floor that would allow her to work it free.

But there was nothing. Nothing at all.

Matt could hear Kelly whispering to him. The words were indistinct at first, muffled by the darkness that kept him from seeing her. But though he couldn't quite distinguish the individual words, there was a yearning in her voice that stirred something deep inside him.

He felt a burning heat spread through his loins.

He reached out in the darkness, searching for her.

Her words became clearer:

"Matt? Where are you? I need you, Matt."

He called out to her, but his words were no more

than a whisper, and when he tried to call again, his breath caught in his throat, his words dying before they could be formed. He struggled to fill his lungs, but his chest felt bound by steel straps wound so tight his ribs ached and even the slightest movement sent stabs of pain shooting into his body. Then, as he reached out to her again, he felt her.

His fingers touched her flesh, and a new sensation flowed through his body.

"Yes," she whispered. "Oh, yes, Matt."

Though he still couldn't see her, he could feel all of her now, feel her body pressed against his, feel her fingers exploring him, feel his body responding to her touch.

She was whispering to him again, her lips pressed against his ear, the words nothing more than sounds that penetrated deep inside him. The pain in his chest eased, and his breathing grew stronger, more rhythmic.

He could feel her tongue now, flicking over his skin, tracing the curve of his ear, then creeping over his cheek. Her lips touched his eyes so gently that almost before he was aware it was happening, they had moved on to his lips.

Now he felt her tongue again, slipping through his lips, probing into his mouth. He breathed deeply, sucking the air from her lungs into his own and sending it back, his body writhing against hers as their breath mingled. Then his body felt as if it were burning; her touch traced patterns of fire on his skin, and just as he thought he could stand no more, her mouth left his and her tongue began moving down, flicking over his chest, moving down his stomach.

He moaned, partly from the pleasure of the sensations coursing through his body, but partly from a deep sense of guilt that was welling up within him. "No," he whispered, his body writhing as her lips and fingers caressed him. "No, Kelly, we shouldn't —" His words died as her lips closed and for a moment he wanted to give in, to let the wave of pleasure crash over him and carry him away. But he pulled away, his hands moving Kelly up, and then rolled over until he could feel his body pressing down on hers. Her arms wrapped around him, pulling him even closer. Her legs opened, then they too were wrapped around him. Her body began to twist and writhe beneath him, and again he felt himself sinking into a bottomless morass of pleasure.

Once again he was on the brink of giving in, of hurling himself into the joys of the body beneath him.

And again he veered away.

"No!" he whispered. "Don't! Don't do this!"

Her legs only wrapped tighter around him, and Matt felt the terrible straps tighten around his chest once again. But now he knew they weren't steel at all — they were flesh and bone, muscle and tendon. And they were twisting more and more tightly around him, until he knew that if he didn't escape in the next instant, he would never be able to free himself at all.

His hands closed around Kelly's neck, and his fingers began squeezing.

She continued to cling to him, but then his hands tightened around her throat, and something in her moaning changed. The ecstasy began to fade, and a new note crept in.

A note of fear.

He squeezed harder, and slowly the grip of her arms and legs around his torso loosened.

Now, through Kelly's moans, he heard another voice, a familiar voice, whispering to, him in the dark.

The familiar, musky scent filled his nostrils.

"That's right," his aunt voice whispered. *"Do it, Matt. Do what you need to do . . . do what you want to do. . . ."*

Kelly was thrashing against him now, but no longer writhing with passion and pleasure. She was twisting first one way, then another, her legs kicking, her arms lashing, as she struggled to escape his grasp.

He was killing Kelly!

He tried to let go, to release her from his grip, but another force — one far stronger than himself — seemed to have taken control of him.

"Do it, Matt," he heard his aunt whisper. *"Kill her, Matt. Kill her for me. . . ."*

He felt Kelly's fingernails dig into his back and rake through his flesh as she struggled to escape his grip, but his fingers only squeezed harder, crushing her throat until her terrified moans were cut off.

"*Yes!*" he heard his aunt cry out. "*Yes, Matt! Yes!*"

As the heat in Matt's loins built, his body trembled with the sensations that flowed through it. Then a howl erupted from his throat, the heat in his groin exploded, and for a few seconds — seconds that seemed like hours — he lay gasping and panting, his body shaking, his skin clammy with sweat.

And slowly — very slowly — the dream faded away.

It wasn't Kelly Conroe he was clutching, but his own pillow, knotted in his hands.

The impenetrable darkness in which he had reached out for Kelly had lifted, and he could see the window of his room.

A dream! It had only been a dream.

He lay still in the darkness, his breathing slowly returning to normal.

The sweat on his body slowly drying.

Yet even as he caught his breath, he knew it hadn't all been a dream, for there was still an unmistakable odor in the air. The heavy, musky scent of Nightshade, his aunt's perfume.

He reached out and switched on the light, and for a moment lay blinking in the glare. When his eyes adjusted to the light, he left his bed and went to the door of his closet. Pulling it open, he stared at his reflection in the mirror. His face was flushed, his hair damp.

And when he turned, peering over his shoulder to look at his back, he could see them.

The welts were bright red, and swollen.

Eight of them, four to the left of his spine, four to the right.

He shuddered, recalling the last moments of the dream, when his hands had closed inexorably around Kelly Conroe's neck, and her fingers — fighting against the death that already held her in its grip — slashed down his back.

So it hadn't been a dream, not all of it.

Part of it, at least, had really happened.

Chapter 22

The sky was incongruously bright the next morning. There should have been clouds — roiling thunderheads as black and heavy as his mood, Matt thought. He felt as if he hadn't slept at all; his body ached with a fatigue that ten minutes under the hot shower, followed by a minute of ice-cold needle spray, did not alleviate. Nor did the towel he'd heated over the radiator while he stood under the steaming water do anything to thaw the chill in his body, for the cold he was feeling came not so much from the exhaustion in his body as the confusion in his mind. The dream — the terrible dream in which he'd made love to Kelly Conroe, only to kill her a moment later — was still so fresh in his mind that he shuddered as he stood with the towel wrapped around him.

Though he wanted to go back to bed, to hide from whatever the day might bring, he knew it was impossible. To stay at home — to hide in his room — would only make things worse, and whatever reality awaited him, whatever accusations he would have to face at school, couldn't be worse than the dream that was still etched in his thoughts. Throwing the soggy towel in the hamper, he went back to his room, dressed, and headed toward the stairs. But as he came to the closed door to the guest room, he paused.

The dream came back to him, his aunt's voice whispering to him, urging him on as he tightened his hands around Kelly Conroe's throat. But his aunt was dead — he'd never even met her! So how could he know it was her voice he'd heard? He reached out, twisted the knob, and pushed the door open. In an instant his nostrils filled with the musky odor of her perfume, and strange images began tumbling through his mind.

His father, caught in the crosshairs of the telescopic sight of his rifle.

No! Not his father! *It was a deer he'd shot!*

His grandmother, moving down the hallway, calling out to someone who wasn't there, following her long-dead daughter down the stairs.

And Kelly, struggling to free herself from —

No! He tried to reject the images, to separate the memories from the dreams. But his mind was as tired as his body, and even as he tried to sort them out, they tumbled together again. He stood frozen in the doorway, unconsciously holding his breath, his eyes fixing on the portrait of his aunt, the scent of her perfume pervasive.

He could almost feel her now, and then more images leaped out of his subconscious.

She was in his room — in his bed — touching him, pressing her flesh close to his —

But it hadn't happened! He'd only been dreaming!

349

His mind reeled, and then, suddenly, he felt it again.

Her touch.

Her body against his.

Her voice, whispering in his ear.

Recoiling from the images he was certain could have come only from his dreams, from the scent of the perfume in the air, from the whispering in his ear — and most of all from the touch of the dead woman's flesh — he slammed the door shut and spun around.

And there she was — so close that he nearly lost his balance as an involuntary sound erupted from his throat.

"Matt? Matt, what is it?"

His mother! Not his aunt at all, but his mother. "I — I — you just surprised me," he stammered, flustered. "I was just —"

His mother's eyes shifted to the door he'd just slammed closed, and when she spoke, there was a harshness in her voice Matt had never heard before. "I'm going to get rid of all that stuff," she said. I'm going to get rid of it today."

"But what if Gram comes —" Matt began, but the words died on his lips as his mother's eyes narrowed.

"I don't care," she said, her eyes fixed on the closed door to the guest room. "It doesn't have anything to do with —" Matt waited for her to continue, but she didn't. Then, at last tearing her eyes from the door, she smiled at him and laid her hand on his cheek. "It doesn't have anything to do with you," she said, this time finishing what she'd started to say a moment before.

When he left for school an hour later, Matt's mood was as dark as when he'd gotten up. At the foot of the driveway, before turning toward town, he automatically glanced in the direction of the Conroes' house, to see if Kelly might be coming along the road to meet him. But then he remembered that she wouldn't.

If she had come home late last night, someone would have called to tell his mother. If not the Conroes, then Dan Pullman. The chill he'd felt when he got up that morning gripped him again, and the image of the dream rose in his mind. But this time there was something else: the gap in his memory of yesterday afternoon, when he thought he'd only walked over to Mr. Rudman's, left the stag's head, then come home.

In fact, he'd been gone an hour, for what should have been a fifteen minute errand.

Where had the other forty-five minutes gone?

And why had he looked for Kelly at the waterfall?

A few minutes later, standing across the street from the school with no memory of the walk that had brought him there, he felt a wave of panic.

Was it the same thing that had happened yesterday, when he lost forty-five minutes? But no — today he'd been walking along a route so familiar he could have done it in his sleep, and his mind was so occupied with other things that he'd simply paid no attention to where he was going.

As he crossed the street, Matt felt the other students' eyes on him. But it wasn't like yesterday, when they had watched him suspiciously, turning away when he looked directly at them. Today they were glaring at him, and he could see the anger in their eyes.

They think I did it, he thought. *They think I killed Kelly.*

Killed. The word, straight out of the dream, hung in his mind.

Again the images tumbled through his mind.

Which were real?

Which were dreams?

Worst of all, which were memories?

As he stepped through the doors of the school, Matt knew that wherever he turned, wherever he went, he would hear people whispering accusations that he knew, deep in his heart, he could no longer deny.

Call him back! Call him back now, before it's too late!

The urge was almost irresistible, but even as Joan thought it, she knew she wouldn't do it. Besides, it was already too late — Matt had disappeared around the bend in the driveway minutes ago, and by now was on his way to school.

Leaving her alone in the house.

Except she wasn't alone. She knew it now, knew it with a terrible certainty that could no longer be denied. The strange words she'd heard her sister speak before she'd gone to bed last night were echoing in her mind when she awoke this morning: *Everything you have is mine. . . . I'm taking it back. . . . I'm taking it all back.*

The sour taste of fear had remained strong in her mouth, and her mind felt bound up with a panic she hadn't at first been able to identify. Then the terrible memory of her sister's visitation came back to her, and the panic had grown.

She was losing her mind.

A paralysis came over her then, and she wanted nothing more than to sink back into sleep, to disappear into unconsciousness. But as she lay in bed, Joan knew that unconsciousness would be no escape.

It didn't happen, she told herself. It was impossible — it was only a dream!

Cynthia couldn't be in the house, couldn't have talked to her, certainly couldn't have touched her. But as she denied the possibility, she heard her sister's mocking laughter.

Laughter that followed her into the bathroom as she tried to wash the sour taste of fear from her mouth.

Laughter that taunted her as she made coffee and tried to eat a piece of toast in the kitchen.

Laughter that turned to victorious peals as Matt left for school.

Laughter that had kept her pinned against the window like a bug in a display case.

How had it happened? How had Cynthia escaped from her grave?

What did she want?

But Joan knew the answer to that. Cynthia had told her last night: *"Everything you have is mine. . . . I'm taking it back. . . . I'm taking it all back."*

The words lashing at her, Joan spun around as if to face her tormentor. "No!" she screamed. "It's not true! It's not!" And realizing she was screaming at an empty room, she fell suddenly silent, her eyes flicking over the kitchen like those of a trapped animal searching for its stalker.

But Cynthia's mocking laughter still hung in the air.

Joan fled from the kitchen, bursting through the door to the dining room, knocking a crystal candelabrum from the sideboard as she passed. It crashed to the floor, shattering into a thousand pieces, but Cynthia's laughter drowned out the sound as Joan pushed through into the entry hall, slamming the dining room door behind her.

"Doors can't shut me out," Cynthia's voice whispered. *"But you don't understand, do you? You never understood!"*

"Leave me alone!" Joan screamed, and fled through the living room, then into the library. But Cynthia was there too, her laughter echoing off the walls.

Joan felt her mind beginning to crack. "Bill?" she called out. "Bill, help me. Please help me . . ."

But as she called out her husband's name, something sounded wrong. Her voice was muffled, as in a nightmare in which she tried to call out for help but the words died in her throat, and no matter

354

how hard she tried, no sound emerged from her mouth.

"He won't help you," Cynthia whispered. *"Why would he help you? He didn't love you — he never loved you!"*

"He did," Joan sobbed, sinking onto the wing-back chair next to the fireplace. "It's not true. He loved me . . . he always loved me."

Her sister's voice turned venomous. *"He didn't,"* she whispered. *"Nobody loved you, Joan. Not Mama, not Daddy, not Bill — not anyone!"*

"They did," Joan protested, but even as she uttered the words, she knew they weren't true.

"Daddy left us. Don't you remember? When you were still a baby, Daddy left us! He left us because of you! That's why Mama hated you!"

"She didn't," Joan cried. "It isn't true — none of it is true!" She covered her ears, trying to shut out the sound, but she couldn't blot out her sister's relentless voice.

"It is true. You know it's all true!"

"No!" Joan screamed, rising to her feet. "You're lying! It's all lies!" She stumbled toward the door, but there was no escape from her sister's voice.

No escape from her terrible accusation.

"Your fault, Joan," Cynthia whispered. *"Your fault! All of it is your fault!"*

Joan shambled through the living room, then came to the foot of the stairs. Cynthia's voice was coming from everywhere, and now she could see her too: standing at the top of the stairs, gazing down at her, her lips twisted into the cruel smile

355

Joan hadn't seen since she was a child. "I'll kill you," she screamed, staring up at the looming visage. "I swear to God, I'll kill you!"

As peals of Cynthia's mocking laughter filled the house, Joan started up the stairs.

And with every step she took, she felt a little more of her sanity slipping away.

In his first year as Chief of the Five-Man Force, Dan Pullman had discovered that the ire of those who considered themselves the town's leading citizens wasn't reserved for those they perceived as underlings, such as his deputies. "In the end, you're responsible," the Gerry Conroes, Marty Holmeses, and Bill Hapgoods of the town had explained during the years he'd headed the department. On the other hand, he'd noticed that though they held him responsible for anything they considered a failure on the part of the department, they rarely gave him any credit for its successes. He'd been smart enough never to complain about that, which he thought was probably the reason he'd held the job of police chief longer than any of his predecessors.

So now, though his mood was as foul as a midwinter storm, and had been since the tongue-lashing he'd taken from Gerry Conroe the evening before, Dan Pullman understood that no explanation of why he couldn't immediately devote his entire energies to searching for Kelly Conroe would satisfy Gerry. Not as editor and publisher of the local paper, and certainly not as the missing girl's father.

But what did annoy Pullman, and accounted for the mood he was in this morning, was the continuous stream of phone calls that had ruined his chances of getting any sleep at all last night. And he'd needed the sleep.

From the moment he left the Conroe house last night, he'd been examining Kelly Conroe's disappearance from every angle. Despite his reassurances to Gerry and Nancy, which were at least statistically accurate, he agreed with them that Kelly probably hadn't simply taken off somewhere. Over the years, he and every man on the force had come to know each kid in Granite Falls, and whenever something happened — some minor theft or vandalism — the town's cops usually knew where to look first. Most of the problems stemmed from only a handful of kids, while the rest rarely got involved in anything more serious than the traditional — if illegal — keg party that invariably followed high school graduation. And until now, Kelly Conroe had never been in any kind of trouble whatsoever. Her family was stable, and it would be hard to find a soul in Granite Falls who wished her ill. So, despite what he'd told Gerry and Nancy last night, Pullman figured the odds of her having simply run away as being somewhere between slim and none.

Still, as he drove home last night, he knew it wasn't feasible to mount an effective search effort until morning. And then after being kept awake by considering where Kelly might have gone, his sleep had been interrupted by the constant stream of phone calls from irate parents demanding action.

Before midnight, the callers had identified themselves, and were at least somewhat rational. They were worried, and though Pullman was careful not to say anything that would make them more worried, he tended to agree that they might have something to worry about.

After midnight, the calls had been anonymous, and the message varied only in the number and variety of obscenities the callers used to make their point: "If we can't sleep tonight, why should you?" Pullman, using the caller I.D. feature of his phone, mentally noted which of the crank callers were rudest, but had not bothered to actually write down any of the names. Still, by the time dawn broke, he'd had no sleep, and figured out he was thoroughly pissed off at about ten percent of the town's population. Had he been in a mood to reason more clearly, he would have calculated the true figure as closer to a tiny fraction of one percent. On the other hand, most of the callers were related to at least a few dozen other people, every one of whom would be urged to vote against him come next election.

Unless he found Kelly Conroe. Alive. This morning.

And that, he was one hundred percent sure, was not going to happen.

As soon as it was light enough he called Tony Petrocelli, and the two of them went over the route Kelly would have followed from the school to her house, searching for a sign that she'd run into trouble — a dropped book, maybe a handkerchief, anything that might have been hers. They examined both sides of the road leading from the edge of town out to the Conroe house and found nothing. In the town itself, it would have been nearly impossible for Kelly to have run into trouble without someone noticing; if not from a car, then from one of the houses.

Now, like Eric Holmes and Pete Arneson — and Matt Moore — Pullman was out by the waterfall, repeating a search that was eerily similar to the one for Emily Moore that had been abandoned only the day before. As they had with the road, Pullman and Petrocelli split the area in two, each of them searching half of it, then switching and searching the area the other one had already gone over. The only signs of violence they saw were a few spatters of blood in the area where the fight between Matt and Pete Arneson had taken place. As Petrocelli photographed the area, Pullman carefully collected as many samples as he could scrape from the rock. The lab in Manchester would quickly tell them if any of the samples could have come from Kelly Conroe.

Once they were finished with the area immediately adjacent to the pool and falls, they began working their way along the trail leading to the Hapgood house.

"But if I were Matt, and I was dragging Kelly Conroe, I wouldn't use the trail," Tony Petrocelli objected. "Anybody could have come along."

Pullman shook his head. "That's the whole point — according to Matt, he was looking for Kelly, not carrying her or dragging her. And if he was looking for her in the dark, he'd sure use the path. Which means we should find footprints going both ways, and they should be very fresh, and they should match the shoes Matt was wearing last night, which looked like Doc Martens, maybe about a size nine, or ten." He stopped abruptly. "Like these," he said, squatting down.

Petrocelli hunkered down beside him, and both men studied the clear imprint that a deeply cleated shoe had left in the soft earth. It was recent enough that the brand name and a logo were clearly visible, along with the sole pattern. It took only a moment for Pullman to decipher the mirror image of the brand name: Redwing. The logo, set in the center of the heel, looked like a spider, or maybe a large tick. Pullman sighed. "Well, so much for my theory that they were Doc Martens."

"Nearly the same thing," Petrocelli replied. "Redwings are Australian — good for hiking, and look almost like Doc Martens." He carefully placed his own size twelve foot alongside the print. "About the right size too."

They moved farther down the path, searching for more prints, and now that they knew what they were looking for, it didn't take long to find them.

And every one of them pointed toward the Hapgood house, not away.

"So if these match Matt's shoes," Petrocelli said as they came in view of the house, "then we know

Matt used the path only to go home."

Pullman said grimly, "Time to see if we can find the shoes Matt was wearing last night."

Chapter 23

Crazy.

She was going crazy.

She was going crazy, and she knew she was going crazy, and there was nothing she could do about it.

Cynthia's voice was everywhere now, following Joan wherever she went, laughing at her, taunting her, mocking her.

"Never yours," Cynthia kept repeating. *"Don't you understand, Joanie-baby?"* she whispered, using the belittling nickname Joan had always hated. *"Nothing you have was ever yours. It's mine. All of it! Bill is mine, and this house is mine, and everything in it is mine. I was only letting you use it! But now I'm taking it back!"*

A whimpering moan escaped Joan's lips, and her head felt like it would explode from the pressure of the churning emotions building inside her. "No," she whispered brokenly. "It isn't true. None of it's true. Bill loved me. He wanted me. He —" But her words died in the cacophony of Cynthia's scornful laugh.

Destroy her! That's what she had to do! She had to destroy Cynthia.

Obliterate her from the guest room.

362

Obliterate her from the house.

Obliterate her from her mind.

"You can't," Cynthia whispered, as if she'd read Joan's thoughts. *"You can never get rid of me, Joanie-baby. Never!"*

Joan came to the top of the stairs. She was only a few feet from the closed door to the guest room — Cynthia's room — and she could feel the nearness of her sister's spirit.

"Go ahead," Cynthia taunted. *"Try it. Try it, Joanie-baby, and see what happens."*

A strangled cry of fury erupting from her throat, Joan lunged toward the door, twisting the knob and hurling it open so hard it crashed against the wall, cracking the plaster and shattering the glass knob.

Ignoring the glass shards on the floor, she went to the closet where her sister's clothes, arranged by color to form a brilliant rainbow, hung on their padded hangers — clothes her mother had cared for so perfectly that they looked like they'd never been worn. "Why didn't you take care of *me* like this?" she cried out, her voice choking on her sobs. "Why couldn't you love me even as much as you loved her damned clothes?" Snatching one of the dresses off its hanger, she ripped its bodice with one quick jerk, then hurled it aside as she grabbed another one. One after another she tore the dresses from their hangers, until she stood in the midst of a tangle of torn and mangled material.

Material that could never again be put back on the hangers as a memorial to her sister.

"They're only clothes. They're not me, Joanie-baby," Cynthia whispered.

"Don't call me that!" Joan screamed. She reeled away from the closet and began ripping the pictures from the walls, hurling them to the floor, the glass covering the photographs shattering.

Cynthia only laughed.

Joan moved on to the desk, sweeping the surface clean, sending her sister's books and pens, her stuffed animals and favorite Barbie doll, skittering across the floor.

Then, through the turbulence of her own emotions, she heard something. She froze, and a strange silence fell over the house. Then she heard it again.

The doorbell.

Someone was ringing the doorbell.

A wave of panic crashed over her. What should she do? She glanced at herself in the mirror — her face was ashen, her hair a tangled mess. Maybe she shouldn't answer the door — maybe she should just wait for whoever it was to go away.

The doorbell sounded again, as if to deny the possibility that whoever awaited would leave.

What if they came in?

What if they came in and found her like this?

What if they told her mother she was playing with Cynthia's things?

Her mother would beat her again, and lock her in the cedar chest in the basement.

No! Don't let them catch you! Don't let them tell on you!

364

She ran from Cynthia's room, hurried down the stairs, then paused in the entry hall, trying to catch her breath. She ran her fingers through her hair, clumsily brushing it away from her face.

The doorbell sounded again, and at last — knowing she could put it off no longer — she turned the knob and pulled the door open just wide enough to peek out.

A policeman!

A policeman, wearing a uniform.

She wanted to slam the door and run and hide in her room. But even if she could hide from the policeman, she couldn't hide from her mother. Her mother would find her and —

Fear galvanized Joan's mind, pulling its fragments back together, jerking her out of the past and the memories that had held her in thrall. Hearing her name, she pulled the door open wider and recognized Dan Pullman standing next to Tony Petrocelli.

"Can we come in for a moment, Joan?" the police chief asked.

Matt, she thought. *They want to ask Matt more questions.* "I — Matt's not here, and I —" Her mind cleared further, and she remembered what her lawyer had said last night. "I don't think I'd better talk to you until I talk to Trip Wainwright. He said —"

"I know what he said, Joan," Dan Pullman said quickly, sensing that she was about to shut the door. "I was just wondering — does Matt have a pair of Redwing shoes?"

A veil of suspicion dropped over Joan's face, and her eyes flicked from Pullman to Petrocelli, then back to the chief. "I'm not really sure," she said. "I don't pick Matt's shoes out for him."

She heard Cynthia's laugh.

"Maybe if you could —" Pullman began, but before he could finish, Joan shook her head.

"I'm sorry," she said, starting to close the door. "I'm not supposed to talk to you."

"All I want —"

Joan shook her head. "I'm not supposed to," she said again. "I'm just not supposed to!"

A second later Dan Pullman and Tom Petrocelli were facing a closed door, and both of them were certain that no matter how long they rang the bell, she wouldn't open it again.

"Lawyers," Pullman said bitterly. "Damn all lawyers."

But as they started back toward the waterfall, Tony Petrocelli turned to look back at the house. "Did she sound okay to you?" he asked, cocking his head. To him, Joan Hapgood had sounded almost like a child to him. A child about five years old, who was afraid of doing something wrong.

Pullman shrugged. "She's just doing what Trip Wainwright told her to do. And he's just doing his job. So let's you and I go do ours."

From the house, Joan watched them disappear into the woods.

They hadn't found out. They didn't know she'd been in Cynthia's room, so they couldn't tell her mother.

"But I can," Cynthia whispered. *"I can tell Mother anything I want."*

Joan's eyes widened. "No!" she screamed. "I'll kill you! I swear to God, I'll kill you!"

Gerry Conroe's fist crashed down on his desk, barely missing the keyboard he'd been tapping on with steadily increasing frustration and fury for most of the morning. "God damn it! What the hell is going on here?"

Eleanor Austin, who for nearly fifteen years had been Gerry's secretary, administrative assistant, editor, and general factotum, had not reacted when he smashed his desk with his fist, but she was so startled by his curses that she slopped her coffee onto the story she was editing. "Take it easy, Gerry. Breaking the computer isn't going to help."

"It's starting to look like nothing's going to help," he growled. "I hate the damn thing, and I hate the Internet even more."

"That's today," Eleanor observed, the soothing tone of her voice only exacerbating his frustration. "Yesterday you said you could find anything you needed to know on the Net. 'The greatest tool ever invented by mankind,' I believe is what you said."

"Well, I was wrong," Conroe muttered, his eyes narrowing as he studied the screen in front of him, which was currently displaying the latest of what had been an unending series of messages informing him of the result of his search:

0 occurrences found.

"Why the hell doesn't it just say it can't find what I'm looking for? Somebody should teach this thing to speak English."

Eleanor quickly cast around in her mind for some way to divert Gerry before he launched into a diatribe against all things modern. "Why does it matter so much who Matt's father was?" she ventured, then recognizing her error at once, anticipated his reply: *If you know the father, you know the son! The apple never falls far from the tree.* Which means mothers don't count at all, Eleanor added to herself.

But instead of what she'd expected, her employer said, "The thing is, Matt Moore doesn't seem to come from any tree at all." He gestured toward the computer. "According to this, he doesn't even exist!"

Eleanor couldn't contain a smug smile. "You mean maybe the Internet isn't quite the greatest tool ever invented by mankind after all?"

"No!" Gerry said, shoving his chair back and standing up. "I mean that something phony is going on around here, just like I've been telling everyone. And I'm going to find out what it is!"

Walking out of the office, he strode to the corner of Main and Chestnut, cut diagonally across the intersection — pausing only long enough to glare at the two drivers who honked at him — brushed past Agnes Fenster, who served Trip Wainwright in more or less the same capacity as Eleanor Austin functioned for him — and shoved open the door to Trip Wainwright's office. "What the hell is going on?" he demanded.

The lawyer looked up from the will he was working on, his features automatically falling into a neutral expression that hid whatever he might have been thinking. "I'm not sure I follow you, Gerry." He rose from his chair, offered his unannounced visitor his hand, and when Conroe refused to shake it, smoothly used it to gesture toward the client's chair in front of his desk. "May I assume you don't approve of me looking out for my client's interests last night?"

Suddenly Conroe understood Dan Pullman's refusal to go after Matt Moore: Wainwright must have intimidated him. "You get in the way of finding my daughter, and I swear I'll make you so miserable you'll wish you'd never been born."

Wainwright sighed as he lowered himself back into his chair. He'd known this visit was going to happen — could practically have predicted Gerry Conroe's exact words. That was both the blessing and the curse of living in a town as small as Granite Falls. But at least knowing what was going to happen this morning had allowed him time to prepare for it. "Look, Gerry," he began, "I'm very, very sorry about Kelly. But until we know exactly what happened to her, I can't let you or anybody else try to convict Matthew Moore of doing anything to her. For all you or anyone else knows, he had absolutely nothing to do with anything that might have happened." Gerry Conroe's jaw tightened, but before he could say anything, Wainwright held up a hand as if to hold off the torrent he knew was about to break. "And don't put me in a position where I have to recommend that either Matt or Joan sue you either. I hate it when my clients wind up in court, especially when they have to sue my friends. So why don't you tell me what's on your mind, and try to keep your temper out of it."

Conroe said nothing for a moment, trying to gauge how much of Wainwright's words were bluff. Though he couldn't imagine Trip recommending that Joan actually sue him, he couldn't be entirely certain he wouldn't either, and the lawyer's expression gave away nothing. Finally, he lowered himself into the chair. "I just want to know where that kid came from," he said.

Wainwright frowned. "Matt? We all know where he came from — he's Joan's son. As for his father . . ." His voice faded, and he shrugged dismissively. "I suppose if you want to know that, you'll have to ask Joan. She's never told me, but on the other hand, I've never asked."

"What makes you think Joan would know?" Conroe countered. As Wainwright's face finally registered an expression — even if only of puzzlement — Conroe's lips compressed into a grim line. "As far as I can tell, she's not his mother."

Wainwright blinked. "I beg your pardon?"

"She's not his mother," Conroe repeated. "I've been on the Net since lunch, and I'll bet I know more about Joan Moore Hapgood than she knows about herself. And I can tell you for a fact that her medical records don't show that she ever gave birth to anybody. As for Matthew Moore, I've

370

checked the records of every state in the East, and there's no birth certificate for him. According to everything I've seen, he never officially existed at all until Joan registered him in school here after she came back from New York. Before that — nothing! No birth records, no adoption records, anything! So what's going on? Who is he? Where did he come from? And how come all of a sudden his stepfather is dead, and his grandmother and my daughter are both missing?"

"Even if everything you say about Matt not being Joan's son is true — and I'm not saying it is," the lawyer countered, "I don't see how it's germane to anything else. Even if Joan adopted Matt, it doesn't follow that —"

"She didn't adopt him!" Conroe cut in. "I don't know where the hell she got him. But I'm by God going to find out, and I suspect that when I do, a lot of what's going on in this town is going to be a lot clearer. And if that kid's done something to my daughter, you can bet I won't rest until he pays for it." He raised a finger and pointed it at the lawyer's head. "And don't try to get in my way. You're protecting a murderer, Wainwright. He shot his own stepfather, damn it! And nobody's doing anything about it! Do they have to find my little girl's body before they lock him up?" Before the lawyer could respond, Conroe was on his feet again. "You tell your 'client' that if anything's happened to Kelly, he's going to wish that he'd never been born at all! And tell him that's not a threat, Wainwright. It's just a plain, simple statement of fact."

371

A second later he was gone, and five seconds after that, Wainwright saw him march across the street — oblivious to the blaring of horns — and disappear into the police station. And when he was done there, there would be only one other place he would go. Picking up the phone, Wainwright dialed Joan's number, his fingers drumming impatiently as he waited for her to pick up at the other end. But when he finally heard her voice, it was a recording on the answering machine.

Joan sat at Cynthia's vanity, her eyes fixed on the image in the mirror. But it wasn't her face she saw — at least not the face that Dan Pullman and Tony Petrocelli had seen a few minutes ago. Instead she saw the face that had been hers years ago, when she still lived in the house on Burlington Avenue, after Cynthia left, when her mother had forbidden her even to go into her sister's room, let alone to sit at her vanity or use her cosmetics. But Mother wasn't home now, and Cynthia had gone away, and she was alone in the house.

"No one to tell," she said softly. "No one to tell on me."

"I'll tell," Cynthia whispered. *"I'll tell Mama, and you know what she'll do."*

"I'll kill you if you tell," Joan replied. "I'll kill you, and maybe I'll kill Mother too!" She picked up a tube of Cynthia's foundation — a brand-new one that had never been opened — and carefully unscrewed the lid. Using a sponge she found in the top drawer of the vanity, she carefully applied the cosmetic until every bit of her face was covered. She paused then, gazing at the blank canvas her visage had become. "I can be pretty too," she said. "I can be as pretty as you."

Her sister laughed, but Joan ignored it, turning her attention to the array of colors spread across the top of the vanity. Choosing a shade of lavender that reminded her of the fuchsias that grew in the pots hanging from her mother's front porch — her favorite flowers in the whole world — she carefully applied the color to her eyelids.

Next she chose a pot of rouge that would add color to her cheeks, and tried to put it on just the way Cynthia always had, accentuating her cheek-bones.

She brightened her lips with a brilliant scarlet that was Cynthia's favorite, then carefully outlined them.

Just like Cynthia.

In the top right-hand drawer she found the eye-lashes Cynthia had loved to collect, and chose a pair of extra long ones that she'd been dying to try on ever since Cynthia showed them to her. Lifting them from their plastic case, she painstakingly pressed them to her eyelids, then applied a coat of mascara to make them look even thicker.

"Pretty," she whispered, staring at the face in the mirror. "I'm just as pretty as you are!" Her jaw tightened and her eyes narrowed as she heard her sister's peal of laughter. "Don't laugh," she whispered. "Don't you dare laugh at me!"

The laughter rang out again, and Joan's anger

grew. All her life — for as long as she could remember — she'd had to live with Cynthia's laughter. But not now. Not anymore. Opening the bottom drawer of Cynthia's vanity, she took out the gloves she'd taken from her mother a few days ago, the gloves her mother could never wear again, the gloves whose leather would never again scar her face. She pulled them on slowly, stretching them to fit over her larger hands, her thicker fingers. She gazed once more at the face in the mirror.

She saw nothing of the grotesque gargoyle that stared back at her, its eyes painted a hideous purple, its cheeks clumsily smudged with bright red, its lips an open wound the color of blood.

Instead she saw a face that was radiant with youth, and even more beautiful than Cynthia's had ever been. She looked as if she were ready for a formal dance, complete with perfect white gloves that came to her wrists.

Only one thing was missing — she hadn't yet put on her perfume. A moment later her fingers closed on the bottle of Nightshade. She shook it, then lifted the stopper from the vial's neck. As the room filled with the heavy, musky scent — the sensuous aroma that had always been Cynthia's favorite — Joan dabbed fluid on her neck. The heavy fragrance hanging around her like a cloud, she rose from the vanity and left the room, feeling a tingling sense of eagerness, as if some beau — someone who truly loved her — might be waiting for her downstairs.

When she came out on the landing, she looked down for the man who should be waiting for her, smiling at her, extending his hand toward her.

But there was no man.

There was no one.

There was only Cynthia.

Cynthia, and her terrible, mocking, taunting, cruel laughter.

As it pealed in Joan's ears, slashing at her spirit, tearing at her soul, she flinched. Then, with decades of suppressed rage boiling inside her, she started down the stairs.

What little hope Kelly Conroe had been able to cling to was quickly fading. Though she could barely feel her hands or feet, it felt as if someone were slowly twisting off her arms and legs, ripping her limbs from her shoulders and hips. Though she'd managed to scrape the tape from her mouth, it had done nothing more than allow her to breathe more easily, for her throat and mouth were so parched with thirst that she could barely manage to speak, let alone scream. Not that she believed anyone would hear her. Not even Mrs. Moore, who had stopped muttering and hadn't answered at all when she had finally rid herself of the gag and spoken to the old woman. Kelly had given up imagining what might lie beyond the blackness, given up wondering how she might escape. She was going to die, and even that didn't really frighten her anymore, for at least it would be an escape from the pain that gripped her body.

Suddenly, a shaft of light appeared from above, and Kelly instinctively reacted like a creature of the dark, trying to scuttle out of the light, to escape from it back into the safety of the darkness. But then her eyes began to adjust to the glare.

The chamber in which she'd been imprisoned was no more than a dozen feet square and eight feet high, and looked exactly as she'd imagined it would — the floor packed earth, the walls rough-hewn wood. Then Kelly caught sight of Emily Moore and her stomach contracted into a convulsive retching. Mrs. Moore lay curled against one of the walls, her back toward her. The old woman's wrists were bound just as hers had been, but instead of hands, there were hideous stumps of putrefying flesh where the hands should have been. A pool of muck lay around Emily Moore's lifeless body, and as Kelly realized that it could only be the old woman's congealed blood, her belly heaved again, and her throat and mouth burned with the acid her stomach ejected.

A sound jerked her attention away from the corpse of Matt's grandmother, and she saw that a ladder had been lowered through the hole in the ceiling through which the light still glowed.

Rescued!

She was being rescued!

But a moment later, seeing a figure come down the ladder, her brief moment of hope was extinguished. Then the figure was looming above her, and even though the face was shrouded in shadow, she could see that it was covered with grotesque makeup, and contorted with fury.

The figure spoke, and Kelly knew who it was.

"How do you like it?" Joan hissed. She drew her foot back and kicked Kelly. "How do you like being locked up in the dark?" She kicked again, and as the shoe struck Kelly's ribs, the girl screamed with agony and attempted to scramble away. But Joan followed her, hissing down at her. "Now you know how it felt! Now you know how I felt when Mother locked me in the cedar chest! And now you're going to know how it felt when she hit me! See how you like it, Cynthia! See how you like it!" As Kelly cowered in abject terror, Joan raised her hand, and as it hovered in the glow of the light spilling in through the hole in the ceiling, Kelly saw that Joan Hapgood was wearing some kind of glove.

A pale glove that almost looked like —

The hand descended, smashing against Kelly's face. She screamed and again tried to writhe away, but the hand rose again, and this time, as the light illuminated it, she saw that it wasn't a glove at all.

It was the skin of Emily Moore's hand, stretched tight over Joan's own, the old woman's cracked and yellowed nails looking like claws.

A second later Kelly felt the nails dig into her cheek, and she screamed from the burning pain of the scratches.

"See how you like it," Joan hissed again and again as she lashed out at Kelly. "See how you like what Mother did to me. What you let her do to me! See how much of it you can stand!" Joan's kick

377

sank deep into Kelly's gut, and more blows rained down, pounding at her until her face was bleeding and she could feel the bruises swelling.

Barely conscious, she only dimly realized that tape was again being pressed across her mouth. I'm going to die, Kelly thought. I'm going to die, and nobody's ever going to find me. . . .

Chapter 24

On any other day, Becky Adams would have gone directly from her final period geometry class to the room in the basement where Mr. Addington taught photography and the darkroom was located. There, she would have either checked out a camera, to take pictures for either the school newspaper or the yearbook, or spent an hour or two in the darkroom.

"I don't understand it," her father had said when she decided to sign up for Mr. Addington's advanced class this year after taking a summer school course from him. "Why would a pretty girl like you want to hide behind a camera or in a darkroom?" Though she hadn't even tried to answer his question, Becky knew exactly why she liked photography: Until now, she'd never felt like she was a genuine part of the school. Everybody else — everybody she'd grown up with — had lots of friends and were involved in all kinds of things: sports teams, the cheerleading squad, the band or the choir. Everyone else seemed to have found a place to fit in. But it wasn't until she discovered photography that Becky had found her own place: even though she still wasn't a part of any of the groups in the school, she could at least photograph them.

But the best hours were the ones she spent in the darkroom, where she didn't have to try to fit in with anyone else.

Today she was supposed to have photographed the football team for the yearbook, but that had been cancelled, and Becky knew why: it was because of the bruises on Pete Arneson's face. That, and the fact that no one wanted to be in the picture with Matt Moore.

All day long she had overheard the gossip. It seemed like everywhere she went — in the classrooms, in the halls, in the cafeteria, even in the library during her fifth period study hall — everyone was whispering about what Matt had done. By the time the final bell rang, all Becky wanted to do was get away from it. But while she was getting her books out of her locker she couldn't help overhearing Jessica Amberson talking to Tammy Brewster.

"I'm not going to go anywhere by myself. Nowhere at all!" Jessica was saying. "I can't believe I used to want to go out with him." Her eyes widened as she thought of the possibilities. "My God, Tammy, it could be me Matt murdered instead of Kelly!"

Becky slammed her locker shut so hard that Jessica and Tammy jumped as if she'd stuck a pin in them. "Nobody knows Matt did anything!" she told them. "And I don't care what anyone says, I don't believe he hurt Kelly, or his grandmother, or anyone else."

Tammy fixed Becky with her most patronizing

look. "Well, if you're so sure he didn't do anything, why don't you just go with him right now?"
Tammy tipped her head toward the front doors,
and Becky turned around just in time to see Matt
push them open and hurry down the steps, his
head down.

"Maybe I will!" she shot back. Turning away
from Jessica and Tammy, she hurried down the
corridor, through the door, and outside. Matt was
already across the street, and she called out as she
started down the steps. "Matt, wait up!" He didn't
turn around — didn't seem to hear her at all —
and Becky broke into a jog, crossed the street, and
caught up with him before he reached the corner.
Finally he turned to look at her.

His face was pale and his eyes were clouded with
suspicion — and anger.

"What do you want, Becky?" he asked, his voice
as guarded as his expression.

"I thought maybe we could walk together. I
mean, at least as far as my house." When Matt
made no reply, she nervously went on. "I mean, if
you're going that way."

Matt's eyes narrowed. "What did you do, take a
dare from Jess and Tammy?"

Becky gasped. "No! I —" But then she hesitated.
In a way, wasn't that exactly what she'd done? If
she hadn't heard them talking about Matt, would
she be here right now? She was about to turn away
when she remembered all the times people had
turned away from her, and how bad it had always
made her feel. But Matt had never turned away

381

from her. Maybe they weren't as close as when they lived across the street from each other, but unlike everyone else, he'd never been mean to her. And right now she knew he must be feeling as she had most of her life. In fact, he must be feeling a lot worse: at least no one had ever accused her of killing anyone. "I don't think you did anything," she said.

A frown creased Matt's brow. "How come you're so sure?"

Becky shrugged. "I just am. You wouldn't do anything like they're saying you did."

Matt started walking again, and when Becky fell in beside him, he made no objection. It wasn't until they'd come to the corner of Burlington Avenue that he spoke again, his voice so low that Becky could hardly hear him. "Do you think it's possible to do something and not remember it?"

"You mean like —" She hesitated, then finished her question. "You mean like kill someone?"

Matt didn't answer for a moment, then shrugged noncommittally.

Becky remembered reading a book once, about hypnotism, and how even when someone was hypnotized, they wouldn't do something they really didn't want to do. But if Matt had been angry at Kelly — really angry —

No! she thought. *He wouldn't! Not Matt!*

"I don't think so," she finally replied. "I think if you did something that bad, you'd remember it."

Matt stopped walking and turned to face her. The anger she'd seen before was gone, replaced by pain and confusion. "But what about all those people you hear about? The ones who suddenly remember the awful things that happened to them when they were little kids?"

They were across the street from Becky's house now, and she glanced uneasily toward the curtained window of the small living room, wondering if her mother was looking out, watching her. "I don't believe it. I think if something terrible happens, you remember it. Especially if you did it yourself." She thought she saw a glimmer of hope flicker in Matt's eyes. "You didn't do anything, Matt," she said again. "You couldn't have. I've known you my whole life, and I just know you couldn't have done anything like what everybody's saying." Impulsively, she put her arms around him and kissed him on the cheek. "Maybe nobody else believes you," she said. "But I do."

As Becky's arms tightened around Matt, he hugged her close. "Thanks," he said. "And I don't care what anyone else thinks. You're better than all the rest of them put together."

Her eyes suddenly filling with tears she didn't want Matt to see, Becky pulled away from him. "I've got to go," she said. "See you tomorrow."

Before Matt could reply, she was gone, running across the street and disappearing into her house. He was still looking at her front door when a movement at one of the windows caught his eye. He thought for an instant that it might be Becky, but then knew it wasn't.

It was her mother, and even through the glass

and across the distance that separated them, Matt could read her thoughts as clearly as if she'd shouted them at him.

Killer . . . murderer . . .

The words echoed in his mind, and suddenly he was running, fleeing down Burlington Avenue, trying to escape the awful accusations that were ringing in his head.

But there was no escape.

Not now.

Not ever.

Joan's eyes fixed on the blinking red light on the answering machine as if it were an alien creature — vaguely familiar, but at the same time utterly incomprehensible. Why should it be flashing? Didn't it only go on if someone had called her? And no one had — she'd been home all day — never left the house at all — and the phone hadn't rung.

Why would it? No one wanted to talk to her anymore.

"No one ever wanted to talk to you, Joanie-baby," Cynthia whispered. *"They wanted to talk to me. Don't you remember? The phone was always ringing, but it was never for you. It was always for me."*

"Shut up," Joan whimpered, pressing her hands over her ears as if to shut out the relentless voice of her sister. But it was useless — Cynthia's voice held her in its thrall.

"Everything was for me, Joanie-baby. Everything."

The red light kept blinking, and as Joan stared at it, it took on an ominous look. Ominous, but at the same time mocking. As mocking as her sister's laughter.

"You're afraid," something whispered. *"You're afraid to listen. Afraid to hear what might be there."*

Her sister's voice?

Her mother's?

No! It was only a machine! It had no voice, couldn't possibly be speaking to her. But the whole house seemed filled with voices now. They seemed to be coming from everywhere. "No!" she blurted, though there was no one there to hear her. "I'm not afraid! I'm not!"

As Cynthia's throaty laugh boiled up out of nowhere, Joan stabbed at the flashing button with a shaking finger, and a moment later heard Trip Wainwright's familiar voice.

"It's Trip, Joan . . . Look, Gerry Conroe might come out there, and I don't think you ought to talk to him. He's got some nutty idea that you're not Matt's mother. It's nonsense, of course, but there's no reason for you to have to listen to it. So if he shows up — and if you're there — just don't even answer the door. And call me when you get this, okay?" An uncertain silence followed, as if he were wondering what to say next, and then nothing.

For a moment Joan stood frozen, her eyes wide, staring at the machine as if it were a cobra that had just struck her. Then she heard her sister's voice again.

"He knows, Joan. He knows everything!"

"No!" Joan shrieked, again clamping her hands

over her ears. "He doesn't know anything! He doesn't!"

"*Stupid!*" Now it was her mother's voice jabbing at her. "*Cynthia was always the smart one! Why did she have to die? Why couldn't it have been you? Then everything would be the way it should be!*"

"No," Joan wailed again. "No! It's not true! I won't hear it!"

Then she heard another voice: Matt's voice.

"Mom?"

She spun around, half expecting him not to be there at all. But there he was — her perfect son. She started toward him, her arms outstretched, needing to feel him, to touch him, if only to prove to herself that he wasn't just another phantom like the voices that were torturing her. But he drew back, his eyes clouding, his face paling.

"Mom?"

Joan caught a glimpse of her reflection in the glass front of a display case. The image was hazy, but for an instant it seemed as though she was looking not at herself, but at Cynthia. She felt an awful sense of vertigo then, as if she were dropping away into a bottomless pit from which she might never emerge.

She reached out to Matt again, struggling to speak, searching for her voice, but he seemed to be pulling farther and farther away from her.

She was going to lose him — lose it all — lose everything she'd ever wanted —

Then a sound broke through the confusion in her mind, and the illusion that a moment ago had held her in its grip fell away.

The doorbell!

Don't even answer the door.

But she had to answer the door. If she didn't, Matt would. And then — "Go upstairs," she said, "and let me take care of this!"

Matt stared at his mother. Her face was streaked with makeup — garish makeup — the kind street whores on television wore. And what was she talking about? What was she going to take care of? What was happening?

"It's Kelly's father!" she told him as she started toward the front door. "You don't want to talk to him, do you?" She was close to Matt now, and his nostrils filled with the powerful scent of the perfume she wore.

The perfume he'd smelled so many times before.

His aunt's perfume.

"Do it!" his mother commanded him. "Go upstairs!"

As if acting under the volition of some force outside himself, Matt started up the stairs. But as he heard the front door open and Kelly's father begin to shout, he froze.

"Who is he, Joan?" Gerry Conroe demanded. "Who is Matt?"

"He's my son!" Joan replied.

Conroe's expression, already contorted with a mixture of exhaustion, frustration, and fear, hardened. "Don't tell me that!" His voice trembled as he hurled the words at her: "I know he's not your son, Joan! I don't know who he is, but I know who he's not. So you tell me — what the hell is going on here?"

Joan covered her ears to shut out his furious accusations. "What is it, Joan? Did Bill find out Matt's not your son? Did he find out where he really came from? That's why he left, isn't it? He was through with you, and he was through with Matt! So Matt shot him!"

"No!" Joan cried. She was cowering now, trying to push the door closed, but Gerry Conroe held it open. "No . . . no . . ."

"Tell me," he said. "Tell me, Joan. Tell me the truth!"

Something broke inside her then, and when she spoke again, her voice had taken on a strangely childish tone. "I don't have to!" she insisted. "I don't have to tell you anything I don't want to, and you can't make me!"

Finally she succeeded in shoving the door shut, but even through the heavy mahogany, she could still hear Gerry Conroe's voice: "I'll find out, Joan. I'll find out the truth!"

Then her eyes fell on a mirror and locked onto the reflection in the glass, and she no longer heard him. It was a reflection not of her, but of her sister, and as Joan stared at it she knew what had to happen.

Cynthia, once again, had to die.

But it would be different this time.

This time she would not only kill Cynthia, but destroy her.

"Who is he? Who is Matt? Tell me . . . tell me the truth . . ."

The words hung in the air, pinning Matt to the spot. What was he talking about? He knew who his mother was — she was standing in the entry hall, looking at herself in the mirror! Then, as he watched, she turned away from the mirror and looked up at him.

Except she wasn't looking at him. She was looking at something else — something behind him. But except for the two of them, the house was empty! "Mother?" he said uncertainly.

She was starting up the stairs now, coming toward him, but her eyes — bloodshot and made larger by the garish makeup — were still fixed on something beyond him. As she drew closer, Matt finally snapped out of the paralysis induced by Gerry Conroe's words. Instinctively, he backed away, then turned and hurried up the rest of the stairs. Without thinking, he went to his room, closed the door, locked it.

Who is he? Tell me the truth!

The words hammered at Matt. What had Mr. Conroe been talking about?

Then he heard his mother's voice, coming from beyond the heavy wooden door he'd locked a moment ago.

"I'll kill you . . . this time I'll really kill you!"

Matt's heart pounded, and a terrible hopelessness rose within him.

He must be guilty!

Mr. Conroe thought so. So did Dan Pullman. He was pretty sure Trip Wainwright did too. Otherwise, why would the lawyer be so worried about what he might say to Mr. Pullman?

And now even his mother thought so.

Maybe he should just unlock the door and go out in the hall and face it. Face his mother.

Face everything.

He reached for the key, turned it, and pulled the door open a few inches.

The hall was empty, and silent.

Where was she? Where had she gone? "Mom?" he breathed, so softly the word was lost in the silence of the house. Then he heard a voice, muffled, barely audible at all.

"He's mine! He'll always be mine!"

Drawn toward the voice, Matt moved down the hall until he was standing outside his aunt's room.

"He's not yours," he heard his mother say. "You gave him to me!"

Matt heard the sound of laughter then, but there was no joy in it. It was a harsh sound, a cruel sound. "Never! You took him! You took him like you took everything else! You did what you wanted to do. . . ."

And as the sound of the second voice came through the closed door, it echoed out of Matt's memory —

. . . *what you want to do.*

Out of his dreams —

. . . *do what you want to do . . .*

Out of his nightmares —

. . . what you want to do . . .

His aunt's voice — he was hearing his aunt's voice! But that wasn't possible — she was dead — she'd been dead since before he was born!

He backed away from the door, stumbling to the head of the stairs.

The terrible echoes from his nightmares tumbling through his mind, he started down.

The mascara from her eyelashes streaking her cheeks, her makeup smeared, the scissors from her mother's sewing box clutched in her hand, Joan fairly shook with rage as she faced her sister. "You can't take him back!" she screamed. "It's too late!"

"I don't have to take him back!" Cynthia replied. *"I never gave him to you in the first place!"*

"Liar!" Joan screeched. She raised the scissors high, then plunged them deep into Cynthia's cheek, slashing through skin and flesh until the point stuck in the bone beneath.

Cynthia only laughed. *"You stole him. You stole him like you stole my whole life. No wonder Mama hated you."*

Joan jerked the scissors free, then slashed again. "She loved me! She always loved me! She only punished me because she loved me!"

"You were nothing," Cynthia shot back. *"You were stupid, and ugly, and no one ever wanted you. Not me, not Mama, not Bill, not anyone!"*

The terrible mocking laugh rose again, and once more Joan slashed at her sister's face. But the voice went inexorably on. *"You can't have it, Joan. You can't have my life and you can't have my son! I'm taking it back! I'm taking it all back!"*

Suddenly Joan was back in New York, back in the apartment where Cynthia had hidden herself away to have her baby. Even when she'd gone into labor, she refused to go to a hospital, refused even to let Joan call a doctor. . . .

"Mama will find out," she insisted. "Mama will find out, and then she'll hate me! She'll hate me the way she hates you!"

"But what if something happens?" Joan begged. "What if something goes wrong?"

"Nothing will go wrong," Cynthia said. "I'll have the baby, and you'll get rid of it, and then I can go home."

But something did go wrong — right after the baby had been born, something went terribly wrong.

Cynthia started to bleed.

"I'm going to call a doctor," Joan insisted, but Cynthia shook her head and pointed at the baby.

"Not until you get rid of it."

Joan looked down at the tiny child in her arms. "I can't. I can't hurt him. I can't —"

"He's not yours," Cynthia hissed. "He's mine. I'll decide what to do with him."

Joan backed away, holding the baby closer. "Let me have him," she pleaded. "Let me be his mother."

Fury and venom spewed from Cynthia's tongue as freely as the blood that was flowing from her womb. "Never! He's mine, and he'll always be mine!"

"But you don't want him!"

392

"*And you can't have him!*" Cynthia pulled herself up, her arms stretched out as if to snatch the baby away from Joan. "*He's mine, and he'll always be mine!*" Spent, Cynthia flopped back against the pillow, her chest heaving as she tried to catch her breath. As Joan watched, her face grew paler, her breathing more shallow.

A moment later her breathing stopped and she lay still.

Joan stood staring at her sister, holding the baby close to her breast. What should she do? Should she call a doctor?

Too late.

The police?

What if they took the baby away?

Go away. Just take the baby and go away.

The idea seemed to come out of nowhere, and at first she dismissed it. But then she thought about it.

No one knew who Cynthia was. She had taken the apartment — a grubby, furnished room in a building filled with drug addicts and whores — under another name. She'd even gotten identification under that name. "*After I get rid of the baby, I'll just go home,*" she told Joan. "*The person who lives here will just cease to exist, and I can go back to my life. But you can bet I won't get pregnant again!*"

Now, as Joan stood staring at her sister's body, she tried to think of a reason not to simply walk away from the dingy room, as Cynthia had intended to do. No one knew she was here — even people who might have seen her had no idea who she was. She held the baby tighter, gazing down into its perfect face. "Everything will be

393

all right now," she whispered. "I'll be your mother, and I'll love you. And your grandmother will love you too." And Mother will love me now, she thought. When she sees the baby, she'll love him, and she'll love me too. She edged toward the door. It would work! She'd take the baby, and in a few months — just long enough so no one would wonder why she hadn't looked pregnant when she left — she would go back home. Everything would be perfect! Her mother would love her, and the baby would love her.

But a few minutes later, as she was leaving, she thought she heard her sister's voice: "It won't work, Joanie-baby. You can't be me. You can never be me."

"I can be you!" she screamed, raising the scissors yet again. "I can! I can!" Over and over the scissors slashed into the portrait until, like everything else that had been Cynthia's, it lay in tatters on the floor. Her rage finally spent, Joan turned away from the destruction she'd created and went back to Cynthia's vanity table. "I can be you," she said. "I can."

She cleaned away the smeared makeup, then set to work once more. But as she applied the makeup this time, she worked quickly and efficiently.

As quickly and efficiently as Cynthia herself . . .

Chapter 25

The house closed around Matt, making him feel like a trapped animal. He moved restlessly from room to room, but wherever he went the voice followed him.

Suddenly, he felt an overwhelming urge to escape, to free himself from the confines of the walls around him, and the terrors they contained. He started toward the front door, then paused. Where would he go? Where would he be safe?

He had no friends — no one except Becky Adams.

No family, except for his mother.

Nowhere — no one — to turn to.

Turning away from the front door, he went into the living room, then into the den.

His eyes fell on his stepfather's desk. In an instant he was a little boy again — only five years old — and it was the day he'd come to live in this house. It was so big it frightened him, but his stepfather took his hand and led him through all the rooms, showing him everything, encouraging him to open every closet, every drawer, so he'd know what was inside. By the time they went through the house, he hadn't been frightened anymore.

But there was one drawer — the bottom

drawer on the right-hand side of his stepfather's desk — that hadn't opened. He tried, but it was locked.

When he asked about it, his stepfather smiled at him. "Everybody has to have a few secrets," he said, winking mysteriously. "And that drawer contains mine."

From then on Matt had wondered what might be hidden in that bottom drawer, but his stepfather had never told him. "You'll find out someday. When the time's right, I'll show you everything that's in that drawer."

Then, last week, his stepfather had said something else. They'd been talking about his birthday, and his stepfather grinned at him. "Maybe I'll give you something really special," he said, and Matt had wondered if his dad was going to come home. But that dream had lasted no more than a second. "Maybe I'll finally show you what's in my secret drawer," his father went on, his expression turning serious.

Matt didn't tell him that he'd stopped wondering about the drawer years ago, when he decided there probably wasn't anything in it at all — at least nothing really wonderful. Probably just a bunch of old papers.

But now, as he gazed at the drawer, the memory of his aunt's words came back to him, *"He's mine . . . he's always been mine."* And he wondered if there might actually be something in the drawer.

Something about him.

Now Gerry Conroe's shouted words came back to him. "Who is he? Who is Matt? Tell me the truth!"

Was that what his stepfather had hidden in the drawer? The truth? His pulse quickening, Matt knelt down and pulled at the drawer.

It was locked.

He pulled open the other drawers, searching for a key, but there was none. But the lock looked simple — very much like the lock on his own desk upstairs.

A lock that had never had a key, but that he'd figured out how to pick when he was only ten years old. All it took was a paper clip — one of the big ones, that wouldn't bend easily.

He rummaged through the top drawer of the desk again and quickly found what he was looking for, almost lost in a jumble of rubber bands so old they were crumbling. Straightening the paper clip, he carefully inserted about three-eighths of an inch of its end into the crack between one of the drawers and the desk's frame, then bent it ninety degrees. Inserting the bent end into the lock, he carefully rotated one way and then the other, feeling for the familiar resistance of the locking device. When the end of the pick caught, he tested it a couple of times, then gave the paper clip a quick twist.

The lock clicked open.

Matt pulled the drawer open, not knowing what to expect.

What he found was a file folder.

Lifting it out, he set it on top of the desk and opened it.

Photographs.

Photographs of himself.

In two of them he couldn't have been more than two or three years old. Then there was one in which he looked to be about five, and in the others he was a little older.

But something wasn't right. He looked more closely at the photos, and in an instant he knew: they weren't of him. He didn't recognize the backgrounds in any of them, or the other people who appeared in two of them. And now that he looked more closely, the boy looked most like him in those in which he was youngest. In the last one, where the boy looked to be about the same age as Matt was now, the resemblance was still strong, but it was clear that whoever the boy was, it wasn't him.

Then who? Matt wondered Where had the pictures come from? What did they mean?

He was going through them again, examining them even more closely, when he smelled it: his aunt's perfume, filling his nostrils with its musky scent. He froze. He could feel her now — she was right behind him!

But that was impossible! She wasn't real! She was dead! But as the scent in his nostrils grew stronger, he turned around.

His eyes widened in shock as he stared up at the figure that loomed above him. She looked almost exactly like the portrait of his aunt that hung in the guest room upstairs. Her hair — her makeup —

everything about her looked the same. "Aunt Cynth—" But before he could finish, the figure spoke.

"I'm not your aunt! I'm your mother! And I'll never let you go! Never!"

Only now did Matt see the fireplace poker raised high and arcing down toward his head.

"You're mine," he heard. "You'll always be mine."

The weapon struck, and Matt crumpled to the floor.

Becky Adams read the page of her history text for what seemed the hundredth time, but it made no more sense to her now than it had an hour ago, when she first slammed the door of her room — not quite in her mother's face, but almost — and flopped down on her bed to study. Except she hadn't been studying at all; she'd been seeing the words, but the meaning hadn't registered. Finally giving up, she tossed the book aside, skootched farther down on the bed, and stared up at the ceiling. The plaster was spider-webbed with a network of cracks that, over the years, had provided her with hours of lonely entertainment as she searched for new pictures or traced new routes through an imaginary maze. But this afternoon even the patterns on the ceiling couldn't lift her spirits.

And she'd felt so good when she came in after Matt walked her home from school, the warmth of his kiss still warm on her lips. But that good feeling hadn't lasted after she closed the front door behind her.

"You come in here right this minute, Rebecca Anne!" her mother had commanded from the living room.

Her mother's use of both her names told Becky she was angry. Then she saw the small glass of sherry on the table next to her mother's chair and understood. She tried to pull her eyes away from the nearly empty glass, but it was too late.

"Don't you get that look on your face, young lady," Phyllis Adams said, the edge in her voice telling Becky this wasn't her mother's first glass of wine. "If I want to have a little treat for myself in the afternoon, it's nobody's business but my own."

"I didn't say anything —" Becky began.

"You didn't have to! Don't you think I can see?" Before Becky could answer, she plunged on. "I can see far better than you think I can." Her eyes fixed accusingly on her daughter. "I saw you kissing that *boy*." She spat the last word out as if it tasted bad.

"What do you mean, 'that *boy?*'" Becky protested, mimicking her mother's tone, and realizing her mistake too late to avoid it. "It was Matt Moore. You like Matt! You've always liked him!"

"Don't you sass me, Rebecca Anne." Phyllis had pulled back the curtain over the front window just far enough to peer out, as if to make certain Matt was no longer there. "Everybody knows what Matt did to his father and grandmother. And now poor Kelly Conroe's missing — I feel so bad for Nancy Conroe, I can hardly bear it." Her eyes glistened

400

with sudden tears, and she picked up the decanter that stood next to her glass, pouring enough to raise the level in the glass past the halfway point. "How could you kiss him?" she asked. "If he gets the wrong idea about you —" She shuddered, unable even to bring herself to articulate what might happen to her daughter.

But Becky had had enough. "You don't even know what you're talking about, Mother."

"Don't you take that tone with me, young lady."

"Then don't talk about things you don't know anything about! Especially not when you've been drinking."

Even now, Becky could remember the look of outrage that came over her mother's face, a look so seemingly genuine that if Becky hadn't seen it a hundred times before — when her mother had been so drunk she could hardly stand up — she might have believed it.

"How dare you?" Phyllis raged. "Just because I might have a little sip every now and then doesn't mean —"

"Fine, Mother," Becky said, holding up her hands as if to stop the denials she knew might well go on for several minutes. "But you're still wrong about Matt. He's —"

"He's a killer, and a rapist, and God only knows what else! And when your father gets home —"

That was when Becky had gone to her room, slammed the door, and flopped down onto the bed to study. Why bother to listen to it anymore? She knew what would happen when her father got home. He'd hear her mother out, let her ramble on until she ran out of steam, then come in and try to gloss over the whole thing, managing to apologize to his daughter without quite condemning his wife. "Your mother's a little high-strung sometimes," he'd say. "You just have to try not to upset her."

Now, still sprawled out on her bed, Becky heard her father's car pull into the driveway. She heard its door slam, the back door open and close, and her father call out to her mother. Then she heard the murmur of voices drifting in from the living room. She could practically count the seconds until she'd hear the soft knock that meant it was time for her father's not-quite-apology for her mother. Except that when it finally came, it wasn't a soft knock at all. It was a sharp rap, followed immediately by her father opening the door and stepping into her room.

"Your mother tells me you were with Matt Moore this afternoon," Frank Adams began, his forehead creased with deep worry lines.

Becky's jaw almost dropped open in surprise, and she sat up, swinging around to face her father. As the anticipation of his apology faded, she felt the anger that had been simmering for the last hour surge to a boil. "I don't believe it! You've always liked Matt — in fact, you've always wanted to know why I don't go out with him!"

Frank Adams's eyes narrowed defensively. "That was before —" he said, but his daughter was on her feet now.

"Before what?" she demanded, her voice rising. "Before everybody decided he did all kinds of horrible things? Well, if he did them all, how come he hasn't been arrested?" The memory of the misery in Matt's face and voice as they'd stood on the sidewalk while he confessed his own doubts rose to the forefront of Becky's mind. "He didn't do anything, Daddy! If he had, he'd have told —" She cut her words off abruptly, but it was too late.

"Told who?" her father asked. "Told you? Why would he do that? And if he didn't do anything, then what happened to Bill Hapgood? He was there when Bill got shot! He was standing right there, and he shot a deer that was between him and Bill! It doesn't take a genius to figure it out. I'm not saying he did anything to Emily Moore — God knows she might have just wandered off. But what about Kelly Conroe? She wasn't the kind of girl who'd just take off, so something must have happened to her. And Matt is the only person that makes sense!"

Becky's eyes glittered with fury. "It does not!" she insisted. "Maybe Matt did shoot his dad. But even if he did, it was just an accident! And anybody could have picked up Kelly — if she was walking home by herself, anyone could have come along and picked her up!"

"That's not what happened," Frank Adams insisted.

Becky's temper snapped. "How would you know what happened?" she shot back. "You don't even know what happens in your own house! You

403

don't even know that Mom's drunk all the time! All she has to do is deny it — just claim she had a 'bad day' or something — and you make every excuse you can think of for her! But not for Matt! Even though you've known him all his life, and always told me he's exactly the kind of boy I should marry. Well, guess what, Daddy? I'm not going to marry Matt, because he's never going to ask me! Why would he, with the kind of parents I have?"

When she stormed out of the house, neither of her parents made a move to stop her. Her father was too stunned by her outburst to do anything but watch her go. Her mother was too drunk even to know she'd gone.

Her fury still raging, Becky set off down the street. If she was the only friend Matt still had, he was also the only friend she had.

Cynthia Moore moved slowly through the house, carefully examining each of the rooms, deciding what she would keep and what must be changed. Some of the pieces were really quite good — she recognized them as family heirlooms that had undoubtedly been in the Hapgood family for generations. But others — both the Queen Anne chair in the living room, which was obviously a reproduction, and the not-quite-Chippendale sideboard that stood gracelessly in the dining room — would have to go. Not that she was surprised to find the less than perfect furnishings: Joan had never had any taste, and undoubtedly had never noticed that the pieces she'd put in the house simply weren't up to standard. What she did find surprising was that Bill Hapgood had allowed Joan's taste to taint the house so badly.

When she finished her tour of the downstairs rooms, she returned to the second floor. First she went to the master suite, into which she would move her things this very day. Going to the closet, she pulled a large suitcase off the top shelf — second rate, like everything else Joan had surrounded herself with — and began filling it with the contents of Joan's dresser. Not all of it had to go, of course. There were a few things — some lingerie, a few silk blouses, and some very good cashmere sweaters — that she recognized as having been gifts from Bill Hapgood. But the things Joan herself had bought all disappeared into the suitcase, just as Joan herself had vanished a little more than an hour ago, when Cynthia had finally come to the end of her patience and decided to take over completely. Having made room for her things in the dresser, Cynthia started back to the guest room to deal with the mess Joan had made. Her hand was on the knob when she heard the front doorbell chime softly from below. For a moment she was tempted not to answer it at all — the house was hardly in condition for her to receive visitors yet. But when the doorbell rang a second time, she sighed, went downstairs, carefully put on her most gracious smile, and opened the door.

The girl standing on the porch was about Matt's age, and struck her as unfortunately plain, her hair as badly done as Joan's had always been. She wore clothing Cynthia considered drab, the kind of clothing she had always hated. She was about to close the door, but before she did, she decided to retrieve a name for the girl from Joan's memory and talk to her, if only for a moment.

Becky.

Becky Adams.

She opened the door a little wider, adjusting her smile to project a degree of cordiality, if not quite friendliness. The girl, after all, was not the sort of person toward whom Cynthia Moore would ever have been more than polite.

Becky Adams looked uncertainly at Joan Hapgood. Though she recognized her immediately, she appeared different to Becky than the last time she'd seen her, at Mr. Hapgood's funeral. She had changed the way she did her hair, putting it up in a French twist, and her makeup was different too. It almost looked like she wasn't wearing any, except that her cheekbones seemed a little higher, and her eyes looked wider apart.

Though Becky had always thought Matt's mother was pretty, she now seemed truly beautiful. Even the way she stood made her look different, and left Becky feeling self-conscious about her own plain features and slumping posture.

"What is it, Becky?"

Becky frowned uncertainly. Even Mrs. Hapgood's voice sounded different — low, and sort of throaty. "Is — I was wondering if Matt's home," she said, her voice faltering.

Cynthia hesitated, then pulled the door further

open and stepped back. "I'm afraid he's upstairs in the shower, but I'm sure he'll want to see you. Won't you come in?"

Becky remained where she was for a moment. It almost seemed to her that the woman inviting her into the house wasn't Mrs. Hapgood at all. But of course she could see that it was. She stepped inside.

"Perhaps you'd like to wait in here," Cynthia said, guiding her through the wide archway that led to the spacious living room. She gestured Becky into one of the wing-backed chairs that flanked the fireplace, and lowered herself onto the edge of the one opposite it. "I'm sure Matt won't be more than a few minutes," she said, her eyes fixing on Becky.

Becky fidgeted under her gaze. "Maybe I should come back some other time," she said, starting to get up. "Or you could just have Matt call me."

Cynthia leaned forward, holding out her hand as if to stop Becky. "Oh, no," she insisted. "You mustn't go — you just got here, and I know Matt wouldn't want to miss you."

Uncertain what to do, Becky nervously eased herself back into the chair. Then the demeanor of the woman sitting opposite her changed.

"You're in love with my son, aren't you?" Cynthia Moore asked, her eyes hardening, her voice suddenly cold.

"No!" Becky protested. "I —"

"Of course you are. It shows all over you. But it

won't do you any good. He belongs to me!"

Becky's stomach suddenly felt hollow, and a chill ran through her. What was Mrs. Hapgood talking about? In a cold sweat that made her body feel clammy, Becky stood up. She was so frightened, her legs would barely support her. "I better go home," she said, her voice quavering.

Opposite her, Mrs. Hapgood rose from her chair, her eyes still fixed on her, but it seemed to Becky that she was seeing something, or someone, else.

Joan wanted him," she said, "and Bill wanted him, and that terrible Conroe girl. They all wanted Matt, but none of them could have him." Her eyes bored into Becky, who was trembling now. "You can't have him either, you pathetic child. He's mine, and he always will be."

Becky tried to back away, tried to turn and run to the front door, but her body refused to obey her. It wasn't until Mrs. Hapgood moved toward her, her hands reaching out, that Becky finally came back to life and wheeled away. But her foot caught on the thick Oriental rug and she fell, sprawling facedown. She tried to scramble to her feet, but by then Mrs. Hapgood was on top of her, sitting astride her, pinning her to the floor.

Then she felt the woman's hands clutching at her hair, pulling her head up.

"Do you understand?" Cynthia screamed. "You can't have him!" She slammed Becky's head onto the floor, then raised it. "I won't let you have him!"

Again she slammed Becky's face into the carpet,

and a howl of pain and terror erupted from the girl's throat.

"No one can have him!"

She smashed Becky's head against the floor again.

"He's mine . . . he'll always be mine . . . I'll never let anyone take him away again."

When Cynthia's fury was finally spent, Becky Adams lay still on the carpet.

Chapter 26

Half carrying, half dragging Becky Adams, Cynthia made her way down the stairs into the basement. She didn't like the basement — it was far too dark and dirty for her tastes — but it didn't hold the terror for her that it held for Joan. But Joan had always been a fraidy-cat, screaming the moment she'd first been put in the cedar chest in the basement of the house on Burlington Avenue all those years ago. Cynthia had almost felt sorry for her the first time their mother did it, but she knew that if she did anything — even said anything — she would be the one her mother locked up.

It had actually happened once, when she was very young. She couldn't even remember anymore what her infraction had been, but remembered that after her mother was finished slapping her — hard — she was taken down to the basement and put in the cedar chest.

Then the lid was closed.

Cynthia had been terrified, not only of the dark, but of the awful feeling that the box might actually crush her.

But she hadn't let herself scream.

She hadn't even let herself move. Instead, she'd forced herself to lie perfectly still and close her eyes and pretend she wasn't in the box at all. And she made up her mind that no matter what she had to do, she would never let her mother slap her again.

She would never let herself be put in the box again.

And she would get even.

Some day — some way — she would make her mother feel the pain and fear she herself had felt that day.

From then on, Cynthia said whatever she had to say, did whatever she had to do, to keep her mother from punishing her.

She didn't let herself get slapped.

She didn't let herself get put back in the cedar chest.

For a while it had been hard — she had to be so careful about what she did that most of the time she just didn't do anything at all — but after Joan was born, it got a lot easier. As soon as Joan was old enough to crawl, Cynthia began blaming things on her; she was already a good enough liar that her mother always believed her. From then on, it was Joan who took the punishment for whatever Cynthia did — and screamed through every minute of it.

Now, as Cynthia dragged Becky across the floor to the trapdoor that was the only entrance to the old root cellar, she wondered what would have happened if Joan had summoned up the courage to come down here — or, even worse, if Joan had managed to regain control before she had finally become strong enough to take over completely.

Maybe Joan would have been happy, seeing what she'd done to their mother. But probably not; for some reason — some reason that she had never been able to understand — Joan kept loving their mother. It never seemed to matter how cruel the old woman was, Joan always managed to make excuses for her.

Weak. That's what Joan had always been — just plain weak!

Heaving the trapdoor open, Cynthia peered down into the black pit below. Her nostrils filled with the putrid odor of rotting flesh mixed with urine and feces, but she paid no attention to the vile stench as she pushed Becky through the opening, barely waiting for the girl's body to drop to the dirt floor before closing the trapdoor and returning to the bright rooms upstairs.

Climbing to the second floor, she went to the guest room to clean up the mess Joan had made. Most of the clothes would be all right — she could find a seamstress to fix the damage, and after they were cleaned and pressed, they would be almost as good as new. But as she tried to put the pictures back together — the wonderful images of herself that she'd always kept on her walls, and in frames on her desk, and next to her bed — her anger toward Joan grew stronger than ever.

The pictures were ruined!

She remembered, then, the album her mother kept hidden in the drawer of her nightstand. The album that was filled with copies of every picture Cynthia had, and dozens more. Leaving the guest

412

room, Cynthia went through the bathroom to the room next door. Her mother's nightstand was gone! She felt a flash of panic. Was it possible that every picture of her — every image of her beauty — could be gone?

No! Of course not! The nightstand wasn't here, but her mother would have saved the album.

Frantically, Cynthia began searching for it. Beginning with the dresser that stood against the wall opposite the foot of the bed, she pulled open one drawer after another, scattering their contents across the floor until the rug was strewn with a jumble of nightgowns, underwear, sweaters, and stockings — things her mother hadn't worn in years, but had refused to give up.

Finally, in the third drawer of the bureau that stood next to the window, Cynthia found it. The album was covered with cheap leatherette that had long ago worn away to reveal the cardboard beneath, but Cynthia handled it with as much care as if it were a Gutenberg Bible. Lifting it from the drawer, she laid it carefully on a table, opened it, and began turning the pages.

They were all there. Every photograph she remembered, from the first one, taken when she was only a month old, to the last, taken just before she had gone away to New York. Even though the baby hadn't been showing yet, she could see the radiance in her eyes the day the photo was taken. It was a lovely photograph — far too lovely to be hidden away in her mother's old photo album. It should be downstairs!

Cynthia knew where she wanted it to be. Not just this one, but all of them. She took the album downstairs and into the den. Rummaging in the top drawer of Bill's desk, she found a pair of scissors, then carefully set to work.

One by one she removed the photographs that sat on top of Bill Hapgood's desk — photographs of his wedding, and his wife, and his family — and carefully cut out the images of Joan. Then, equally carefully, she cut her own face from the photographs in the album.

For the formal portrait taken the day Joan and Bill were married, she chose a photograph of herself as homecoming queen, taken during her last year of high school. The dress she'd worn had been white, its panels and bodice embroidered with rhinestones. It had looked almost like a wedding dress, and as she carefully placed it over the cutout where Joan's image had been, Cynthia knew the image of herself was finally in its rightful place.

"It should have been me anyway," she murmured as she slipped the altered photo back into its frame. Standing it up, she stepped back, cocked her head, and gazed at her work with a critical eye. From only six feet away, the picture looked totally genuine.

Not only genuine, but right.

Then she moved on to the photographs on the desk, replacing the cutouts of Joan's face and figure with images of herself from the album until all the photographs on Bill's desk had been altered.

Bill and Cynthia at their wedding, their son

414

standing next to his mother.

Cynthia and Matt, on the Eiffel Tower, gazing out over Paris. Looking at the picture, Cynthia could almost see the view herself, as clearly as if it she had been there instead of Joan.

Bill, Cynthia, and Matt, riding horses five years ago.

"Perfect," she whispered as she gazed at the photographs, now put back in the positions Bill had left them. "Now it's right. Now it's the way it should have been. . . ."

Matt drifted back to consciousness, the line between sleep and wakefulness so blurred that he wasn't sure where one state ended and the other began. Pain was the first thing he became aware of — pain that seemed to have seized every nerve of his body.

His head ached — a dull, throbbing ache that intensified every time his heart beat. Instinctively, he reached up to touch his head, but his shoulder protested, sending a searing tongue of agony down not only his arm, but his body as well. He groaned out loud, then made himself lie still as the spasm slowly eased.

Where was he? The blackness around him was so deep he could feel it closing in on him as if it were something physical. Claustrophobia gripped him then, and he lashed out in panic with his feet, as if to kick at an unseen enemy. But when his feet touched nothing, the claustrophobia lost its grip and his panic subsided.

His nostrils filled with a foul odor then — urine and feces, mixed with something else, something he couldn't quite identify, but that made his skin crawl and his stomach heave. Steeling himself against the revolting stench, he tried moving again, experimenting with his limbs one by one. His legs were sore, but the pain began to ease as he moved them. Satisfied that they weren't broken, he tested his arms. They felt all right, except for the pain in his shoulders. In fact, his shoulders felt like they had when he slammed into a practice bag too hard a couple of weeks ago. They'd ached for a couple of hours, but nothing was broken. So now he thought that he must have run into something, or fallen.

He reached up to touch his head again, moving slowly this time, working through the pain in his shoulder. He felt something sticky matting his hair, brought his fingers to his mouth and licked them. The salty taste of blood spread across his tongue.

He touched his head again, and felt a swollen, spongy knob. A cut across the top of the knob stung when his fingers encountered the raw nerves exposed by his torn scalp.

Hit by something.

Something hard, and with an edge sharp enough to —

An image flashed into his mind. *Aunt Cynthia!* He'd been in the den — at his father's desk — and his nostrils had filled with the scent of his aunt's perfume. He'd looked up, and —

And seen her!

She'd been there, looming above him, holding a

fireplace poker. But that was impossible! His aunt was dead.

Struggling to hold on to the image before it could fade away from his memory like the wispy vestiges of a dream, he suddenly saw it. Not his aunt — his mother! That's who it had been!

Her face had been covered with makeup, and she'd twisted her hair up the way his aunt's was in the big picture hanging in the guest room, but behind the makeup, it had been his mother's face.

Memories of dreams tumbled through his mind, dreams in which his aunt had come to him in the night, and he'd heard her voice whispering to him, telling him she loved him.

Felt her fingers on his flesh.

Felt her slipping into bed beside him, caressing him, touching him.

Not dreams!

It had never been dreams!

A wave of nausea rose inside him as the truth sank in. How many times had it happened? How many times had his mother crept into his bed in the middle of the night?

Three times?

Six?

A dozen?

No! Not that many! It couldn't have been that many. He struggled to remember, but all the memories seemed twisted together.

He lay still in the darkness, wanting to shut out the terrible memories of what he and his mother had done. Again he told himself it had only been a dream, that his mother couldn't possibly have done the things he was remembering, but even as his mind struggled to repress it all, his body remembered, and merely the memory of her touch brought back the stirring heat in his groin.

With the excitement came guilt. Was it possible that he'd actually liked it? No! No, he couldn't have!

But if he hadn't liked it, why had he let her come back?

A sob caught in his throat, and he wished he could die in the blackness, wished the darkness could swallow him up so he would never have to be exposed to the light again, never again have to be seen by anyone.

A sense that he wasn't alone suddenly overwhelmed Matt, pulling him from his thoughts. He felt an unseen presence, lurking in the darkness nearby.

He tensed stopped breathing for a moment as he waited in the dark for the familiar scent of his aunt Cynthia's musky perfume.

Then he heard a soft, muffled groan.

Pulling himself to his hands and knees, ignoring the pain in his shoulders and his head, Matt crawled through the darkness. "Who is it?" he whispered. "Who's here?"

Again he heard the muffled sound, closer now. He groped in the darkness, and a moment later touched something. It moved, and his hand reflexively jerked away. Once again he heard it, it sounded as if someone were trying to say something. He reached out, and this time when his hand brushed against something, he didn't pull away.

"It's all right," he whispered. "I won't hurt you." He reached out with his other hand and felt an arm . . . an arm in a sleeve.

He moved his hands up the arm until his fingers brushed against bare skin. Hearing a muffled cry, he understood. Whoever he'd touched was gagged.

Quickly, he groped in the darkness until his fingers found a face, and felt the duct tape over the mouth. Carefully, he worked a corner of the tape loose, then slowly began peeling it away. Before he finished, the head jerked back, leaving the tape hanging in his fingers.

"Matt? Is that you?"

It was Kelly!

"What happened?" he asked. "What are you doing here?"

Sobbing, her voice barely audible, Kelly tried to tell him what had happened. "I was coming to see you . . . I just hated the way everyone was treating you, and — and —" She broke off, her voice choking as relieved sobs overtook her.

"But what happened?" Matt repeated.

"Your mother," Kelly said when her sobs subsided enough so she could speak again. "She — I think she killed your grandmother. And she kicked me so hard I think my arm is broken." Matt reached out to her, but when he started to put his arms around her, she whimpered with pain. "Just hold my hand," she begged. "Hold my hand and tell me where we are."

"I don't know. I was in the den, and she — she —" He faltered, but made himself finish. "I think she wanted to kill me too," he whispered hollowly. He told her what had happened.

"There's someone else here too," Kelly said when he finished. "She opened the trapdoor again a little while ago and pushed somebody down."

"Trapdoor?" Matt echoed. "You mean, like in the ceiling?"

"Yes. There's a ladder she uses when she comes down, and —"

"I know!" Matt blurted. "I know where we are — the old root cellar in the basement of our house!" He was silent a moment. "But Mom won't even go down in the basement — she hates it. She says it gives her claustrophobia!" He stood up and moved around in the darkness, feeling for the walls.

Twice his feet struck objects on the floor and he stumbled. The first time, he knelt down and found a corpse, its flesh cold, and he knew what had caused the stench he smelled when he woke up a few minutes ago.

It was the stink of rotting flesh.

The second time he stumbled, it was another body, but when he knelt down, he felt the warmth of life. The body stirred under his touch, and he heard a soft moan.

"Who is it?" he asked. "Who are you?"

There was a silence, and then he heard a voice,

barely audible, whimpering.

"Don't hurt me. Please don't hurt me."

"Becky?" Matt breathed. "Is that you?"

Becky Adams's only response was to beg him again not to hurt her.

"It's okay," he assured her. "I'm going to get you out. I'm going to get all of us out."

But he knew the root cellar, could picture it as clearly as if it were illuminated with a halogen lamp. Its walls were bare and featureless. The ceiling was more than eight feet above the floor. The trapdoor — the only way to enter the chamber — was in the center of that ceiling. Even if he could find some way to reach it, how would he open it? It was impossible.

There was no way out.

Though the TV was on, Dan Pullman was neither watching it nor listening to the vacuously pretty blonde who was earnestly reporting the news of a low-sodium diet in the same solemn tones in which she'd discussed a plane crash a few moments earlier. Instead, the police chief's attention was fixed on the special edition of the *Granite Falls Ledger* that had been on his doorstep when he arrived home ten minutes ago. Most of the front page was taken up by an unsigned piece, obviously written by Gerry Conroe, suggesting that if the local police were unable to solve the disappearances of both Emily Moore and Kelly Conroe within the next twenty-four hours, it would be time "to look to new leadership at our police department." The *Ledger* was certainly keeping accounts tonight, Pullman thought sourly. Why not just demand that he resign right now and be done with it?

His phone rang as he tossed the paper aside, and for a moment he was tempted to ignore it; Heather's friends knew better than to call on his line, and if it were something important from the department, the message would come over the radio that sat on the end table next to his recliner. When the phone rang at his house, it was usually either someone calling to criticize something he'd done, or to demand that he deal with a situation that was beyond the purview of his department. On the other hand, he knew there was a remote possibility that this particular call might be from someone as fed up with Gerry Conroe as he was, and phoning to offer support. Which wasn't really fair, he silently chided himself as he reached for the receiver. This time, at least, Conroe had a legitimate reason to be unreasonable.

"Hello?"

"Becky's gone, Dan." The man at the other end of the line spoke only the three words, but Dan recognized Frank Adams's voice at the first syllable. Frank had been his best friend since they'd had a fight in second grade, and hardly a day had gone by since then that they hadn't talked to each other.

"Tell me exactly what happened," Dan said.

Frank Adams reconstructed the fight Becky had with her mother. "I'm not going to pretend Becky hasn't ever taken off before," he said. "She has, and frankly, there have been times when I couldn't blame her. God knows I've wanted to take off myself plenty of times over the years. But before, she's always cooled off in an hour or so and come back home. You know Becky — she's a good kid, but she doesn't have a lot of friends. The only place I thought that she might go was out to the Hapgoods' to see Matt."

"Did you call there?" Dan asked.

"That's why I'm calling you. Joan said she hasn't seen Becky, but she also told me that Matt's not there. And after what happened to Kelly Conroe . . ." Frank Adams's voice trailed off, but he didn't have to finish his sentence for his friend to get the message.

"Frank, there's absolutely no hard evidence that Matt's done anything wrong. Just a lot of gossip and innuendo, and people wanting quick answers."

It occurred to him to give Frank the same speech he'd given Gerry Conroe last night, but he knew he couldn't do it. Frank Adams wasn't Gerry Conroe, and in all the years he'd been running the Granite Falls police department, Frank had never presumed on their friendship for any kind of favor. Once, he'd even insisted on being given a speeding ticket Tony Petrocelli was about to tear up on the basis of his friendship with the chief. "You do that, and I'll report you to Dan myself," Frank warned Petrocelli. Though Frank had never told Dan about the incident, Petrocelli had.

"Let me make a few calls, and see what I can find out," Pullman said now.

"I know I shouldn't be calling you yet —" Frank began.

"You shouldn't call your best friend when your daughter's missing?" Pullman cut in. "If that's all you think of me, maybe I don't want to be your friend anymore." He started to hang up, then added one more word, just to let Frank know he wasn't really mad at him: "Jerk!"

"Asshole," Frank replied, just as he had since the fight in second grade.

Both men hung up, and Pullman immediately picked up the phone and dialed Joan Hapgood's number.

Cynthia was just pouring herself a glass of Bill's favorite sherry — something Joan had always declined when he'd offered it — when the phone rang. For a moment Cynthia was tempted to ignore it; she hadn't liked the way Frank Adams spoke to her when he called a few minutes ago, and had no wish to speak to him again. He hadn't been rude, precisely, but she heard an accusatory note in his voice. Still, if she didn't answer, he might take it into his head to drive out here, which appealed to her even less than speaking to him on the phone. She picked up the receiver on the fourth ring, and was careful to keep her voice neutral. Not cold, but not overly friendly either. "Hello?"

There was a moment's hesitation, then: "Joan?"

Not Frank Adams.

Reaching into her sister's memory, Cynthia quickly identified the voice of the police chief. "Oh dear, Dan," she said, her voice taking on an overtone of concern. "Is this about the little Adams girl?"

"Frank just called me," Pullman replied. "He tells me Matt isn't there?"

The question hung in the air for a few seconds before Cynthia responded. "No, I'm afraid he isn't. He came home from school, but then went out again."

"Do you know where he went?"

Cynthia felt a twinge of annoyance. "No, I don't. But surely you don't believe he could be interested in Becky Adams, do you? Such a —" She was about to say "homely girl" but quickly edited herself. "— shy little thing. Not the sort Matt would be interested in, no matter how much she chased him."

Dan Pullman's brow furrowed deeply. What was Joan talking about? Becky chasing Matt? He couldn't imagine Becky Adams chasing any boy, least of all Matt Moore, whom she'd known all her life. And there was something strange in her voice too. Though it sounded like Joan, it didn't sound quite right. "What makes you think she was chasing him?" he asked.

There was a barely perceptible silence before he heard Joan Hapgood's voice again. "All the girls chase him, Dan. Just like all the boys used to chase my sister. Don't you remember? The boys always flocked around Cynthia just the way the girls flock around Matt."

Pullman's puzzlement deepened. Cynthia? He hadn't heard her name mentioned in quite a while. And didn't she know that the boys had sniffed around her sister because Cynthia had a reputation for doing pretty much anything any of them had in mind? "I'd never really thought Matt was much like his aunt," he said carefully.

"Don't be silly," Cynthia replied. "He's exactly like Cynthia! Good looking, and charming and —" She caught herself. "But of course you're not interested in Matt, are you? It's that Adams girl you called about. But I'm afraid I can't help you any more than I could help her father. I simply haven't seen her."

Dan was about to hang up when he realized that Joan hadn't asked about her mother. In fact, Joan hadn't called all afternoon to ask whether he'd found any sign of Emily Moore. "Joan, are you all right?" he asked.

"Of course I'm all right," Cynthia replied, and after a moment added, "I mean, given the circumstances."

Even after he hung up, Pullman's eyes remained fixed on the phone. Something wasn't right. Everything Joan Hapgood had said sounded a bit off, as if there were someone else in the room with her, making her try to act as if nothing was wrong.

But who? Matt?

But Matt was barely sixteen years old, and as far as Pullman knew, neither his mother nor anyone else had ever been the least bit intimidated by him. No one, anyway, except Eric Holmes, and Pullman was no more inclined to believe Eric's story now than he had been last night. But he was certain that something was wrong at the Hapgood house. Getting out of his chair, he tiredly began putting his uniform back on, meanwhile working on a mental list of things to do before he actually went back out to see Joan Hapgood. Given what her attorney had told him just last night, he knew he'd better have a lot more to go on than just a feeling that something wasn't right out there. So first he would have a talk with Frank Adams, and Phyllis too, if she was sober enough to be coherent. Then he'd have a look around and see if he could find Becky in the usual places kids went. And finally he would call Trip Wainwright — better to take him along than have Joan call him herself.

It was going to be a long evening.

He didn't believe me, Cynthia thought as she put the phone down. He's going to come out here and try to take my son away from me. But he won't . . . he won't take Matt away.

I won't let him.

Chapter 27

Fingers of panic reached out of the darkness toward Matt, but before they could find a hold on the fringes of his mind, he managed to pull away, to force himself to ignore the suffocating blackness that had not only blinded him, but threatened to drive him into a terror so deep he knew he might never escape. The panic had become a living thing — he could feel its presence circling him in the darkness, relentlessly stalking him as it waited for a moment of weakness in which it would be able to slip through the barriers he'd put up.

Escape.

He had to find some way to escape, to get to the trapdoor in the ceiling. Kelly Conroe, with one of her arms broken and her body so badly bruised that she couldn't bear the pain, had retreated back into the sanctuary of unconsciousness. Matt was certain that if he didn't find a way to get her out, she would die.

Like his grandmother had died.

Twice, he'd made a circuit of the perimeter of the chamber, feeling his way along the wall like a rat sniffing its way through a sewer. Twice, he'd come to his grandmother's corpse. Twice, he'd felt his fingers sink into her cold flesh. The first time,

428

his belly had contracted in a spasm of retching, and his mouth filled with bile.

"What's wrong?" Becky had whispered, hearing him coughing and gagging. Though she'd kept her voice so low it was almost inaudible, it seemed to Matt to echo off the walls, resounding so loudly that he was certain his mother would appear at any moment.

"It's okay," he whispered back when he trusted himself to speak. "I — I just ran into something, that's all."

The second time he touched his grandmother's rotting flesh, he shuddered silently but managed to control his belly.

But how much longer could he hold the panic at bay? It grew stronger, loomed larger in the blackness. He could feel it sinking its talons into his mind, but as he shook it off, he lost his orientation. Then every direction seemed the same, and when he once more found a wall, he had no more idea of where he was than he'd had before. "Becky?"

"I'm over here."

Her voice seemed to be off to the right, but Matt wasn't certain. "Where?" he asked. "Keep talking. I have to find you." As Becky continued whispering, he moved toward her voice, reaching out into the darkness. Finally he touched her, and felt her recoil in the blackness. "It's only me," he said. "Don't be scared."

"What are we going to do?" she asked.

"I have an idea," Matt said. "I don't know if it

will work, but I can't think of anything else."

"What is it?"

"We'll start from one of the corners. You'll get on my shoulders, and when we get to the trapdoor, you can lift it up."

"I'll fall!" Becky protested.

"No, you won't," Matt assured her. "I can hold you up, and you can balance yourself by holding on to the ceiling."

"But what if —" Becky began, but Matt didn't let her finish, afraid that if he didn't assert himself, he might lose what little confidence the darkness hadn't yet robbed him of.

"We have to try it," he said. "Come on." Holding Becky's hand, he groped his way through the darkness until he came to one of the walls, then edged around it until he was in a corner. He knelt down, crouching low, facing the wall. "Climb up on my shoulders," he told her. "Put your right foot up first, and lean against the wall. When I tell you, pull your other foot up. Then straighten up, and once you can balance yourself, I'll stand up. Okay?"

"I — I guess," Becky stammered.

Matt crouched down, and a moment later felt one of Becky's feet touch his back. "Higher," he said. She lifted it up, and he used his hand to guide it onto his shoulder. "Okay, now lean forward, and pull your other foot up." He felt Becky's weight bear down on him, and then, just as he thought he might collapse under the pressure on his right shoulder, she quickly lifted her other foot, found his left shoulder, and balanced her weight.

430

"Good," Matt grunted. "Now, try to stand up. Just do it slowly, and feel your way along."

"Okay," she said a few seconds later. "I'm standing up. Now what?"

"Now I'm going to hold onto your ankles, and try to stand up," Matt told her. Straightening his back, he flexed his knees. For a second he thought it wouldn't work, but then he was able to straighten up until he was standing upright. "Can you touch the ceiling?"

"Uh-huh," Becky grunted.

"Okay. I think I know where the trapdoor is, but you'll have to tell me when you feel it." He took a step away from the corner of the room, then another. He concentrated on moving toward the center of the room, but in the absence of light, he couldn't be sure exactly where he was.

After he'd taken four steps, Becky said, "I feel it!"

"Try to lift it!" Matt replied. He straightened up, locking his knees, and she shoved at the door.

It rose just enough for a faint glimmer of gray light to show through a crack, then fell back into its frame.

"What happened?" he gasped.

"I can't lift it," Becky moaned. "It's too heavy!"

"Try again," Matt said.

Once again Becky struggled to raise the trapdoor, but again its weight defeated her. This time she lost her balance, but as she dropped down, he managed to break her fall by wrapping his arms around her.

431

"I'm sorry," she said, her voice choking as she clung to him. "I just couldn't do it!"

"It's okay," he replied, trying to think of another solution. There was only one he could come up with. "You're going to have to hold me."

"I can't!" Becky protested.

"You can," Matt insisted. "There isn't any other way."

They worked their way back to the corner, and this time it was Becky who crouched down in the darkness. Matt took off his shoes, felt in the darkness until his fingers touched her, then gingerly placed his right foot on her shoulder.

"Okay," he said. "This is going to be the worst part. I'm going to push off with my left foot really hard, and you try to stand up at the same time. As soon as you feel my left foot, grab my ankles. I'll steady us both. Ready?"

Becky said nothing, but he heard her take a deep breath. Then, as he said "Go!" and lunged upward, he felt her body tense. He surged up the corner, bracing himself against the ninety-degree angle with both hands. Becky trembled beneath him, and for a moment he thought she was going to collapse, but then she steadied herself.

A second later she began turning around. "I don't know if I can —"

"Don't talk," Matt told her. "Just start working your way out toward the middle."

Then Becky was moving, though so slowly Matt thought her strength would give out long before they made it to the center of the room and the trapdoor. But after what seemed a long time, but couldn't have been more than thirty seconds, the fingers of his right hand brushed against the frame of the trapdoor.

"Another couple of steps," he said. "We're almost there." Becky edged forward, and finally Matt felt the door above him. "Okay, make yourself as rigid as you can." He could feel Becky's body tense beneath his feet and her hands tighten on his ankles.

"Now," she whispered, her voice strangling on the tension in her neck.

Matt shoved hard, and as the trapdoor lifted, he thrust one arm through just as he heard Becky yelp with pain, then collapse beneath him. For a moment he hung there, dangling, then managed to force his other arm through the crack as well. "I've got it!" he said, hauling himself up. He swung his body and lifted the trapdoor just enough with his shoulder to jam his knee through. A second later he was slithering through the gap between the basement floor and edge of the trapdoor. As he pulled his left leg free, the door dropped into place and he heard Becky's muffled voice calling out to him. Grasping the handle of the door, he pulled it all the way up so the hole in the root cellar's ceiling was fully opened. He groped for the string that would turn on the light above the trapdoor, found it, and pulled. Brilliant yellow light flooded the basement, and Matt blinked in its glare.

"Get me out," Becky pleaded. She was huddled

on the floor, staring up at him, squinting against the bright light.

"What happened?" Matt asked.

"I twisted my ankle. I don't think I can stand on it."

Matt scanned the basement and spotted the aluminum extension ladder lying on the floor a few feet away. He pulled it over to the trapdoor, lifted it up and lowered one end into the chamber below. When it rested on the ground, Becky grabbed onto it and began pulling herself up. Then she was on her feet, working her way up the ladder, hanging from each rung as she pulled her good leg up, transferred her weight to it, and reached for the next rung. She was almost at the top, reaching for Matt's extended hand, when her eyes widened and she tried to speak.

Too late.

Matt had just sensed the presence behind him when something crashed against his head. Grunting, he let go of Becky's hand and slumped to the floor.

Becky screamed as she dropped back into the root cellar. As the terrifying figure of Joan Hapgood began climbing down the ladder, clutching the shovel with which she'd just struck Matt, Becky tried to scuttle away into the shadows in the corner. But it was too late — a moment later Joan was looming over her, the shovel raised high. Becky held up her hands as the shovel arced downward, its blade slashing at her face. Clutching at the tear in her cheek, Becky tried to roll away from the shovel, but it rose and fell over and over again, its blade ripping through her flesh, smashing at her skull until she lay huddled against the wall, unmoving, her face streaming with blood.

Reaching down, Cynthia rolled Becky's body over, ripping the pocket of Becky's blouse as she did. As the pool of blood around Becky spread, Cynthia turned to peer at the body of her mother. "Look what Joan did," she whispered. "It wasn't my fault, Mama. Joan did it . . . Joan did it all. . . ."

Turning away from the bodies on the floor of the root cellar, Cynthia climbed the ladder up to the basement.

She blinked in the bright light.

Where Matt had been only a few moments ago, there was now only a smear of blood.

Her son — her perfect son — her beloved son — was gone.

Matt reeled through the door at the top of the basement stairs, oblivious to his surroundings, his mind still seared by what he'd seen in the root cellar. Stunned by the blow from the shovel, he'd collapsed on the floor next to the trapdoor, his body convulsing as waves of pain rolled through him. Then a scream cut through the pain, a terrified scream that rose into a howl of agony. Pulling himself up to his hands and knees, he peered down through the trapdoor. What he saw made his stomach heave.

Lying against one wall, her hands cut off so her arms ended in ragged stumps of decaying flesh and mangled bones, was the body of his grandmother, her nightgown stained with congealed blood, her eyes, wide-open, staring up at him.

A few feet to her left lay Kelly Conroe, curled up, her left hand clutching at her broken right arm, her face covered with bruises, a cut on her lip encrusted with a thick scab.

In the opposite corner, sprawled against the wall, was Becky Adams, blood gushing from deep gashes in her mouth and throat. Her arms and legs twitched spasmodically, and as Matt watched his mother slash at her with the shovel, his throat constricted, turning his own cry into a choking sob that was all but inaudible. Blind to everything but the vision of the carnage below the cellar's floor, he'd stumbled toward the stairs and started up.

Now he stood numb and trembling in the kitchen, his mind refusing to work, his reason washed away by the flood of horror he'd just witnessed.

Then, through the numbness in his mind, he heard: "Matt? Matt, where are you?"

His mother's voice.

But not quite his mother's voice.

His aunt's voice — the voice he'd so often heard whispering to him in the night.

The voice that should have existed only in his dreams.

Then there were footsteps coming up the basement stairs, and the voice was louder.

He had to get away! He had to escape!

Matt stumbled across the kitchen, through the

mud room, and out the back door. Late afternoon had given way to evening, and he froze on the porch for a moment, blinded now by the sudden darkness. Then the crash of the door at the top of the basement stairs galvanized him, and he charged down the steps, taking them two at a time.

The road! If he could get to the road, he would be safe.

He stumbled down the driveway, unable to shake the vision of the carnage in the basement. It drowned out any other thoughts, paralyzing his ability to reason, so that when he heard the roar of an automobile engine behind him, the sound only spurred him on, sent him pounding harder down the driveway toward the gates. He was almost there, almost within reach of his goal, when the car struck him.

He went down hard, his shoulder and then his head slamming against the driveway, knocking him unconscious.

The car screeched to a stop, and then a figure was crouched over him.

"My baby," Cynthia whispered. "My poor baby." She gently lifted Matt's head and cradled it against her breast, her finger stroking his cheek as she gazed down into his face. "But it's all right, my darling. We'll be together now." Her lips pressed close to his ear. "Now we'll always be together."

Gently easing Matt's head back onto the driveway, Cynthia straightened up. Leaving the car where it was, she walked quickly back up the driveway toward the house, and when she came back the shovel — the one she'd used to put an end to Becky Adams's life — was in her hand. Stooping down, she placed the handle in Matt's right hand, closing his fingers around the polished oak, his fingerprints covering her own. Then she moved his other hand up and down the shovel's oaken handle, so his fingerprints were everywhere. Satisfied, she let his left arm drop again, then placed a scrap of material in his left hand.

Bloody material, which had been torn from Becky Adams's blouse.

"I have to leave you now, my darling," Cynthia whispered. "But not for long. And when I come back, we'll never be parted again. We'll be together. We'll be together forever."

Joan Hapgood felt as if she were waking up from a deep sleep, but as her mind began to clear, her confusion only deepened. What was she doing outside? And why was it dark? The last thing she remembered was —

What?

Her memory seemed to have vanished, but then it began creeping back:

She'd been in Cynthia's room, getting rid of her things.

Not getting rid of them — destroying them. She turned toward the house, her eyes going to the window of the last room she remembered being in, the room on the second floor where her mother had insisted on putting all of Cynthia's things. And then —

And then there was nothing! Just a terrible, blank void, as if she'd suddenly fallen into a deep sleep. Except she hadn't been asleep. She'd been ridding herself of her sister, finally and forever. Ridding herself of Cynthia's clothes, her pictures, everything!

Then what happened? Her glance shifted from the house to the car. What was she doing out here? And why was the car —

Out of the corner of her eye she saw something on the ground, and turned in that direction.

She saw Matt, lying motionless on the driveway. How — Why —

"Matt!" She screamed his name as she dropped down beside him. On her knees, she reached out and gathered him into her arms, rocking him as she sobbed. What had happened? How had it happened? The shovel fell from his hand, drawing her attention as it fell to the ground. In the light of the rising full moon, she could see the bloodstains on the blade, but didn't grasp what they were. Then, as she looked down at herself and saw the blood that stained her own clothes, a strangled scream erupted from her throat.

What had happened? What had Matt done? What had she done?

Help!

She had to get help!

Leaving Matt where he was, she raced toward the house, slamming the back door open so hard its window shattered. Ignoring the shards of glass that sprayed across the mud room floor, she stumbled into the kitchen, found the phone, and fumbled with the buttons, forcing her trembling fingers to press 911. "Help," she begged when the emergency operator came on the line. "Oh, God, please send someone to help me. It's my son — oh, God, I think my son is dead. . . ."

Gerry and Nancy Conroe were just finishing their dinner when the police scanner on Gerry's desk came alive. Ordinarily, neither of the Conroes would have heard it, for they usually ate in the dining room, where Nancy had banned the scanner years ago. "Dinner should be a family event," she had decreed the one time Gerry brought it into the room. "It's one of the few times we're all together, and if you have that thing on, none of us will talk. We might as well stop using the dining room, and eat on TV trays in the den." Which was exactly what Nancy and Gerry were doing that evening, unable to face the prospect of sitting at the dining room table without Kelly. The TV was on, tuned to the national news, but neither of them could have repeated a word of what the anchorman was saying, any more than they could have said what they'd been eating.

Nor were they talking. Instead, consciously or unconsciously, they were both listening to the police scanner, waiting for it to begin crackling, hoping it would bring them word that their daughter had been found. Thus, when the voice of the dispatcher suddenly erupted from the tinny speaker, both of them froze, their eyes turning toward the small plastic radio on Gerry's desk.

They listened in silence as what seemed to Nancy to be an unintelligible stream of words spewed from the scanner. But even she understood the import of the last few words:

"Proceed to 1326 Manchester Road. Repeat, one-three-two-six Manchester Road."

"That's Bill and Joan's house," Nancy said. "What's —"

Gerry held up a hand to silence her as they both recognized Dan Pullman's voice come on the speaker.

"This is Unit One," Pullman said. "I'm on my way. Unit Two, you copy?"

"Unit Two copies." Tony Petrocelli's voice was barely audible, almost lost in a haze of static.

"Meet me there," Pullman ordered. The radio abruptly fell silent.

"What's going on?" Nancy asked. "What's happening?"

Gerry Conroe was on his feet. "They're sending an ambulance over there. It sounded like someone's down in the driveway." He headed toward the front door, and Nancy hurried after him.

"Down?" she echoed uncertainly. "What —"

"Injured," Gerry said, his voice grim as he pulled on a light jacket. "Or dead."

As he pulled open the front door, they heard a siren wailing in the distance and growing steadily louder.

"I'm coming with you," Nancy said, pulling her jacket from the coat tree next to the front door.

Gerry made no argument, and a moment later they were in his car, the wheels spitting gravel as he shot around the circle and started down their driveway toward Manchester Road. For once, Nancy didn't tell her husband to slow down.

Phyllis Adams's head came up as she heard the sound of a siren screaming along Prospect Street, growing louder as it approached the corner of Burlington, then rapidly fading away to a lonely wail. "It's Becky," she said, reaching for the decanter to refill her empty glass. "I know it's Becky."

"You don't know anything of the sort," Frank growled, picking up the decanter an instant before his wife's fingers closed on it.

"What are you doing?" Phyllis demanded.

"Do you really want to be drunk when Becky comes home?"

Phyllis eyed her husband blearily. She was almost sure Becky wasn't coming home — half an hour ago she'd had a strong feeling that came out of nowhere, and knew that something terrible had happened to her daughter. "She's dead," she'd wailed, her eyes tearing. "I know my baby's dead." Frank had only glared at her, and she could tell that he thought she was drunk. And maybe she was, but that didn't mean her intuition wasn't right.

Now, as the siren faded into the darkness beyond the front window, she stood up, steadying herself against the table next to her chair. "We should go out there," she said.

"We're not going anywhere," her husband retorted. "We're going to sit here and wait. If Dan Pullman finds anything — or even hears anything — he'll call us." His eyed his wife balefully. "And it would help if you were sober when that happens."

Phyllis seemed about to argue with him, but then turned and headed for the kitchen. "I'll make some coffee," she said, seeing no point in mentioning the bottle of cooking sherry she kept behind the coffee can on the next-to-the-top shelf of the pantry.

Dan Pullman pulled through the gates of Hapgood Farm right behind the ambulance. He could see Tony Petrocelli's squad car stopped halfway to the house, its lights flashing. As he pulled his car off the drive so as not to block the ambulance when it left, he saw Tony himself squatting next to Matt's body. Crouched on the other side of Matt, leaning against the Range Rover, was Joan Hapgood.

As the paramedics took over for him, Tony Petrocelli stood up and drew his boss aside. "He's still alive," he said. "But I sure don't get what's going on."

"What did Joan tell you?"

Petrocelli shrugged. "She says she can't remember what happened."

Pullman's eyes flicked toward Joan, then returned to his deputy. "Can't remember? She was driving the car, wasn't she?"

Petrocelli spread his hands helplessly. "She says she doesn't know."

"What the hell does she mean, she doesn't know?"

Holding his hand up to shield his eyes from the glare of a pair of headlights that had appeared at the foot of the driveway, Pullman shook his head impatiently. "Find out who that is, and make them go away," he growled. "And make sure nobody else comes in here, okay?" As the deputy moved toward the car that had pulled to a stop just behind the ambulance, Pullman shifted his attention to Joan Hapgood.

"Joan?" He took her arm and gently drew her to her feet, only seeing the blood on her clothes as she stepped into the glare of the ambulance's head-lights. "Are you hurt?"

Joan shook her head but said nothing, her eyes fixed on Matt, who was still lying exactly as he had been when she found him a little while ago.

"I — I don't think so," she stammered.

As she finally tore her eyes away from Matt and looked at the police chief, Pullman could see the confusion in her face. "Can you tell me what happened?"

Joan shook her head.

Pullman frowned. Was it that she didn't know, or didn't want to tell him? "Would you like me to call Trip Wainwright?" he asked. For a moment he didn't think she'd even heard him, but then she shook her head again.

"It doesn't matter," she said. Her gaze went back

to Matt. "I've killed him, haven't I?" she asked, her voice breaking. "I've killed my son."

Suddenly Gerry Conroe appeared at Pullman's side. "What the hell is going on around here?" he demanded. "Tony Petrocelli just tried to order me off the —" His eyes fell on Joan Hapgood's bloody clothing. "Jesus! He tried to kill you too, didn't he?"

"We don't know what happened, Gerry," Pullman said before Joan could respond. "And I was the one who told Tony to get you out of here."

Conroe's face flushed with anger. "I've got every right to be here. My daughter is still —"

"Not now, Gerry," Pullman said, deciding he'd had enough to silence the other man. "Stay if you want, but keep out of my way. If you don't —"

"We need to get him into the ambulance," one of the medics called out to him. "Is that okay?"

Pullman moved to Matt and looked down at him. The shovel — no longer in his hands — lay on the driveway at his side, and in his other hand was a scrap of blood-soaked cloth.

"We've already taken pictures of everything," the medic said as Dan crouched down next to the boy.

Reaching into the inside pocket of his jacket, Pullman pulled out one of the Ziploc bags he always carried. Touching only a single corner of the scrap of cloth, he carefully drew it out of Matt's hand and put it in the bag. As he was sealing the bag he noticed the monogram on the material: FAT.

He recognized it right away, for he had been with Frank Adams the first time his friend ordered a monogram on his shirt. A monogram that had subsequently appeared on every shirt Frank Adams owned, including the ones his daughter had taken to wearing a year ago. "Oh, Jesus," he whispered, and though his words were barely audible, they caught the attention not only of the medics who were about to transfer Matt to a stretcher, but of Gerry Conroe as well.

"What is it?" Conroe demanded. "What did you find?"

Pullman ignored him, concentrating instead on Matthew Moore. "What did you do?" he asked the unconscious boy. "What did you do to Becky Adams?"

With Tony Petrocelli's help, the two EMTs lifted Matt onto the stretcher. "Careful," one of the medics told the deputy as a low moan escaped Matt's lips. "It looks like his shoulder might be broken." They eased Matt onto the stretcher as gently as they could, then lifted the stretcher onto the waiting gurney. As one of the medics began strapping Matt down, he groaned again.

"Hold it!" Pullman snapped, stepping to the head of the gurney and looking down into the boy's face. "Talk to me, Matt!" he said, still clutching the Ziploc bag containing the scrap of material from Frank Adam's shirt. "Tell me what happened!"

"Take it easy, Chief," one of the medics said. "He can't hear you."

Pullman's eyes didn't leave the boy's face. "Come on, Matt!" Another moan drifted from the boy's lips, and Pullman thought he saw a twitch. "Talk to me!"

Then Joan appeared next to the stretcher, looming over Matt. "Leave him alone," she cried. "Just leave him alone!" Her gaze shifted from Dan Pullman to her son. "I'm here, Matt," she whispered. "I'm here. And I'll never leave you. I'll never leave you again."

As she uttered the last words, Matthew Moore's eyes snapped open, and a different sound erupted from his throat.

It was not a moan. It was a scream, an anguished scream carrying so much pain that it froze everyone who had gathered around the stretcher.

Chapter 28

He was back in the root cellar.

The blackness was even deeper than before, the walls of the chamber so close around him that every breath was a painful struggle. The stench of death was in his nostrils, and every nerve in his body felt as if it were on fire. From somewhere in the darkness he thought he could hear the wailing of the dead.

But he'd gotten away from the root cellar! He'd stood on Becky's shoulders and —

Suddenly he was there again, pushing up, struggling to raise the trapdoor. The wailing had stopped, and he was almost out — almost free — almost —

He grunted as the shovel crashed down on him, stunning him.

Now he was stumbling through the darkness, running down a driveway that seemed to go on forever toward gates that never appeared any nearer. Then something was behind him, some unseen menace, coming closer and closer. He struggled to run faster, but his feet seemed mired in mud, and now the gate — the gate that was his only escape from the menace closing in behind him — was farther away then ever.

The car struck him with no warning, and he moaned as a sharp pain shot through his shoulder.

He stumbled, then felt himself falling.

He tumbled through the blackness, sinking deeper and deeper into it.

A voice.

His mother's voice.

"I'm here, Matt . . ." *The stench of death in his nostrils gave way to the musky aroma of her perfume.* "I'm here. . . ." *The odor grew stronger, and he could feel her fingers reaching out to him, feel them begin their caresses.* "I'll never leave you . . . I'll never leave you again."

Sensing that if he let her touch him — if he submitted to her this one last time — he would be lost forever, Matt summoned the last of his strength. Ignoring the pain that tore at his body, he sucked his lungs full and opened his mouth.

His own scream washed away the nightmare of memories that had held him in a prison of blackness, and his eyes blinked open.

She was there!

His mother was there, next to him, staring down at him, reaching out to him.

"No!" he screamed. "No! Don't touch me. Don't ever touch me."

His mother's hand froze, and for a moment her eyes met his. Once again he seemed to be caught up in the nightmare, for suddenly he was no longer looking at his mother.

He was looking at his aunt.

Another scream rose in his throat, but before it could erupt into the night he heard a man's voice: "Talk to me, Matt. Talk to me!"

Matt tore his eyes away from the strange visage of his aunt, and saw Dan Pullman looming above him. "B-basement . . ." he managed.

"You don't have to tell them. You don't have to say anything." Again her fingers reached out to touch him, and again he shrank away.

"In the basement . . ." he said, summoning the last of his strength. "In the root cellar!" He tried to sit up, but the pain in his shoulder tore through him, draining the last of his resources, and he collapsed back down onto the stretcher.

"Okay," Dan Pullman barked to the medics. "Take him to the clinic. Tony, come with me." As the medics wheeled Matt to the ambulance, Joan Hapgood started to follow the stretcher, but Pullman stopped her. "Not yet," he said. "First I want you to show me the root cellar he was talking about."

Joan's face paled. "I don't go into the cellar." The fear in her eyes was almost palpable. "I'm afraid of it — it's so dark and feels so closed in, and —"

"Show us," Dan Pullman cut in, signaling Tony Petrocelli to follow him as he took Joan's elbow and began steering her toward the house. When Gerry Conroe started after him, Pullman almost ordered him back, then changed his mind. Depending on what they found, it might be better to have Gerry Conroe with them.

Something about the house had changed since Pullman had been here earlier in the day. At first he wasn't sure what it was; perhaps it was only in his imagination, given what Matt had said a few moments before. But then he decided it was more than that. There was a dark aura about the house, and from the moment he followed Joan Hapgood inside, with Gerry Conroe and then Tony Petrocelli behind him, he had a feeling of terrible foreboding.

As they moved through the mud room into the kitchen, Conroe paused and reached out to touch his shoulder. "What's that smell?" he asked.

The tremor in Conroe's voice told the police chief that the other man already had a pretty good idea of what the odor must be.

It was the scent of death.

Instead of answering Conroe's question, Pullman grimly scanned the kitchen, his gaze instantly drawn to an open door next to the refrigerator. "That lead to the basement?" he asked.

Joan stopped short. "Don't make me go down there. Please don't make me."

There was a pleading, almost childish note in her voice that surprised Pullman. Now, looking at her in the bright kitchen instead of the glow of headlights that had been the only illumination in the driveway, he saw that it wasn't only the house that had changed.

Joan Hapgood had too.

Her hair was arranged differently, pulled back from her face in a tight twist he didn't remember seeing before. And instead of the pale lipstick that was all Joan usually wore, tonight her face was

451

made up as if she'd been preparing to go out. The colors she'd chosen — the turquoise eye shadow and bright lip gloss — made her look as if she were wearing a mask. Something was wrong with the clothes too. They didn't quite seem to fit her, and they looked dated, and in a style that might have appeared right on a girl in her teens, but made Joan look as if she'd dressed for a costume party.

Gerry Conroe, whispered, speaking softly, as if to himself "Jesus." His eyes were fixed on Joan Hapgood as if he were seeing a ghost. "What the hell is going on?"

Pullman and Tony Petrocelli exchanged a glance, and the police chief made a quick decision. "Stay up here with Joan," he told the deputy. "I'll go down and take a look."

"I'm coming with you," Conroe said. When Pullman hesitated, Conroe pushed harder. "My daughter might be down there, Dan."

Pullman reluctantly nodded. "Okay. But you do exactly as I say. And you touch nothing."

A moment later the two men started down the stairs, moving slowly as Pullman searched for signs of blood. Wherever there were reddish smears, he altered Conroe to avoid them. At the bottom of the stairs the smell of rotting flesh was stronger, over-powering the musty scent of mildew that they would have recognized from their own basements. Pullman paused, and noticed an opening in the floor, almost hidden behind the furnace at the far end of the room. Moving closer he saw the open trapdoor, and the ladder protruding from the three-foot-square hole. There was a large blood-stain on the floor near the ladder, and as Conroe moved toward it, Pullman held out an arm to stop him. "Stay here," he said, his voice low but carrying a note of authority. "Let me take a look first."

Reluctantly, Gerry complied, and Pullman stepped forward and gazed down into the dark pit beneath the basement floor.

For a moment he saw nothing, but then, protruding out of the darkness surrounding the shaft of light coming through the trapdoor, he saw a leg. Flicking on his flashlight, he probed with the beam, moving from the leg up to a white shirt.

A white shirt that was soaked with blood.

His stomach knotting, he climbed down the ladder, careful to touch as little of it as possible. At the bottom, he crouched over the crumpled body that was clad in the bloody white shirt and jeans. Though the face was badly slashed and covered with blood, he recognized Becky Adams. He reached out and touched her neck, searching for a pulse.

There was none.

Struggling against the nausea that was threatening to overwhelm him, Pullman turned the light away from Becky Adams, and a moment later was staring into the face of Emily Moore.

Or, more accurately, at what had once been her face. Her skin was torn and bruised, and dried blood was crusted around her mouth and nostrils. Pullman's pulse quickened when he saw a movement, and then he realized that it wasn't a movement at all, but a mass of ants that were already feeding off the old woman's corpse.

He moved the beam, again and saw Kelly Conroe.

She too was lying still, her face bruised and bloodied, but when he reached out to feel for a pulse, she jerked away from his touch.

"No . . ." she whispered. "Please . . . no more."

"Kelly?" Gerry Conroe cried out from above. "Oh, God! Kelly!" A moment later, ignoring Dan Pullman's orders, he was at the bottom of the ladder, kneeling over his daughter, reaching out to touch her, but hesitating at the last second, as if afraid he might hurt her.

Kelly was silent for a moment, and then, with a soft moan, opened one of her swollen eyes. "Daddy?" she whispered, reaching out to him.

As Conroe gathered his daughter into his arms, he looked up at Dan Pullman, his eyes glittering with rage. "I'll kill that son of a bitch. I swear, I'll kill him for what he did!"

Kelly's hand closed on her father's in a weak squeeze. "No!" she whimpered. "N-not Matt! His mother! It was his mother. . . ." Then, the realization that she was finally safe sinking in, she began to sob quietly.

As Gerry Conroe tried to soothe his daughter, stroking her hair and cradling her as if she were a baby, Dan Pullman used his radio to issue orders. "We've got a real mess out here," he said after telling the dispatcher to get a second ambulance out to Hapgood Farm. "Make sure someone gets on the gate right away — the last thing we need is a bunch of rubberneckers up here." Putting the radio back in its holster, his gaze shifted to Gerry Conroe. "What was that all about up there?" he asked. "When we were with Joan."

Conroe's eyes stayed on his daughter. "It was her clothes — her hair — everything," he replied softly, his glance flicking toward Pullman before returning to his daughter's bloodstained face. "When I first saw her in the light, I thought I was looking at her sister. I mean, I could swear that dress was Cynthia's, and the way she's got her hair and her makeup . . ." His voice trailed off and he shook his head. "I just don't know," he finished. "It was almost like seeing a ghost."

Pullman was silent for a few seconds, then rose to his feet. "Will you be okay if I leave you alone down here?"

Conroe nodded, and a moment later the police chief climbed back up out of the root cellar.

"Why can't I go to the hospital?" Joan Hapgood was seated at the kitchen table, her body was tense, and when she spoke her voice was as tight as an overwound clock spring. "Why can't I see my son?"

"Let's just wait until Trip Wainwright gets here," Dan Pullman said for the third time in the last five minutes.

When he'd emerged from the basement, Pullman said nothing to Joan Hapgood. He went directly to the telephone on the kitchen counter and called her attorney. "I think we're going to need you," he told Wainwright. "I want to talk to Joan, but I don't want anyone saying I questioned her improperly."

Joan, who heard him as he spoke to her lawyer, tried to protest. "Why are you calling him? I already told you — I can't remember what happened. I just want to see my son. Can't he meet us at the clinic?"

Pullman had said nothing. Hanging up, he sat down at the kitchen table, resisting the impulse to go through the house looking for something that might explain what had happened. What he'd found in the basement provided far more than the legal definition of "probable cause," but he knew that without a warrant, Trip Wainwright could tie up for months whatever evidence he might find.

Better to wait a few minutes for Wainwright now than churn through paperwork for months later. Better to do it by the book.

The attorney arrived on the heels of the ambulance that came to pick up Kelly Conroe. As the medics, followed by two state troopers, disappeared down the basement stairs, Joan Hapgood's eyes widened in surprise.

Surprise that looked to Dan Pullman to be absolutely genuine.

"What are they doing?" she asked. "What did you find down there?"

Before Pullman replied, Trip Wainwright broke in. "Would you mind telling me exactly what's

456

going on here, Dan? I thought we agreed that you wouldn't talk to either Matt or Joan without me being present."

As briefly as he could, the police chief explained what had happened to Matt Moore. "I haven't talked to Joan," he said. "I just asked her to show me where the entrance to the basement was, and I didn't need a warrant for that, given what Matt said."

Wainwright's eyes narrowed suspiciously. "And did you find anything?"

His eyes fixed on Joan Hapgood, Pullman said, "I found Emily Moore, Becky Adams, and Kelly Conroe."

Joan Hapgood gasped, and her hand flew reflexively up to cover her mouth. "M-Mother?" she stammered, standing up and taking a step toward the basement door. "My mother is down there?" Pullman nodded, and she uttered an unintelligible cry.

"Sit down, Joan," Pullman said.

The gentleness in his voice caught Joan's attention, and she froze. Then, the horror in her eyes dissolving into fear, she sank back onto her chair. Wainwright took a seat next to her, at the table.

"She's dead, Joan," Pullman went on, his eyes remaining on her. "So is Becky Adams. And Kelly Conroe has been beaten so badly she can barely speak."

As the horror returned to Joan's eyes, Wainwright slipped a protective arm around his client. "Is there any proof that Matt did it?" he asked. "I

457

mean any real proof?"

Again Pullman's eyes stayed on Joan as he spoke. "When we found him, there was a shovel lying next to him, smeared with bloody finger-prints that I suspect will match Matt's. And there was a piece of the shirt Becky Adams is wearing, with her father's monogram."

Wainwright's lips compressed as he digested this. "There has to be an explanation —"

"Kelly Conroe says it wasn't Matt." Pullman went on, still watching Joan. "She says it was you."

Again the look of shock on Joan's face seemed genuine. "No!" she cried. "How could she —"

"She did," Pullman interrupted. "She said, 'Not Matt. His mother. It was his mother . . .' " As he re-peated the words Kelly Conroe had spoken, he saw a change come into Joan's eyes. The horror — and the confusion — seemed to clear. She shifted posi-tion, and the dress she wore somehow seemed to fit her better. And when she spoke, her voice was calm and clear.

"The Conroe girl said I did it?" she demanded. "That's ridiculous."

Trip Wainwright put a restraining hand on her arm. "You don't have to say anything at all," he cautioned, but she brushed his hand aside and gave him a withering look.

"I hardly think I need your help," she said, then turned back to Pullman. "It was Joan," she said. "It was always Joan."

Wainwright was about to say something, and Pullman silenced him with a gesture. "And who

458

are you?" he asked softly, though he was certain he already knew the answer.

"I'm Matt's mother," the woman sitting at the kitchen table said. "I'm Cynthia Moore."

The color drained from Trip Wainwright's face, and his eyes flicked between Dan Pullman and the woman he knew as Joan Hapgood. Pullman broke the silence that had fallen over the room. "Do you know why she did it?" he asked.

"He was going to take Matt away," Cynthia said.

Pullman frowned. "Who? Who was going to take Matt away?"

"His father," Cynthia replied. "Bill Hapgood."

"I thought Bill Hapgood wasn't his father —" Pullman began, but Cynthia Moore, her nostrils flaring angrily, cut him short.

"Don't you think I know who the father of my own son is?" she asked, her voice suddenly turning bitter. "Let me show you something."

She stood up, and Wainwright was suddenly on his feet too. "Joan, I don't think this is a good idea. Before you show him anything, or say anything else, we have to talk."

Cynthia ignored him. Slipping her arm through Dan Pullman's, she drew him with her as she moved toward the dining room. Turning on the chandelier that hung over the table, she glanced around the room, her eyes lingering on the glass-fronted cabinet that held the half-dozen sets of fine china the Hapgood family had amassed over the generations, along with dozens of crystal goblets in different sizes and patterns. "All this should have been mine, you know," she said to Pullman. "He never loved Joan — not like he loved me."

They moved on, passing through the entry hall and into the living room. It was Trip Wainwright who first noticed the photographs on the piano. There were three, of Bill and Joan Hapgood.

Except that Joan's image was gone, replaced by Cynthia's.

"I'm going to call Dr. Henderson," Wainwright said softly as Cynthia led them into the den and his eyes moved from one picture to another, each one altered in the same manner as the ones on the piano in the living room.

Pullman nodded in silent agreement as Cynthia went to the desk, picked up a file folder, and handed it to him. He opened it and saw a letter from a laboratory in New York City. It confirmed that DNA tests on samples of both Matthew Moore's tissue and William Hapgood's established the relationship of the man and the boy.

"He was going to take him away," Cynthia said as Pullman read through the file. "I couldn't let that happen. Don't you see? That's why I had to make Joan kill him. Otherwise he was going to take Matt away from me."

Pullman looked at her uncertainly. "You 'made' *Joan* kill Bill? But it was Matt who —"

"He was there," Cynthia told him. "But it was Joan who made him pull the trigger." Her eyes took on a faraway look. "She stood behind him, with her arms around him. She loved to hold him, you know. She loved to go into his room at night, to

460

watch him sleep." Her voice grew husky. "And touch him. She loved to feel his skin against hers, his body . . ." Her voice trailed off, then she looked anxiously into Pullman's eyes. "They both loved me," she whispered. "Bill and Matt both loved me. But she took them away."

Tony Petrocelli appeared at the door. "Dan?" he said. "We're ready to bring them up."

Pullman signaled curtly, but before Petrocelli left the room, Cynthia said, "Mama? Is he talking about Mama?" Before anyone could answer, she turned back to Dan Pullman and spoke to him with a pleading tone. "I want to see her. Please? Can't I see my mama?"

Wainwright had returned to the room, and Pullman's eyes met his, an unspoken message passing between them. The lawyer nodded. "I don't have any objection."

They got back to the kitchen as two state troopers emerged from the basement, carrying a stretcher. Pullman asked if they were carrying Emily Moore, and, after the trooper nodded, the police chief eased the sheet off the old woman's face so her daughter could look down at it.

"It was Joan," Cynthia Moore said, as she always had when she'd done something wrong. "It wasn't my fault, Mama. It was Joan . . . it was always Joan. . . ."

Epilogue

Karl Rhinemann's various degrees hung in gilt-framed splendor against his office's rich, oiled-walnut paneling. His diploma from Harvard, denoting a Bachelor of Arts degree in biochemistry, hung in the center. Surrounding it were the rest. The medical diploma from Harvard Medical School. The Ph.D. in psychology from Columbia. The L.L.D. and J.D., also from Columbia. But neither the years of schooling nor his equal number of years in practice had prepared him for the woman who sat across the desk from him, perched nervously on the edge of the deep red leather wingback chair that usually made his subjects feel more relaxed than they had any right to be. Rhinemann's practice was in forensic psychiatry, and on this day it had fallen upon him to do an initial evaluation of Joan Moore Hapgood.

As his subject watched him warily, he quickly reread the file in front of him. According to the report made out by Daniel Pullman, who had been the chief investigator of the crimes Joan Hapgood was accused of committing, she had killed her husband, her mother, and an unrelated teenage girl, attempted the murder of her son, and battered a second, unrelated teenage girl.

His eyes shifted from the file to the woman who sat before him. She did not look like the monster the file depicted. Indeed, she did not look like any sort of monster, but like a very frightened, very worried woman, whose face was etched by a grief that was engulfing her prettiness. "Would you like to tell me what happened?" Rhinemann asked, leaning forward and resting his chin on his folded hands, his attentiveness letting her know he would see through any lies she might tell.

"I don't know what happened," Joan Hapgood said softly. Her eyes, wide and frightened, met his with no hesitation. "I know what they say I did, but I don't believe I did any of it. I loved my husband and my mother. I still love my son."

"And the girls?" Rhinemann asked. "How did you feel about them?"

"Kelly Conroe is my best friend's daughter. I loved her. I —" She faltered. "— I hardly knew Becky Adams. But I know she was a sweet girl. Shy, but very sweet. When we lived across the street from her, I always liked her very much."

Rhinemann leaned back in his chair, unfolding his hands and idly picking up a pencil he had no intention of using. Whatever notes he took would be committed to paper after the subject was gone. "Would you like to tell me what happened the day your son had to go to the hospital?" Joan Hapgood tensed, and he could see her debating something in her mind. He nodded — an almost imperceptible gesture that he knew would probably not even register in the subject's consciousness. It would, however, suggest to her subconscious that she could trust him. Sure enough, she shifted in her chair, making herself more comfortable.

"You'll think I'm crazy," she said.

Rhinemann shrugged noncommittally. "Try me."

"I — I was clearing my sister's things out of my house. . . ."

"Cynthia's things?" Rhinemann had studied Dan Pullman's account of his conversation with Joan Hapgood on the night she was arrested so many times that he could have repeated it verbatim, had no need to ask Joan to identify her sister. It was his way of prodding her. When she nodded but still said nothing, he added, "And she didn't want you to do that?"

Joan bit down on her lip as if to prevent herself from speaking, then shook her head. "She said it should have been her house. Then —" She took a deep breath and continued. "Then she started laughing at me."

"Laughing at you?" Rhinemann repeated, deliberately lending his voice a touch of mockery. As he had intended, the subject exhibited the first signs of anger. "Did she laugh at you often?"

For the first time, Joan Hapgood's eyes moved away from him, and she began picking at the seam of her dress. "She always laughed at me. As long as I can remember, she always laughed."

"Why would she do that? Why would she laugh at you?"

Joan's eyes met his again and when she spoke,

464

Rhinemann could hear her anger in her voice. "She always thought she was better than I was. And she always said that even though I wanted to be her, I never could. She said I could never be as pretty as her, or as smart as her. She said Mother would never love me the way she loved her."

"And that was true, wasn't it?" Rhinemann asked, his voice bland though his pulse was quickening as he saw the subject's rage growing.

"No!" Joan shouted. "It wasn't Cynthia that Bill Hapgood loved — it was me! And even if I didn't give birth to Matt, I was his mother. Not Cynthia! Me!"

"But it was always Cynthia your mother loved best, wasn't it? And no matter what you did, you couldn't be as pretty or as smart as your sister."

Joan's voice hardened. "I could! I could be everything she was. I could have been just as beautiful as she was. And just as smart and popular too!"

"But you couldn't make your mother love you, could you?"

Joan flinched as if she'd been struck.

"Is that what it was about? That you could never make your mother love you?"

Again Joan flinched, and then, abruptly she straightened, seeming to grow taller in the chair. Her expression shifted too, but more than that, her features now appeared more refined, her cheekbones higher, her eyes more widely spaced. And her lips curled into a smile so cold that it made Karl Rhinemann's skin crawl.

"Of course Mother never loved her," the woman who sat across from him said. "I saw to that. I saw to everything."

Rhinemann regarded her without speaking for several seconds, wondering how to proceed. Finally, he asked, "Does Joan know about you? Does she know what you've done?"

Cynthia smiled enigmatically. "That all depends, doesn't it?"

"Depends on what?" Rhinemann countered.

Cynthia Moore shrugged. "Oh, come now, Doctor. I'm not a fool, and neither are you. We both know that what happens to Joan depends entirely on what you say in the report you're going to write as soon as Joan is taken back to her room. So what is it going to be?" The forefinger of her right hand touched its counterpart on her left hand. "It's quite possible that Joan is totally insane, isn't it? After all, the way Mama beat her and locked her in the cedar chest in the basement when she was little could account for a lot, couldn't it? Certainly it would account for her fear of the basement at Hapgood Farm. And it would account for the way she beat Mama and Becky Adams to death. And it would certainly account for me — Joan wouldn't be the first person to develop a second personality, would she?" She cocked her head knowingly. "Someone had to take the abuse that she couldn't stand. And who better to come up with than me?" Her smile turned brittle. "After all, Doctor, you and I both know that no matter how much she professes to love me, deep down she must hate me.

466

Why wouldn't she? I'm everything she never was. I'm everything she ever wanted to be. And she was my whipping boy from the day she learned to crawl. Without me, she never would have gotten those beatings." Cynthia laughed a cold, harsh sound. "But there's another possibility, too, isn't there?"

Rhinemann raised his brows in a silent invitation for her to go on.

The woman's right forefinger moved on to the middle finger of her left hand. "Perhaps Cynthia doesn't really exist at all — maybe I'm Joan, simply pretending to be Cynthia. After all, is it really reasonable to believe that Cynthia simply 'appeared' whenever I needed to be rid of someone? Don't forget — Bill had left me, and told me he was going to take Matt away from me — he showed me the proof that he'd fathered him. He even told me that the only reason he married me was because he began to suspect that Matt really was his son. His, and Cynthia's! So why wouldn't I kill him? He was going to take my son away from me. And why wouldn't I kill Mother, after everything she'd done to me?"

"And the girls?" Rhinemann asked.

The woman shrugged as if what she'd done to the two teenagers was barely worth explaining. "They wanted Matt. They wanted him, just like Bill wanted him."

"So you killed one of them and beat the other," Rhinemann continued. "Just like your mother beat you."

The woman's head tipped forward as if she were a teacher acknowledging the correctness of a pupil's answer. "So what are you going to do, Doctor?" she asked. "What is Joan's fate to be?"

"What do you think I should do?" he countered.

The woman leaned back in the chair and crossed her legs, and when she spoke again, her voice was soft, her smile easy. "For all I care, you can find her totally sane and do whatever you want to her. But the trial will be difficult, since Joan won't be able to answer anybody's questions about much of anything. And I won't be around to help."

Rhinemann allowed himself a small smile. "Oh, I suspect if the questioning were handled properly, you'd find it impossible to resist coming out."

The woman refused to rise to the bait. "If I were you, I wouldn't put my reputation at stake by trying." Her eyes and smile hardened. "I told her I'd never let her have my baby. She didn't believe me. And then I took Matt away from her, just like she took him away from me. And she'll never get him back. Never." As the psychologist was about to ask one more question, she said, "Good-bye, Dr. Rhinemann. And say good-bye to Joan for me too. I don't ever expect to see her again. Not her, and not you either."

As the psychologist watched, the woman opposite him changed again. She seemed to deflate, her body sagging in the chair, her features losing definition.

"Mother would have loved me," Joan whispered, her eyes tearing. "If it hadn't been for Cynthia,

468

Mother would have loved me." Her eyes fixed on the doctor's. "Whatever happened," she said, "I'm sure it's all Cynthia's fault."

Two weeks later, Joan Moore Hapgood was once again sitting in the chair across from Karl Rhinemann. As he went through the file in front of him — a file three inches thicker than when he first got it — he glanced occasionally at her. She looked exactly as she had at the end of their first interview: grief-stricken and confused.

For two weeks he'd interviewed her, given her numerous personality tests, and with her permission and cooperation had put her under hypnosis. He's also administered drugs that would have made it impossible for her to tell him anything but the truth, at least as she knew it.

And he had found nothing.

There had not been a trace of the Cynthia Moore personality he'd spoken to during that first interview.

Joan Hapgood was unable to account for anything that occurred in the basement, except to repeat what she'd said at the end of their first interview: ". . . It's Cynthia's fault . . . it's all Cynthia's fault."

As he finished perusing the file and leaned back in his chair, Joan spoke for the first time since being brought to his office a few minutes earlier. "What's going to happen to me?"

Rhinemann pursed his lips and tented his fingers over them for a moment, then shrugged helplessly. "I have no choice but to keep you here."

"But I didn't do anything," Joan protested.

"You don't remember doing anything," Rhinemann corrected. "And I agree that you truly don't remember. But your son and Kelly Conroe both remember, and aside from your confession — which your own lawyer agrees that you made in front of him and the investigating officer —"

"Dan Pullman," Joan supplied.

Rhinemann tipped his head. "Dan Pullman, yes. Aside from that confession, traces of your fingerprints were found on the shovel and the blood of all three victims was found in your clothes. While there's no evidence that you pulled the trigger while your son aimed the rifle at your husband, you yourself said you did."

"But I didn't —"

Rhinemann held up his hands to stop her. "Whether you did or didn't kill your husband makes no difference. I see no way you can be held accountable for things you can no longer remember having done, but at the same time I can't agree to release you from the hospital. With the endorsement of the evaluation review committee, I'm recommending that the court remand you to this hospital until such time as you are deemed fit to stand trial."

A gasp escaped Joan's lips. "How long will that be?"

Karl Rhinemann rose from his desk, moved around it and put his hands gently on Joan Hapgood's shoulders. "I don't know," he said softly. "But you might be here for the rest of your life."

As Joan's body shook with a strangled sob, a thought flitted through Karl Rhinemann's mind: *She's won. By not appearing again, Cynthia has won.*

It wasn't until he was once more alone in his office that he realized that his conclusion had been unreasonable. After all, Cynthia Moore only existed in the mind of Joan Moore Hapgood.

Cynthia herself had been dead for sixteen years.

How could she possibly have won anything at all?

"You don't have to do this if you don't want to," Matt told Kelly Conroe. They were outside the gates at the foot of the Hapgood driveway. The last of the leaves had been torn from the trees by a storm that passed through Granite Falls a week ago, and through the skeletal branches of the ancient oaks and maples, they could see the looming form of the house neither of them had gone into since the day Joan Hapgood had tried to kill Matt. His shoulder still hurt, but nothing was left of the cut on his head but a pale white scar.

Kelly's wounds, too, had begun healing in the month since her father gently lifted her out of the root cellar beneath the basement floor. But though her body no longer ached and the cuts no longer stung, she still woke up in the middle of the night, the soft cloak of sleep torn away by nightmares filled with images she could barely repress

471

in the full light of day. She slept with a nightlight now, unwilling to awaken in darkness even though she knew that the terrors she had survived in the basement of Hapgood Farm could no longer reach her.

After spending three days in the clinic, Matt had gone to stay with the Conroes. "Bill Hapgood was my best friend," Kelly's father had told him. "You're his son — you'll stay with us as long as you need to, and you'll always have a home here. You don't ever have to go back to the farm again." But when he and Kelly had returned to school a week later, passing the gates to Hapgood Farm every day, Matt knew he would eventually have to return to the house he'd lived in since he was five years old, have to sort through everything that had been left to him — not just the house and its contents, but all the memories too.

This morning, he had decided there was no point in putting it off any longer, and when he told Kelly she insisted on going with him.

"Maybe if I see it all again," she said, "maybe if I make myself go down to the basement and look at that place she put us in — I won't have the night-mares anymore."

And now they stood just outside the gates, and Matt could see the nervousness in her eyes. "I can do it by myself," he assured her. "You really don't have to come with me." He could see Kelly wavering, but then she shook her head.

"You can't go back in there by yourself. We'll do it together."

She slipped her hand into his and they started up the driveway. Their pace didn't falter until they came to the spot where the driveway forked, one branch leading to the circular drive in front of the house, the other to the carriage house behind. They headed toward the front door as if by common consent, though no words passed between them. When they were on the porch, they stopped and looked at each other. "You really don't have to —" Matt said again, but Kelly didn't let him finish.

"Open the door, Matt."

He slipped the key into the lock, twisted it, and pushed the door open. They stepped through quickly, as if afraid they might lose their nerve entirely if they hesitated.

The house did not have the feeling Matt had expected. Indeed, as he closed the door behind him, he had the sensation that they were not alone. He glanced at Kelly and saw that she sensed it too.

"Maybe we shouldn't do this," she said, her voice so soft it almost vanished into the silence of the house. "Maybe we should just go home."

Matt shook his head. "I have to do it. I have to try to find out why my mother —"

"She wasn't your mother," Kelly broke in. "She was never your mother, Matt. She was your aunt."

Matt said nothing. He hadn't yet told anyone about the dreams — dreams that he was now almost certain had not been dreams at all — in which his mother came into his room in the dark-

473

ness of night. Came into his room, and into his bed, and —

Not his mother.

Joan Hapgood had *not* been his mother. Had never been his mother. Was that why she crept into his bed? Had she somehow thought that would bind him to her? He shuddered at the memory.

Face it, he told himself. *Face all of it.*

Steeling himself, he moved into the living room, with Kelly still by his side, and he saw the photograph of Joan and Bill Hapgood that had been taken on their wedding day, the photograph he'd previously assumed was of his mother and stepfather.

Now he knew better: it was his aunt and his father. Except as he moved closer, he saw that it had been altered. Instead of Joan Hapgood's face, there now was an image of Cynthia Moore.

He was looking at a picture of his parents.

His mother and father, both dead, and now together in a way they had never been in life. His eyes stung with tears as he gazed at the photo. What might his life had been like if his true parents had married? He bit his lip to hold back the sob that rose in his throat. His hand tightening on Kelly's, he moved on through the rooms on the first floor, then started up the stairs. He stopped at the door to the guest room, where all of Cynthia Moore's things — his mother's things — had once been preserved by his grandmother and they were nearly destroyed by his aunt.

Face it, he repeated to himself. *You have to face it.*

Still holding Kelly Conroe's hand, he stepped into the room. And smelled his mother's musky perfume.

Then he heard his mother's voice. *"You're here,"* she whispered. *"You've come back to me."*

Matt froze as the words sank in, and then, as he stood rooted to the spot, he felt it.

His mother's touch on the back of his neck.

"No," he whispered. "Don't . . . please don't. . . ."

The finger on his neck moved to his cheek, then his lips. As his heart pounded and panic rose within him, the familiar darkness — the darkness in which his aunt had seduced him — began to close around him. *Don't,* he told himself. *Don't give in to it again.*

"Do it," he heard his mother whisper, as he'd heard her whisper so many times before. *"Do what you have to do . . . do what you want to do. . . ."*

The fingers caressing his lips moved lower, slipping between the buttons of his shirt to touch his chest. As his body responded to the familiar touch, his resolve began to crumble. But just before he lost himself to the scent, the touch, and the voice of his mother, he steeled himself and spun around.

He was facing Kelly Conroe.

But it was not quite Kelly. Where before Kelly's eyes had always been clear and sparkling, now they were burning.

Burning as her fingers — now stroking his cheek . . . touching his skin — were burning.

"Love me, Matt," she whispered, her voice husky, her eyes smoldering. "Love me here. Love me now." Her hands were under his shirt again, peeling it back until it fell from his shoulders, and then Kelly's body was pressed against his. "Please," she whispered. "Love me."

Matt's heart throbbed as his body responded to Kelly's touch. Almost of their own volition, his arms went around her, pulling her close.

Her lips found his, and as the scent of his mother's perfume spread through his body, he felt himself drifting once more into the dark pleasures she had brought him. *"Do it,"* he heard her whisper once more. *"Do what you want to do. . . ."* But as her arms tightened around him, as her body pressed against his, images began boiling up out of his memory.

The deer — his father — his grandmother and Becky — all of them dead.

The scent of his mother's perfume gave way to the smell of blood.

"No!" Matt moaned. Twisting free of Kelly's embrace, he grabbed her by the arm and began pulling her toward the door. "We have to get out of here," he told her. "Now!"

He heard his mother cry out. *"No! Don't leave me! Please don't leave me!"*

He ignored her cries, pulling Kelly out the door and toward the top of the stairs, then lifting her into his arms and carrying her down the long flight toward the entry hall and the open front door.

"No . . ." his mother's voice whimpered, pleading

with him as he had so often pleaded with her. *"Please . . . no . . ."*

Matt shut his mind to his mother's imprecations, but he could feel her reaching out to him, trying to keep him with her. And then he was through the front door, across the porch, and down the steps.

Standing in the driveway, he finally lowered Kelly to the ground. Gently, he turned her so she was facing him, and looked into her eyes.

It was the eyes of his friend.

Putting his arms around Kelly, he held her close. "It's going to be all right," he said. "It's finally going to be all right."

Kelly looked up at him uncertainly. The last thing she remembered was being in the guest room, looking at Cynthia Moore's things. And then —

Nothing.

"What happened?" she asked. "We were in the guest room and —"

Matt put a finger over her lips. "Nothing happened," he told her. "I just saw a ghost, that's all."

His arm wrapped protectively around Kelly, he turned his back not only on the house, but on all of its ghosts as well.

The employees of G.K. Hall hope you have e
joyed this Large Print book. All our Large Pri
titles are designed for easy reading, and all o
books are made to last. Other G.K. Hall boo
are available at your library, through select
bookstores, or directly from us.

For information about titles, please call:

(800) 257-5157

To share your comments, please write:

Publisher
G.K. Hall & Co.
P.O. Box 159
Thorndike, ME 04986

7sw
18X